Frederic Lindsay was born in Glasgow, and attended university both in that city and in Edinburgh, where he now lives. Since becoming a full-time writer, he has written plays for the theatre, radio and television, including the three part serial adaptation of his first novel *Brond* which was shown on Channel 4. His third novel, *A Charm Against Drowning*, was published by Andre Deutsch in Spring 1988. Currently, he is working on his next novel and on the script for a film of *Jill Rips*, the rights of which have been sold.

Also by Frederic Lindsay

BROND

and published by Corgi Books

JILL RIPS

Frederic Lindsay

CORGI BOOKS

All the characters in this novel and any similarity in name, rank etc. to serving or retired members of Strathclyde Police or any other police force is purely coincidental.

JILL RIPS

A CORGI BOOK   0 552 13284 5

Originally published in Great Britain by Andre Deutsch Limited

PRINTING HISTORY

Andre Deutsch edition published 1987
Corgi edition published 1988

This book is set in 10/11pt Plantin.

Corgi Books are published by Transworld Publishers Ltd.,
61-63 Uxbridge Road, Ealing, London W5 5SA, in Australia by
Transworld Publishers (Australia) Pty. Ltd., 15-23 Helles
Avenue, Moorebank, NSW 2170, and in New Zealand by Transworld
Publishers (N.Z.) Ltd., Cnr. Moselle and Waipareira Avenues,
Henderson, Auckland.

Printed and bound in Great Britain by
Cox & Wyman Ltd, Reading

In memory of
Catherine Stevenson Lindsay

CONTENTS

In the Whitechapel district of London on 31st August, 1888, the body of Polly Nicholls was found on the street. A week later on 8th September, Dark Annie Chapman was killed, also by the knife; within three quarters of an hour on the night of 29th September, Long Liz Stride and Catherine Eddowes were murdered; the last victim, twenty-five year old Mary Jane Kelly, was discovered in her room on the 9th of November. All of the women engaged in prostitution; all were mutilated and, given time and privacy, the butchering of Mary Kelly in particular was grotesquely thorough. In a series of letters, the murders were claimed by someone signing himself 'Jack the Ripper'. The murders ended as suddenly as they had begun and, despite theory and rumour, the killer's identity remains unknown.

Prologue

ONE DAY IN THE BEGINNING

One day in the beginning, Jamie said to her, 'If I put my wee bobbie into your vagina, you'd get a rare tickle.'

She knew what his bobbie was; it was one of the names the boys used for that part of themselves. All of the small ones, the five year olds or the six year olds like Jamie, when they got excited or worried would absent-mindedly clutch themselves there. Because she was a year older, and for other reasons, she felt superior to Jamie. When she told Miss Sturrock what Jamie had said, Miss Sturrock pretended to be too busy to listen.

'I don't have time for your nonsense,' Miss Sturrock said.

She looked at Miss Sturrock's neck; it had gone red at the front, all the way down to where it went into her blouse out of sight.

'I know what his bobbie is,' she said, watching Miss Sturrock's neck, 'but what does "vagina" mean?'

'That's not a word you're allowed to use. It's a rude word,' Miss Sturrock said.

'I don't think Jamie should be allowed to use rude words to me,' she told Miss Sturrock.

Miss Sturrock pretended not to hear.

'I don't think,' she said, 'Jamie should be allowed to use rude words like—'

'Stop it!' Miss Sturrock cried, not pretending any more. Her eyes were watering as if she was getting ready to cry. 'I don't believe Jamie said any of that to you. He didn't say any such thing at all!'

13

It made the rest of the morning interesting, trying to get Miss Sturrock to explain what the word meant, and wondering why she would not give Jamie a row.

At the end of the day, she took her coat off the peg and put it on. There were twenty pegs on each side but only fourteen children in the school. She counted the pegs on her side. When she had taken her coat, all the pegs were empty. In the quietness, she could hear the sounds of Miss Sturrock tidying away. Softly, she turned the handle on the door of Miss Sturrock's toilet and peeped in but was disappointed. It was nothing – only a lavatory seat like the girls' ones only bigger and a wash-hand basin. A sound behind her made her turn round.

'Go away,' Miss Sturrock said. She was standing at the end of the corridor by the classroom door. Her hands were hanging by her sides, and she didn't look or sound angry. She said: 'Just go away. Why can't you be like your sister? Why can't you be like anybody else?'

When she came into the playground, they were waiting for her.

'You're a clype,' Peter said. He had a fat round face and thick red hands that looked as if they were swollen. 'You've been trying to get our Jamie into trouble.' He was Jamie's cousin, but everybody was everybody's cousin. Except her. And Francesca, of course.

'You are a crapule.' She said it carefully, making the word sound exactly the way her mother used to say it.

His mouth gaped at her, like a fish in a box at their stupid harbour. The thought made her smile and at once without any warning he kicked her on the front of the leg. She screamed tears and rage; and over that, as if she were listening for some other sound, she heard one of the boys sniggering.

They were all round her, laughing and pushing, and then they were going away. So quickly that her mouth had not emptied of its screams, they were all gone, running off round to the side of the shed. In the quietness, she looked up and

14

Miss Sturrock was watching at the window; the teacher's face made a white circle and the brooch swinging below it sparkled through her tears.

The school and the field beside it were at the top of the hill and that was the end of the village. The Woman whom now Francesca and she were supposed to call Mummy stayed in a house at the bottom of the road that wound down to the flat ground beside the harbour in two loops. Halfway down, Fat Chae was crouched by the hedge, but his mother wasn't with him. Although he was almost grown up, his mother was always with him.

'Hurt poor wee thing it's hurt.' It wasn't easy to follow what he was trying to say, since even his tongue was fat and flopped between his lips as he spoke.

She hunkered down beside him to get a better look. The feathers on one side were all puffed out so the bird looked fat and round, but the other side was broken and the wing was pulled half off. Two yellow legs stuck out thin and stiff. The fish lorry coming down the hill threw a streak of brown mud on to the white feathers.

'You are stupid,' she said. She stood up and stirred the bird in the broken place with her foot. 'It's not hurt, it's dead.' A soft smear came out of the dead body of the bird across the shining toe of her shoe.

Fat Chae struggled to his feet. She heard his breath wheezing in his chest. 'I've got a sweetie in my pocket do you want a sweetie?' His lips mumbled then as if each word were a plump gobbet of sweetness.

She shook her head. The thought of eating anything he gave her made her sick.

'Money,' he said. 'I've got money in there you can have it in there.' He pointed at his trouser pocket and pulled it open with one finger. With money she could buy sweets of her own, they would be nothing to do with him; but when she pushed her hand into his pocket, having to squeeze hard against the fat thrust and straining of his thigh, there was no bottom to the pocket and she touched the soft bulging place between his legs. She tried to pull her hand out and

15

for a moment it was held by the tightness of the cloth as if she was in a trap.

'I hate you,' she said. She bent and wiped the soft dead stuff from her shoe, but even when she shook her fingers some of it clung to them. She reached out and rubbed them clean on the ragged sleeve of Fat Chae's jersey.

He stared at the mark puzzled. 'It was a joke boys do it told me to.'

'I hate you. Fat pig.'

He looked up at her. 'Your mother was a whore,' he said clearly, spacing out the words as if he had borrowed a voice for an effect of mimicry.

Don't you talk about my mother! The words in her mind were like the screams which had come from her mouth when Jamie's cousin kicked her, but she had learned not to say them aloud when anyone spoke of Mother.

'Your mother,' he said, and hesitated, trying to get it right, 'your mother was your mother was murdered.'

Straight above the harbour the sky was grey but beyond the church it was black. That was like the sea which was grey near the land and black as black far out. Only where it met the sky there was a thin strip of whitey cloud like an eyelid.

Somebody's hit the world, and it's got a sore face.

When she came into the kitchen, the Woman looked round from the oven and asked, 'Why are you limping? What's up with your leg?'

'I don't remember,' she said.

She could not think of a reason then why her leg should be sore.

'Was it the boys?' the Woman asked anxiously. She lifted a tray from the oven with a big shape wrapped and hidden. The kitchen was heavy with warmth. 'Have they been tormenting you again?'

'I pay them no attention.' She watched as the Woman set the tray on the big wooden table. 'They're just common fishermen's sons.'

'Don't let your daddy hear you saying that! He wouldn't

think it was funny,' the Woman said, staring at her in fright. That was stupid, the Woman's husband was not her father; that was stupid, stupid, but she said nothing, watching as the Woman unwrapped the shape on the tray.

'A lovely bird.' The Woman patted it with the backs of her fingers.

A bird? It was nothing like the puffed staring brokenness under the hedge; and yet, there were the legs – but it had no wings to fly. It was uglier than the bird under the hedge.

As she watched, the Woman peeled strips that hung curling from her fingers. 'Bits of bacon. That keeps it moist and sweet.' She took a long clean knife and starting at the top cut down until a wall of white meat toppled over and did that twice more and then took smaller pieces and at last with the tip of the knife pushed out curls from the bony corners. Looking up, she laughed, 'You've been here before. A wee old woman.' She turned the tray and did it all again, the white walls dropped in the same way and again with the tip of the knife she pushed out the last twists and curls of the meat.

'Here.' The Woman held out a dangling length and she opened her mouth and the Woman dropped it warm on to her tongue.

'No more, mind.'

She watched and the Woman took one of the legs and bent it and twisted until it pulled loose. Where it tore free red liquid gathered under the torn place.

'Oh, it could have been doing with a while longer.'

With her fingers the Woman worked at the gap, and brown chunks and red strands were piled on another plate. The pool of red widened.

'We'll do something with those bits. To be on the safe side.'

'What's that? The red stuff?'

'It shouldn't be there. It's a big bird, right enough.'

Blood. It was blood.

The piece she had started to swallow came up her throat

17

and she would be sick but nothing came. She spat out the chewed horror from her mouth.

'You wee bitch!' the Woman cried. 'Get out of this kitchen! That was deliberate badness. You did that out of badness!'

At the gate she watched the boats hurry nearer through the dark water. The one who tried to make her call him Daddy would be on one of them bringing back the big-clawed poos caught in a crib. He would drop the poo into boiling water and it would die. When it was dead, he took it out and broke the shell with a spoon and took out the pink and brown stuff inside.

Was there no blood in it?

Fat Chae, who liked to watch the boats come back, was walking down to the harbour beside his mother. They walked slowly without speaking. His mother was always with him though he was almost grown up.

'You're there,' the Woman said. She had come to the door. 'Come back in here.'

When she went inside, the Woman gave her a kiss.

'I shouldn't have lost my temper with you.' She felt the Woman stroke her hair. 'Poor thing. Poor lamb. Poor motherless bairn.'

The best thing was to smile and put your head against her. She felt the hand stroke, stroke her hair.

'You're a good girl. You're my girl now. That's what you're going to be,' the Woman said. 'I don't pay any heed to what they say. I know you'll grow up to be a good girl.'

It was silly to be afraid of blood. I won't scream, she thought, not even if it is coming off her fingers on to my hair.

BOOK ONE

CHAPTER ONE
After Midnight

SATURDAY, AUGUST 25TH

After midnight; Murray Wilson kept his head down and climbed towards Sunday bells and an old woman's voice.

It had been an unprofitable week; there had been too many like that on the string recently. That day, however, he had worked at his trade. After lunch, he had taken a bus out into the country. Half an hour was enough to change worlds. Among the neat bungalows, he found the right neat bungalow and at his knock a nice suburban lady shading forty, in green slacks and a halter top, appeared. Her smile was pleasant, but there was too much caution in it, which let him know that he was at the right house.

'Mrs Jerrold?'

'Yes?'

She made it into a question, but the lack of a denial was all he needed. She watched his hand as he pulled out the envelope. He held it up and her eyes moved as she read what was scrawled across the front: Gone Away.

'Your writing? Or Mr Jerrold's? Anyway here you are and here I am, and you've probably had one of these before.' With a natural movement, he passed her the envelope. 'Would you like to write a cheque for me now? If you don't, the only place your husband will be going away to will be court.'

'I couldn't give you a cheque,' she said. 'My husband handles the money – anything to do with money.'

'He wouldn't mind,' he said. 'If it has to be done, maybe he'd prefer if you did it.'

'I don't have a cheque book. Don't you see I can't help you?'

'I was trying to make it easier for you,' he said. 'But I don't mind waiting.'

He sat in the front room surrounded by the expensive furnishings for which his clients would like to be paid. At one point in the afternoon, she brought him a cup of tea, and said suddenly as he drank it, 'He tries hard. He doesn't drink or gamble. It's not his fault.' When he went upstairs to the lavatory, all the doors to the bedrooms were closed. He opened each of them: one had a bed and a table, the second was empty, in the last there were mattresses on the floor and children's clothes scattered on the bare boards and stuffed into cardboard boxes, the kind firms use to deliver a washing machine or a television set.

It was his trade to know how to persuade people to give information, to accept documents, to make statements that had to be signed against what they saw at first as their own interests; and this was done not by force but by his understanding of what would influence them: the opinion of neighbours, the effect on their business, the hope of leniency if they co-operated, sometimes shame, conscience perhaps or some picture of the person they had once imagined themselves to be. Part of his trade was to be able to get into a house, and sit, and wait. After a time, two little girls arrived in from school and sat side by side on the couch watching him with wide eyes. 'Play upstairs,' their mother said at last. 'It's only a man who's come to see Daddy.' When Daddy came home from hunting, he wrote a cheque and held it between trembling fingers. 'You won't have any trouble with that,' he said, staring at his signature as if he felt in it some special power to cure what ailed him. It was the woman though who came to the door and asked, 'Are you proud of yourself?' whispering so that her husband would not hear.

It was the kind of trace that should ideally have been fitted in with other enquiries because the fee was small and there would be a low ceiling on expenses. It had been an unimportant routine job.

Murray Wilson kept his head down and climbed towards the old woman's voice; perhaps she would lose her nerve and retreat indoors. The light from the landing came down to meet him and the voice hissed, 'Mr Wilson, I've been watching for you coming.'

'It's late, Miss Timmey.'

'I heard it again, Mr Wilson.'

She caught a pinch of his coat sleeve in her tiny claw. Thinning white hair pulled tight to her skull, nose like a polished bone, she reminded him always of a bird. A wounded bird which fluttered against him on the shadowed landing: 'I heard the child cry out. Oh, it was awful, awful.'

'There's nothing wrong with the child in there, Miss Timmey.'

He nodded at the flat opposite his own, and she put her finger to her lips. 'Oh, sshh. Sshh! It's the *other* child.'

Deliberately, he raised the pitch of his voice. 'They have only one child and, believe me, I had a good look at her after you spoke to me.' It was stupid even to try to persuade her. She was old, touched with senility; she had never been married, never probably been with a man; and she had the bad luck to live next to a pair of the beautiful people, Moirhill version: the girl small and pale and blonde, the man older, in his mid-twenties with very black curly hair: every time you saw them they looked glossy and replete, as if they had just got out of bed. They kept touching. Murray had seen them in the park, locked together on the grass, with the child matter of fact and cheerful playing round them.

It was little wonder they had driven old Miss Timmey demented. She kept hearing a child in pain and need of rescue: she had cast Murray for the part of the white knight, which was his bad luck. He tried again. 'The girl's healthy. She's happy. She's as fat as she can roll. There's nothing wrong. Go to bed.'

Reluctantly, she edged towards the refuge of her own flat, the one in the middle.

'Please,' she whispered. 'They might be listening.'

23

'No,' he said, not lowering his voice. 'They'll be sleeping, and that's what I'm going to be doing in about ten minutes from now. And that's what you're going to do. Go inside. Lock your door. Make yourself a cup of tea. And go to bed.'

'But the child?'

'Is asleep in her bed.'

'But—'

Impatient, he interrupted, 'I hope for your sake that they're not listening,' and she shrank back, yet still hesitated so that it was only after what seemed to be a struggle that she could bring herself to close the door. It occurred to him that in her own way she had shown a lot of courage. It was a pity she had not found a better cause.

He looked at the two closed doors and then turned to open his own. Soon he would be asleep. The couple would be asleep entwined in one another's arms. Their plump little daughter would be asleep. He doubted if Miss Timmey would sleep.

He incorporated the banging on the door into his dream so that he surfaced with the confused impression it was the night in Memphis when Seidman got himself killed. The noise of traffic came and went and the banging stopped and then started up again louder than before. The pillow had got lost out of the bed and one side of his neck ached.

The window showed as a dull glowing patch on the dark. Under it he could make out the shape of the sink and the single ugly line of the cold-water tap. The pilot light on the Ascot water heater offered a tiny blue reflection.

With a groan he came fully awake and rolled out of bed.

The voice roared, ending on a bang, 'It's Eddy Stewart. I've brought you a present, Murray.'

He took the chain off and opened the door. 'Close your mouth,' he said. 'I have a nervous neighbour.'

Stewart was lying against the wall. He lifted his head and showed one eye shut and dried scabs of blood like tribal scars on the cheek underneath it.

'I need a kip for the night.'

'This isn't a doss-house,' Murray said, but he turned and led the way back into the kitchen where he had been sleeping. Yawning, he went over to the sink and turned on the water heater. The gas under the tank lit with a soft explosion. 'One coffee to sober up on and then out.' Behind him, he heard the creak of the rocker chair. 'That's where I sit, Eddy. Find somewhere else.'

'Somewhere else?' Stewart looked around without showing pleasure. The rocker he was sitting in was one of the old kind with a fixed base and a spring; the back and the arms were covered in faded green velvet; beside it a low table supported a chess board and an arrangement of pieces. As Murray continued to stare at him, he got up and took one of the two plain wooden chairs beside the kitchen table. Apart from a cooker beside the sink at the window end of the room, there was nothing else in the way of furniture. There were no pictures or photographs on the walls. 'This place needs a woman's touch.'

'I'll leave that to you, Eddy,' Murray said, taking a mug from a hook and putting in a couple of heaped spoonfuls of instant coffee.

Stewart rested his elbows on the table and put his head in his hands like a man who wanted to go to sleep. 'You should have seen this one tonight. We finished up in her flat. The place was practically empty. In the bedroom, there was just a mattress on the floor, know what I mean?'

'I've seen a room like that.' He put the cup of coffee between Stewart's elbows.

'But you haven't seen a woman like this one. She was black – smooth, smooth skin – Jesus, when you've been married as long as I have, you need to see a woman's belly without stretch marks. We made it on this mattress on the floor, and then she took off the evening dress, a long gown, red and cut low so that, you know, you could see her tits. And then she got this floor brush and she started marching up and down with it over her shoulder. I mean the bitch was stark naked, marching up and down and singing. Black as the earl of hell's waistcoat and singing, ''The Campbells

25

are Coming''. She wanted me to get up and join her –
'shun, quick march, right turn – form bloody fours, I
shouldn't be surprised. Mad! But what a body – black,
did I say she was black? She'd even have made you forget
you were a monk, Murray.'

'If you want to have a wet dream, go home,' Murray said,
taking his seat in the rocker by the chess board. 'You know
I don't listen to that stuff.'

Stewart wiped his hand across his mouth. 'You never had
a pro? Don't try to kid a kidder. You forget I've known
you a long time. I remember what you did when we were
on the beat together twenty years ago. Before Billy Graham
converted you.'

'Drink your coffee.'

Distracted for a moment, Stewart stared at his cup. 'Are
you not having any?'

'I don't drink that muck. I'll have a cup of tea after I've
got rid of you.'

'Oh, yeah. Scented tea from bloody China. You're an old
maid, man.'

Murray yawned and held up the fingers of his right hand.
'Five minutes.'

'I remember after you got converted how you rounded
up the whores on Bath Street and walked them down to
the Sally Anns at the corner of West Campbell Street. You
made them stand there and sing hymns in their bare feet.
And the rain was pissing down.'

'No, Eddy. You've got me mixed up with somebody else.'

Stewart gave him a grin of satisfaction. 'Is that right?
Could be.'

'Why don't you go home to Lynda? She'll be waiting for
you, God knows why.'

Stewart stopped smiling. 'When I said that bitch tonight
was in evening dress, didn't you wonder why?'

'It's time for you to go home, Eddy.'

'I met her in the line of duty.' As he waited, Murray
leaned forward, ignoring him, and slid the queen along
one of the board's diagonals. 'I thought you might be

interested. Are you not curious about what your wee brother gets up to?'

Looking up abruptly, Murray caught Stewart grimacing at him, pulling back his upper lip like a dog showing its teeth. As he watched, Stewart's face settled itself again into the habitual folds creased by tiredness and drink, familiar as a mask.

The mask said: 'We've been targeting Blair Heathers.'

'So?'

'Heathers threw a party tonight. John Merchant was at it, your brother Malcolm's boss.'

'From what I hear a lot of people go to Heathers' parties.'

'That's right. And for the last month we've been taking a note of all of them. New name tonight. Your brother Malcolm got his invitation.'

'And Irene?' Murray asked. The words were out before he could think about them. 'My brother's wife.'

'She was there. Only she left early. On her own. When she came out, she looked annoyed. Maybe they had a quarrel about something.'

'I wouldn't know,' Murray said.

'Give us time and we'll know,' Stewart said. The grin had come back. 'Everything goes on the big computer in the sky. Anyway, after another hour your brother came out.' He paused.

'With the black woman,' Murray said. It wasn't a question.

'You're such a quick bastard,' Stewart said in irritation. 'You should have been a detective. I went after them – being a friend of yours.'

'Did you recognise her?'

'She's new, but she works for Heathers all right. Not directly, of course. The little bastard may be a millionaire, but he came from Moirhill and he still has his contacts. He's never had any bother getting as many women as he needed to sweeten a deal.'

'What deal's he sweetening here?' Murray asked, but that was too direct.

'Come on Murray. Peerse is my gaffer on this one. He'd cut my balls off if I told you anything. If I told anybody anything – but especially you. You know how he feels about you.'

'You want more coffee?' Murray asked.

'I wouldn't have time to drink it – not in five minutes.'

'Stay if you like. You can sleep in here. I'll sleep on the couch through there.'

'In the office, eh? Frightened I get a look in the filing cabinet?'

The only secret of the filing cabinet, Murray thought, was how little was in it. He wondered if that was what Stewart meant. He said, 'You haven't explained how, if the woman came out with Malcolm, she finished up with you.'

'He changed his mind maybe.' Stewart stood up. 'Look, I think I'll go home right enough. I've got a little bit left to give the wife.'

Because there was so little space, when Murray stood up he crowded close to Stewart. 'Not till you explain.'

'Suppose I shove you out of the way and walk out?'

'Don't be silly,' Murray said quietly. 'You couldn't have done that on your best day – and that was a long time ago.'

The big detective licked his lips. 'Take a joke, Murray. I'm not stupid enough to get into any go with you.' He glanced away. 'More sense than your brother – he got into a – he got a doing. Not from me!'

'No. You wouldn't be stupid enough to come here if it was you.'

'I followed the two of them. Your brother's wife had taken his car, so they took a taxi. Through the tunnel. Got out at Moirhill Road. Maybe he'd changed his mind. They were talking and two plainclothes guys came over from across the street. They didn't see me. I recognised one of them – a young guy – you wouldn't know him, well after your time. But you'd know the type, a head-banger. Whatever your brother said, this guy hit him once and put the boot in a couple of times when he went down. It wasn't any big deal. I came forward and broke it up. That's all there was to it.' Stewart shrugged. 'I did your brother a favour.'

'What happened then?'

'That was it. Your brother got a taxi. I took the girl home – since I'd stuck my nose in, I thought I'd combine business with pleasure. See if she'd talk.'

'Did she?'

Stewart shook his head. 'We're back to Peerse again, Murray. You're over the line. That's not your business.'

After a moment, Murray nodded; accepting.

'It's a lousy job. You know that,' Stewart said unexpectedly. 'Did I ever tell you when I was a kid my mother went to see our local Councillor? She wanted to send me to a fee-paying school and went to ask him about it. He said to her, That kind of place isn't for people like you. Some fucking Socialist, eh?'

'John Merchant.'

'I have told you before. That wasn't yesterday . . . Now the bastard's in line to be Lord Provost. They'll make him a Sir – Sir John Merchant.' He laughed. 'Some fucking Socialist, eh?'

'And is Heathers going to make him rich?'

'You never stop trying, do you? I'm going home.'

Murray walked him along the narrow corridor to the front door. Stewart took a step out on to the landing then turned back.

'I had to talk that plainclothes guy out of taking your brother in to the shop. He wanted to give him a doing where he wouldn't be interrupted.'

When there was no response, he tapped on the board that had been nailed across the upper panel of the door. 'What happened to your glass?'

'Kids.'

'Nice advert.'

Lettered on the board were the words: Wilson Enquiry Agency – Discretion Guaranteed.

'Nowadays,' Murray said, 'who can control kids? If one of them grows up to be a bad debtor, then I'll get him.'

Stewart grinned. 'I did your brother a favour.'

'You told me.'

'And you – Peerse would break my back, if he knew I'd done you a favour.'

'Peerse!' Murray made the name sound like one of the swear words he avoided.

'Sure! But he's still my gaffer. Funny to think it was Peerse got the promotions.'

'Somebody has to be clever, Eddy.'

'Cleverer than you, Murray?'

'I got out. That's where I was clever.'

Stewart looked at the mended door and the dark passage beyond it.

'Yeah,' he said.

CHAPTER TWO
The Guard

TUESDAY, AUGUST 28TH

The old Chambers Building filled one side of the Square. It had been built out of nineteenth-century riches and confidence. Murray had read up on it when he was a raw policeman on duty there, young and enough of a stranger to be excited by the city; and so, as he crossed the entrance hall, he knew that the marble under his feet was Numidian and black Irish. He knew that of the two giant nudes which guarded the main staircase one was named Purity and the other Honour. As he climbed, he knew the staircase was of marble and its balustrade of alabaster with pillars from Italy and Derbyshire. The mosaics on the wall had been imported from Venice; the lamps were copies of the one in St Mark's. From the old days, he remembered where the Committees met and went along a lobby roofed and lined with majolica from Staffordshire. There were rooms of satin-wood from Ceylon, amber-wood from South America and mahogany from Cuba and St Domingo. The city had levied tribute from the world, but then there had been giants on the earth in those days.

'You're in the wrong place,' Merchant said. 'Where are you looking for?'

It might have been the foreign inflection, still there despite the years of exile, which made the question sound abrupt; but it was, in any case, the tone Murray would have expected from him. Merchant had the reputation of being an arrogant man. He had been a power in the City Chambers for more than twenty years, and even after the Region had been set up preferred to spend as much of his time as possible in familiar surroundings rather than in the new bureaucracy's prematurely tarnished tower of concrete and glass.

He remained to that extent a European of a certain kind, a man of taste.

The narrow silver skull inclined again over the file of papers spread on the table before him. After a moment, he looked up as if in surprise and made a gesture of impatience. 'I really don't have time to waste.'

The windowless room was small, a side chamber off one of the lesser committee rooms, wood-panelled and smelling of wax polish. The table and four upright seats with green leather backs provided its only furniture. Murray took the seat that faced Merchant, and when he sat leaned forward with his elbows on the table. 'I'm Malcolm Wilson's brother,' he said, and felt the unwelcome anger pressing up for release.

'Malcolm Wilson,' Merchant repeated and, shutting his eyes, seemed to recall the name. 'A promising young man. He's the type who will go far.' He looked down again at the file in front of him. Unexpectedly, he sounded tired.

'If he takes your advice,' Murray said, 'he's going to go further than he expects to. Maybe, all of you are.'

Merchant leaned back. 'I think that is something you had better try to explain.'

Murray hesitated. He had thought through what he had to do, but caution suggested that he get what he wanted with as little pressure as possible. Whatever happened, by coming here and making an enemy of Merchant, he had probably finished himself in this city.

'I work as a private detective,' he began. 'It's part of my business to hear things. I have contacts.'

'Wait a minute.' Merchant rubbed a finger between his brows. 'Wilson's brother. Yes . . . you're older than he is. You were a policeman here in the city . . . You went off without the formality of a resignation. Some years later, you turned up in Manchester where you set yourself up as a detective. But you had been in the United States before that.

You worked for a criminal called Seidman. And now you're back favouring us.'

'Seidman wasn't a criminal,' Murray said. It was foolish to have that as his first reaction: what difference could it make, this much later and so far away, to the memory of a good, brave man? 'But you've asked questions about me. Never mind whether the answers were right or not, that means you had to check up on me – because you had to check up on Malcolm. That means you've got involved in something.'

'If I did ask questions about you,' Merchant said, but with the same touch of weariness he had shown when talking of Murray's past – like a parlour trick he was running through only out of old habit – 'who do you imagine gave me the answers? Anything I know about you, I learned from your brother.'

'Yes,' Murray said flatly. He could believe that. 'Let me tell you something then you didn't know. Your deal's sour. It's time to get out of it.'

'Have you said this to your brother?' Merchant wondered.

'Not yet.'

'Why come to me? Why not simply warn your brother, if you're so concerned?'

'Because I don't know whether he could get himself out. You're the one who can find a way to bury the bodies. I'm telling you that you have to do that – and not just for yourself – for Malcolm too.'

'Are you threatening me? You're not being absurd enough to threaten me *here*?' Merchant glanced around the quiet panelled room, full of territorial certainty like a man in his own place. 'A private detective . . . of sorts. Not successful.' He bent his head to his papers and continued without looking up: 'There should be a licensing system. There seems to be no way of preventing unsuitable people from going in for security or crime prevention. Sometimes I don't understand this country.'

It was a common enough expression: not to understand what was going on in the country. Murray had used it himself. The difference was that Murray knew himself to be native born.

'This country,' he repeated and something in his tone made the older man's head snap up.

'Oh, that has the real policeman's sound,' Merchant said. 'You don't like foreigners. Blacks. Jews? How do you feel about Jews? The first election I won in the country was getting into Lairds Hill Golf Club. My God, I was pleased. By that time I thought even my accent was almost gone. And then by the worst of bad luck, I heard someone boasting after a round. They didn't let Jews into Lairds Hill – all these years later, they still don't. I handed in my resignation the next day. I was heartbroken, but in those days I wanted to make a stand.'

'I didn't know you were Jewish,' Murray said, and caught a look of something like contempt in response. Hurried on: 'I'm not interested in the past. I'm someone who takes family seriously. I don't want Malcolm involved.'

'Families can be a great embarrassment. I've seen the wrong kind of family ruin a man's career – A well-meaning brother. Even an attractive wife.' Merchant smiled. 'I've met your brother's wife recently.'

'On Saturday night,' Murray said, 'at Blair Heathers. I heard that from a policeman – a real one. Since you make me, I'll spell it out. The police have targetted Heathers. He's under surveillance, him, the people he sees. That contact of mine, that policeman, he mentioned you, he mentioned my brother. He even mentioned Irene.'

'Blair was charmed by her,' Merchant said. There was no alteration in his voice, but Murray saw a sudden blankness in his eyes, the same absence he had seen in the eyes of opponents in the moment before they dropped unconscious in the ring. 'Your brother's wife is charming.'

'It wasn't even hard,' Murray said, 'once I'd been given the tip, to work out what the deal must be. You're the politician; Malcolm works for the Region. Which contract from the Region is going to make Heathers even richer? It has to be something to do with the Underpass.' It was the same feeling as when the last blow struck bone and the man began to fall. 'I'm a better detective than you thought.'

'I'm not a Jew,' Merchant said. He rubbed his fingers between his brows in the same unconscious effort of recollection. 'When the Nazis came to Poland, they had two plans for extermination, but only one was for the Jews – the other was for the intellectuals. After the massacre at Bromberg on Bloody Sunday, all the politicals were gathered in the camp at Soldavo – that was in the winter of 1939. I was only nineteen – a boy at University – but I had made the mistake of being the President of a left-wing student society. Heydrich had personally ordered that the activists should be killed. We didn't know all that naturally. We were the victims. I saw a guard kill a boy. I saw worse things later but because that was the first I would not forget him. It wasn't what he did to the boy, it was the noise. There's a noise a baby makes crying.'

A muscle in Murray's thigh had cramped. It was if he had been sitting very still for a long time. Cautiously, he eased it, while Merchant talked on as if compelled about that lost time. He wondered if the older man was ill, and even, fantastically, if it was possible that he had been told he was going to die.

'All that stuff,' Murray said, 'it's the past,' and fell silent.

'No,' Merchant said. 'The guard who killed the boy is here in the city. I saw him on Saturday night. I knew him at once.'

His voice trailed away and he sat looking at his hands like a discarded prayer folded over the file of official papers.

'All that stuff,' Murray said almost gently, the way you talk to someone who is sick, 'about being a Jew in the camps. Nobody wants to hear about that Jewish stuff. All the Socialists are flying the PLO flag now. Don't you understand nobody cares about that stuff any more?'

'You don't listen,' Merchant said. 'It didn't happen to me because I was a Jew.'

CHAPTER THREE
Irene and I

WEDNESDAY, AUGUST 29TH

Inside, Malcolm Wilson found the air heavy and still with the dry taste of electric heaters in hot weather. In the bright sunshine the site was a scooped saucer raked brown with claw marks and alive with ant men and lego toys. Inside, blue smoke from Blair Heathers' cigars trailed from the lamps like festive streamers.

'Thank God it's Friday.' Heathers laughed, showing teeth so splendid and so clean that they could only be false, the right kind of expensive dentistry having arrived too late in a self-made life. 'That's what you lot with your bums behind desks say – and the grafters out there aren't any different. You have that in common. T.G.I.F.'

He was in high spirits, it seemed. Despite the gloss on his skin, the jewellery on his plump white fingers, the exclusive barbering, he looked at home here close to the raked earth and the machines.

'They won't find much difference down there,' the heavy man standing next to Malcolm objected. Malcolm tried to recall his name. 'They're on shifts round the clock. Sunday or Friday makes no bloody difference.'

And then he smiled at Heathers to show how that was to be taken; 'We keep them at it'; and Malcolm remembered: Chalmers, the site manager, which made him like the rest a Heathers' employee.

'Into the golden hours,' Heathers said. 'They'll be earning more than I do.'

Malcolm glanced round the beefy competent men indicating

their appreciation of the joke. They were all of a type except himself and the odd-looking man with the foreign name.

'And this is Mr Kujavià. He's a business consultant,' Heathers had said.

Kujavia? It was foreign, of course, but of what country — Russia? Perhaps Poland. He was in the same kind of business suit as the others, a thickset man under the average height with a lumpy potato face and spikes of black hair standing up on his head. Mr Kujavia the business consultant. Where had he seen him before?

'Malcolm here is the man who's paying for it all,' Heathers was saying.

'Oh, no,' Malcolm said, and felt his foolishness when there was a general response of laughter. 'I help with little pieces of the local red tape.'

'And that,' Heathers smiled, 'helps to pay the bit the government and the EEC leave over.'

It was afternoon and it seemed to Malcolm, looking out through the long glass panels, that despite what had been said about working round the clock there was a change to be observed and that the patterns outside were altering into something not slower but somehow looser, like metal coins yielding up their tension.

'Everybody finished?' Heathers asked. 'Don't let me rush anybody. Only I'm going right now.'

There was a general setting down of glasses.

'Right. We'll have the Cook's Tour then.'

Someone hurried to open the door and they filed out into the dry dusty air. It felt arid and overheated like the temporary structure they had left, as if the entire site had been baked on a whim of Heathers.

In the open vehicle, they were crowded together. Startling but unmistakable, he caught the smell of an unwashed body. Involuntarily, he turned his head in surprise and realized he was beside Kujavia. The man's linen was clean where it showed, even the face and hands seemed clean, but again the air between them was oiled with the choking offence of human dirt. The muscles of his throat rose and perhaps he made some noise for the man looked round. The impression was of a pure and terrible malevolence and Malcolm's shoulders contracted as if ducking from a blow. Even when Kujavia glanced away, it took an effort to straighten from that spontaneous and uncontrollable reaction. Humiliated, he wondered if any of these bulky stolid men surrounding him had noticed. He took deep breaths of the clean air that blew warm against them and willed his heart to beat more slowly. He tried to imagine in what kind of business Mr Kujavia might act as a consultant to Heathers, whose voice dominated over the engine and the racket of the site as they bumped down towards the bottom of the saucer.

'—like God. It helps those who help themselves. If you try to farm the top of Ben Nevis, what do you expect to harvest except bloody snow? Look round when you get down . . . bloody amazing . . . technology . . . That's the future . . .'

It was a royal progress. Seated up at the front, Heathers nodded to left and right without at all interrupting the flow of his talk. Men lifted a hand in salute as he passed. There did not seem to be anyone who failed to recognize him. Malcolm remembered how on Saturday night he had said, 'I have a minute for everybody. Even the brickies. They respect me for that.'

'You don't mind going down into the tunnel?'

Chalmers' voice broke into his thoughts.

'Why should I?' Malcolm asked.

'Some people do. You'd be surprised.'

'I'm looking forward to it. I gather it's a new technology.'

'New enough,' the site manager said. 'We don't handle that part of it. It's contracted to an outside firm. Specialists.'

As he spoke, they rolled inside the tunnel entrance to the Underpass. After the controlled confusion of men getting out of a crowded vehicle, they gathered in a group. Malcolm patted the chinstrap on his safety helmet, and noticed how many of the others went through the same reassuring ritual.

'We're going to walk down,' Heathers said. 'It gives you

the feel of it better. And the exercise won't do anybody any harm.'

Even just inside, voices echoed. As they went forward, the tunnel was lit from the roof with a white brilliancy that stretched black-edged shadows beside them for company. The sense of descending was kinetic, a tightness at the front of the thigh with every step. Malcolm, looking over his shoulder, expected to see daylight, but it was gone though the tunnel seemed so straight. Some people can't come underground, Chalmers had said.

'Feel anything?' Heathers grinned back at them from under the helmet stamped with his initials in gold. 'Feel anything yet?'

It was cold, and the group milled to a halt and Heathers was saying, '—shamed the Government into the go ahead. Community cash. The most sophisticated transport link in any inner city in Europe,' and the curtain of broad backs parted and the man behind Malcolm muttered, 'Jesus wept!' and sounded reverent.

Heathers guffawed. 'That's the kind of thing you see in the real world when you come out from behind your desk, George.'

'That's real?' George asked.

It was a cavern of ice.

'So cold,' Chalmers the site manager said, 'they've to stop every ten minutes to thaw out.'

Ahead of them a trench ran the length of the tunnel floor. The earth beside it glistened. Pipes curved down into the trench and over a wheel on the nearest a workman bent, winding it down by slow turns.

'After five or ten minutes, they go numb from the waist down,' Chalmers went on quietly as Malcolm, hardly conscious of what he was doing, moved forward until he was at the front of the group. He was in the grip of a powerful and unexpected emotion. The ice vault, the cold, the stillness, above all the movements of the men which were so slow and seemingly noiseless, produced this effect. Nothing in his experience, apart from sex, had taught him to imagine he might be lost and carried out of himself. 'Liquified nitrogen freezes at ninety-six degrees below zero. You can see why it's cold out there. They're pumping it into the ground – later the soil will be excavated and the concrete will go in wrapped in a fibreglass shield – hundreds of tons of it. When the ground thaws out again, they'll have given us a foundation. But that's later. Right now they're working in sixty degrees below freezing. You're watching the coldest men in the world.'

It could not have lasted. Anyway, the voice reciting facts and figures brought it to an end. The significance of his mood was gone like the meaning of a dream that is sensed but lost in the margin between night and day. He was surprised to find himself at the front of the group with Chalmers and Kujavia on either side.

Chalmers shook his head. He was smiling as if he understood. 'I shouldn't go any further,' he said.

When Kujavia took him by the arm just above the elbow, the grip was enormusly strong, but it was the remnant of the mood which made him walk forward unresistingly. After only a few steps, the outcry of voices behind sounded very far away. He heard it as a distant confusion shot through with glittering points of noise like ice crystals. The group working around the trench had stopped to watch. Gloved, helmeted, turning the white blankness of faces, in its stillness it seemed to be composed of sculptures rather than men.

They came to a place where the air around them changed. At that invisible boundary, the cold stopped being something outside them. It moved inside, encasing every organ of the body. Malcolm felt his heart like a bird struggling to escape. Clothed as they were, it was impossible to go any further.

The man who had been crouched over the wheel came towards them. He spread his arms as he approached in the natural gesture of a boy herding geese out of a garden. Under the yellow helmet, the face was made of angles and tight pulled skin. He drew off his right glove using the pit of the other arm to drag it clear. As they watched, he tilted back his helmet and broke off a piece of his hair. The brittle strands snapped between his fingers.

'It's cold here.' White breath puffed from his lips. 'You shouldn't be here.'

'I am sixty years,' Kujavia said. 'More old than sixty. But I am a lion.'

The air came into the lungs like knives.

But when they returned, Kujavia stood apart seemingly ignored as the men eddied in a slow unease.

'I don't know,' Chalmers muttered. 'I don't know. I never saw him before.'

On the other side, Heathers did not interfere but watched with no expression Malcolm could read. He felt the weight of the older man's gaze.

Going back, there was no hint of daylight until, as if a corner were turned although the tunnel appeared undeviatingly straight, they were at the entrance. Moments later they were seated and being run into the dazzling light of the sun.

'You'd have missed an experience if you hadn't come,' Heathers said. On the bench seat his fat thigh pressed hard against Malcolm. 'I was surprised that you hadn't wanted to come.'

'I don't understand why my brother phoned you. He had no right to do that.'

He waited for Heathers to respond but met the same blank gaze as if what he had been saying did not make sense. The hot pressure of the thigh next to his made him uncomfortable. His ribs ached where the policeman had punched him on Saturday night. He wanted to be rich and safe, so safe nothing like that could ever happen to him again.

'I haven't even seen my brother in a week,' he said. 'Maybe he tried to get in touch last night. My wife and I were out late. But even so . . . It doesn't make sense.'

'I was told you phoned to say you wouldn't come,' Heathers said.

When the vehicle stopped outside the site office, there

was an odd hesitation before people moved to get out. Since the incident in the tunnel, most of the men had been watchfully silent. Now they got out in the same subdued fashion. Malcolm saw that Kujavia alone remained seated, lolling back, eyes closed like a cat in the sun.

'Merchant phoned to say he couldn't come,' Heathers said in his hard nasal drawl. 'This business of not coming – I got frightened it was catching.'

He took Malcolm's arm in a way that reminded him unpleasantly of what had happened in the tunnel. 'If you came in a taxi, I'll give you a lift.' They were walking to where Heathers' car was parked. Malcolm caught an acrid whiff of his own sweat and from Heathers the cloying sweetness of a deodorant. The chauffeur, who was sitting with his back to the site and head bowed as if reading, must have been keeping one eye on his mirror for as they approached he jumped out and opened the door.

There was no reasonable way to refuse. Malcolm got in and slid over to leave room. Heathers followed him and the opposite door opened and Kujavia came in on the other side.

'What—' Malcolm began, but in his fright it came out, Wait!

The car moved off, picking up speed as it came on to the paved road and became part of the flow of traffic moving towards the city.

'How can I do business if I can't rely on people?' Heathers asked.

He did not seem to want any answer to that, and Malcolm watched the buildings go by and tried to pretend Kujavia was not there.

'How do you like being the boss of the Department, Malcolm? Does it suit you?'

'I'm only in charge of things temporarily,' Malcolm said. 'Until Mr Bradley gets back to work.'

'You know better than that. I made it my business to see the hospital reports. He's dying. He's gone rotten here.' With the same pale plump hand that had grasped Malcolm's arm, Heathers rubbed his belly. 'As of now, you're Johnny on the Spot. The man that matters.'

'If anything did happen to Mr Bradley,' Malcolm said carefully, 'I'd certainly hope to be on the short list. After all, I know what the job involves . . .'

Heathers stared at him, little blue eyes very bright above the red cheeks.

'You're too young,' he said. 'They'll bring in somebody from outside. It's the way the Region's mind works. If you've got somebody good, you've got them, so look outside and see if you can bring another good one in. You can't expect politicians to know anything about management.'

The casual verdict physically sickened Malcolm who wanted his share, his opportunity at the pork barrel Bradley had delved into up to the elbows. If Bradley had sold himself, he had taken care the price should be right. Malcolm remembered him saying, 'Some plumber or carpenter grafts away, studies, gets a leg up and becomes that wonderful beast, a Master of Works. First thing he's being invited out for a game of golf. No clubs? Don't worry – my son's bag's going spare in the boot. And you'll have a drink? Come to think of it – what about a meal? You can't pay here – it's club members' treat here. That kind of thing's nice – especially when you're not used to it. Oh, you're a popular chap. Then comes the day you're overseeing a job, a school or a hospital like as not, and the concrete's not what it should be or they've scamped the wiring and you should have a word with the contractor. It's a good job you're seeing him at the weekend for a round of golf and dinner at the club. He's right glad you mentioned it. He'll see to it – no problem. And if things don't improve, you don't like to keep narking on, do you? Not a popular chap like you, a chap who fits in so well. Not with him being a personal friend, like.' Bradley shook his head in disgust and his accent broadened. 'That's what the public would never credit – how cheap most of those buggers come.' It was six weeks and a day before the routine medical check-up gave the first hint that something was wrong. The big Yorkshireman's eyes were clear and his skin had a very healthy look from the open air and all the good holidays he had taken where you could be sure of the sun. There was no way of telling that he had gone rotten inside.

'I always got on well with Willie Bradley,' Heathers was saying. 'I could work with him. It wouldn't be reasonable of me to say you could count on his job – not at your age. But you've got a great chance to make a good impression. You're a lucky young man.'

With the venomous clarity of hope deferred, it occurred to Malcolm that, despite the car and the chauffeur and the rings on those plump fingers, Heathers' accent was exactly still like the one his mother would have described as that of a keelie, a boy from the slums of Moirhill. The hostility of the thought frightened him; it wasn't something he had planned for; it didn't fit in with what he wanted for himself. Sweat trickled down between his shoulder blades.

'Mr Heathers—'

'Blair. That's all the respect I need. Just Blair. My father now, he was different. When I was a kid, I saw him getting into an argument with a rent collector who'd been calling him "Heathers" – without any "mister" in front of it. He knocked him down. I'll be honest with you, he kicked him in the head.' Heathers smiled. 'I don't offend easily. But then I'm a more successful man than my father.'

Glancing away, Malcolm saw Kujavia leaning back in the corner with his eyes shut. There was no way of telling if he was awake and listening.

'Denny!' Heathers leaned forward to the driver. 'I'll need you again in about half an hour – after you take Mr Wilson back to his work.'

'There's no need,' Malcolm said.

As he spoke, the car came to a halt. Without waiting for the driver, Heathers opened the door himself and swung round to get out.

'Really, there's no need.' He did not want to be left alone with this ugly ill-smelling old man. 'I can make my own way.'

44

'Did I promise you a run back?' Heathers held up one soft white hand in admonishment. 'People have to keep their promises to one another. Otherwise it would be all take and no give. That wouldn't be right.'

As they pulled away, he glimpsed Heathers trotting up the broad steps in front of his buiding. Success made you healthy, energetic, slow to take offence. Turning, he found that Kujavia had opened his eyes and was watching him. The moment of recognition followed at once.

'Why you look at me like that?' Kujavia growled.

'I've just remembered where I saw you before.'

On Saturday night. Arriving at Heathers' house; as he got out of the car with Irene, the first person he noticed was John Merchant. The tall figure of the Convenor was bent forward with an odd intent stillness. Following his gaze – a car pulled up at the entrance – a big car but shabby, with one wing crumpled. A woman getting out – and Merchant looking not at her but at the man inside, whom you glimpsed: white face, spiked black hair, a lumpy ugliness. But glimpsed only for a moment before your attention was entirely taken by the black woman. It was as if everything Heathers' money might obtain for you had been gathered in a single fleshly image.

'You don't know me.' As he spoke, Kujavia leaned forward and closed the glass panel that shut off the driver.

'You didn't go into the party,' Malcolm said. 'You brought the black girl – Rafaella . . .' He couldn't remember the second name she had given. 'You brought her and then you drove away.'

'What bloody party?'

'On Saturday night at Mr Heathers. There were a lot of people there, dozens of people. But you just brought the woman and then drove away.'

'Why I do a thing like that?'

'Because you'd brought her for me,' Malcom said, and something in the other man's stillness told him that what he had suspected was true.

—My family are Nigerian, she had said. The taxi tilted

45

and they rushed down into the tunnel under the river; a lorry hurtled past them in the slow lane, hung the echoing clamour of its wheels over them like some crazy fairground machine; and her eyes shone as she turned to him. My family are Nigerian. My father was killed in an accident, and my mother did not send for me to bring me home. My mother would have sent for me but she was not able though she kept wanting.

Black satin skin, extraordinary breasts in the low-cut red gown, the delicate luxury of her perfume; but when they got out of the taxi, the pavement was broken and uneven under a litter of glass and soiled rubbish.

—I thought you were in a hurry, she had said. Under the expensive perfume, there was the sudden tang of sweat. In the cold night she smelled of fear.

'I wasn't that interesting – not for a woman as beautiful as that,' he told Kujavia. 'It was too easy. I know I don't look rich.'

And then, too, if from the taxi he had not glimpsed the street sign: Moirhill Road; or if she had taken him to a better district or if they had stopped outside a hotel . . . Desire and suspicion had pulled opposite ways. If she could have found a familiar phrase to say to him, something he recognized out of his own background, he would have gone with her like one of those toys that march down an incline at the touch of a finger.

—You won't regret it, she had said. Anything you want.

Kujavia leaned forward and banged on the glass with the edge of his fist. The driver looked round and at a peremptory chopping gesture from his passenger brought the car to a stop by the kerb.

'I want to see the girl,' Malcolm said.

Over his shoulder, as he got out, Kujavia said, 'You don't know what you want.'

But he did. It was as if the policeman's feet had beaten fear out of him and left only the taste of her lips, when she had kissed him in the taxi, and the length of her tongue in

46

his mouth. Next morning, aching and bruised, he wakened with a swollen erection.

'Wait here?' The driver made a sour sceptical movement with his mouth. 'The kids'll have the wheels off the motor if I sit here.'

Jackal children, however, gathering for a fresh kill angled away, ostentatiously unconcerned, as they caught sight of Kujavia. None of them would touch the car.

He registered the poverty of the street as he hurried after Kujavia, but it was different in daylight. What harm could come to him in daylight? As Kujavia turned into a close, however, and he followed and climbed the stairs in pursuit, his legs began to shake under him. Somewhere above, he heard a door close. The noise echoed in the stone box of the stair.

There were three doors on the landing, two with brass nameplates beside the old-fashioned bell pulls. He did not recognise the names and so it was on the third bare door that he knocked. Almost instantly, it was opened but only for a few inches. Across the gap he saw the dull line of a chain. From inside, a woman's voice, thin and piping like a girl's, asked, 'Who's there? What do you want?'

'Mr Kujavia?' he wondered hesitantly. 'Is this where Mr Kujavia lives?'

In the silence, he could hear her breathing, odd little gasping sounds.

'If he's there, would you tell him I'm willing to pay for the information – where she is – the person I mentioned to him?'

A man's voice muffled from inside shouted something, the chain rattled coming off and the door swung wide. From the woman and the passage beyond her, there came the same smell, oily, sweet, unmistakably, of human dirt. Her bare forearms shone like larded sides of bacon. She was enormously, obscenely fat.

In the lobby the outer door closing made the worst sound in the world. He understood that he had tricked himself. There was no way that the elegant black girl from Heathers'

47

party could be in this place. Soiled light spilled from a door at the end of the passage and as he went towards it he was startled by a hellish outburst at his back.

'It's just the dog in the back room,' the woman wheezed. 'He can't get out.'

The room was small, a kitchen of sorts with a sink under the window and a cooker loaded with dirty pots. The shape of it put into Malcolm's head a memory of his brother's flat, his brother's poverty—This is my only chance, he would tell Murray. Don't spoil it for me.

When he turned his head, the bed was in the recess where he might have expected to see it, and the black girl Rafaella across it with a sheet thrown over to cover her from the waist. It was nothing to do with his will, it was automatic, that he saw the nakedness of her breasts – and would have his response to their size and shape as part of what he felt when he remembered – before he realized what the stain on the sheet was at the junction of her parted thighs. In the stillness of her face only her eyes moved watching Kujavia.

'Miss Palamas had a job to do,' the ugly little man explained. 'She was supposed to be very good. I don't like monkeys, so I didn't care how good she was. And she wasn't one of my girls. And then she's not good after all. So now she'll be one of my girls. Even if I don't like monkeys.'

He picked a bottle up from the table. It was a wine bottle and the long neck stood out from his fist. At the sight of it, the girl whimpered.

'Even a monkey can learn.' He leaned on the bed with one hand and bent over her. 'Because she wasn't one of my girls then, I teach a *little* lesson. Only have a few friends in and make some fun for them.'

Malcolm had risked himself for this girl before. On the Saturday night with the two plainclothes policemen: 'Lovers' quarrel?' / 'You go home sir . . . You're seeing the young lady home? Know her well, do you? . . . What close does the . . . lady live in along there? The number? What's the name on the door? . . . You leave the young lady to us. We'll see her home . . . Don't give us a hard

48

time . . . sir! / 'Joe! He's had enough! He's had enough! Knock it off, you daft bugger!' / Clockwork man, he had marched down the incline, defying them; they could treat a man who had come from one of Blair Heathers' parties as if he was nobody. 'I'll see the young lady home,' he had said. The younger man, thin faced, sharp nosed, had watched him and grinned. The older one, beefy and smelling of drink, had stared at the girl, smacking his lips as if tasting something sweet. It had been the young one who had used his fists and then his feet, shoe caps like black gleaming hands that flew at him as he curled tight, tight, until everything that was black flowed together and the voices stopped.

—This is my chance, he would tell Murray. Don't spoil it for me.

It was the decisive moment of his life; but it did not feel as he lived it that he had any kind of choice at all. He had thought of himself as greedy and had dramatized it to himself as an adventurer's greed for life and possessions. In this squalid place, he learned that his greediest need was for something as shabby and uncertain as security.

—This is my chance.

But he tried.

'Mr Heathers would never tell you to do anything like that.'

Kujavia did not deny it. 'Nobody tells me what to do,' touching his chest with the tips of his fingers. '*Mister* Heathers is a rich man. But there isn't anything I don't know about women.' He showed his yellow teeth in a smile. 'Next time I break it off inside her.'

The fat woman blocked the lobby. She did not move aside and for a sick instant he thought she was trying to stop him from leaving. As he squeezed past, she hugged him with her belly.

'I thought you were going to pay,' she said.

When he got outside, there was no sign of the car. In his mind, ideas plaited like colours making one thing out of light: he had not been afraid of Kujavia; there had been too much at stake; the girl, the poor girl; he was not a coward; he was a coward; not afraid of being hurt himself, afraid of sharing in what Kujavia might do . . . anything you want, she had said; the girl, the poor naked girl. Out of the muddle, a strange idea; Irene and I have made a world in which Kujavia can exist.

Irene and I . . .

As he walked the long street among the watchful children, he kept expecting the car to appear until it occurred to him that the driver had never intended to wait.

CHAPTER FOUR
Tasting Blood

WEDNESDAY, AUGUST 29TH

In the car, Blair Heathers was unwise enough to close his eyes. Blood in his temples leapt in tiny explosions of forked lightning. In fright, he popped open his eyes and stared at the back of the chauffeur's head.

'You were quick back, Denny.'

'You said to make it fast, Mr H.'

Heathers caught the chauffeur's glance in the mirror, and wondered if the man had seen him open his eyes so suddenly. He had been with him for a long time; perhaps he had remarked on that movement before and speculated about it. Heathers found that thought unpleasant and said abruptly, 'So I did. You'll be looking for a productivity bonus, Denny.'

The chauffeur laughed dismissively. He practised an exactly calculated independence since both of them knew that was the form of obsequiousness Heathers found most comfortable. He kept silence then until the car drew to a halt. 'That's it on the left – the house should be about halfway down going by the number – it doesn't seem all that long a street.' He squinted at the house on the opposite corner. 'I can't read the numbers from here.'

'Bloody little people,' Heathers said. 'They hide their number in wee iron knots on the gate. Put bloody silly names over the door. Pretend they're in the middle of an estate park hoatching with sheep and gamekeepers.'

This time it seemed to Heathers his chauffeur's laugh was genuine.

'I'll carry on straight ahead,' the man said. 'Find the first place on this side of the road.'

'You do that,' Heathers said, preparing to get out.

'One of these days when I'm sitting reading my paper, somebody'll think I'm getting ready to bag his house – and call the police.'

'That'll be right,' Heathers said drily. 'First thing that would occur to anybody seeing a car like this.'

The joke put him in a good humour with himself as he processed between the semi-detacheds, small family houses built in the thirties. Some had put a dormer window in the attic to get a third or fourth bedroom; at one time, somebody had set a fashion for adding a porch. The garages took up most of the space between neighbours. 'Ravenscraig'. 'Beechcroft'. In Gaelic: 'Sky and Sea'. It was easy to miss the numbers.

When she opened the door, he could smell the mingled scent of flowers and furniture polish.

Inside there was a fitted carpet with a hard-wearing dark pattern, a low table for the telephone fitted with a padded seat, a stand bearing a vase of yellow tea roses. There was even a barometer on the wall. In the living room, looking at a piece of polished wood that seemed to be an imitation of the kind of tourist junk he had seen for sale in African airports, he said, 'Malcolm's a lucky man. I hadn't realized – I hadn't expected you to be the perfect housewife.'

'You don't know anything about me,' she said.

'Malcolm – does he know all about you? How long have you been married, a year is it, two? I wouldn't be surprised if there's a lot about you he doesn't know.'

'If you want to wait until he comes home,' she said, 'you can discuss it with him.'

'It was you I wanted to see. That's why I phoned to find out if you'd be in.'

'Not you,' she said. 'It was your secretary who phoned.'

He shrugged then, as a thought struck him, smiled. '*Confidential* secretary. She knows when to keep her mouth shut.'

Irene Wilson was sitting on the couch in the full light from the deep picture window. From the comfortable chair – which had a fitted cover, of course, in a floral pattern and tied underneath with tapes – he studied her legs and was pleased with what he saw. She's better looking than I remember, he thought; like an actress.

'Most people will do what you tell them,' Irene Wilson said. 'And not just because you're rich. They can see you expect to have your own way.' Taking him by surprise, she laughed.

'What is it?'

'When I said that, you put your head on one side. You were like a cat having his ears rubbed.'

'You rub and I'll purr,' he said; but could not resist adding, 'I'm the same man I've always been. I've never changed.'

'Just after I met Malcolm,' she said, 'we'd just got married, and he brought me here from London. You were almost the first person I saw on the local television. You were talking about your childhood in Moirhill, and how poor you had been.'

'We were all poor then.'

'That's right,' she said, delighted. 'You said that then. I remember.' Her voice took on the faintest colouring of the broad drawling accent of Moirhill, which he knew he had never lost. 'We were all poor then, but we were happy. There was a great sense of sharing. I think that's what the young people have lost.'

'I say more than my prayers,' he said, not hiding his pleasure. 'But if you ask me my philosophy, I'll tell you – make time for people. I'll pass the time with a brickie's labourer, if I feel like it. I can tell what foot a man kicks with – what religion he is, understand? – just by looking at him. It's a kind of instinct. Crack a joke. I can tell a Paddy before he opens his mouth. And I talk to them the way I talk to you. They respect me for it. I can get on with the highest and the lowest – that's good business – and it's not bad Christianity either.'

'It's odd,' she said. 'You remind me of a man I knew – oh years ago.'

He stood up, very easily for a man of his age considering that the chair was low and well cushioned; but then he had had the foresight to manoeuvre himself to the edge first. Things were going well. She would not be the first wife of an ambitious man who, while the driver Denny read his paper somewhere, had obliged him. Only, with changing places to sit beside her on the couch, he found himself looking at the chair he had been in and the little bookcase beside it and the window behind. Side by side on the three cushions, facing the same view, they might have been a couple sitting together on one of those long seats just by the entrance when you got on to one of the old tramcars. The idea distracted him, but he could not share it; even if she had belonged to the city, she was too young ever to have seen the high trams sway and rattle through its streets. With an effort, he reminded himself of what she had said.

'I hope you liked him.'

When she laughed, the little muscles moved in her throat. Something sharper, less willed, less under his control, added itself to his usual anticipation. His mouth dried.

'He was a businessman too. I thought he was rich, but living in a village what did I know? Once we were in London, the money soon went. Rich one day, poor the next. My sister told me later he'd left debts everywhere round the village. He'd have been bankrupt if he hadn't run off with me. Or they'd have put him in jail.'

'Your sister?' He was surprised. For some reason, he had taken it for granted that she was someone alone, without ties from the past.

'That was years later,' she said casually. 'I didn't see her for years after I had run off.'

'What age were you then?'

'Sixteen. I was sweet sixteen.'

Had she been drinking? She seemed different from the woman he had met on Saturday night at his party. He had

54

known wives who drank to pass the endless boredom of afternoons.

'I can't picture your sister,' he said. 'Is she like you?' He laughed out of his dry mouth. 'If she was here, I could sit between you on this couch. It's big enough. It's the right size.'

'No, that wouldn't be possible. My sister is dead.'

Her mouth turned down as if she would weep.

'I'm sorry.'

And she laughed. 'I don't have a sister. A friend told me that – about running off with a businessman. I never had a sister.'

He stared at her in bewilderment. He became angry. Behind all this assurance, his body knew that it was old. He did not understand this change in her. She glittered with suppressed excitement. It made him angry that she should remind him he was old.

'You didn't stay long on Saturday. Too many people for you? I like a lot of people round me on a Saturday night. You left early. Were you fighting with Malcolm?'

'I didn't really feel like going at all.' She looked at him thoughtfully. 'Malcolm felt I should.'

Malcolm would. 'A pretty wife like you – he'd want to show you off,' he said, feeling better. Probing if she could be hurt, he went on, 'I was glad Malcolm stayed on. No sense in the night being spoiled for both of you. When he'd said to me you weren't coming, I told him, Don't worry – you won't lack for company at my house.'

'Do you make sure people have . . . company?'

'I'm a good host. I like to be sure everybody enjoys himself.'

Faintly, he caught her perfume; she was close to him with her long neck and little breasts. He had a partiality for the kind of women he described to himself as lady-like, and a particular way of dealing with them in bed. 'God, I'd forgotten what it was like,' that corrupt bastard of a policeman Eddy Stewart had said to him the other day, 'to get a young one under you. It's a different thing altogether.'

It had been good to hear that from a man half his age; he had never had to do without young flesh.

'I didn't know you'd left on Saturday,' he said. 'I was looking for you and they told me you'd gone. I'd have seen you home.'

'Why would you do that?'

'The good host . . .'

What had he expected on Saturday night? Malcolm Wilson was a familiar type; at first sight, the wife had been too. With that mass of black hair, better looking maybe than he'd expected – would have expected if he'd given it more than a casual thought – but not beautiful, not even really his type. He'd seen better, had better; no lack of them. She had argued with him, saying it was wrong for any man to be too rich. Even that, though, he had encountered before; some women took that line to catch your interest; it was, after all, only another kind of flattery. He had told John Merchant: 'This lady here's been talking politics at me. Trying to convert me.' Merchant, smooth as ever (and slippery . . . a shadow of worry . . .), had said, 'That is a process of two steps, first you become as a little child and then Mrs Wilson has to find a way for you to pass through the eye of a needle.' And he had said . . . yes, 'I'm a kid at heart. And Irene and me are going to be such friends, I think she might provide the eye of a needle for me yet.' Not subtle, but with the wives of ambitious young men you didn't have to be. Only, she had gone early, disappeared, and he hadn't been able to get her out of his head since. She had a trick of looking at a man that excluded everyone else in the world.

'Oh, I'd have seen you home. Since your husband was busy. What was it you said a minute ago? "Rich one day, poor the next?" Your husband wants to get on in the world. He's ambitious. Wouldn't you like to see your husband making a bit of money?'

'Malcolm.'

'You don't have to remind me – I know his name.' He thought: She imagines I'm an old man who forgets names.

'Believe me, when I do business with a man, there isn't much I don't know about him. That's twenty-four hours a day I mean. Like you not wanting him to come today and see what we were doing at the Underpass.'

'Was that where he was today?'

She seemed so genuinely puzzled that, believing her, he felt offended. 'I'm surprised he didn't tell you. It's his future we're talking about here.'

But when she laughed again, even before she spoke, he understood that it was some kind of game she was playing with him. His anger, unexpectedly even his sense of foolishness, sharpened his lust.

'Of course he told me,' she said. 'He was terribly pleased with himself. You know what he's like.'

'His brother phoned to say he wouldn't come. Malcolm tells me he didn't know anything about it. I wondered if he'd told his brother to do that, and then lost his nerve? Why would his brother phone off his own bat?'

'You can ask him yourself. He's coming here this afternoon.'

'Why?'

She shrugged. 'To see Malcolm. I was surprised. They don't go out of their way to see one another. They don't get on well. Maybe he wants to talk to Malcolm about this Underpass of yours.'

'Your husband wouldn't be stupid enough to listen to him. He has a future if he plays his cards right. You tell him that, keep him right, be a good wife to him.'

He put his hand on her leg and felt the warmth of her in his palm. She giggled; a surprising noise, very warm and amused.

'I had a bet with myself you'd do that about now,' she said and lifted his hand from her. Strangely, for a second as she held it, he seemed to see his own hand through her eyes: plump, very white, wrinkled on the wrist like a used glove. At the firmness of her touch, he felt a weakening pleasure and made no resistance, but his anger increased.

'Do you want all the nice things as much as he does?

57

Christ, I recognized him as soon as I met him. Men like him – I've been buying them all my life.' It wasn't what he had meant to say. It was stupid to talk like this to her. He could not help himself. 'Buying them or frightening them. Sometimes they have to be frightened.'

The tip of her tongue wiped her bottom lip and the corner of her mouth. Where it had passed, her lips shone. It was in his power to arrange for people to be hurt; even if he was old. It made no sense for him to be uncertain or to feel that he was not in control.

'You want all those nice things,' he said. 'I can tell. A pretty girl like you. You're ambitious. Just like him.'

He put his hand on her breast. When she did not flinch, he gradually tightened his grip, looking all the time into her face. With his other hand, he grasped her by the jaw and began to draw her towards his mouth. She sank her teeth into the web of wrinkled flesh that hung at the root of his thumb. It was no nip but a real bite that took meat out of his hand as he tore it away.

He heard a voice whimpering with shock.

'As if I cared about any of that,' he heard her say.

He was on his feet looking down at her and there was a noise. It took him a moment to understand that someone was knocking at the outer door.

'The bell's out of order,' she said. 'Malcolm keeps intending to have it fixed. If I hadn't been expecting you, you might still have been standing on the step trying to ring it.'

His uninjured hand made itself into a fist, and then it would only be a matter of moving it through the air. Her eyes shone as she looked up at him. The crazy idea came into his head that she wanted him to hit her. By the side of her mouth, there was a smear of bright blood. When his fist opened, his two hands shook.

'I could have you cut,' he said stupidly.

He had no help from his anger or his lust. That night both were with him as he imagined what he might have done to her and followed each refinement with another until he climaxed and slipped into a troubled sleep. But when it mattered, he let himself be led through the hall past the telephone and tea roses. When the door opened, the man outside had reacted very fast, like a fighter, taking a half step back. Before he could stop him, the man had caught his injured hand, turning it so that he could look at the wound. 'It's all right, Murray,' the woman had said. 'He's just leaving.'

The sun struck signals off the windows of cars. His legs and belly ached. It was hard to walk. He felt a great temptation to rest on one of the stone steps that led up into the neat little gardens. When the Underpass is finished, he thought. I'll deal with her then – and him. Afterwards – when I don't need him; that made sense, it was smart; he had been smart. The pain of his hand cut through his confusion, making him feel sick. Where he had cradled it, the blood had spread across his shirt as if he had been wounded in the chest. He hid it in his pocket and with his good hand he drew the jacket across to hide the stain. He tried to think how long he had been in the house. Soon he would come on the parked car. Had he been long enough in the house? Would Denny think it had been long enough?

He was very tired and the sun beat on his unprotected head. He tried to understand why he had submitted to being led out of the house, but with each effort instead of an explanation he received an image of her mouth with the smear of blood as she said, 'As if I cared.'

It was not possible that what he had felt was fear. He dismissed the idea of fear, stumbling along in the heat, looking around for the car and, fierce veins beating in his skull, worrying about how he would explain himself to Denny his chauffeur.

CHAPTER FIVE
The First Victim

THURSDAY, AUGUST 30TH

Then his name did not matter. He was fifty-one years old and in good shape apart from the regular discomfort produced by a stomach ulcer. He believed there was more risk in visiting doctors than in staying away from them. He could not forget how as a boy he had seen his mother come back from the hospital unable to raise her head from her chest because treatment had destroyed the muscles of her neck. As a result he swallowed quantities of tablets and powders he got from the local chemist, and died without ever discovering the cause of his discomfort. There was no way of knowing how many of the lines round his eyes had been scored by the ulcer and how many by the process of his marriage going bad.

From ten days earlier, when his wife left him, he had been explaining to neighbours that she was gone to visit their married daughter in Shreveport, a city in Louisiana, which is one of the Southern states of the United States. As it happened, most of his neighbours knew where Louisiana was. He told the truth elaborately because he was a rather dull, meticulously honest man, and because he was missing out the one thing that mattered which was that she had explained to him with some force why she did not intend to come back.

On that Thursday morning, he had told his employer he was taking leave of absence. There had been some unpleasantness and he was not certain that his job would be there when he wanted it again. Previously he had taken the surrender value of his life assurance policies and in his pocket he had an airline ticket to the United States. He had been disappointed by the sum he had realized on the policies but it was enough, and fortunately he was in sound health, apart from the unsuspected ulcer and a long history of trouble with his teeth. Later, when his name mattered, the record of so much dental work was helpful.

Tomorrow he would catch a plane, tonight he could not face an empty house. He ordered a beer and asked what was available to eat, settling for two rolls sad enough to have been left over from the lunch offering. Steadily he chewed on them as if he could masticate the years of his marriage, purge what had been wrong and take only the best of it with him across the Atlantic to his wife. It was a fool's sacrament, tasting of chemicals, to whiten, to aerate, to speed fermentation. There was nothing in it of wheat. If it was a penance, he served it.

Perhaps he made a special kind of face reflecting on all of that for when he looked up the woman was already watching him.

He had been married to the same woman most of his adult life and been faithful. Even during the bad last years, he had not turned to another woman. The kind of life he lived did not throw him into the company of anyone likely, and he had lost the courage or the knack of hopefulness needed to offer himself to a stranger. It was more than three years since he had made love to his wife, although they continued all that time out of old habit to share a bed. His manhood was dry.

Yet when he saw the woman watching, he left his place at the bar and joined her. He gave himself no time to think, which was extraordinary, and as he listened to her a knot of fear and excitement tightened and unwound and tightened inside him. It was as if even at his age a man might change and become somehow new.

'It would have been our thirtieth anniversary next month.'

Close up, she was younger than he had thought. He had made a judgement on the woman sitting alone watching him which did not fit the girl opposite. She was certainly under thirty with very blonde hair cut short and dark big eyes. She had a good jaw and clearly marked cheekbones, things which he associated with character. For some reason, it seemed to him like the face of a country girl – and then she looked to the side and down and it was a beautiful face.

'Would have been? Is your wife dead?'

At her tone, the faintest disturbance moved in him like the shadow of one of those fish which are misshapen by the pressure of living far under the surface. According to his ideas if you misunderstood and spoke to someone of a near relative who was dead as if the person still lived then you would offer, even perfunctorily, some convention of apology. There had been nothing of that. Her voice was pleasant and curious, but there was no place in it for remorse.

'Oh, no, not dead. She's gone to Shreveport.

'. . . It's a town. In Louisiana. That's in the south – of the United States.'

She held out her glass and smiled.

When the drinks came, he waved away the change. The size of the tip he had given alarmed and pleased him. Out of character, anything was possible.

'Shreveport,' he explained, 'is more like a city really. It's quite interesting how it got it's name. A riverboat captain cleared a logjam that had blocked the whole river. They named the place after him. His name was Shreeve, you see. That was in 1836.'

'You have a good memory for dates.'

It seemed that no one had ever listened to him so attentively as this stranger. She made him feel as if they were alone in the room.

'My daughter lives there and she wrote long letters telling . . us about the history of the place and what industries it has and about how funny it was at first to see the policemen going around with guns. She wanted us to share it all.'

'That sounds nice. Did she write you separate letters?'

'What?'

'I mean one to you then one to your wife – or just all the time to both of you "Dear Mummy and Daddy".'

'All her letters were to both of us,' he said and felt tears press behind his eyes which made him angry until he remembered. She doesn't know Clare's left me.

'That doesn't seem fair.'

He felt old, bitter and wise. As if any of it had to be fair.

'People are different,' she said. 'You can't make them one thing, it's dull. Not that it's exciting here. Would you like to come to my place? We could have a drink there just as well as here.'

When he had been young, men wanted and girls refused. It had been a battle in which you led attacks and devised stratagems; getting your hand to the top of a leg had been a major victory and typically brought the campaign to an abrupt halt. He had claimed one complete success, and had taken it for granted he should marry. Everyone had been younger then – himself, the girls – all of them younger than this woman beside whom he was an old man.

'You don't know me,' he began, 'and even nowadays—'

'My name is Frances,' she said. 'That better?'

He told her his name, and blundered on. 'Even nowadays – perhaps more than the old days – there's a risk involved for a girl. I mean with a stranger.' He was anxious to persuade her that she should not do this kind of thing again. 'Terrible things happen – you read of them in the papers.'

'You're nice,' she said. 'You're a very nice man. I wouldn't be taking any risk with you.'

They took a taxi; his car, since he did not believe in drinking and driving, was tucked safely out of sight in the garage at home. The elephant-grey legs of the flyover flicked past. 'They say,' she said, 'there's a woman buried in one of those. She was killed by a man and then her body was put in there. Next morning the workmen poured concrete on her. They didn't know she was there, you see.'

He was amused. 'I've heard that story before.'

'Do you think it's true? My – a friend told me that.'

'Heard it about somewhere else, I mean. I expect stories

63

like that get made up about those things wherever they build them. It's because concrete is so ugly.'

She looked vaguely offended. 'No matter how much talk there was, there would be no way of finding out. The person would be buried until it didn't matter.'

'I think it would always matter,' he said, and then, afraid that would sound dull and moralizing, hurried on, 'I don't think the police ever close the file on an unsolved murder.' What had first occurred to him, however, what he had meant, being serious-minded and something of a moralist, was that time had nothing to do with it; it would never stop mattering that a soul had been deprived of life. 'Anyway, there couldn't be a body in all of them,' he explained reasonably. 'It's just like the old days in the country when every tree and hill had a story about a suicide . . . or a murder come to that. Girls who killed their babies so no one would know. But you come from the country, don't you?' She had the rising inflections and, still, some of the vowels of one of the rural parts of the East Coast.

'From a fishing village,' she said.

'Plenty of superstitions there. It's not any different in the city. People think they're different, but human nature doesn't change.'

'You must have done a lot of travelling to find out so much.'

'No!' He felt that he had let down his guard and she might be laughing at him. 'It's just that I grew up in the country. I haven't travelled much. What chance have I had? I've been with the same firm for almost thirty years – twenty-eight years and, eh, five months to be exact.' She smiled and, realizing, he wanted to say to her: You're right; what does it matter, five months, six months? He had always been exact. 'What chance have I had? Clerk, chief clerk. I couldn't have done so well if I'd moved. I began to take the exams – but I had to stop – I was warned about my eyesight. In the end, I was running the place.'

'You've done well,' she said. 'Now you own the business, isn't that right?'

'It's a family firm.' There had been a time when he thought he would get on the board of MacKinlays. 'The father still runs it – he's nearly eighty. I can still see him the way he was on the day he interviewed me for the job. Sometimes I think he's never changed. I changed – and the firm. It got bigger, and I helped.'

'I can see you'd be pleased,' she said, and yawned.

'He has two sons . . . never give your life to a family firm.'

Shamefully, tears prickled in the corners of his eyes. It had been a nasty little scene. 'I can't see what good it will do for you to run after her,' the old man had said angrily. 'It's such a bad time for you to go. I feel let down.' He was glad of the excuse, he thought suddenly; he wanted to get rid of me.

'His older son never liked me.' He stared blankly at the passing street. There was a corner shop, closed and shuttered; and a pub with narrow high-set windows like a fort. He realised they had left the main road behind. 'In that kind of work, the main thing is being able to cost a job properly. That's how you manage to make a profit. When he started, he couldn't do it, no matter how hard he tried. He couldn't get the hang of it. He made a botch of everything. It was me that tidied up after him. If you want a crime, that was my crime. It would have been better for the old man if I'd been his son.' Appalled, he fell silent. '. . . That was, oh, years ago.'

When they got out of the taxi, it was a street of tenements. The impression was shabby only, not of a slum, nothing degraded. Yet he was disturbed.

'I don't know where we are,' he said.

'My flat's on the first floor. It's nice.'

'What district is this? What street is it?'

'It's quiet here.' She was fumbling in her bag. 'That big place over there belongs to a builder. And here – look – I have to unlock this gate. That's how safe it is.'

The close entrance was shut off by a tall structure of bars.

'What would you do if you forgot the key for the gate?'

She closed it behind them and went in front of him

without answering. The passage was brightly lit and the walls were tiled to shoulder height, blue tiles with a single white flower on each. As he climbed behind her, he asked again, 'If you hadn't your key, would you be able to attract a neighbour's attention? Would someone come down and let you in?'

'No chance of that.' They were on the first landing and as she opened her door she nodded at the one opposite. 'That's a jewellery repair workshop. And upstairs it's a dental mechanic's and I don't know what else. There's no one but me here at night.'

In the flat, he asked, 'Doesn't it frighten you being alone in the building?'

Embarrassed, he took only a vague impression of the room. Decoration, carpet, furniture, all of it seemed new. He had the feeling he disliked in an hotel room or a guest-house: that it could belong to no one, since it was made for strangers. He was by nature a home-loving man. The one exception to this impersonality was a painting on the wall opposite where he was standing. It showed a brown and orange landscape of low hills with a pale fragment of moon or sun low in the sky. The frame was wide and painted gold, and the picture seemed to have come there by accident from a different life.

'What makes you think I live alone?' she asked.

The question startled him with a queasy vision of a husband appearing from the next room.

'It's all right,' she said, 'my friend doesn't live here. Never mind him.'

He followed her into the inner room. It was tiny and the bed seemed enormous, but she went past it and opened a second door.

'See?' she said. But he didn't until she pointed. 'There's a mirror on the ceiling over the bath.' As he looked up, puzzled by it, she laughed at him. 'What good would it be covered in steam? Doesn't it make you wonder what kind of people they were?'

'People?' he repeated in bewilderment.

66

'Oh, this place doesn't belong to him. We're fairly sure of that. We think it's one of the little presents he's picked up for being co-operative.'

'I don't understand.'

'Why should you? Don't you think I know why you came here?' She took his hand and laid it upon her breast. 'Like this?' she asked softly. 'Isn't this what you wanted?'

At the touch of her separate flesh, a shock ran through him. Trembling, he brought his face close to hers.

She pulled back.

'I don't allow that,' she said. 'Anything else, but I don't let people kiss me on the mouth.'

It had been too long. As they lay together naked on the bed in the tiny room, he knew that he would fail. He had thought his manhood was gone, but he responded and, even when with a sudden shuddering he lost control, she made him respond again and he entered her and she moved under him as if he was a man. When it was over, he was weeping and it did not matter that perhaps he had not emptied his seed for a second time.

'Who is Clare?' she whispered warm against his ear.

Appalled, he kept silence.

'Is that your wife's name? You kept saying it all the time.'

He turned his head from her. 'Why did you – why did you let me? You can't have found me attractive. I'm an old man. I shouldn't be in bed with you.'

'Because you wanted it so badly.' She stretched like a cat. 'It was the way you looked at me. You were so frightened.'

He caressed her shoulder with his lips. 'I'm not frightened any more.' Hearing his own words, he believed them. It was true that fear had become a habit, faint and unacknowledged as a fluttering in the blood. Sometimes a sound can go on for so long that you only realise it is gone when suddenly you feel the silence like a presence. He was full of gratitude.

'You don't have to worry. We won't see one another again,' she said. 'You can go home to your wife.'

'My wife's gone away,' he reminded her. 'To Shreveport – in Louisiana.'

Hadn't he explained that to her earlier? Like an impulse of disloyalty, he put aside the idea that she might be stupid. 'I'm going out there to join her.' To the New World. 'I don't think I'll ever come back. Why should I – why should we come back?' If Clare would not have him, he would find a place to live; he would find a job. It was not as if he had no skills or was a man with nothing to offer. 'A man wants to be where he has ties – and my daughter lives there.'

'Ties?'

'To someone you love.' Tentatively, he murmured, 'Like you perhaps and the friend who comes here.'

'Last night, lying where you are.' He felt the warmth of her pressed along his side. 'He told me this joke. It was about a butcher who was asked to circumcise a little Jewish boy on a desert island – only he didn't know what "circumcise" meant, and he did something else. You can imagine.'

He did not want to. 'I don't know why someone would want to tell a joke like that.'

'It saved his life. He was in a concentration camp and a lot of them broke through the wire. This was in the winter, he says, and in the middle of a forest. At first he could hear the others moving all round him and then it was quiet. He fell into a hole full of snow and thought he wasn't going to be able to crawl out. They hadn't been given much to eat – that's what he said. In the morning some peasants found him, an old father and three sons. They had been going about all night hunting for the prisoners and killing them. They didn't like Jews. Lying on the ground the first thing he saw, when they came out from among the trees, was the blood on their boots. They would have kicked him to death too, but he remembered this joke and it made them laugh. He said it was the only joke he ever remembered, and that was because the boy who had told it to him when he was at school had made fun of him for not understanding it. He isn't Jewish, you see.'

Had he thought he was charming her into taking him into her home? A word came into his head – seduction –

an old word – and tears of humiliation threatened him.

'I'm sorry,' he said. 'I need – I'm not . . .'

He stumbled over saying that he was unwell.

'You know where it is,' she said. 'Would you like me to come with you? Would you like me to wash it for you?'

He sat on the furred cover of the lavatory and spat a curd of vomit, all that he could manage, into the basin. He told himself that when he felt better he would leave with dignity. The brown-yellow smear slipped into the smooth porcelain. He turned on the tap gently so there would be no noise and the water slid down and took most of it away. With the edge of his finger he pushed the last of it into the stream. He wished that he could go home and that Clare would be there. He stood up and pressed a towel against his face. It was warm from the rail and he took comfort from it. He wanted his wife and she had left him alone. From the round mirror about the rail, circled by its single coil of fluorescent light, his face stared back at him. Clare had gone away. No one could blame him. Whatever happened now, the stranger watching with a white circle in each eye told him, nobody could blame you.

When he came out the small bedroom was in darkness. From the passage beyond came the sound of voices. A voice which he recognized as that of the woman who called herself Frances said something and then another voice spoke.

'You take such chances,' the second woman said. It sounded very different to him from the voice of Frances: more . . . educated, not a country accent, one from a town or a city, southern English, perhaps London?'

'I needed company.'

'Company! That's another name for it. What happened last night anyway?'

'That's why I sent for you,' Frances said. 'He was in a funny mood from the minute he got here.' She lowered her voice and he moved by an ordinary impulse of curiosity nearer to the narrow crack of the door's opening. 'Soldavo . . . one of the guards.'

'Do you think it can be true?'

'He saw him! There wasn't any chance of a mistake – that's what he said.'

'What name? Didn't he give you a name?'

'I tried to get it out of him. You know what he's like – he didn't think it would be right to tell me – he didn't think it would be safe for—'

She stopped speaking suddenly as if at a signal.

When the light came on, the room appeared momentarily not small but vast. Turning acres of light pinned him alone and isolated in the centre of an enormous room. Conscious of his nakedness, he covered himself with his hands.

'I'm sorry,' he said.

There were two women. Frances was naked like himself but without shame. The other woman was clothed and had dark hair, and it was to her he spoke as if she had come to judge him. 'I didn't mean any harm. I couldn't help hearing what you were saying. But Frances told me about her friend. I know what a terrible thing happened to him.' She was young and beautiful and passed judgement on him.

'My sister doesn't fuck,' the blonde woman said. 'But you can come to bed with me. And she'll help. You'll be surprised at the way she can help.'

He wished that he could go home and Clare would be there, but she had abandoned him.

Whatever happened now would be her fault.

CHAPTER SIX
A Sense of Vocation

FRIDAY, AUGUST 31ST

There had been giants on the earth in those days, and two of them had been set naked on either side of the marble staircase. Approaching them, it annoyed Murray that he couldn't any longer remember which of them was Purity and which Honour. As he put his foot on the first step, a hand caught him by the shoulder. Turning, the movement with which he knocked the grip loose was instinctive.

'Don't be a mug,' Eddy Stewart said. 'I'm not here as a friend.'

'They've made you a Councillor.'

'It's not a joke. There's been a complaint.'

They had to move aside as a group of visitors, smiling and jostling, white teeth in black faces, one or two of them in national costume, came towards the staircase.

'I'm listening.'

'You've been making a nuisance of yourself trying to see John Merchant.'

'And he got in touch with the police?' Murray was puzzled.

Stewart hesitated. 'There was a complaint.'

'Heathers call you? What does that make you, Eddy?' As long ago as their time together on the beat, Murray had judged Stewart could be bought by someone some day when the price was right. Perhaps, it was possible, he had known that before Stewart did. 'Just another hard man for hire. I don't think you could stop me if I wanted to go up and try to see Merchant again.'

'You're not an easy bloody man to help,' Stewart's heavy

face flushed an ugly red. 'I'm trying to mark your card for you before you see Peerse.'

. . . Which made it a different proposition altogether. 'He's here?'

'You know Peerse. He makes it his business to hear anything about you. He takes a personal interest.' Stewart began to cross the hall to the entrance and Murray fell into step beside him. 'You want to watch that mouth of yours. One day it'll get you into trouble.'

As they approached the car, the door swung open and a voice complained genteelly, 'Hurry it up.'

Stewart went in front beside the driver, a pale fat man Murray did not recognize. Peerse was so tall that he had to bend his head slightly to avoid the roof. He sat in the farthest corner of the bench seat with his back very straight although he had to bend his head. A detective inspector, he had not finished climbing the promotion ladder. He had too much talent not to be a man with a future. Murray found that hard to accept. When they had been young policemen, he had regarded Peerse, beaten up twice in the early months, so ludicrously tall and thin, as a joke. He had been like one of those daddy-long-legs, appalling and fragile, that shed legs at a touch. Now, expensively suited, authoritative, with silver wings of hair that made him look more like an ambassador than a policeman, it was their shared misfortune that more than anyone else in the world, apparently, the sight of Murray reminded him of what he disliked about that past. He leaned across Murray and pulled the door closed. At once the car moved away accompanied by the urgent double note of the siren.

'What's the hurry?' Stewart asked, but Murray caught only a few words of the driver's reply.

Stewart turned in his seat. 'Should we drop him?' He nodded at Murray.

Instead of answering, Peerse flicked the middle finger of his right hand as if gesturing away a servant. Stewart faced to the front and Murray watched with interest the vivid stain that rose and ebbed on the side of his neck. Eddy was not having a good day.

Had the driver said something about a body?

Façades of mean dullness flowed past, pubs, betting shops, gap sites and boarded windows. Out of the driver's words Murray had picked a name – Deacon Street. That meant Moirhill; a tougher district now than when Blair Heathers had left it; more derelict, without the sense of community there had been then among the poverty. If there had been a killing, Peerse would want to get there fast, before the Northern shop boys—

'Explain,' Peerse broke his silence suddenly. He had small eyes, very blue like splinters of ice.

Murray yawned.

'Waiting,' Peerse said.

'I used to know you when you could talk in sentences, Ian.'

'Last warning. Cut out the first name – that's cheeky. You don't want to cross the line.'

It was Murray's turn to look out of the window and let a flare of temper come under control. 'I don't believe John Merchant complained. Maybe someone else did.'

'Who would that be?'

Murray cursed his own stupidity. Peerse was the last policeman in the world he would want to take an interest in the connection between Malcolm and Heathers. If Peerse was targetting Blair Heathers, he would be as honest as a salt scoured bone; there was no way of corrupting that arrogance.

'Nobody. Maybe Merchant did – but I only saw him once. He didn't seem bothered.'

'You tried to see him again yesterday – and you were back again today.'

'He's a busy man. It's not easy to catch him.'

'Why did you want to see him?'

'There were a couple of details I wanted to clear up.'

'That's not an answer.'

'It's the only one you're going to get,' Murray said. 'I was working for a client. That makes it confidential.'

Peerse leaned forward and tapped Stewart, waiting till he faced right about before saying, 'He thinks he's still in America. No – it's better than that. He thinks he's on television in America;' and whickered air through that long narrow nose, the sound that passed with him for amusement.

Avoiding Murray's eye, Stewart made a show of joining in the joke.

Satisfied, Peerse sat back as the driver brought the car to a halt. They had drawn into a side street and ahead of them a crowd was gathered round the entrance to a lane. Beyond that police cars were already parked.

'I don't think we can take the car right in, sir,' the driver volunteered. His voice was surprisingly light and hasty for such a big man.

'Obviously,' Peerse said sourly. He opened the door and unfolded his length from the car. Bending, he warned Murray, 'I haven't finished with you.'

Left with the fat driver, Murray watched as Peerse cut through the crowd with Stewart in his wake. Erect, immaculate, towering so far above the slatternly women and gaunt unshaven men, he appeared like a representative of some different species.

'Here!' the fat driver shrilled. 'Where the hell do you think you're going?'

'Don't give yourself a hard time,' Murray said quietly. 'Don't you know when your gaffer's kidding an old friend?'

As he got out, he saw across the crowd the young constable who was stationed at the mouth of the lane watching him. He heard the fat driver fumbling with the handle of his door. On impulse, he crossed towards the lane. The crowd opened a path. 'Is it a lassie?' 'Is it right she was raped?' 'You lot are no bloody use—'

'Keep back,' the constable cried. His eyes were bright and his face flushed and sweating. 'They're right at the end, sir. Round the corner.'

Out of the sun, it was extremely cold in the alley. Brick walls on either side, the dusty cobbles, even the blank line of barred windows, soaked up the light. Whoever had died

74

in here seemed already buried. He put back his head and there high above was a stripe of afternoon sky, summer blue and chilled. A deep grave open to the sky.

When he looked down, it seemed darker and the man had popped out from beyond the corner abruptly as a conjuring trick.

'This one's going to be a bugger.'

'Aren't they all?'

'Wait till you see this joker.'

'Was she raped?'

'Eh?'

The man's grunt was more puzzled than suspicious, but Murray knew he was on the edge of pushing his luck too far. Having no choice, he went round the corner. In front of him the alley ended in a turning circle and a service platform below which a group of men were gathered. Inspection lamps had been set up and under their white unsparing glare a man knelt over a shape on the ground. By some accident, the watching men were perfectly silent. The police examiner moved to one side and he saw that where the head of the shape should be there was a ruin of pulp drawn away from the body in a brief stripe of red. It was so quiet that from behind a barred window to the right someone could be heard whistling 'The Blue Danube'. There was a hollow echo to it as if it came from an empty room. The way the body had been turned, one arm lay out to the side under the bright light of the lamp.

One of the men turned his head – Stewart. With a comic carefulness, he eased his way out of the group round the corpse.

It was only when they were back round the corner safely out of sight that he spoke: 'You must be clean off your nut. Peerse would've gutted you if he'd seen you there.' Before Murray could answer, Stewart exclaimed, 'Not another one!'

The *Citizen* columnist Billy Shanks was being nodded in his turn past the young constable. He came towards them grinning widely.

'Hold it, Billy,' Stewart said. 'You're not on.'

'There's no chance of a quick look? You could pretend you haven't seen me.'

'One mug's enough, Billy. Put it in reverse.'

Billy Shanks gave a grin of inexhaustible good nature. His long arms waved as if under separate instructions, a parallel conversation using a code whose semaphore was lost.

'Don't blame the constable, Eddy. You shouldn't have a boy doing a man's job.'

They walked slowly back towards the mouth of the alley. Stewart spoke very fast and softly. 'Man in his fifties – Doc Pritchard's having a look at him now. He's got stab wounds – I suppose one of them killed him. No idea when yet. A van man found him. Maybe it happened last night, small hours this morning. Oh, one other thing – when the doc was looking, I saw cuts on him – he'd been ripped about the lower body.'

'Sexually?' Billy Shanks asked hopefully.

'His ornaments are still there if that's what you mean. But he's got cuts – like I say, on the belly.'

The constable made a business of clearing a way for them into the crowd.

'He's doing a grand job.'

'Little Boy Blue,' Stewart said unexpectedly and laughed.

The driver was dithering beside the car. When he saw Stewart with Murray, he blew out his plump cheeks in a sigh of relief.

'Another bloody eedjit!' Stewart said, as if in disbelief that the world could hold so many.

Ignoring the driver, they walked on a few paces beyond the car before stopping.

'Have you any identification?'

'He just had on a shirt and trousers – nothing there to give a hint who he is – was.'

'Just? You mean that was all?'

'The lot.'

'It's a picture job then. Show it around till somebody recognizes him.'

At this, Stewart took a quick look at the listening Murray who said, 'Yes – I saw it.'

76

'What?' Shanks asked.

'The bloody van,' Stewart said and started to laugh. 'The driver must have been half asleep. Didn't stop till he felt a bump. He ran a wheel over the poor bugger's face.'

Grinning, he walked away. In the tenements opposite, women hung out of the windows, their elbows on the ledges as if spectating at a play.

'Your usually reliable source has a great sense of humour,' Murray said watching him make his way back through the crowd around the alley.

'Ah, Eddy's not the worst.'

'One of the best – laughing all the way to the bank.'

'Don't be like that,' Shanks said seriously. 'So he drops a hint for old times' sake,' one long arm made a complicated explanatory loop, 'why not? "Eat up, eat up, yer growin' boys!" You remember?' And as Murray stared at him, reverted to the same parodic voice, ' "Eat up, boys, you'll never find better digs than at Ma Donelly's." '

'Ma Donelly's food was lousy,' Murray said, remembering. 'I'd forgotten it and her. Anyway it was me that had to eat it not you.'

'And Eddy and I would come round and bum supper.'

'Can you give me a run back into town?'

'Everybody was nicer then,' Shanks said nostalgically. At the same time, however, he looped across one long arm and gave Murray a business-like tap on the shoulder. 'What are you doing here anyway?'

'I was just a passenger. The call came through while I was talking to Peerse.'

After waiting for a moment to see if there was any more, Shanks said in a tone of deepest scepticism, 'And you and Peerse are such good friends. You wouldn't like to tell me what you were talking about?'

'That's right.' Murray looked at his watch. 'I have things to do. Can we get on our way?'

'Not right now. I'd like to ask some more questions. Get the feel of it. Maybe put a name to that van driver.'

'Why you? You left the crime beat a long time ago.'

'Oh . . . the "Cit" will send one of the usual men,' Shanks said vaguely. 'Connolly probably or young Robertson.'

'So?'

'I . . . caught the call on the radio in the car. I was talking about murders yesterday in the Shot with Tommy Gregory. You know him!' Murray shook his head. 'Interesting guy . . . anyway, when I heard the call, I took a notion. And you're here. And then Peerse. God intends me to take an interest in this one.' He waited for a response to that; gave up on Murray's silence. 'A dead man – half dressed – with no shoes. He didn't have shoes on, did he? It looks as if he was killed somewhere else and brought there, eh? You're the detective – don't you feel it's a strange one?'

Murray shrugged. 'I'm only a detective when someone pays me.'

'Why is it then I feel you have an interest in this one too? You didn't recognize him as a client?'

For answer, Murray rubbed his hand down his face and scowled.

'Oh, that's right, the van smashed his face in. If it was the van . . . What do you think?'

'I need a run back into town. The paper will send a real reporter out on this – why not give me a lift?'

'You lack a sense of vocation . . .' Shanks, rising to the bait, wagged an arm in distress. 'I've forgotten more than young Robertson will ever have the wits to learn. Anyway, for the column I need an angle. I need a handle – something that lets me pick this thing up. There's something about it . . .'

Murray pretended to think. 'I did hear the word rape mentioned.'

Shanks blinked, struck by the idea. 'Did they say that? The guy had been raped? Could Pritchard be sure of that – without tests? I wouldn't have—'

'Billy! Billy – you have vocation enough for both of us.'

And then he had to walk back. Moirhill Road was long; if he turned north, it would have taken him all the way to the suburbs and green fields; but his way lay in the opposite

78

direction towards William's Cross, taking one at a time the shoddy fronts that had passed so easily glimpsed from a car. His flat was on the first floor of the last close in the Road before the Cross: the other marker he used for first-time visitors was that it was next to the Chinese take-away. He stopped to read the menu in the window. He did this regularly but had never been inside since he had a prejudice against such places based on the fate of an alsatian when he had been a young policeman. When he had finished reading the list, he went into the fish and chip shop round the corner and bought a supper. As an afterthought, he got them to add a meat pie on top.

The phone was ringing when he opened the door of the flat. He listened to a Mr Foley complain in his ear while he unpicked the newspaper parcel one-handed and extracted the pie. Mr Foley was voluble concerning the importance of finding his ex-partner Beddowes, his embezzled money, even his wife – though this last sounded most like an attempt to enlist sympathy. He had a lot to say and Murray bit into the pie and gazed bleakly at the desk with the phone and the old Adler portable, the pair of chairs for clients, the filing cabinet with the reference books on top.

'We're making progress. I've no doubt we'll find Bed-dowes – and your wife.' Not to mention the money. He cleaned a piece of pie out of a back tooth as the voice got excited. 'I'll be submitting a written report . . . tomorrow. No, I can't be more definite . . . That's your privilege . . .'

In the back room, he turned on the water heater. He managed half the fish but the chips had waited too long. Slippery and lukewarm, they were wadded into the paper and dropped in the bucket under the sink. His prejudice where tea was concerned favoured Chinese and he drank the first of too many cups, its perfume tickling his nostrils, and wondered how he could keep Mr Foley going, and thought about Merchant, and the man in the lane and the bad joke played on him in death by the van driver's wheel. Merchant's story of the butcher who did not know the meaning of circumcision came into his head and ran there like an offensive tune which would not be dislodged. Eddy Stewart had a sociable memory for jokes; he wondered if he had heard the one about the butcher. Every day was an anniversary of something. For Merchant there would be a day in every year which was the anniversary of the guard from the camp: 'I saw worse things later but because it was the first I never forgot him.' And now Merchant was claiming to have seen the man again, in a different time, a different place, a different world. Crazy. He thought about how too many anniversaries might make you crazy. He wondered what had driven his neighbour Miss Timmey crazy. 'It wasn't what he did to the boy,' Merchant had said. 'It was the noise. There's a noise a baby makes crying.' He thought about Miss Timmey and why her madness should take the form of accusing the young couple across the landing, who were so crazy for one another, and might now be lying entwined on the bed—

And it was time then to stop thinking. Solitary is not lonely. Loneliness, as much as water on stone, will wear away the hardest substance.

He set up the chess board with a problem he had worked before. It was a conversation with a familiar acquaintance. After a time, he moved a piece, but as he reflected on the responses that made possible, the unwanted image came to him of a couple entwined on a bed. How could a woman, a woman on her own, kill a man? Even if the pain had been unexpected and terrible, would he not have defended himself by instinct? How could she have been sure, a woman on her own, that she could kill him? Crazy. The woman – crazy idea – carried the man's hand to her mouth and bit at the soft webbing beside the thumb. Perhaps he was expecting to be fondled; perhaps he was smiling. Like an animal, she tore out his flesh. Murray stared at a ruined face given one hard edge by the inspection lamp and at the hand thrown out under its glare and at the half moon of blackened flesh torn from the root of his thumb, and remembering drove away the maggot ideas silence bred sometimes until the room darkened and the pieces on the board withdrew into the shadows.

CHAPTER SEVEN
Clients

SATURDAY, SEPTEMBER 1ST

'I'm a busy man,' Superintendent Standers said.

'I'm sorry your time's being wasted like this,' Murray said. 'It was stupid of me going into the lane. I did it on impulse and I can't apologize any more than I have done. I was out of line. But it isn't anything to do with the murder – I don't know why Peerse bothered you with it.'

'*Inspector* Peerse. And let me decide what's a waste of time.'

Meaty hands folded in front of him, the Superintendent had a countryman's complexion, though scored with lines in the cheeks and the deep pouches under the eyes that seemed to come with the job. He was new into the city and, recognizing the type, Murray guessed at an uneventful progress with the neighbouring county force from constable to Training School to Chief Inspector until regionalization had put several forces into one command structure and brought him into town as Superintendent of the Moirhill sub-division of Northern. Through the half-open door came the sound of people talking and moving about, the ringing of telephones, all of it echoing under the high roof of the school hall.

A man in shirt sleeves holding a clipboard appeared in the opening. 'It seems it's okay for the bottom jaw,' he said. 'So that's good news, sir.'

'What the hell are you talking about?' Standers asked.

The man with the clipboard looked flustered. He had been standing with one hand resting on the handle of the door as if able to pause only for a moment in mid-flight. Now he came another step or two into the room.

'The victim, sir. It seemed as if there might not be any help at all from the teeth – but it turns out they've got the front of the lower jaw and most of the right side still attached. And he had quite a bit of work done. It should help to confirm an identification.'

'Once we find out who he is,' Standers said. Unexpectedly then, he smiled and said on a different note, 'That's a good bit of news . . . eh, Tom. Things are beginning to move. Carry on.'

Puzzled by the altered tone, Murray looked towards the door and saw beyond the shirt-sleeved detective the hovering ramshackle figure of Billy Shanks. Glancing back, he found Standers' eye upon him.

'You can go,' the Superintendent said. 'And shut the door on your way out.'

'Not for a ticking off. What gave you that idea?' Standers said. He tapped the newspaper lying folded open on the corner of the desk. 'I think this could be useful to us.'

From where he sat, folded into a chair to which he anchored himself by one long tendril leg, Billy Shanks could see under the Superintendent's finger that morning's copy of the 'World of the Streets' column.

'I'm glad about that. When I got your call, I was worried,' he said. 'You shouldn't have to waste your time. I wouldn't want to have written anything that caused a problem – not on a murder case.'

'Most cases of homicide,' Standers said, taking the tone of a man accustomed to them, 'are over before they start. It's the boyfriend or the father or son – the wife who's taken one kicking too many. Most murders are family affairs, you could say. Or pub jobs – when a broken glass catches the other guy in the wrong place.' He touched his neck. 'Cut there and jump back before the blood hits you in the eye. This one could be more complicated . . .'

'That's quite an incident room you're setting up out

there.' Shanks wrinkled his nose at the memory of the smell that had stung his nostrils in the entrance corridor. Generations of children had left it to haunt the place, poverty's equivalent of clanking chains. It oozed from walls painted institutional green and hovered uneasily outside the headmaster's door, whose reversed title he could make out worked in spidery silvery tracery on the opaque glass which separated them for the moment from the bustle of activity. 'It surprised me to see the school opened up.'

'It was before,' Standers said, and paused as if for a response. 'For the Robertson case.'

'Of course.' Twin girls, Shanks remembered, and only eleven years old.

'It was my decision to set up here,' Standers said. 'It could be easier in the long run . . . if things get complicated.'

'The way they did in the Robertson case,' Billy Shanks said in a carefully neutral tone. The killing of the twins had been linked to three other child deaths, one of them years previously; it had attracted national attention. The case had promoted the officer in charge out of Moirhill.

'This is a very special patch,' Standers said. He got up and took up a position in front of the map. The bastard! Shanks thought, he's dragged me down here to make sure I'll know how to spell his name properly. 'Deacon Street, Carnation Street, Florence Street,' a finger followed their course, 'they make a triangle – with Merse Street lying on top of it and curving back to join Moirhill Road. Put a circle round that lot and you'd cover half the pros and ponces in the city. And the rest of them would be either neds or ne'er-do-wells. It's a human sump. It's a garbage heap. Don't quote me on that, of course – or I'll have some do-gooders complaining.'

Shanks joined him in front of the map. With a wild loop of the arm, he dabbed at it.

'I was born about . . . there,' he said. '14 Florence Street. Two up. Left-hand side.' But could not prevent himself from adding, 'Right enough, it's gone down a lot since then.'

Standers gave him a look of placid indifference.

'The body was dressed in just a shirt and trousers. Pulled on after he was dead — at least that's what forensic guess. His though, they fit well enough. What does a man with his underpants off in Deacon Street suggest to you?'

Shanks discarded the first two answers which occurred to him — the hardest thing he had learned on his way to becoming a professional was when not to be funny — and said seriously, 'Looks as if he was after a bit of fun, right enough.'

'Our present problem,' Standers explained sitting down again, 'is to identify the victim. What he's wearing is good quality, but off the peg.'

'And you can't take a photograph. Have you let the van driver go yet? Or is he still "helping with the enquiries"?'

'He's home. He had his breakfast with us. For a while it just seemed too bloody convenient — him putting his wheel right over the face.'

'But you're satisfied?'

'Accidents happen. What we're left with is a description of height, hair colour, estimated age — no scars or warts, nothing helpful.' He rubbed a hand across his face, moving the heavy flesh under his chin. 'It's a sex killing. If you were writing about it, you could describe it that way.'

'I don't know that I'll be writing about it again,' Billy Shanks said with a pleasant stirring of malice. 'I don't do crime, you know.'

The Superintendent picked up the newspaper and held it out towards the other man as evidence. 'You did this morning.' It had the tone of an interrogation.

'It was the way the body was cut about.' The journalist's hands flew apart as if truth was something measurable between them. 'And the coincidence of the date. And, yes, somebody had been talking to me about Jack the Ripper. It all came together, but that's the way it happens. Just ideas. Just speculation. When you have to find something new every day . . . It's not really got anything to do with your murder case.'

Standers gave him the same placid look as before. 'Jack

the Ripper,' he said, after a pause, 'how many did he see off then?'

Shanks tried to remember what Tommy Gregory had told him. Since it had only been his point of departure for the column, he hadn't even bothered to do any checking. 'Four . . . no, five. One of them was a double murder, two in the same night.'

'I thought there were more,' Standers said with a touch of disappointment or what might have been suspicion. 'All whores, weren't they?'

Before Shanks could answer, there was a tap on the door. To his surprise, Standers got up and went to it instead of calling on whoever was there to come in. He stood in the open doorway and spoke quietly. 'I didn't realize . . . I'll cover that . . . Phone them!' That last phrase came more distinctly with an edge to it, but then his voice fell to a murmur again. When he was finished, he closed the door once more and coming back to his seat behind the desk, said again, 'All whores.'

'That's right.'

The Superintendent studied him for a moment. 'I can't give you much longer.'

'I didn't want to take up your time,' Billy Shanks said blankly. A loose agitation passed through his long frame as if sketching an intention to rise.

'We've got the other half of the package on this one,' Standers went on as if following a line of thought uninterrupted. 'Not the whore. The customer.'

Despite himself, Billy felt a renewal of interest. His quick mind pulled an idea from the air. 'You mean it might be someone who had it in not for the prostitutes but for their clients?' He saw it all at once like a pattern shaken into place. 'A woman who hated what men did to women, the way men exploit them.' He laughed out of pleasure at its neatness. 'A twentieth-century crime just as the Ripper's belonged so well to the nineteenth. Women's lib instead of Victorian exploitation and hypocrisy.'

Standers stared at him. 'A woman? No way a woman

could have killed him. Oh, he was with a woman all right – I'd bet on that. But it was the pimp that killed him.'

Billy Shanks deflated. 'The pimp . . .'

'Stands to reason. A quarrel about money . . . Oh, a nutter as well. I'm not saying he wouldn't be a nutter – those cuts on the body are a bit . . . funny. I'm going to put the squeeze on everybody on the game in Moirhill. Somebody'll talk for peace and quiet.'

'They're not great talkers.'

'Too much pressure is bad for business. Somebody'll drop a whisper.'

'Unless,' Shanks muttered out of his concealed irritation, 'the killer frightens them more than you do.'

'You wouldn't care to give me a name?'

'There are some frighteners round here,' Shanks said uncomfortably. 'You'd know them better than me.'

'I'm always willing to listen. I haven't been on this patch long,' Standers said complacently, 'but I listen. I'll give you a name. I keep hearing about a man called Kujavia—'

Shanks' two long arms flew up of their own volition, wig-wagging distress. 'Not from me. You haven't heard of him from me.'

'He frightens you,' Standers said with satisfaction. 'I've heard he's good at that. It's his speciality. Only he overdoes it. I've been told that. Once particularly – he overdid it and killed a woman. Only a brass – but he got away with it and that's . . .' He made a face. It was plain they handled things better in the country.

To Billy Shanks it seemed that the Superintendent, who was new to the city, was too fond of the sound of his own voice. To get away from the subject of Kujavia rather than because he cared, he wondered aloud, 'Will frightening the girls work? I seem to remember that when Peter Sutcliffe was murdering one a month round Yorkshire, the red-light districts in Leeds and Bradford and the rest were still in business. The girls worked in the afternoon or out of the clubs at night. Most of them have some bread-and-butter regulars they can count on.'

'It worked in the Robertson case,' Standers said. 'This place was swarming with so many policemen somebody talked. It was bad for trade.'

'That was the big one. By the time it finished, men were being transferred in from all over the Region . . .'

'It'll frighten away the customers,' Standers said. He patted a meaty hand on the folded newspaper. 'Suppose the idea got about that somebody was topping the clients? Like you were saying a minute ago . . . It's even better. If they thought it was a whore doing it – who could a man trust? It would put the notion of getting on the job out of your head.' And he smiled like a man sharing a joke.

At last it seemed to Billy Shanks that he saw the light. 'That's the line you want me to take in the column? That the murder was done by a woman. And that it might happen again.'

Standers shook his head. 'I'm not *telling* you to say anything. You know I don't think a woman did it. But if – for the sake of argument – *you* took that line, well, it would help to keep the customers away. Keep them away and somebody might drop a hint. And if the brass who was there when the victim died gets it into her head it's her we're after . . . that's pressure too, isn't it? She comes to us to cover her own back – or he starts worrying in case she does. It's all pressure.'

'It's some idea,' Billy Shanks said, keeping his tone carefully neutral. 'I'll think about it.'

Standing up, the Superintendent looked more impressive, a heavy, fleshy man with the big frame inherited from generations of agricultural labourers. He laid a hand on Billy's shoulder as he walked him to the door. 'Remember,' he said, 'I'm not telling you to say anything.'

From the hall, an echoing bustle filled the room suddenly carrying with it, pervasive and unforgettable, that stinging smell of corruption and poverty Billy Shanks had thought belonged to the past.

'The window was down,' Murray said, 'so I got in to wait

for you.' He had explained why Standers had called him in, and now he was explaining how he had got into the car.

'I put it down because of the heat,' Shanks said.

The sun beat down on the roof of the car and there was no wind to stir the litter scattered across what would once have been the children's playground. A shirt-sleeved detective standing on the school steps stretched and, yawning, looked across the yard to where they were parked.

Murray eased one buttock off the clinging warmth of the plastic sea. 'I wouldn't mind if you wanted to drive away.'

'Jesus!' Shanks said, giving no sign of reaching for the key. 'That was the headmaster's room. I've stood in front of that desk as a kid. I got the belt there – plenty of times. I was too tall, it was easy to pick me out.' He scowled. 'Pressure! Did I tell you what he said about "pressure"? Clown! He's a clown.'

'You told me. He thinks it's going to be another Robertson case. He wants you to make him famous, Billy.'

'And what do you want, Murray?'

'A lift into town – when you're ready.'

'Now you're in a hurry,' Shanks said. 'You sat and waited till I came out, you sat and listened while I shot my mouth off, now you're in a hurry. There's something about this story . . . Peerse and you. Why are you interested in it?'

'Peerse can't be involved with it. He's not free. He's—' Murray stopped abruptly. Targetting Blair Heathers, he had been going to say. And John Merchant . . . and my brother. It must be the heat, he thought; I've been sitting too long here in the heat.

'He's what?'

'Can we go? I'm too dry to spit.'

'Don't bet Peerse won't get in on the act. If that clown is right and this did get to be a big case, Peerse will get in on it somehow – like a blowfly round shite.'

'Big case, big deal. Somebody killed in Moirhill – big deal. Nobody's going to care. You don't care, Billy. Whatever you told Standers, you're not going to write about it again in your column.'

'Probably not.' And at last, reaching forward, he turned the key and brought the car to life. 'Unless . . .'

Murray had to wait while the yellow Datsun spasmed across the yard and rushed on the gate, narrowly missing the stone pillar on the left. Taking a breath, he prodded, 'Unless?'

Billy Shanks swung into the turn. 'Unless it happens again,' he cried. 'And if it happened on the right date — magic!' He jolted into top gear. 'Then it would be big.'

He glanced to the side, but for some reason Murray had turned away and there was no way of telling what he thought about that.

CHAPTER EIGHT
Visiting Mother

SUNDAY, SEPTEMBER 2ND

'Mum Wilson,' Irene called her, which never sounded entirely appropriate. Not that the old lady – though born in the first years of the century on an island in the grey heaving Atlantic among a Sabbatarian people – huddled gaunt into a black shawl. If there had been any possibility of that, it had died with her husband. His death was a junction at which her life had taken a different road; so that, for example, as a change representative of all the others, she had not crossed the threshold of a church since that time. Altogether, with her good complexion and upright carriage, in a dress of light colours, she made of old age a reassuringly modern icon. Yet one still somehow unsuited to being called 'Mum Wilson' in Irene's light clear tone. Perhaps for no better reason than that her sons called her Mother. Perhaps because Irene never called her just Mum; it was always in full 'Mum Wilson'. To an unreasonable extent it got on Murray's nerves.

'Mum Wilson, as usual we apologize.' Her voice rang through the tiny flat. 'Or I apologize for him. He didn't want to be hurried this morning. Sunday's his day for lying in bed and worrying.'

'Worrying?' The old lady fixed her gaze on her younger son. Her eyes were extraordinary, being palest blue against her brown skin and the nested wrinkles of age. They had the milky appearance of the near blind, but in reality her vision was perfectly good. Against this, as she aged, she had become increasingly deaf. By habit, voices were raised in

90

her presence. 'What is it? What's wrong?' And her tone had sharpened with an anxiety that was instant, apprehensive and hovering.

'Not a thing, Mother.' Malcolm brushed a kiss against her cheek, and went through into the sitting room assuring her over his shoulder, 'Everything's fine.'

'What did you say?'

'He says everything's fine, Mother,' Murray said raising his voice, before dropping it again to ask, 'Why do you do that? You know she can't hear you if you walk away from her.'

'What is it?' Mother asked him. 'How can I hear what Malcolm's saying if you keep talking?'

'Look at Malcolm,' Irene cried into the silence. 'You can see how well he's looking, Mum Wilson.'

'No,' the old woman said. 'He's not.'

She stared at her son who had spent a lot of time outdoors in this good summer; the paleness slid behind his tan made him yellow. He had the look of an old man who has slept badly.

'Don't fuss, Mother,' he said irritably, and then to Irene more quietly, 'Don't you think I've had enough?'

'Speak so Mother can hear,' Murray burst out.

At which all three turned to look at him.

'What is it?' Mother asked. 'What are you keeping from me?'

It was the start of a Sunday visit familiar to them. The table had been opened out and set for dinner since midday. Now, two hours later, Malcolm and Irene had arrived. There had been plenty of time while they waited for Murray to listen to his mother's concern over whether Malcolm was well, happy, untroubled. Meticulously, she did not relate any of these speculations to Malcolm's wife. Since her younger son's marriage two years earlier, she had, after the first shock, come to terms with Irene for her own reasons. Mostly that day she had fretted over his reason for missing the previous Sunday's visit.

'They don't come every week, Mother,' Murray had said. 'Even I don't manage every Sunday. Things happen.'

She widened her strange blind-seeming eyes on him and said, 'No, he's been very faithful about coming. He doesn't often miss a Sunday now.'

'Not since he got married.'

'Irene keeps him up to the mark,' she said seriously. 'She's been good for him.'

For some reason, he covered his mouth with his hand. He felt the hard pressure of his teeth against the drawn tightness of flesh at the root of his thumb. Thinking of the reach of her ambition for her younger son, he said, 'Malcolm needed to marry a lady.'

'Irene?' His mother surprised him. 'You're the detective. I'm only an old woman. She is a good wife for Malcolm – he needs someone to give him a push, he's not as confident as he seems – but she isn't a lady. I wish she was.'.

A memory had made him smile. 'Do you remember, years ago, when the plane crashed on Breagda? There was no one on the island – you had all left it long before and so though they searched it was weeks before they found him. He had been alone piloting his own plane. That seemed marvellous to me, to have your own plane, to be as rich as that. But I overheard you saying to my father, "Oh, he was not one of the gentry. No. He was just an ordinary fellow." '

'I know what I mean even if you can't see it,' Mother said. 'Behind all her airs, there's a common woman.'

Now they had come, she hurried them to the table. She kept the flat tidy and resented the woman whom the brothers paid to come in twice a week. She cooked for herself and enjoyed preparing these Sunday lunches. There was soup first and then sliced ham with peas, tomatoes, potato crisps of which she was fond. Malcolm had developed the habit of bringing a bottle of wine and he would open it and set it on the table, pouring a glass for his mother, Irene and himself. To Murray, who remembered an earlier time, his mother raising the wine glass to her lips, the slight flush that coloured her cheeks, gave him a sense of unreality. For Malcolm, born at the junction time of his father's death, it was different.

'Pull your chair in,' Mother said. She insisted on serving the meal herself. 'You've pushed your seat back, and I can't get past you.'

The soup had been eaten, and now she brought through their plates, the portions decided, there was no question of setting out bowls from which they could choose. She gave more to the men, and if one slice seemed sappier, more succulent, it might be that it went to her younger son. For herself, she was at an age when a little would satisfy her, but she expected each of their plates to be cleared.

'It's the piano,' Murray said, hitching his chair forward.

'I don't know why you keep it,' Malcolm said. 'There would be plenty of room if you got rid of it, Mother.'

Irene, however, was not to be diverted. 'I don't know why it should make you so angry,' she said, accepting her plate. 'Usually you like him, I've heard you laughing aloud while you read him.'

'It didn't make me angry,' Malcolm said. 'Angry, for God's sake!' His face had gone red. 'You asked me to read it – I read it. You're the one who's fascinated by it.'

Murray didn't have to ask; before Irene spoke, looking across the table at him and smiling, he knew. 'Did you read it yesterday, Murray? What that friend of yours wrote in his column?'

Mother rested her hand on Malcolm's shoulder. 'What friend is that, Murray?'

'Billy Shanks,' he told her, but without taking his eyes from the younger woman.

'Murray knows someone famous,' Irene said laughing. 'Yet I had never heard of him till I came here. He's famous here.'

'Famous!' Mother exclaimed in what sounded like contempt. While her husband was alive, she had lived in isolated places. She had never acquired the habit of newspapers. Now she was addicted to television. Only someone who appeared on television could be famous.

'A man was killed,' Irene said. Sitting opposite, Murray saw a circle of light surrounding her. The sun had found a gap in a drifting sky of clouds, and struck into this room in the cliff wall of the high-rise to surround her with its dazzling brightness. Like an actor picked out upon a stage, she cried to them, 'He was found dead in Moirhill – near where Murray used to live – where he became friends with the famous Billy Shanks. Years ago. After you ran away from home, Murray – when you were only a boy, really.'

What was it John Merchant had said? – Anything I know about you, I learned from your brother.

Malcolm flushed a deeper red. 'It doesn't matter where he was found, does it?' he asked, avoiding Murray's glance. 'Who wants to talk about a murder? We're supposed to be having dinner, for God's sake!'

'According to Billy Shanks,' Irene said, raising her voice to be heard, 'it's exactly a hundred years ago since Jack the Ripper committed his first murder – that was in Whitechapel, you know – in London. It's exactly a hundred years ago—'

'It's not,' Malcolm said. 'If we must talk about it, at least get it right.'

Mother gave Murray, who had unconsciously eased his chair back again, a little tap so that he moved forward. She laid down her own plate and sat down. As she did so, Murray caught in her glance at Irene a shadow of confusion. It was like a premonition of the slackening and bewilderment of the mind which comes with senility. Despite her age, the possibility of such a thing for her had never occurred to him until that exact moment. 'I waited a long time for that piano,' she said inconsequentially.

It was Irene who responded. 'When did you buy it?' she asked.

There was a silence which went on too long and then lengthened again as not one of them was quick-witted enough to fill it with an answer.

'Was it after Malcolm's father died?' she wondered pleasantly.

'Yes, after,' the old lady said.

'Perhaps he wasn't fond of music?'

'None of us play the piano,' Murray heard himself say. 'What does it matter?'

'I wanted it for Malcolm,' Mother said.

'But when I got old enough to learn, I hated the lessons,' Malcolm said. Unexpectedly he smiled, as if the memory had put him into a better humour.

They talked then about other things. As Murray ate, he kept looking at his sister-in-law and glancing away. He would have been ashamed to have it seem he was envious of his brother. She had dark hair that shone; she must be very healthy, only the hair of the well and the young glistened like that; he wondered what it would feel like under his hand. He could hardly believe that she was sitting opposite him, or in her reason for being there. She was married to his brother, who had met her in London, where she had been a secretary, something like that. Malcolm had gone on holiday and had come back with her; then they were married. Her mother and father were dead. She had no relatives. It had not been convenient for any of her friends to come up for the wedding. He realized with a kind of shock that he knew nothing of her background, and yet it was his daily business to find out such things about strangers. Malcolm would know, he supposed. It did not seem possible that people could fall in love and marry without offering each other the past to share; yet he was not sure. He found that he was looking at her breasts, and when he raised his eyes she was smiling.

As Mother got up to fetch the next course, little bowls of sweet pudding, Irene said, 'Of course, Polly Nicholls — that was the name. I've been sitting trying to remember.'

'Let it rest,' Malcolm said.

'Something in Billy's column yesterday,' Murray guessed. 'The one Mother and I haven't read.'

'Clever.' Irene held out her hand to him across the table as if inviting him to touch her.

'Polly Nicholls . . .' It wasn't difficult to take the next step. 'The Ripper's first victim.'

'In Whitechapel a hundred years ago. A prostitute,' she

95

said. 'And not glamorous at all. She was a tiny woman, and five of her front teeth had been knocked out in a fight. When they make a film of it, the women don't look anything like that.'

'I don't understand,' Mother said. 'A film of what?'

'About Jack the Ripper,' Irene cried, her eyes sparkling. 'With fog and hansom cabs and beautiful young actresses arranged under the street lights, just pretending. In real life, Polly Nicholls had been thrown out of her doss-house because she didn't have fourpence for a bed. She hadn't eaten all day before she was killed.'

'This week Billy Shanks didn't make me laugh,' Malcolm said sourly, with a side glance at Murray as if in some obscure way the fault was his.

'Billy Shanks,' his wife ignored the interruption, 'describes how he walked down the lane and saw the body of the man spread out on the ground and the doctor examining it. He makes you see it all. It's what reality is like, he says.'

'Billy saw all of that . . .' Murray shook his head. 'I wish now I'd read it.'

'Prostitutes and murder! There must be something better to talk about than filth like that.' Malcolm made a movement of disgust. The yellow under his tan made him look ill.

As he turned his head, his mother stopped him with the back of her hand against his chin. 'Your poor face!'

On his cheek the last visible bruise of the beating he had taken after Heathers' party was fading.

'I fell.' He put up his hand as if to shade his eyes.

'When? You didn't say anything to me about falling.'

As she reached for his hand, he pushed hers away. It rose up trembling as if in protest, before falling to her side.

'Yes,' and she went round into the kitchen, but was quickly back saying as she came, 'Anyway, isn't it silly? If it was a man killed like you said, and didn't Jack the Ripper kill women? And in London at that. Wasn't it a man killed?'

96

Irene laughed. Her eyes shone with the joke of it. 'That's a change for the better, Mum Wilson.'

'No,' Mother said, 'there's nothing better about a man being killed. Whatever sort of man he was.'

That was impressive, but as Murray looked at her with her hand resting on Malcolm's shoulder he was afraid for her. For her second son she had such a ferocity of concern, like a young woman bending over a cradle. It defied her age; it made her vulnerable. He could not imagine how she would survive if anything happened to Malcolm.

BOOK TWO

CHAPTER NINE
A Letter from Jill

MONDAY, SEPTEMBER 3RD

Murray got a tomato juice at the bar and made his way over to the table in the left alcove at the back. Billy Shanks had two rules: he never stood a drink or let one be bought for him and never made introductions. One of the two men already there was tall and heavy with a full prophetic beard flecked with white; the other, an ageing youth of forty or so, had a narrow sweating face that looked as if it had been moulded out of used blotting paper.

'Why are you asking for an opinion, if you're so sure it's from a crank?' the Prophet was asking.

'Why?' Billy Shanks' arms flew up, endangering the tableload of glasses. 'Because I want everyone to tell me I'm right, of course. There's always crank mail on a Monday. People have too much time on their hands at the weekend. They brood.'

' "Modern days Jill rips Jack." I like that,' the Prophet said, looking at the sheet of paper he held. 'Only it should have been in red ink. Jack's were.'

'It was,' Shanks said. 'The colour doesn't show on a photostat.'

'It was worth passing on to the police then?'

'Routine.' Billy Shanks' laughter had a false sound.

'You're sure the original wasn't in blood?' the Prophet asked hopefully.

'Christ, no!'

'In his first letter to the police Jack talked about saving what he called the proper red stuff in a ginger-beer bottle.

101

Only it went thick,' the Prophet said, 'and he couldn't use it.'

Murray decided against asking to look at the letter. He had no reason to be interested in it. Yet he leaned forward unobtrusively and saw it was printed in block capitals, each carefully shaped as if by a child. Even if somewhere you had seen the person's normal writing, there would be no way of recognizing it from this.

'It's all rubbish,' the ageing youth sneered. A drop of water on the end of his nose swung from its precarious position over his beer into Murray's direction. 'Do you not think it's rubbish?'

'Theo thinks everything is rubbish,' Shanks said by way of explanation.

'It's not likely,' Murray said, thinking aloud, 'what you have there was written by any murderer. Billy's right. Some old lady − or a kid left too much on his own.'

Billy Shanks launched a hand soaring that turned like a tern in mid-flight to retrieve the photostat. 'Right! Jack the Ripper didn't write *his* letters, I'll bet. And Peter Sutcliffe didn't send that tape to the police in the Yorkshire Ripper case. They still haven't found whoever did that.' He nodded in triumph. 'Murder's one trade, drama's another. Different trades, different talents.'

'Oh, the real Jack wrote some of his letters,' the Prophet said. ' "I am down on whores and I shan't quit ripping them till I do get buckled." Or − "From hell, Mr Lusk, sir, I send you half the kidney I took from one woman, preserved it for you, t'other piece I fried and ate it; it was very nice." ' He had a voice like a preacher, or an actor, paced and resonant. It was odd how even in the warmth and noise of the bar, the words of the old letter made a pause. 'I can't see that being written by an old woman − or a kid.'

But the watery Theo sniffed, 'I don't know. I've got a girlfriend whose kid plays at hanging his Action Man.'

'. . . I could believe that,' the Prophet said.

'Anyway,' Billy Shanks intervened across their mutual dislike, 'it looks as if whoever wrote our letter was trying

102

to imitate the style the Ripper used.' He swept a wide gesture of relief. 'I can't imagine Jack the Ripper – or even Jill – sitting in a library taking notes.'

'Can you not?' The Prophet was taken by the spirit of contradiction. 'That's because you imagine him – or let's say her,' he smiled benignly malicious on Shanks, 'only at the moment of the crime. A knife that moves in the dark, no other reality, out of the shadows into the darkness. It's that defect of our imagination that will keep her safe, for she'll have another existence, sit next to you at the office, come to supper, seem the most ordinary person in the world.' He was the rare kind of talker who exerts a spell. Murray thought about the ones who went on Sundays to visit. 'It's like the story by Le Fanu about the man who feels himself to be haunted by something he senses but can't see, by a presence. There's just a hint that he has some reason to suffer from guilt. He runs away abroad and thinks he's escaped from it, but it comes back. He retreats to his own country, into the most isolated place, and takes with him just one person who loves him and will guard him. The story is called "The Familiar". Mr Le Fanu had his own ending for it . . . but the one I wanted would have had our hero waking up one night in his secure refuge to find the loved one leaning over him, mad and demonic. That's the real horror.'

'I like it,' Billy Shanks said.

'The Watcher,' the Prophet said. 'You'll find a surprising number of stories with that theme. It was one of the ideas that haunted the nineteenth century – the Watcher – or wakening out of a fit to find you'd been buried alive.'

'Bollocks!' Theo snarled. 'What does that nineteenth-century bollocks mean to your average punter? You want to fucking wake up. Nineteenth century? We're nearly out of the fucking twentieth century.'

'I'll give you a twentieth-century ghost story, if you'd like one.' The Prophet transfixed Theo. 'You and I are alone in a house in the country. Oh, not a Gothic mansion, but, let's say, an old manse, painted, refurbished, Rentokilled from end to end. You'd buy it in a moment. Only it has a cellar − you can guess the kind, with a door and a flight of steps down into the dark. You have to give me those − put anything you like in the cellar, mushrooms, wine, but as an investment, that's modern enough. We've been arguing about ghosts and you begin to press the notion that there's "something down there". Something predatory and unnatural down there. But the victim − in this case myself − knows that it's only a foolishness, a joke that would like to be cruel. And so − being much stronger than you − I tie you up and leave you by the cellar door. I mean to come back, of course, after the second cigarette. Only, while you're lying there not able to move, comes the knock and slithering of something climbing the steps . . . I would call it "Charley-in-the-Cellar".'

Theo rolled a white eye at him like a spooked horse. 'I don't have to listen to this crap,' he said.

It was the Prophet, however, who got up and bent impressively over them. ' "The shallowest of mortals is able now to laugh at the notion of a personal devil." That's not me − a dry stick of a nineteenth-century civil servant said that. "Yet the horror at evil which could find no other expression than in the creation of a devil is no subject for laughter, and if it doesn't survive in some shape or other, then the race itself will not survive." He lived to be eighty-four and died the year before the First World War started. He wasn't far wrong, eh, boys?'

'That's a wonderful bloody man,' Billy Shanks said, gazing after him affectionately.

Murray decided that rather than hearing Theo's response, he would prefer to go to the lavatory.

Two men were relieving themselves in consort. The nearer looked quickly round as Murray stood into the wall. Tall and solidly built with a high red colour in his cheeks and prematurely white hair, he seemed healthy and prosperous. 'All right, so Parker is from the Bible Belt,' he boomed at his companion, 'but don't tell me his religious observances require him to drink coke and eat hamburgers exclusively.

It's just that when he comes over here, he enjoys making the hostesses squirm. Coke and hamburgers every time when they're longing to do the *nouvelle cuisine* bit – and everybody has to eat them – all the ambitious shits chewing away and smiling. But when I was at head office, he had me out for Thanksgiving and that was frightfully traditional – sausage forcemeat and turkey. The wine, though, was Californian.' 'Lucky turkeys,' his companion said, giving himself a hygienic shake.

'You're on your own then,' Murray said, remarking on the obvious as he sat down again.

'Alone at last,' Shanks grinned. 'The poet has folded up his tent.'

'You know some strange people. I've never heard a guy talk quite like that one, but then I don't know many poets.'

Shanks laughed. 'Poet? You mean Tommy Beltane?'

'The big guy. With the beard.'

'Ah, it's the beard that does it. And he is a marvellous bloody talker. If you could work a typewriter with your tongue, Tom would be rich. He's a clerk with the Region. I get the odd juicy bit from Tom.'

'That'll help to keep him in biros.'

'No, it's not like that. Tommy Beltane wouldn't take money.' Shanks signalled reproof with one palm pushed away flat against the air. 'But he likes to talk.'

'So it was the other one who was the poet. The crap merchant.'

'One of the gifted. Theo is bidding to be the bard of our fair city.'

'He seemed a right idiot.'

'Oh, he's a complete cunt,' Shanks agreed. 'Never mind him. What do you want to ask me?'

'Maybe I just looked in for the pleasure of your company.' Murray smiled briefly. 'I've heard a rumour John Merchant keeps a girlfriend. Would you know anything about that?'

'I could give you a name and address – if you'd tell me why you want to know.'

'I couldn't do that. It's for a client.'

Shanks studied him thoughtfully. 'You've got the wrong idea, I'm the one who's supposed to get told things. It strikes me, Murray, that with you everything goes one way.'

'I'll buy you a drink.'

'It would be a dear whisky.' Shanks chewed his lip. 'Would this be anything to do with Blair Heathers?'

'You didn't hear me say anything about Blair Heathers.'

'If it was, I might give you that name.'

Murray shrugged and waited.

'I keep hoping somebody will nail that evil old bastard,' Billy Shanks said. 'And if Merchant got flushed down the tubes as the message boy that would be a bonus.'

'I thought you only got angry in print.'

'Shows you're not a regular reader. I don't get too angry in print any more. Not after Heathers sued.'

'Sued you?'

'The paper — it happened before you came back. Judges have a weakness for millionaires. Particularly that judge. He felt it was really wrong of me to write about a children's home where rain came in on the beds and the floors buckled and they had to rip out the heating and try again. Writing stuff like that can damage a man's reputation. So we lost and I still get to write the column and everything's the same. I work hard at making it look the same. And nobody sees any difference except me. Me and Tommy Beltane and a few thousand others. It's our secret.'

'Nothing to do with padding your expense account . . .' Murray said unsympathetically. 'So you'll tell me who Merchant's girlfriend is?'

'After I get something to drink,' Shanks said. But when he came back, sipping his drink, he remarked instead, 'Imagine them using Southpark again for a murder enquiry. When I was at school there, the father of a mate of mine was the janitor. This girl Muriel and I could get into the school at night. It was an adolescent's bloody dream world. We fucked in the gym and the ladies' staffroom, we even did it in the lavatory, but mostly we went into the headmaster's room. God, he couldn't have had any sense

106

of smell that headie or he'd have sent for the police.'

'Can we talk about Merchant's girlfriend?' Murray scowled. He disliked this kind of reminiscence, and Billy knew it.

'It wasn't all my fault, Murray. Nobody should meet a girl who'll do anything – not when you're fifteen. I did things with her I've never done again in my whole life with grown-up women. I used to sit and try to work out what else I could do to her. Books have got a lot to answer for, Murray. I even went in the back door there on the carpet in front of the headmaster's desk. I kept looking at it while Standers was talking to me. It looked like the same carpet.'

As Murray felt his face being studied for a reaction, it occurred to him that he was being punished for casting doubt on Billy's expense account. After a pause, however, as if the act of remembering had set something unexpected going in him, Shanks went on, 'Muriel was younger than me. One day I got together a bit of money and we played truant and took a train down the coast. She was a good swimmer – big made with long legs. She stood in the water splashing me – a big daft kid . . . The thing is I've always had a bad conscience about Muriel. I felt I'd – stupid bloody word! – corrupted her.' And it was true he got out the word 'corrupted' only with difficulty, as if it stuck in his throat.

While he spoke the last few sentences, he had been fiddling with one of the empty glasses. Now he looked up, blinking.

'Don't worry,' Murray said with authority. 'Muriel's conscience will be clear. If ever you meet her, she'll be too respectable to talk to you. She'll be some nice guy's old lady.'

Immediately, unreasonably, Shanks looked relieved.

'I wouldn't tell stuff like that to anyone else, Murray . . . Frances Fernie.' He scribbled down the name and the address under it. 'It's a street off Moirhill Road – further out, on the respectable side.'

'I'll find her.'

Having got what he wanted, Murray stood up. Shanks looked up at him.

'That stuff about Jack the Ripper in Saturday's column. It's what I use now to hide what's missing. Who cares about a children's home? Nobody wants to read the small print – not in contracts or Acts of Parliament – it's boring. When the century gets its tombstone, that's what'll be written on it: They got bored too easily.'

Murray picked up his glass of tomato juice and finished what was left in it.

'Here's to Muriel,' he said.

He didn't really like tomato juice.

CHAPTER TEN
Whores are Different

WEDNESDAY, SEPTEMBER 5TH

It didn't bother Murray that old Barney wiped a finger under his nose before folding the paper and passing it over. Situated at the Cross, selling papers every day of the week in all weathers, the old man was a storehouse of local knowledge and a magnet for gossip. It was worth putting up with his idiosyncrasies. Anyway, it was another voice to make a pattern of the days; living alone, that counted for something.

'Where you off to then?' Barney asked.

'Up the Road a bit.'

'A fair step?'

'So so . . . up past the canal,' Murray conceded.

'You're going to see somebody?' The old man hazarded a guess. He had a voice like vinegar and razor blades from too many wet mornings and fogbound afternoons.

'That's right,' but went on since it was part of the game to give something, 'I've been trying to get her in since Monday.'

'Her,' the old man repeated. 'It's a woman then.' Honour satisfied, he reverted to a favourite topic, 'All the people you have to see, you should get a motor.'

'The sun's shining,' Murray said. 'It's a good day for a walk.'

'Ay, but,' Barney said, wiping his nose again, 'in business, time is money.'

Speaking as one businessman to another . . . which was funny, but didn't provide a car to replace the Cortina which had failed its test — 'if it was a horse, ye'd shoot it,' the mechanic had said; or shorten the dusty length of Moirhill Road on the day of a bus strike. Time being money, he walked too fast, so that when for the third time he turned into the street where John Merchant's girlfriend was supposed to live his temper was sour and his collar stuck to his neck with the heat.

The metal grille at the entrance to the close was unlocked and folded back which was an improvement. The walls were lined with blue tiles each with a white flower and it was suddenly cold out of the warmth of the sun. As he came to the first landing, a man was coming down from above carrying a parcel clumsily wrapped in brown paper and Murray watched him out of sight before knocking.

For a deceptive moment, Murray thought that he knew the woman. She had blonde hair cut short and a narrow pretty face with high cheekbones. It was only when she tentatively smiled showing crooked slightly overlapping teeth that the impression of a resemblance vanished.

'John sent me.'

'No,' she said, 'he didn't,' and started to close the door. He pushed it back and forced her before him into the flat.

The sun had found its difficult angle between the cliffs of tenements and the room was flooded with light. It was clean and the carpet was a wound brightness of pink and green. There was an easy chair and a couch with a woman's magazine laid open on a cushion. On the wall opposite him a painting of a landscape altered as the sunlight fell across it warming its colours. Through an open door he glimpsed a bed neatly made with its cover smoothed over and hanging straight. It was tidier and more comfortable than where he lived.

It was nothing like the whores' rooms he remembered.

'John,' he said, 'likes his meat well wrapped. I can see that.'

He pointed at the chair and the edge of the uncertainty that he had begun to feel left him when she sat down without arguing. She gave no indication of the resistance even timorous people offer as a token when they are in their own homes buttressed by a sense of possession.

'I haven't had any man up here,' she said suddenly. Muscles in her throat worked as if out of a dry mouth she was trying to swallow.

'One man. This one man I'm thinking of.'

If John Merchant refused to see him, then it seemed to Murray that he had to apply pressure here: to the hidden part of Merchant's life, where he wouldn't want to have the police run interference for him.

'I wouldn't hurt anybody,' she said. 'You won't prove I've hurt anybody.'

He saw that her upper lip was shining with sweat. The woman was terrified. Why was she so afraid? It was as if they were talking about two different things.

'What do you call yourself, Frances? Is it Mrs or Miss Fernie?' The truth was that he wasn't even sure any more that he had the right woman, the one named for him by Billy Shanks.

'I'm not married,' she said. 'Why are you here? Are you not the police?'

'You're not very bright,' he said. 'You're not very bright at all, Frances.'

She wiped her hand across her lips. Crouched on the chair, she was wearing a black sweater and dark grey tight cord trousers. Her feet were bare apart from plain black slippers like ballet pumps. There was something of a dancer's slimness and tone to her body, its breasts small and high with the nipples standing out under the light sweater. Standing over her, he caught the salt smell of her fear.

'Not bright,' he said and walked through into the bedroom. Besides the neatly made bed, there was a wardrobe against the wall, two chairs, one cushioned and set before a dressing table which had a scatter of brushes, bottles, little boxes and a decorative fan in garish colours spread half open. He began to throw the clothes from the wardrobe on to the floor. At the sound she came to the door watching in silence without a protest.

111

'He's generous,' he said and waited for a moment as if it was a question she might answer. He began on the drawers of the dressing table, pouring out first from the small ones on either side of the mirror rings and a watch and a necklace of plump amber-coloured beads. From two larger drawers he tipped out scarves and tubes of pills and ointments, one of which fell clear of the mess and rolled to rest with 'haemorrhoids' lettered in blue on the upper side. At the bottom there were two long drawers and from them he threw down jerseys and soft coils of underwear. Last of all under everything else as if hidden, he came on a doll damaged by time and with most of its yellow hair missing. It fell on all that had gone before and watched him from its remaining eye.

'John doesn't like anything too flashy,' Murray said and stirred the tangle with a shoe smeared by the oily dust of his long walk. 'And he likes things kept tidy. I bet you even have to take a bath regularly.'

'I don't need anybody to make me take a bath,' she said.

'I wonder if he likes that voice of yours. What is it – east coast?' She had retreated into a watchful silence. 'There's no way John's going to take you out on his arm – not where he'd meet anybody that mattered. He's a bit of a gentleman, John, maybe a wee bit of a snob, eh?' His voice kept the same quiet insistent pitch as he moved closer to her, uncomfortably close. 'You're all right, but not anything special. Why you? Is it something he does to you? Eh? Or the other way round? Is that it? I think that's it.'

For a second, crowding her close, it was possible to believe she would spill them out, the indignities which would give him a hold on Merchant and let him protect his brother.

'I don't talk any worse than you.' That was unexpected, like a cat twisting under his hand. 'The Highland way you talk,' and at her own words she blinked and something changed in her eyes.

There would be no secrets, but he didn't stop trying. 'How did you come to meet John Merchant in the first place? Did somebody pass you on to him?' A useful

112

possibility occurred to him. 'Was it Blair Heathers – did he pass you on?' Something about her had left him in no doubt from the first glance that she was a professional.

Frances Fernie circled the tangle of her possessions fastidiously before settling on the edge of the bed. She nibbled at the corner of a thumbnail. 'I don't know anybody called Heathers,' she said without looking up. 'But you're right about somebody introducing me to John. You're right about that.'

'So?'

'You wouldn't know him,' she said. 'I met John through this friend of mine, Malcolm Wilson. But you wouldn't know him.'

Despite the shock he took a habit of self-control for granted. Ideas spun through his mind too fast to be made use of or grasped. He thought his expression would give nothing away and then he realized that somehow he had brought his face close to hers. Her eyes widened impossibly and came near and then went from him, rushed out into some inconceivable distance. He was filled by a murderous rage. Carefully, one step at a time, he moved back from her.

'Why tell me then?'

Her lips were white and she shook her head but seemed unable to speak. There was no way of telling what it was she denied.

'You're a whore,' he said. 'For a whore you take too many chances.'

He stared in a kind of stupidity at the stuff he had thrown on the floor to remind her that a whore was different and that no matter how much money a whore gathered it could not buy her peace or any place to be secure.

In the lavatory, the lid had a fur cover, slick under his fingers as he lifted the seat and began to relieve himself. As if by accident, the thick yellow stream strayed on the edge of the bowl and he stared as it sprayed soiling the carpet and it seemed as if the hard jet falling out of him would never cease. Like a sleep-walker, he ran hot water into the basin and washed his hands. He soaped and rinsed them

113

and did the same again and a third time. The towel from
the rail was warm and he held it against his throat. Through
the open door, he watched the woman gathering up the
yellow-haired doll with a twisting protective movement that
kept her gaze fixed on him.

By the basin a round mirror was fixed. When he pulled
the cord, a coil of fluorescent light came on around it. The
mirror tilted at his touch and he saw reflected in the depths
of his eyes two perfect circles of white.

CHAPTER ELEVEN
Second Death

SATURDAY, SEPTEMBER 8TH

Not dreaming, but drifting against the morning light, Murray saw his brother's wife with a knife in her hand and she came near and then turned and went from him into the distance. It wasn't true that he was angry; and then, unbidden, his father appeared and poor Seidman killed in Memphis; muddled images of the dead.

When he opened his eyes, he saw a grey beetle nested in balls of fluff on the carpet. He waited for it to move, but it turned suddenly into an eraser that had been knocked off the desk and with that he knew he was in the front room and remembered why he was sleeping there.

'Can I come in, Murray?'

'What time is it? It's the middle of the night.'

'It's called working unsocial hours.'

'You get paid for them. I don't.'

As they went into the back room, Eddy Stewart staggered against the lintel.

'You're drunk.'

'Tired.' Uninvited, Stewart half fell into the rocker. It squealed back under the impact. Murray lifted him by the arm – 'That's where I sit, remember?' – and dropped him into one of the upright seats at the table.

'You're not a kind man,' Stewart said thoughtfully. 'Always liked you, Murray. Always from the old days. I never cared what they said about you. But you're not a kind man. Couldn't say that. Not being honest . . . honestly.'

'How drunk are you, Eddy? I thought that was a sponge you kept in your throat.'

'Ach!' Stewart made a throaty exclamation of disgust and resting his head on his hand seemed to go to sleep. Murray knocked the elbow off the table.

'What the—' Stewart spluttered as his head jerked up. He groaned and rubbed the sagging flesh on his face into deep folds. 'Can I stay here for the night?'

'Not a chance,' Murray said. 'This is private. People come here when they're invited. You're breaking a rule, Eddy.'

'I haven't had all that much drink. A share of a couple of bottles to help them celebrate.' Abruptly, he said, 'I can't face going home.'

'Find another blackbird and get her to sing for you.'

'You can get tired of putting it to whores.'

'So go home.'

'Fucking Moirhill! They're all peddling their meat up there or they're tealeafs or just thick and too bone bloody idle to live anywhere else. If you weren't just a toytown copper, you'd have stayed long enough to knock a few doors. You didn't stay long enough to learn, Murray. You don't know how many shits there are in the world.'

'Next time bring your violin. Come on. Out. I've got work in the morning, and you're a big time detective with a boss. Peerse'll be looking for you.'

'Peerse can go and—' Stewart made an explicit gesture of explanation, 'sideways. Another bloody teetotaller. I was helping the Northern team celebrate. They got a confession.'

A confession. Murray went still.

'For the guy that got offed in Deacon Street,' Stewart said. 'You were there. Turns out he was a queer. Met the wrong little friend. The kid's been done a couple of times before for queer-bashing. This time he went too far.' Rubbing a finger in one eye, he squinted at Murray sceptically. 'What's making you so happy?'

'It's the way you tell them, Eddy,' Murray said.

'Stuff you too.' Stewart yawned. 'I'm shattered.'

116

'You can put your head down here – but this is the last time.'

As Eddy Stewart gaped in mid yawn, the concession taking him by surprise, Murray despite himself felt his grin widening, a thing out of his control. No more worry; no more crazy suspicions.

They had a confession.

He rolled over and shut out the light with an arm. Outside a bus crashed gears as the signal on the corner went to green. He wondered if Stewart was still sleeping, and then must have dozed for when he opened his eyes the big detective was resting his behind on the edge of the desk. 'I can't find the coffee. And I can't face that perfumed piss you drink.'

Murray kicked his way out of the sleeping bag. 'You're not meant to. That's good tea. Too expensive to waste.' He gathered up the papers scattered on the desk and turned them face down.

Stewart looked on with amusement. 'Secrets, eh? If you'd had them locked away, you could have let me sleep in here and you could have had the bed. What's happened to the girl that used to work for you – the one with the big tits?'

'Marge.' Murray frowned. 'Her mother took her away.'

'I can't believe it,' Stewart said with relish, preparing himself to be persuaded. 'Not you, Murray. What'd you do to her?'

It was a sore point. 'The stupid woman thought the whole place was an office. When she found out I lived in the back room, she didn't think it was suitable.'

'Just as well, you can get into trouble with them at that age. What age was she – fifteen?'

'Seventeen – don't be stupid. She'd sat her exams in typing and shorthand. Didn't pass right enough – but for what I can pay, I was lucky to get her.'

As they went through the lobby into the back room, Stewart said, 'Seventeen . . .' lingering on the word.

Murray put on the heater and brought out tea and coffee. 'She was just starting to cope. I can't be here all the time.

117

How can I run a business without somebody here to answer the phone?'

'Seventeen,' Stewart said as if to himself. He sat at the table and waited until Murray passed him a cup of coffee. 'There's something about their tits at that age . . .'

'Last night you were sitting in that chair crying,' Murray said. When he felt his temper slip, he spoke more quietly. 'You didn't want to go home to Lynda. You've been married over twenty years but you'd have slept on the floor here rather than go back and face her.'

For a horrible moment, Stewart's tough morning face crumpled into the abject mask of the previous night. He bent his head and sipped the scalding coffee. When he looked up, he had managed a smile. 'Billy Graham has a hell of a lot to answer for. Do you remember when you rounded up all the whores in Bath Street and walked them down to the evangelist meeting on the corner? You made them take off their shoes and walk down. It was raining and they had to stand there in their bare feet and sing hymns.'

'Every time you're drunk . . . I'm starting to think that guy was you.'

They looked at one another in silence.

'I've felt like killing myself,' Stewart said. 'Doing it all the way. You're not the only one with a conscience . . . But this woman I'm going with isn't just another easy ride. She's special. I'm due a wee bit of happiness.'

'Happiness.' There wasn't any expression in the way Murray said the word. It might have come from a language he had not learned.

'It's wee Sally that's killing me. Jenny's just a cow – she's past helping. That bastard she works for just laughed when I said I'd report him to the Law Society. What can I do? I can't fill in a fucking lawyer. It'll end up with another abortion. And Peter's going to hell – I wanted him to follow me, but, oh, no! All right, I said, what about the army then? But he says he doesn't want to get shot in Ireland – little shit! Sitting about the house . . . Let me catch you with

118

drugs, I said to him, and I'll put you inside myself. Bugger them. It's not my fault — I've always been firm with them. It's Sally,' his voice glutted with tears, 'she's just a magic wee kid. She loves her daddy.'

'She's lucky there right enough.'

'How could I expect you to understand? You'd have to be a father to know how I feel.'

It was a relief when the extension bell announced that the phone was ringing in the front room. It was a long time, years, since Murray had seen Eddy's wife. If he hadn't quit the police and left the city so abruptly, he would have been the best man at her wedding. Leaning against the desk, looking down at the traffic, he listened to her voice.

'Stupid cunt!' Stewart exclaimed when he came back from speaking to her. His face was red with rage. 'Peerse phoned a couple of hours ago. He'll be wondering where the hell I am.'

'She did well finding you at all,' Murray reminded him.

'The last bloody place she tried.' He knotted his tie with trembling fingers. 'Peerse is such a bastard.'

Murray watched him with amusement. 'Everybody's entitled to a day off.'

'Maybe — but that stupid bitch told him I was in bed sleeping and she was just away to waken me. Two hours ago!'

It was a long time since Murray had laughed aloud. It was a good feeling, and unfortunate that Stewart should spoil it at once. Red-faced with the effort of bending to tie his laces, he muttered, 'Anyway I don't get it. What does Peerse want me over at Florence Street for? What's it to do with us even if they have found another body?'

Florence Street . . . where Billy Shanks' old school was . . . the school they had been using as the incident room for the murder enquiry.

'You told me there had been a confession,' Murray said.

In the car, however, having accepted Murray's excuse that he had business in Moirhill and needed a lift, Stewart explained, 'The kid that confessed was just a head banger. He runs with the Valley, and they'd picked him up for some

119

stupid thing or other. You know the style — a wee bald head full of billiard chalk. He wants to be a hard man and when he heard them talking about a murder he thought it was Opportunity Knocks.' He snorted reluctantly with laughter. 'Apparently all he was worried about was getting word back to the Valley. "Big Dunc'll know? Tommy Merry'll know? They didn't think I'd any bottle. They'll not laugh at me now." I tell you, Murray, they should never have abolished hanging. It would do that wee cunt good to get hung — put the nonsense out of his head.'

Murray got out at the end of Florence Street and watched as the car picked up speed and then swung in through the school gate, taking the turn too fast so that the tyres squealed. After waiting for a moment, he went over to the other pavement and walked along until he was opposite the yard. People came out and in and some of them glanced his way. He was too obvious standing there; and so for a while he walked the length of the street back and then forward, but he didn't see anyone he knew and there was no sign of Eddy reappearing. When he looked at his watch, an hour had passed. He knew what he was doing was stupid. If he was challenged, he could give no reason for being there; he was not even sure he could explain it to himself.

In the end, he gave in and went back to his flat. He had time to make a cup of the sweet smelling Chinese tea and then the phone rang.

'I've been trying to get hold of you,' Eddy Stewart's voice complained.

'I'm just in.'

'It was John Merchant they found dead. Bollocks naked not far away from where the first one was found. And cut about the same way in the same place — only an awful lot worse. So the kid's out of the frame — not that he would ever have been in it if it hadn't been for that clown Standers. He was sure he had it wrapped up — all routine but brilliant with it.'

Stewart stopped talking and Murray listened to the silence sing in his ear.

120

'Murray?'

'John Merchant. I heard you.'

'There's something else . . . Because it was Merchant, Peerse and me are on the team now. Blair Heathers is going to have to wait. The thing is, Murray, whatever you think about Peerse . . . he's a clever bugger.'

The telephone static muttered like a premonition.

'The thing is,' Eddy Stewart said, 'they recognized the body right away – Merchant being who he was. And when Peerse heard, he remembered Merchant had a bit on the side and pulled her in.'

He stopped talking again and waited as if for Murray to admit something before he would go on.

'Frances Fernie,' Murray said.

'That's right. And she made a bad impression, she was scared, they were sure they were on to something. Only she has an alibi. She claims she was with some guy all night.'

'What guy?' Murray asked, but he knew the answer before Stewart spoke.

'Your brother Malcolm. That's why I'm phoning you. They've been holding him since this morning. He's "helping with enquiries" – you know the routine. It doesn't look good.'

CHAPTER TWELVE
The Beating

SATURDAY, SEPTEMBER 8TH

'Small world.'

'You're not a lightweight any more, Murray.'

The doorman whose stock in trade was a memory for faces could not hide his pleasure at remembering this one after so many years.

'I'm not seventeen either. You've maybe moved up a division since then yourself.'

The doorman appreciated the joke; he was a man who liked his jokes to be kept simple. 'And the rest. About a hundred and twenty pounds since they days.'

It was late and this was the last of the possibilities his contact had given him. The approach had not been impressive – a dingy passage then, since he had not taken the lift, two flights of cold stairs passing on the first floor a car-insurance office on one side and Wood Art Novelties Ltd on the other. Perhaps it was the contrast with that exterior which had helped to make the club fashionable. A group of three men and two youths came into the vestibule. One of the men said as he passed, 'Hey, George, Louie sent us,' in a fake Bronx accent which made George laugh although the chances were he had been treated to it before.

'The thing is,' he said, turning back to Murray, 'you're not a member.'

He was a big man and they had kitted him out in the kind of suit worn by gangsters in forties movies, wide-shouldered, loud, and with a lot of room in the legs.

122

'I don't want to gamble,' Murray said. 'Just have a drink – maybe something to eat.'

'I couldn't let you go upstairs.'

'That's all right.'

'Anyway it's full of bloody Chinamen up there.'

'I don't want to gamble.'

'Something to eat and drink?'

'That's it.'

In the long room most of the tables were empty and a single couple danced with melancholy absorption to a pianist playing at being Sam playing it again. There was a lot of glitter in the decor and an effect of chrome and red leather. There were imitation machine-guns on the walls and fake bullet holes to match and black and white blow-ups of stylized threat and ritual dying in which George Raft, Bogart and Cagney featured. One end of the bar had a cold table and beyond that a servery labelled The Steak Out.

The barman explained, 'They got a professor from the Art School to design it. And students – some of them helped him. But he was a real professor.'

'Did he design the doorman's suit as well?' Murray asked.

The barman grinned. 'The big fellow hates that gear. He thinks it makes him look like an idiot.'

'He could have something there. What's the food like?'

The barman recited until Murray interrupted, 'What's the difference between that and the other one?'

'A couple of quid. It comes with cheese and strips of bacon on top. They'll give you a side salad if you want it.'

Although he was not on expenses, Murray had to eat. It had been a long day since Eddy Stewart had phoned to tell him about Malcolm. Tomorrow was Sunday when he would visit Mother.

—Let me tell you about Malcolm, Mother. He's helping the police with their enquiries. He may be able to help because a woman called Frances Fernie claims he spent Friday night in bed with her. I don't want you to worry though or get too upset about that; it's quite possible she's lying. Why would she do that? Because if she wasn't sleeping with Malcolm, it's just possible she was murdering John Merchant — that's right — *that* John Merchant. There isn't any kind of doubt she slept with Merchant. She talks like a country girl, but she's been around one city or another for some time; lots of people don't have a good ear for changing how they sound. I don't know why she should claim Malcolm was sleeping with her. I don't know how they could have met.

—What do you think, Irene?

At midnight the comedian did his act. All the tables except one were full. An aggrieved couple were steered away from the empty table. That was the one, Murray decided. The comedian was a long-time performer who had recently made a record that had sold well enough to move him upmarket. In the accent of Moirhill, he told jokes about football, blacks, Irish and Pakistanis. The pianist had been replaced by a group. People danced.

—She has the body of a dancer. A lot of men must have wanted to sleep with her. She slept with John Merchant, an important man. Polish peasants wanted to kill him, but he was lucky, he knew a dirty joke and people like to laugh. Now he's dead. He came a long way to be tortured to death.

When Blair Heathers' party arrived, it made an entrance — but then that unoccupied table on the busiest night of the week had already made its declaration. It was a surprise when the disturbance settled that there were only seven of them. They took up room naturally; their gestures needed space; even the girls taller than Heathers who sat in the middle apple-cheeked and beaming. Like Xmas Eve in the sergeants' mess, Murray thought, pushing himself off the stool in their direction.

As he came up, one of the men and a girl were making their way to the dance floor. He took the girl's seat and looked round. Left at the table with Heathers, who sat almost opposite, were two men and the other three girls, look-alikes more or less for that year's image of the desirable. The men were older than the girls but a lot younger than Heathers, to whom with a common impulse all of them had

124

turned. At that, even the girl who was available to be intrigued realized that Heathers didn't know him either.

'Nobody's sad,' Murray observed in the tone of a man willing to be reasonable.

The nearer of the two men, beak-nosed, beefy jowelled, blared, 'I rather think you've chosen the wrong place to squat. Better if you left again, eh?' The officer whom duty called to the defence of an unspoiled Xmas. Murray studied him thoughtfully but did not bother to reply.

The waiters wore striped shirts to be in character, their sleeves held up with bands of fancy elastic like a barber's shop quartet. Most of the shirts had yellow on purple stripes, but the one who came across had blue on dark brown. Another officer. 'Is everything satisfactory, sir?' he asked, staring across at Murray. 'Is there anything?'

Before Heathers could answer, Murray said, 'If this is a wake for John Merchant, I'm one of the mourners.'

Heathers stared and then, over his shoulder, said, 'Leave it, Peter – for the minute.'

The man in the striped shirt sketched a bow and moved off. From the corner of his eye, Murray saw him, nodding a couple of the waiters discreetly nearer.

Beak Nose enquired generally, 'What? What did he say? I didn't catch his name. Didn't say mourning, did he?'

The girl with the interested smile became solemn. She was prepared for any occasion.

'I can have you lifted right out of the door,' Heathers said. 'I probably will yet. What's this about John Merchant?'

'Did you know he came from Poland?'

'That's not a bloody secret,' Heathers cried. He looked round for the waiters.

'It's a long way to come to die.'

'Die?' It seemed Heathers was persuaded he was dealing with some irrelevant crazy. 'Who died?'

But it was the second man at the table, junior rank but sound, who told him, 'I thought you knew, Blair. I thought you didn't want to discuss it.'

'Knew?' Heathers snarled and balls of spit flew out with

125

the exclamation. 'How am I supposed to know anything? I'm only off the plane an hour.'

'I didnt realize . . . John Merchant's been murdered. I saw it on the news before I came out.'

'God almighty!' Genuinely, Heathers seemed stunned. 'How would John get himself killed?'

It was an odd way to put it, and it was Murray who responded.

'Messily,' he said. 'John got himself killed the hard way. Somebody used a knife on him – in places you wouldn't want me to describe.'

'Oh, please,' the girl said in what could have been protest or anticipation. Not a man to give the benefit of the doubt, Murray watched her lick her shining lips.

'From what I hear,' Murray spoke across the table at Heathers, 'most of the wounds were made while he was still alive.'

'It was a sex crime,' the junior officer explained. 'There was something about a letter, so that they know it was a woman who did it. She must be quite mad. She's killed someone already – in Moirhill. There are brothels there, you know.'

'Let me get this straight. Are you telling me John Merchant was killed by a prostitute?' Heathers sprayed them with his anger.

'I don't think that follows. Not at all – I know he was your friend—'

Heathers ignored him. 'Who are you?'

'Murray Wilson. I'm the brother.'

'You're . . .' Heathers pondered, rubbing thumb and second finger together, slow motion version of finger snapping to remember '. . . the brother . . . the one who's handy with the phone. And now you turn up here.' He smiled unpleasantly. 'Your brother's the one I do business with. I don't have anything for you.'

'I wouldn't count on doing any more business with my brother,' Murray said. 'He's been with the police all day. It's what they call "helping with enquiries".'

For a moment he thought he had the old man going, he could see all the questions he needed to ask, but then Heathers thinned his lips: 'I'm here with friends,' he said. 'You've chosen the wrong time.' Without looking round he beckoned with one finger. It was the gesture of a man who could shrug off his coat knowing somebody would be there to catch it before it hit the ground.

The barber's shop trio gathered behind Murray's chair. On a hot and spicy breath the invitation was breathed into his ear, 'The gentleman's leaving?'

He stood up. 'Leaving for a drink. I'll be over there when you want me.'

'I won't want you,' Heathers said.

The dark brown shirt followed him to the bar. 'You're sure you don't want to leave?'

'I'll leave when Heathers does.'

'I'll tell Mr Heathers that,' the man said, not sounding threatening at all.

With knife cuts there is an initial numbness, often the victim believes he has been struck only with a fist; later the pain comes and if the knife is unclean the wound goes bad. After a time, the way he had been dismissed from Heathers' table went bad in Murray's pride. He stood with his back against the bar and watched them make a long leisurely supper; it would have been unreasonable to think they should go home because Merchant was dead. A rich man was enjoying a night out with his expensive admiring friends. It didn't make any sense that an obscure clerk called Malcolm Wilson could have been allowed to disturb his evening. The bottles came and were emptied and no one seemed to look Murray's way and the band played and at intervals they would dance, one or other of the desirable girls smiling down at Heathers as his plump white hands lifted the cheeks of her buttocks.

And it repented the Lord that he had made man on the earth, and it grieved him at his heart. The quotation came unwanted into his head and with it a memory from childhood. His father had taken him to visit his uncles. Three unmarried brothers, Calum, Iain and Angus, bearded fishermen they had gathered round the child like salt towers. It was the only time his father had ever taken him to see them. At one point, they prayed; they made you kneel on the floor to pray; you had to kneel and lean with your elbows on the seat of your chair to pray. That bit was like something in a dream; he had dreamed about them for a long time afterwards, shouting out in his sleep. He did not think anyone mourned John Merchant or cared about what had happened to him; except possibly Frances Fernie – only he had never put much store by the idea of whores with a heart of gold.

Suddenly he realized that although he could spot the rest of the party among the dancers or at the table Heathers was nowhere to be seen. He circled the floor heading for the vestibule where he remembered there were phones on the wall near the entrance. Heathers was putting the phone down finishing a call, but as he caught sight of Murray watching he lifted it again and, after a moment's hesitation as if making up his mind, dialled again. The phone had a hood around it, and Murray watched the hand gripping the phone and the lips moving as if with a message from outer space.

When he had finished, Heathers made as if to brush past Murray then stopped and swung round. To his satisfaction, Murray saw that the old man's cheeks were mottled red and white with rage.

'I don't know what your game is,' he said. 'You won't help your brother by being stupid.'

'You don't want to get so excited. It could give you a stroke. At your age, that might be fatal.'

Murray's Highland blood made him kin to the second sight, that old gift by which the chosen open a window on the future. He saw Heathers' face, suffused, terrified, staring into the blankness of the moment beyond dying. If not now, yet the hour and the moment would come. Heathers gaped at him as if bewildered, and then a fusion of hatred and terrible fear altered his look like a rabid dog baring its teeth before it would bite.

'You're a very stupid man, mister,' he said.

Over the old man's head, Murray saw the big doorman watching them. 'I'm going to tell you what I told John Merchant,' he said quietly. 'You're a police target — just the way Merchant was. That Underpass deal, the one you were boasting about on television, the pride of the city, it stinks. It could be your mistake, the one that puts you in jail. And you mixed my brother up in it. He's in enough trouble now. I want him off the hook with you. Understand?'

Heathers, however, was shaking his head in a parody of amazement. Any trace of fear had disappeared.

'Police watching me, is that right? You're something else. Who the hell do you think you're talking to? I've been watched by experts all my life, since before you were a tickle in your father's balls. And I'm still here. Did you think you were running in here telling me something I didn't know? Nobody watches me without somebody watching them. Maybe you could surprise John — I didn't tell him anything he didn't need to know — but there's nothing you can tell me.' He held up his hand and rubbed the thumb across the fingers. 'I buy people. I've got good lawyers — and I've bought a policeman or two in my time. There's no way I'll ever be in jail.' He put a fat little hand against Murray's chest. 'You're the one that's just got yourself in trouble.'

It was time to leave, but Murray was stupid and went back to the bar. He watched the dancers, and for some reason remembered Eddy Stewart weeping with remorse — but then Eddy had a bad marriage and that could give a man a case of easy guilt.

Sitting there, he gave off anger like the scent of danger in the jungle. The stool beside him stayed empty till it was taken by George the doorman.

'Do they let the help drink with the customers?' Murray wondered.

'I don't always do what I'm told.'

The barman set a pint glass of beer and a whisky in front of him unasked.

'He,' Murray said nodding at the barman, 'thinks you look like an idiot.'

'It's the same as a boiler suit,' George said, patting his lapels. 'You have to earn your corn.' He emptied half the glass of beer and sighed. 'It gave me a charge seeing you again, Murray. I've been standing out there thinking about the old Northend. First night I went to the Northend I met you. A couple of kids. We didn't know what it was all about.' He paused as if for a response. Murray said nothing. 'There were some good fighters came out of the old Northend. Nearly had the world champion – remember they used to tell us that. Nearly.' He grunted amusement. Even seated on the stool, he was taller than most men. 'It's away now. Closed. Did you know that? . . . It's away now. I trained there when I was a pro. Never got to be world champion.'

'Look,' Murray said, 'I'm not in the mood for old times.'

'Do you want a beer? . . . A short? . . . What *are* you drinking?'

'Lemonade.'

'Murray,' the big man said hitching round comfortably, 'you're the kind of guy who could cause trouble on lemonade. You need the hard stuff to quieten you down.'

'Is this your break or are you finished for the night?'

The big man nodded equably and emptied his glass. 'I'm going back.' He stood up and seemed about to go, then changed his mind. 'Remember the first couple of nights we went to Northend? It was good fun. Then the third night you paid your money – so they put you in with a guy who gave you a hiding. That sickened most of them off but the ones that went back after that they got learned. You and me went back – but it was a hell of a hiding. You and me are getting too old for that stuff. Beam me up, Scotty! You know that joke? They go all shoogley and up they go – no problem. It's an idea, Murray. Lots of guys get a tanking they don't need. I mean in *this* town.'

Unobtrusively the club was emptying. For some reason, the band had stopped playing early and by now half the tables were unoccupied. People were drifting away and a greyness came on the air, something like weariness, something like remorse. Even if he tried – he would not try – to tell Mother about Merchant, about Malcolm and Frances Fernie – and, of course, he did not want her to know about them – she would not believe him; she would not even listen.

The tall girls rose like flowers around Heathers, who was getting ready to leave. Perhaps, like flowers kept fresh by being in water, their sense of his wealth and his power kept them so desirable, so inexhaustibly ready to be entertained. They distracted Murray as he crossed the floor towards them. What good would it do to follow Heathers? He was better than that; better at his trade.

—Not the best in the world, but I know my trade. I trace, I snoop, I find out, the way someone else makes chairs or wires a circuit. If a man has nothing else, he can hold to his trade. I'm a good tradesman, if you must talk of pride.

At the last moment, with the satisfaction of having had Heathers turn abruptly towards him, he veered away. In a corner there were doors marked Dames and Hoods.

As he relieved himself, Humphrey Bogart bared teeth at him from the tiled wall. Here's lookin' at you, kid.

'Get him to close his eyes.' The man standing beside him put a large pale hand across the tiles. Murray finished and stepped back to avoid his contact. The man was tall, heavily built, with a well-fed, fifty-year-old face under a plumage of white hair. Swaying and looking over his shoulder as he stood into the stall, the big cigar in the corner of his mouth curled blue smoke up into his eyes. The computer in Murray's head unasked rattled cards and placed him: one of the gay couple in the Shot Paid talking about a visit to the States. That time too there had been piss on the air. Unexpectedly, the back of his tongue went down in a hidden spasm of retching. He went to the basin and ran water over his hands.

'It's not fair,' the man said. 'Take this afternoon – I was walking from the Square up to St Vincent's following this beautiful thing in jeans. Oh, incredible. A beautiful tight

131

bum and that perfect little gap between the thighs. And blond hair, shining, and worn long. And then I came level with him and he was a girl. God, I felt so upset. What's the world coming to when you can't tell the difference between the boys and the girls?'

'Mister,' Murray said, 'you must be very drunk or very stupid.'

He turned with a sense of release. His hands tightened with the need to hurt, but the first glance told him it was useless. Smiling with shaking lips, the big man was as abruptly sobered as the drunk walking a parapet who realizes the ground a few feet below in the dark is the tops of tall trees.

Murray thumbed the button and felt the stream of hot dry air flow over his hands.

Another man had entered unnoticed. He watched them from the door with blank uncurious eyes. Automatically Murray checked his memory and was sure he had never seen him before. He would not have been difficult to remember: black hair of the solid colour sometimes given by dyeing, standing up in spikes, and a doughy lumpy face; like a cartoon only there was nothing funny about the effect. He moved aside to let the big man escape, carrying his white hair like a flag of surrender.

The newcomer came forward and leaned over the nearest washbasin. He pulled up his lip and picked between his front teeth with a dirty fingernail. 'Two friends making a quarrel?' He spoke with the accent of the city touched with some original foreignness.

With a streetfighter's eye, Murray saw the breadth of shoulder, the unusual length of the arms, the strange lumpy ridges on the face like folds in a dough kneaded with dirty hands. The frustration of that day, of too many days, ached for relief. 'Friends?' he asked and spat into the basin.

The man watched him in the mirror.

'Sorry, pal, I not want to fight you.'

In his muscles disappointed, beyond the disapproval of his mind, Murray released a long breath.

'You're a wise man,' he said contemptuously.

'Sure.'

Murray turned his back on him and the man said, 'You want to fight — you'll find plenty people.'

There was an inner and an outer door with a short flight of steps between. Murray climbed the steps and stepped back into the club through the second door.

In a half ring what seemed at first impression a dozen men waited for him. His reflexes were fast and instantly he threw himself back only to jar against an unyielding resistance. The door he had just passed through was now locked from the inside. The men stood waiting. Beyond them he could see the empty spaces of the deserted club; on the nearest table blue smoke curled up from a cigar left in an ashtray. As he looked round, he saw that the doorman was one of the men on his left. He had tried to give a warning and Murray knew that by his code that was enough. George would not be an ally.

After the first shock, he stood quietly, his feet slightly apart, his arms relaxed at his sides. He was breathing faster but it was controlled. He saw there were no weapons showing and thought that might mean there was a fair chance he would not be fatally injured. The men facing him were used to a man collapsing with fright or rushing them. Their waiting became wary and dangerously heightened.

On his left, between George and an older man with a boxer's bent nose, there was a blond teenager who let fly with a kick for the head karate style. Marginally, the left was the side from which Murray had expected the first move. It was the side most people expected to be the weaker. He twisted, caught the foot by the ankle and threw it from him. He heard the satisfying crack as the blond head smashed into the wall. A boot from the other side caught him on the back of the thigh. It was a practised kick, not swung but pushed out like a punch and if it had landed differently would have broken his leg. He staggered and the whole pack fell on him. There were so many, they got in each other's way. Three trained men like the one who had numbed his leg would have worked more effectively. Crouched he made an awkward target. Mouth open, heaving for air, he pumped his fists. Anything he hit was profit. A heavy blow struck him on the side of the head. He drove his knee up and a rabbit screamed thinly. He fought his way almost clear by aggression and strength. A space opened round him.

It was enough. Someone, perhaps the one who had caught him at the beginning, kicked him on the thigh. Almost on the same place as before, it paralysed the leg. Spinning like a grotesque bird wounded, as they came again he went down.

Testicles, spleen, kidneys, head – there is no way a man on the ground can protect all of them. The only thing in his favour was their number and eagerness. The time came and passed when it would have been better to lose consciousness.

It took a moment to realize the storm was over. Squinting up he saw blurred and enormous like a shape in fog, the strange lumped face of the man who had barred the door on his escape. Like a black halo of spikes, the hair stood out round it. In his hand over Murray's head, he held one of the ice buckets lifted from a table.

'I fix your barrow, you bastard.' The face grew larger, spit from its mouth fell on him. The figure was taller than anyone he had ever seen, taller even than the bearded fishermen who towered over a small boy.

Too quickly for Murray to protect his head, the bucket swung away into the distance and rushed back.

—You don't know what guilt is. You're just an amateur at guilt, Eddy.

Lights flashed from the bucket's polished sides. It filled the world.

BOOK THREE

CHAPTER THIRTEEN
What the World Is

WEDNESDAY, SEPTEMBER 12TH

The stripper was no girl, maybe even over thirty, but her legs were long and well-shaped and her breasts looked firm under the leather gear that still covered them since she was only into the opening bars of her number. She strutted from one side of the small platform to the other, it was almost prancing, it was almost a march. Wherever she was going, she was in a hurry to get there. She gazed above the heads of the audience and with one hand shook the chain that ran from under her armpit to where it was clipped at the top of her thigh. She spread her fingers and vibrated them over her crotch, then marched to the brisk music of her tape back across the platform, leant back and sticking the dog whip through her legs from behind waggled it up and down more or less on the drum beat. For the first time she looked down at them, glancing about as if to catch someone's eye.

'That SM stuff,' Billy Shanks said, gathering a mouthful of mashed potato on to his fork, 'it seems a bit heavy for a working men's club at lunchtime.'

'Poor buggers.' Eddy Stewart looked round at the roomful of men. A blue haze of smoke drifted over the tables. 'A lot of them are having to nurse their beer because they don't have a wage packet. You and me are the working men here.'

'Still,' Billy said, not to be deflected, 'last time you dragged me to this place, it was the schoolgirl routine, a wee performer squatting on her hockey stick. I didn't like it, but I could see why they would. But this high heels and a whip stuff . . .'

'You're a snob,' Stewart said. 'Some of these guys have been round the world — and the rest have seen the videos.'

The stripper bent over and showed them her behind. Billy sighed. 'How is Murray?' he asked.

'He could do with someone to visit him. He's depressed.'

'With Murray, how could you tell?'

Stewart laughed. 'He wasn't his usual cheery self.'

'It's a phobia — I can't bear to go and see somebody I know in hospital. I can go as part of the job, but not privately. I mean, if it's for the column, fine. I used to know a bus conductor like that — every time he got into a car he was travel sick.'

'So make it official.' Stewart chewed with relish. He always enjoyed a lunch that came on Billy Shanks' expense account. 'Do your boy reporter bit and ask him what happened. Even if he doesn't cough why, he'll be glad to see you.'

'With Murray,' Billy repeated himself gloomily, 'how can you tell?'

'You can tell.'

'I don't know . . .' Billy swung an arm in a gesture furtive on his own wild scale. 'He's depressed?'

'They think he might lose an eye.'

'What?'

With Billy shock had the unexpected effect of making him go very still.

'That was early on Sunday — when I went in. But they couldn't find the eye at that point — it's all gone to pulp. The doctor I spoke to wasn't happy about the way it looked. If he gets away with it, he'll have potted the darky in a black ball final.'

'Ah, for God's sake,' Billy groaned. 'If it has to depend on his luck!'

The big policeman forked food in and said broodingly but not very distinctly, 'What's so different about Murray? Most of us have lousy luck.'

Billy, with the intuition of someone who had been born up the next close; played in the same streets when school was something the big ones went to; was even in some second-cousin-twice-removed kind of way related to Stewart; said with only apparent irrelevance, 'I always envied you getting Lynda. She was your luck, Eddy. If she'd had better taste, she'd have married me.'

Like many men born to be bachelors, he had the notion that his state was due to some perfect girl whom he had been denied and who made any other woman second best. Quite often for him, when he thought of her, Lynda filled this romantic niche.

'You're full of piss and wind,' Stewart said, belching himself as if in illustration.

'Probably,' Billy said, 'but I still find it easier at the moment to feel sorry for Murray than I do for you.'

'He might be worse. Jill the Ripper might have got him and cut his balls off.' Stewart snorted, spraying crumbs of aggressive amusement in Billy's direction. 'That's what the old guy who found him thought had happened. The old clown ran up the street with his trousers half up his bum. Slap into Tommy Clarke with his wee notebook for car numbers. All of them standing about every corner in Moirhill with their wee notebooks, only somebody dumped Murray and none of them any the wiser. This silly old bugger had been getting ready for his bed when he looked out and saw Murray on the pavement under the lamp. Corner of Deacon Street – three in a row the old guy thought and away like a bloody fire engine.'

'Very public spirited of him,' Billy reflected. 'Most folk in Moirhill would have kept their noses clean instead of running to look for a policeman.'

'Policeman my arse! He was away to phone the *Citizen* and collect a sweetener.'

Restored, Billy whinnied and flew out his arms jubilantly. 'That's public spirited too. After me, you'd have been the first to know.' He sobered. 'Which still doesn't tell us who did him over – or what he was doing in Moirhill in the first place.'

Murray, standing just inside the entrance, had difficulty

at first in spotting them. It wasn't just that the room was crowded, but that the dark glasses shaded the smoke like mist; the music smashed against him like something physical striking his head; after the drifting isolation of the side ward, it was an assault of people so that what he felt was almost timidity and he had to force himself to walk forward. As he crossed the room, the stripper finished her act, turning her back and shaking her hips in a frenzy until her tight buttocks shimmered in a looseness of the flesh.

It was Billy who saw him first, and reacted spontaneously with dismay that turned at once into relief and concern.

'I signed myself out,' Murray said, answering the question before it was asked. It felt good to sit down; too good, like scurrying into a refuge.

'How's the eye?' Having arrested his fork half-way to his mouth, Stewart completed the movement and started chewing. 'That looks like a bit of raw meat hanging down under your glasses.'

'It's still there.'

'Signed yourself out.' Stewart nodded and sucked a fibre of meat from between his front teeth. 'You're a hard bastard.'

'How did you know we were here?' Billy wondered.

'Phoning.' Murray turned his darkened gaze on Stewart. 'They let Malcolm, my brother, go.'

'Your brother? They let him go home on the Saturday night. Of course, you'd be out of the game by then . . . you wouldn't know.'

'Standers let him go?'

Stewart blew out his lips in the pleasure of contempt. 'Standers! Forget him. As soon as Merchant was found dead, the Chief Constable hit the panic button. It was too hot to leave for a clown like Standers. Jackie McKellar's in charge now.'

'McKellar?' Murray's years out of the city had left him out of touch with a lot of things; he was still catching up.

'Detective Chief Superintendent McKellar,' Billy took a professional pride in explaining. 'Early fifties. There was a planning meeting at Headquarters on Saturday afternoon. Ness – he's the Assistant Chief Constable (Crime) – chaired it. McKern, Standers' boss for Northern, was there. And Frank O'Hara of Central Division.' On the last name, he looked at Murray questioningly, but saw that he understood. Central was the politically dominant of the six divisions into which the city was divided – in it were the main business districts and the centre of local government – so that although they shared the same rank O'Hara was deferred to by the other division chiefs. His presence was an indication of the kind of pressure they expected Merchant's death was going to involve. 'Oh, and Standers was there, but only to give a progress report. Eddy's right, Jackie McKellar's the man in charge now. And he's good – he's got a record of quick results. McKellar knows what he's doing.'

'Peerse doesn't think so,' Stewart said. 'He believes in your Jill the Ripper, Billy – or at least half believes in her. And he more than half believes he knows who she is.'

'He *what*?'

'Merchant's girlfriend – Frances Fernie.'

Billy subsided in disappointment. 'Not possible. Murray's brother was with her in her flat from ten o'clock on the Friday evening until seven the next morning. They know the body was dumped between midnight and five in the morning, which means either your brother's in it too or she's in the clear.'

'McKellar believed your brother's story, Murray,' Stewart said. 'But don't be surprised if Peerse turns up on his doorstep one day soon.'

'How can they be sure when the body was dumped?' Murray asked, ignoring him.

'The Crusader pub – you know, the one in Barnes Street? The bar staff locked up and came out of the side door about midnight. The chargehand and another guy walked down the lane to Carnation Street. There was no body there then – they'll swear to that. It was found just after five by a beat copper making a routine check.'

141

'Only he's not getting any medals,' Stewart said, 'because he skived off earlier in the night instead of doing his rounds, which means they can't narrow the time down more.' He glanced at his watch. 'And it's nearly time I was away. The rest of them are over there working a twenty-hour day and eating sandwiches.'

'Talking about skiving,' Billy said. 'Eddy the fox.'

'I'm tidying up a loose end,' Stewart said with a satisfied grin. 'I've been a long time at this game.'

Murray stopped himself just in time from putting his hand up to press against the pain in his head. He swallowed on a surge of nausea. 'I'm trying to put a name to a face,' he said. 'A guy who has some connection to the casino in Stark Street. That's where I met him.'

'On Saturday night?'

'You know I don't remember anything about Saturday night. I got a bang on the head,' Murray said. 'He's about five eight. Maybe a hundred and seventy pounds. He's got black hair, but it's weird – it stands up in clusters and it looks black enough to be dyed. Sounds funny, but he isn't funny at all. He's, just seeing him, you know he's . . . a real nutter.' *Evil* was a word that would have embarrassed them all. 'Very white in the face. He's got a foreign accent – could be Polish, but he's been here a long time. Might be middle fifties, but I think he's older, could be seventy.'

They looked at him in silence.

'One other thing,' Murray said, 'he could take his orders from Blair Heathers.'

Stewart swore abruptly. 'Jesus, Murray, you want to have more sense. Heathers spends more on haircuts than you earn in a year. You do wee jobs – you've got one coat, and that's the one you were wearing when you got off the train the day you came back. If you hadn't got in tow with that lawyer Bittern, you wouldn't be making enough to keep you in pie suppers. Don't mess with Heathers. That would be like Laighburn Juniors putting a team in the World Cup.'

'It's a while since I've seen you so excited, Eddy,' Murray said. 'You don't want to get so emotional.'

'Nobody's excited.' Stewart wiped a last piece of bread round the plate and pushed it away. The red flush subsided on his cheeks. 'If you had lost that eye, you'd have been too busy looking for a pitch to sell matches to worry about Heathers.'

'Bloody hell!' Billy exclaimed. 'You'd be a great man to say a few words at a funeral. You know how to bury a friend.'

'No use saying one thing and thinking another,' Stewart said, registering a vague discomfort. 'You're a moody bastard, Murray – I reckon we're about the only mates you've got.'

'You and Peerse.'

Stewart laughed. 'You'd be all right with Peerse – he'd buy a box of matches from you any time: Go out of his way to do it.' He stood up; ready to go, he hesitated. 'What I was saying about your brother . . . don't worry about that. It's just Peerse – but you know what Peerse is like. I mean, they're looking for a maniac. Merchant wasn't just killed, he was messed about – even worse then the first one. It was the same weapon, a knife with a long narrow blade. They think he might have got it first in the back of the neck and that paralysed him. After that he'd about thirty cuts round the bum and at the front. Whoever did it peeled his prick like a banana and Forensic think they did it slowly. Like I say – a maniac.'

When he had gone, Murray sat lost in thought. What Eddy Stewart had described seemed different in kind from what had been done to the first victim. From what he understood, the tears on the body in the first case had been made as if the killer had struck and sliced in excitement – and most, perhaps all, seemed to have been done after death. It looked as if Merchant had been tortured. A number of things followed from that. It meant he had been killed indoors, perhaps in a flat, anyway in a place where someone could take their time. Torture could be used to satisfy an impulse of cruelty, Eddy's maniac; but it had another use as well, an old use.

Was it possible someone had tortured Merchant to get

143

information out of him? If so, what kind of information could that have been?

Billy had misunderstood his silence. When he looked up, Billy said, 'You shouldn't let Eddy bother you. Anyway, I think all that stuff about your brother at the end there was his way of apologizing.'

It took Murray a moment to work out what he was talking about, then he said, 'That's just Eddy's style.' He touched a finger to the swollen side of his face. 'If he thinks you're down, he can't resist giving you a kick. He's been in the police too long.'

'He can be a right bastard,' Billy said with a sudden change of mood. 'Before you came, he was going on about my father. Telling me what a fine man my father was. He must imagine there's something wrong with my memory. My father had a silver plate in his head from the war. Eddy and the other boys would follow him about and torment him until he lost the place. Then my mother and I would have to hide with a neighbour or stand in the street while he wrecked the house. Sometimes he would take a fit and fall down and roll about.'

Murray had never heard this before, but he wasn't interested.

'When I described that guy from the casino,' he said, 'Eddy recognized him, I'm sure he did, maybe that's why he started to shout the odds. What about you, Billy? Do you know who he is?'

'You could call Eddy my oldest friend. I've known him longer than anybody else. One night back then, there was this guy lived up the stair from us, Sammy Dudley, and Sammy's hiding in the house because he was frightened to come out and face – what was his name? McConochie. That's right, McConochie, a right ned. It lasted for nearly an hour. Sammy hiding in the house and McConochie running up and hammering on his door and then when he got fed up with that running back down into the street and yelling up at the window – Come out and get what's coming to you, ya yellow shite! And finally Maisie Dudley – she'd be about fifteen then – got so ashamed for her father peeping out between the curtains peeing himself with fright that she put on her old man's jacket and bunnet and ran down the stairs pretending she was her father. She ran out of the close with her fists up and McConochie took a swing and laid her out. Down she went, the bunnet flew off and all her hair spilled out. McConochie shouts, Jesus Christ, it's a lassie! All the women hanging out of the windows enjoying the laugh went crazy. Bastard was the kindest word they had for him. All hell broke loose. He was shirricked right down the street. One-Punch McConochie they cried him after that – until he got so fed up with it that he flitted.'

'One-Punch McConochie,' Murray said neutrally. 'He wouldn't have dyed black hair would he or hang out at the casino in Stark Street?'

'Eh?' Billy made a face of puzzlement. 'My father had been watching out of the window of our flat and when he saw the girl fall down he ran away down the stairs. He charged out of the close waving his arms, threatening McConochie, who turned and ran for it. I was proud of him – but then just as he bent over Maisie he fell down beside her. I could see the foam coming out of his mouth. It was the worst fit he ever threw – at least where other folk could see him.'

Murray said, 'Billy, you're full of piss and wind.' Despite himself, Murray saw a picture of old man Shanks, as tall as his son grew to be, with the same big arm gestures but even less controlled, everything less controlled, the man with the silver plate in his head, the man the kids in the street tormented.

'My father couldn't stand to see anybody being hurt. I stood at the back of the circle round him. I couldn't see him, but I could hear the noises he was making. I thought, this time he's a goner for sure.'

'You recognized the description of that guy in the casino too. Right? What are you frightened about?'

Billy shaped broken clockwork rings with the base of his glass on the table. 'Eddy's a bastard, but it doesn't mean

145

he's not right about some things. You've been battered, Murray. You don't want to risk that again. Let it go.'

'Give me a name.'

Billy sighed. 'Joe Kujavia.'

Something in Murray relaxed. If the figure in the nightmare could be given a name, perhaps it would be easier to sleep. 'Joe Kujavia.' He weighed it carefully, like a thing his hand was taking into its grip.

'From the way you described him, it couldn't be anybody else. There can't be two bastards in the world looking like Kujavia. Was he involved with what happened to you?'

Murray hesitated. 'I had an argument with Blair Heathers. I'm not telling anybody else that. Not Eddy. Not anybody.'

'Don't try to prove the connection,' Billy Shanks said bitterly. 'A respectable businessman like Heathers and scum like that − it's two different worlds. Kujavia's a pimp among other things, he runs girls in Moirhill, and uses an iron bar on them. If he was killed tomorrow, there would be a hell of a lot of people in Moirhill out dancing in the streets.'

'Do you have an address for him?'

'No. And if I did have one, I wouldn't be doing you a favour. This guy's killed people. They've never got him into court, but I know. He battered the woman he was living with to death. Funny, I always remember the priest crying. I was young then. He was a good man though. It was him that looked after the kids − got them adopted.'

'There were kids?'

'The woman had a couple of kids. God knows who the fathers were. She'd been married before she went on the game. Maybe one of the wee girls was Kujavia's. Funny how you remember the first jobs you go out on. That bloody priest sitting there crying. Later you don't let things like that upset you. It's part of the job.'

But suddenly Murray was too tired to talk. He thought about getting back somehow to the flat, getting behind a locked door, going to sleep until the pain stopped.

It was Billy Shanks who started to speak again, breaking the silence between them. 'It's a job you can't do without asking questions . . . What happened to you on Saturday night, did it have anything to do with the Jill murders?'

'Is that what you call them now?'

Billy shrugged. 'Nothing in newspapers exists properly unless you can invent the right label for it. That's part of the job too.'

'The Jill Murders.' He gave it the emphasis of a headline. 'That's what Standers wanted you to call them, wasn't it?'

'I didn't do it for Standers' sake,' Billy said. 'I told you after I saw him that I wouldn't be interested. It was John Merchant getting himself killed — second murder, right date. That did it, Murray. I had a story.'

The ache behind Murray's eye came and went in waves. He had no idea what Shanks meant, and he could not get up the energy to care. He would think about it later, after he had slept. 'I'm glad for you, Billy. But it is nothing to do with me. Okay?'

'It was just a thought,' Billy said.

Murray grunted.

'Even with friends . . . I didn't say it wasn't a lousy job.' Billy smiled, and then put his hand across his mouth like a child apologizing for a lie. 'Sometimes. Mostly it's good, pretty good . . . You look rough, Murray.'

'I'm just going.'

But he sat on. In a little while, he would feel well enough to move.

'If I've a friend,' Billy said, 'Eddy must be the oldest one I've got. And times are when I can't stomach him. He was sitting there an hour ago and tells me they brought Maisie Dudley's daughter into the Northern shop yesterday. Five guys had pulled her away from a bus stop into a condemned tenement. Nobody lives around that bit any more so they could take their time. He said they raped her taking their time. All five of them — all the ways there are.

147

He said she had the same red hair as her mother. You could have warmed your hands at Maisie Dudley's hair.' His hands for once lay still on the table and he looked at them and said, 'I wanted to say to him, It's no good, Eddy, you can't make me foam at the mouth and fall down. I'm not my father. It's my job to know what the world is.'

CHAPTER FOURTEEN
Conferences

FRIDAY, SEPTEMBER 14TH

It was only when he went down into the street and bought a paper from Barney on the corner that Murray realized he had missed Thursday. As he walked into the city centre, he tried to work out how many hours he must have slept. He had fallen into bed on Wednesday afternoon after talking to Billy Shanks, and had been wakened an hour ago by the persistent ringing of the phone. The thing was that as he rolled out of bed and trailed yawning through the lobby to answer it, he had not felt specially refreshed; nothing hinted to him that he had slept for more than forty hours. His only thought as he recognized the voice was that, despite the lousy taste in his mouth, it had been worth the effort since it was Mr Bittern who was calling.

'I tried to get hold of you earlier in the week, Mr Wilson,' the lawyer complained discreetly.

Like all private investigators, Murray depended for his livelihood on having a firm of solicitors who would refer clients to him. As a one-man Johnny-come-lately, he had been lucky to have Bittern, Samuels and Alexander (Incorporating Gibb and MacTaggart) offering him scraps from their crowded table.

Shortly after their first acquaintance, Mr Bittern, the senior partner, had unbent and explained to Murray that crime was caused by boredom; people in the slums, particularly the young, needed to have their energy 'of which they had so much' directed into socially useful channels so

149

that they would not be bored. He had an old man's bleat on the vowels: pee-eeple.

'I sympathize with your difficulties. You are quite well now? Good. But I am afraid that Mr Foley is not one of the world's most patient me-en. I have to say that he feels not enough is being done to find Mr Beddowes.'

'Mr Beddowes . . .'

'And Mrs Foley, of course.'

'And the money.'

'That, according to our information, seems certainly to be with Mr Beddowes . . . and Mrs Foley, presumably.'

Which, Murray knew, was why he had been offered this job; for the same reason as the ones before it; lawyer Bittern had an eye for a bargain. You get what you paid for; and Foley's money had eloped with Beddowes. There was a taste in his mouth as if his gums might have been bleeding while he slept. 'Foley isn't so anxious that he'll go to the police though. Is he afraid they might want to look at the books?'

Wires hummed and clicked disapprovingly into the silence.

'Sorry.' Murray cleared his throat. 'Forget I said that.'

'Ye-es,' Mr Bittern decided; but could not refrain from adding, 'Leaving aside the state of Foley and Beddowes' books, which is not at issue, it is by no means clear that there is or will be occasion for the services of the police. Whatever monies may or may not be missing belonged to the firm and have been removed by a partner . . . may have been removed. If removed, it is plausible that the partner involved might not be Mr Beddowes but Mrs Foley to whom her husband consigned a share when she improved her status from secretary to spouse. In that case, the relation between husband and wife would obtain and whether there were a larceny would depend on the intention of Mrs Foley, who may for all we know expect ultimately to return to Mr Foley.'

'Yes,' said Murray in his turn. His head ached and Bittern had lost him. 'It would help if there was more money available.'

'I think we've covered that.'

'I had to limit the circulars and photographs. A hundred sent out to the likeliest agents − not a letter of instruction, but I had to make the usual promise that a fee and expenses would be paid to anyone who turned something up.'

'That is acceptable.'

'It's not a help that Foley won't let me talk to his neighbours. He's not even happy about me talking to *Beddowes'* neighbours. I found the taxi driver who took them to the station. And Beddowes' ex-wife − you know he'd been divorced? − and—'

'Put it in a report for Mr Foley. Today? It would settle his mind that something is being done. And a copy for me?'

Mr Bittern was a gently unreasonable man and when Murray put down the phone he knew ground was lost that he could not afford to lose.

The train wheels made a rhythm out of loss and afford, and he looked out of the window as they ran on the viaduct level with the top floor of tenements and crossed the river and the houses began to spread out and then came together again as little one-storey semi-detacheds showing vegetable plots and garden sheds and children's swings to the railway line. 'There's a good shopping centre not far away,' Malcolm had explained, 'and I can get into the office by train. It'll do us fine . . . for just now.' Ambitious Malcolm.

When he came up the steps, he was uncertain for a moment which way to turn. Below him the long empty platform seemed glazed and expectant in the sun. He began to walk up the hill towards the main road. Facing down the slope half way up, a Porsche 911 Turbo was parked; it had the big spoiler wing at the back and was the colour of blue the sky took over the desert at sunset. It looked exactly like one he had seen in California, sitting outside an apartment block in a piece of the Mojave that had been watered and tamed and shod with highways. Out of a habit of attention, he noticed that it had been fitted with non-standard BBS wheels; it was someone's toy, and too expensive to be sitting in this neighbourhood. Inside, a man in a white shirt, the cuffs rolled back on his forearms, was reading with the book rested on the wheel in front of him. It didn't need a uniform for Murray to identify him as a chauffeur. He had the air of a man used to waiting. As he turned into Malcolm's road and made his way slowly, as if reluctant, past the tiny cropped lawns and the low gates clamped across each entrance, Murray wondered about that expensive car and where its owner might be while his driver waited so indifferently.

When Irene came to the door, she stared at him as if shocked. They stood intimately close in the warm motionless air, time suspended.

'Have you got a visitor already?' he asked.

'Mmm.' She made a little noise that might have been assent. With her right hand she held the door by its edge as if she might decide to close it, while the other hung strangely passive by her side with the opened palm turned to him. She leaned down from where she stood above him in the entrance to the hall, and cried, 'Your poor face! My God, I had no idea it was so bad.' Standing back as he came into the house, she continued, 'We would have come to see you, but with what happened . . . We would have come to the hospital at the weekend.'

'I signed myself out.'

He spoke over his shoulder, impatient to check on the identity of her visitor. He stepped into the front room; sun inclined in through the wide picture window, islanded the chair and the man's shape in it and painted a white lozenge on the carpet. The air felt heavy, hot as outside, like a barrier to press against.

'Mr Heathers,' Irene said behind him. 'Do you two know one another? This is Malcolm's brother. Mr Heathers came to see if there was anything he could do to help – because of what happened. It was very kind of him.'

She sounded matter of fact as if she meant simply what she said: kind Mr Heathers; what could be more natural?

'I heard you were in hospital,' Heathers said. His voice sounded dry and harsh, but firm; with his back to the light, it was not obvious that he was an old man.

'I signed myself out,' Murray said. He could get tired

152

of explaining that. As he spoke, he circled a step or two moving to the side so that he could see Heathers' face. What he saw was ambiguous, for although the mouth was taut with controlled fright, the old eyes stared with greedy satisfaction at the great bruise that disfigured Murray's cheek below the dark glasses.

'You don't want to do anything stupid,' Heathers said, glancing away.

'Come and sit beside me on the couch,' Irene said. He felt her hand on his arm and let himself be seated. 'What would you like to drink? We were having tea. But there's something stronger, if you'd prefer.'

'Tea would be fine.'

There was a table with two glass panes as a top set at the level of their knees between the chair and the couch. There was a teapot and a little Delft milk jug and cups with a rose on the inside; there was even a plate of sweet biscuits nicely arranged. On the backs of one kind of biscuit, sugar fractions sparkled in the sun. He balanced the cup Irene had fetched, sipped tea, and listened to the harsh accent which sounded confident and even young when the face was shadowed against the light. 'People get the wrong idea when they meet me socially. I couldn't be the man I am at home and do all I've done. In business I'm a man in a man's world. If you want to know me, that's where you come. I'm a businessman,' the voice said.

'What business have you here?' Murray asked. Irene had put milk in the cup without asking him, and the milked tea lingered on his tongue bland and slightly sickly.

'Business?' Irene wondered. 'He came to sympathize about what had happened to Malcolm – but I told him there was no need.'

'The police let Malcolm go,' Murray said. 'I was told that.'

'It wasn't really *that*,' she said. 'Mr Heathers thought I might be upset because Malcolm had been sleeping with another woman. That's what he came to sympathize about.'

'The world didn't stop because John Merchant got himself killed,' Heathers intervened. 'Nobody's indispensable.

153

A little bit of trading, a bit of in-fighting – they'll get themselves a new Convenor. While that's going on, while the new man's finding his feet, your brother could be a little bit more important not less. That's what I was thinking about. Right?' He paused as if expecting to be contradicted. 'And Bradley – him that was your brother's boss – he's dead.' The word fell like something heavy and inert on the carpet with its white pool of sun, and Murray stared down, rubbing the fur of milk on his tongue against his palate. 'Your brother might have a future. But he needs to make friends. You could help your brother.'

'I don't do favours,' Murray said. 'My brother's the one who does the favours.' As soon as the words were out of his mouth, he heard them as being stupid; if he had asked how, he would have learned what Heathers wanted. To ask the right question was part of his trade, when to open your mouth and when to keep it shut; feeling ill wasn't an excuse for being bad at your trade.

'I'm not talking about favours. I'm talking about hiring you.' And when to keep your mouth shut . . . 'From what I hear you're not a bad snooper. You did all right for Billy Milligan.'

It had been his best effort; it hadn't been easy and it had persuaded him he might be able to make a living as an investigator. It had been Milligan, who, out of gratitude, had talked the lawyer Bittern into giving him a chance. A chance at small debt and the maybes of adultery; so it was hardly his fault if nothing afterwards had let him show what he could do.

'Since then my rates have gone up.'

'I know what you charge,' Heathers said. 'I play golf with Andrew Bittern.'

'He's one of the people I work for.'

'I know how many people you work for. And I know how much you charge.'

'I lost some time this week,' Murray said. 'I can't afford to get beaten up. If I don't do anything about it, it could put ideas into people's heads.'

154

'Please, oh, please!' In her excitement, Irene jumped up and laid her hand on Heathers' arm so that the old man startled at her touch. 'It's a wonderful idea. I'm sure that Murray could help. Mr Merchant was a nice man and he was very kind to Malcolm.'

Her eyes shone with emotion. She looks as if she might cry real tears, Murray thought, and to his surprise Heathers gave the appearance of catching the infection. With almost a snuffle, and a shake of the head, he sighed, 'Ah, John was a gentleman. An old friend.'

'Are you asking me to find who killed John Merchant?' Murray wondered.

'Christ, no!' Heathers exclaimed in astonishment. 'There's plenty of policemen to do that.'

'Why did you say you wanted Murray then?' With the excitement gone, Irene's voice sounded flat and oddly disappointed.

'A retainer, I was offering him a retainer. Putting him on the books for a bob or two. And when something turns up for him to do, I'll get him to do it.'

Back to the small debt, Murray reflected wryly; but then Heathers would already have a firm for that.

'If you're going to pay him anyway, why shouldn't he try to find who did the murders?' Irene persisted. 'You said he was a good detective.'

'Computers,' Heathers said as if talking to a child. 'And dozens of detectives. And bloody thousands of man hours – not to mention the overtime.' He wriggled himself forward out of the depths of the chair, leaning forward towards Murray. 'Chances are they'll manage without you. I'll find something for you to do – but not now, that's what a retainer's about. And the thing is, I know what you get paid, mister. That's what I'm offering – and whatever expenses you need. Within reason. And no bloody garbage about lost weeks. I'm running a business not a charity.' The insignificant physical task of getting to the edge of the low chair had cost him a visible effort, and perhaps it was the consciousness of that which made him venomous. He sank

155

back and took his breath. 'If you did hear anything, of course, I'd expect to be told. If John Merchant was tortured, I'd like to know why. But that's only if you happened to hear something. I don't want you going around stirring things up. You try that and the money stops – I don't want things stirred up.'

'Tortured?' Murray wondered.

'That's what your friend Peerse thinks. And he's got brains instead of cow shit between his ears.' As Heathers mouthed the harmless vulgarity, Murray saw his head turn as if he couldn't resist a glance at Irene. Did he think, the old man, he might shock her?

'Business information? Your business?' Murray asked.

'If it was, I'd want to be the one that was told about it,' Heathers said, his voice suddenly flat and ugly. He made a gesture of impatience. 'You won't hear anything. I'm not expecting you to hear anything.'

'You already told me that.'

'I'm telling you again.' Heathers clenched his plump white fists on the arms of the chair and lifted himself to his feet. 'You're getting paid for waiting, that makes you lucky.' With his hands behind his back, he paced to and fro; he strutted as small men sometimes do; if he had been apprehensive when he first saw Murray, the last trace of it seemed to have gone. 'Usually men who work for me work hard. Not as hard as me right enough – not the way I worked, building up everything from nothing, nobody who hasn't done that knows what hard work *is*. But that's me, not you. You take it easy, you'll get a cheque every week. Take time, get over your accident. Think of me as a friend of the family.'

When he had gone, Irene came back from the hall and instead of sitting on the couch again took the seat he had left. After a pause, she said, 'I'm disappointed.'

'His money's as good as anybody else's.'

She thought about that and then said, 'That's not what I meant. I was disappointed because I thought he was going to ask you to find the murderer.'

156

'You heard him — I don't have a computer.'

'But you're going to take his money.'

—It's my trade. Only this time he was to be paid for not practising it.

'When he saw you coming in, he was frightened,' she said. 'It was because of him you were beaten up. That was it, wasn't it? He thought you would hit him.'

'He's an old man.'

'He didn't know you were a gentleman. That must have been why he offered you the money.'

'Why were you disappointed?'

'Because—' she began emphatically, but she had already answered that question. 'If you caught the murderer, we would be the first to know.'

He was tired of sitting on the couch facing the window. His head ached with staring into that brightness.

'When does Malcolm get home?' he asked.

'Didn't you know?' Out of the brightness, her surprise mocked him. 'He's been sent away — to do a course on computers. At the moment, he'll be sitting in the North British in Edinburgh drinking coffee and conferring. They were being kind — sending him away, after all the fuss. Only for a few days. You'll see him at Mum Wilson's on Sunday.'

'All the fuss . . .' He supposed that was one way of describing it when a whore's alibi for murder was that your husband had slept with her. 'Did you know about her? Her name's Frances Fernie. Did you know that?'

'She was a friend of mine,' light, clear, hasty, just the tone in which she cried 'Mum Wilson'. 'In London. After we were married, she turned up here. She came to see me — and met Malcolm. It must have gone on from there. Not that I knew anything about it, of course.'

On an impulse, he held up his hand, stretching the thumb away from the palm so that the flesh at its root grew taut. With the forefinger of his other hand, he touched the drawn skin. 'I saw the body of the first man who was killed, not Merchant, the first one. That was in the lane. I shouldn't have been there. His hand was lying out to the side and it

157

was . . . torn. There, just there. A lot of other things had been done to him, but that was the one I noticed. I haven't been able to get it out of my head. It had been bitten — or it looked like that. As if it had been torn with teeth.'

He got up and the light came out of his eyes and he moved so that he could see her face.

'It doesn't make sense. It sounds stupid when I say it. The thing is, I haven't been able to get it out of my head.'

Unexpectedly, she was smiling.

'Is this how you begin?' she asked. 'It's all new to me.'

CHAPTER FIFTEEN
Fear of Dying

SATURDAY, SEPTEMBER 15TH

'That's some keeker,' old Barney said, admiring the yellow bruising round Murray's eye as he folded the newspaper before handing it over. 'How'd you get it? It's not as though you're married.'

'I got hit by a champagne cork.'

'Eh?'

'Would you believe the bucket?'

'Were you at a wedding? You want to stay away from them. I've seen some terrible fights at weddings.'

It was earlier than the day before, but then, in contrast to what had happened when he first came out of hospital, Murray had hardly slept at all the previous night. He felt hungry but as if food would make him sick. He had breakfasted on cups of tea. It was a fine morning though, bright sun again and windless; he lingered beside the old paper-seller. Two bachelors taking their leisure together, they squinted against the sun.

'You ever hear of a guy called Kujavia, Barney?'

He was conscious of the old man's sudden stillness.

'What was that name again?'

'You heard me.'

Barney spat a yellow loop into the gutter. 'It's not that I don't want to help you, Murray. But I'm out here in the morning and at night on my own. Trouble's what I don't need.'

'You've told me things before. There's never been any comeback. I'm a wall, Barney.'

159

'Aye, right,' Barney said, in what might have been agreement or scepticism. 'But you've never raised that particular name before.'

'There could be a couple of notes in it for you. Not right away – next week. I've got a cheque coming from a client. I'll call you expenses.'

'He's a bad bastard, I'll tell you that for nothing.' But having begun he didn't stop; dribbling out what he knew in a hoarse grunting murmur, never looking directly at Murray and breaking off abruptly not just to sell a paper but whenever anyone came within earshot. It was unpleasant that amount of caution; it smelled of fear. Most of what he told, Murray had already heard from Billy Shanks.

'What about an address?'

'Away to hell, that's over the line. If I knew, I wouldn't tell you.'

'But you don't?'

'He moves around. Know what I mean? A man with enemies.' He sighed as Murray kept silent. His passion was information, and that appetite made it hard for him to keep what he had sterile and unshared. He scraped a hand across the grey bristles on his chin, and said almost angrily, 'There's Mary O'Bannion. She's a pro – built like a bloody mountain. He's with her most of the time. And before you ask me – I don't know where she lives.'

Murray didn't believe that, but he had been given more than he could have expected. As he began to walk up Moirhill Road, he thought about the important thing Barney had told him about Kujavia, the thing Billy Shanks hadn't mentioned.

The bar was functional: a counter, glasses, drink, a lavatory that was a urinal without towels or hot water. The Crusader was a trough in which poverty stuck its snout and found nothing in the way of comfort but alcohol.

And company, of course.

Two men standing together at the bar checked on Murray as he came in, one with no more than a sliding of the eyes, the other with an odd tilting motion of the face like the muzzle of a suspicious dog; an old man sucked toothlessly on a tumbler of red wine; a woman at a table brooded over an empty glass. On the strength of Heathers' expected cheque, Murray bought a whisky. He asked what the lady drank and the barman poured a double. Having accounted for him, the two men lost interest.

It was true the city had some of the ugliest prostitutes in the world; strictly functional – like the Crusader.

Misunderstanding, the woman responded to the dark man's smile. Her teeth showed yellow.

'I'm not looking for trade,' she said.

'Have the drink anyway.'

She emptied the glass with a greedy swallow as if he might change his mind without warning.

'It's just that I have an appointment,' she explained.

'You're going to get your hair styled.'

'No,' she said seriously. 'It's with the doctor. That's why I couldn't break it, like. I need to see him. My stomach's giving me laldie. If it wasn't—'

'Take this – it'll cure you. Save you a visit to the doctor.' He pushed his own glass across to her. She took it but stared at him uncertainly. 'It's okay. I'll get myself another one – in a minute.'

'If it wasn't for the doctor, mind you,' she continued automatically and drank. 'It was a doctor that did it to me. A black doctor in Greenock. He made a mess of me inside.'

'Tough.'

'Have you got a car?'

Murray shook his head.

'You see if you'd wheels . . . I was going to say I could've given you relief, like. And been in time for the doctor. It's time – that's the trouble.'

'You'll make time for another drink though.'

'If you're offering.' She stirred with a dull animal suspicion.

He collected drinks from the silent barman and as he sat down told her, 'I'm looking for somebody.'

161

'I know. love. Listen, what about later—'

'Mary O'Bannion. I'm looking for Mary O'Bannion.'

'Oh. You're a man with a weapon.'

'How would that be?'

'You hit her, and she hits you. I don't do that stuff, darling. I've had too much pain in my life. No offence, like.'

A pulse of pain like anger flared behind his right eye and at the base of his skull. It was bad, but he could cope with it. What troubled him was the unremitting ache; too slight to be painful, it was like the pressure of some small muzzled animal pushing to get out. It had been trying since he had wakened in the hospital.

A man with a weapon . . . There was nothing to smile about in her now. Nothing at all.

'Would fifty pounds make you late for the doctor?'

'I need to see him.' Once an idea had lodged in her head it took time for it to make room for another. Greed began the nudging process. 'Fifty? What would you want?'

'You stand against a wall and let me punch you in the stomach.'

He watched the colour leave her face.

'I wouldn't be surprised if you've got something wrong with your stomach right enough,' he said. 'You should see a doctor.'

'I told you,' she said vacantly. 'I'm going to see him. I told you. That's not on, what you wanted.'

'Not for a hundred?'

'Have you got a ton on you?'

Perhaps deliberately she let her voice rise on the question. From the corner of his eye, Murray caught the tilt of the dog's mask turning. Because of the pain, because he had been offended, he had behaved like a fool.

He laughed easily.

'You must think I'm a clown. It was just a joke. With you going on about having to see the doctor . . . like . . . No offence?'

By mere instinct, she reacted to the aggression he gave off despite himself.

'You want to watch it,' she said with a yellow grimace. 'If I put the boys on to you, you'll get a tanking.'

Murray took a deep breath and sat back. He rubbed a hand over his face.

'I'm sorry, love. I know you're not feeling well. You're worried about the doctor. You've had a rough time. Here I was just wanting to give you a drink – something to take the pain away, eh? A joke can do that too sometimes, isn't that right? But that was a stupid joke. Definitely a stupid joke, eh?'

He offered a monotone of sympathy like a man soothing a spooked horse.

'Definitely,' she said. 'You want to watch your mouth.'

Under the influence of his sympathy, however, everything dull and compliant in her was surfacing. When for the second time he pushed his own glass, still full, across to her, she accepted it without question.

'You need it more than I do,' he said.

'Just so it doesn't go to waste, eh? Oh, Jesus!' She made a face as it went down. 'You're right about me feeling rough.'

'Have another one.'

'I'm going to the doctor,' she said without conviction.

While he was ordering drinks, Murray watched, in the mirror behind the expressionless barman, one of the men cross to the table and bend over the woman. Meticulously taking no interest, the second man stared into what might have been a glass of lemonade, tilting his head and sniffing into the stillness. More than alcohol, a lot of the hard men now who were on drugs craved the sweetness of the mixers.

'Are you a fucking cop?' she asked as he sat down.

'No,' Murray said, keeping it simple.

'You're big enough for one. You're a big fellow.'

'I'm big all over,' Murray offered, suggestively.

'Right enough,' she went on, heeding the warning voice in her head, 'You're not drinking. You're buying, but you're not drinking. And another thing, you don't look like one of Big Mary's regulars. I was surprised when you said you were wanting Big Mary.'

'No,' Murray said, more emphatically this time. 'you weren't surprised. You're just saying that now – but you had it right before. I'm a man with a weapon. Big Mary's the right one for that, okay? So what's the problem? I need her address – it's worth a fiver to me.'

As she thought about it, he made the mistake of pushing: 'Anyway, it takes all kinds to make a world. You're not telling me all Big Mary's customers look the same.'

'They're frightened,' she said. 'They want it and they don't want it.'

Murray blew out his lips contemptuously. 'Some folk are like that and some aren't. Look, if I was a policeman, I wouldn't have to ask you her address. I'd know it, wouldn't I? Stands to reason.'

'Aye, but, if you've been with her . . . you *should* know.' She said this not searchingly but as if she had just worked it out.

'My place. She used to come to my place. But I've moved away from there, so I need to get in touch. She'd be glad if you told me – but even if she wasn't, who's to know? Might be worth more than a fiver . . . That's easy money.'

'I don't know.'

He stood up. 'It's time for your doctor. Come on – I'll walk you to the corner.'

She hesitated, greed and caution pulling opposite ways. 'Where did you say you met Big Mary?'

'Through a friend of mine – Mr Kujavia.'

'Kujavia?' A squeal of rage and disbelief harshened by a raw edge of fear. The squeal hung in the air between them. It was as much his as hers. It burst and echoed inside his head. 'Ya lyin' messan!' One of the two men at the bar had moved to the door; if he tried to leave, he would be caught between them. The barman had come to the end of the counter and, raising the flap, was standing in the opening dabbing at a pint glass with a grey cloth.

After that move into position, everyone waited. All his life Murray had found a release in fighting. He had sometimes been hurt but he had never been afraid. In this endless

164

moment of waiting that was changed. He could not afford to take a blow on the head. It was a knowledge that came without calculation; an instinct of the body. And with it came the fear of dying.

He rose to his feet and moved quietly to the door, stopping where he could see all three of the men. He spoke to the one who was blocking the door.

'You're a good guesser. I've got mates out there on surveillance. You were clocked coming in. If I don't leave here in one piece, you're in a lot of trouble, friend.'

His tone was low and reasonable. There was no threat in it, but rather an undertone of amusement. In the face of his certainty, the man began to move away from the door and then changed his mind and swung around to check the street.

He's a mug, Murray thought, but not enough of a mug to believe me. He knew his best chance would be to make a rush while the man's back was to him, but he could not decide to move. It would only take a moment to check the windows opposite, look for a parked vehicle – some sign of a police presence. Guardian angels.

The man turned abruptly and as Murray braced himself came close. But he was grinning. 'Aye,' he said with contempt, 'you weren't kidding. You've got a right mate out there,' and with a nudge of the shoulder he walked past. In a moment, the alteration was complete. Two men stood drinking quietly, the barman behind his counter reached to fix a bottle on the gantry. A woman slouched at a table staring disappointed into an empty glass.

As Murray went out, he pushed awkwardly at the swing doors and the left one came back striking him on the arm. A big man with a full head of hair and a great jutting beard flecked with white was crossing the pavement to the entrance. As staring he broke step, Murray recognized him. The guy who talked so well, Billy Shanks' friend . . . Tommy Beltane.

The Prophet.

'I've just promoted you,' Murray said, 'to guardian angel.'

CHAPTER SIXTEEN
A Short History of Prostitution

SATURDAY, SEPTEMBER 15TH

'The Romans did their whoring differently,' Tommy Beltane said. 'Like everything they touched they made it sinister and grotesque. The whores of Rome, the *bustuariae*, believed, were persuaded to believe, they were the servants of the Gods of the Dead. They practised their trade in the great cemeteries of Rome and received their lovers lying in the graves which had not yet been filled in.'

'I met one like that back there,' Murray said. 'She looked as if she might have been buried and dug up.'

Wondering how he would take that, Murray glanced at the man by his side. A big man with the appearance of a painted patriarch on the ceiling of an Italian cathedral. People probably turned in the street trying to guess who he was. Nobody. A clerk who worked for the Region. Tommy Beltane, who after the briefest of hesitations had attached himself to Murray outside the Crusader by some attraction of opposites.

'Billy Shanks is,' Beltane pronounced on the full organ note of an actor of the old school, 'a good man but not a brave one.' They hovered on the edge of the pavement and crossed quickly as a break came in the traffic. 'Do you know he hasn't printed a tip from me in weeks? Months? Never libel the rich in this country. As if that bastard Heathers had any reputation among decent men outside the fictions of a courtroom. Even the costs were phenomenal, apparently – and the paper was ordered to pay both sides. God knows why they didn't settle out of court as usual – an expensive rush of principles to the head. You do know about the case?'

Murray nodded.

'I just remembered that you'd not have been here when it happened. You were abroad, weren't you?'

Automatically, Murray accounted to himself for Beltane's embarrassment: it was not at showing he had discussed Murray with Billy Shanks; or because he imagined that Murray had anything to hide about those years away; but simply that for him the idea of choosing to be away from the city at all was a shade disgraceful. For Beltane, Murray suspected, nothing outside this city was quite real.

'Despite all that, you still give him the odd tip,' Murray said, strolling forward at the big man's side in the warm sun, 'even if he hasn't got the guts to use it?'

Beltane shook his head. 'I'm not criticizing him – well, of course, I am. People like Billy should have virtue in the Roman sense. They should have a care for the state.' He stopped abruptly to declaim, '"One on God's side is a majority!"' ignoring the passersby, who in the way of the city made it a point of pride to try to return the compliment, 'Marvellous, eh? But it wasn't a journalist who said that.'

'No,' Murray said, glancing at him from the corner of his eye, 'they wouldn't be brave enough. I can see that.'

'Oh-oh!' Beltane responded and started forward once more, without adding to his double note of disquiet.

'Were you expecting to meet anyone in particular in the Crusader?' Murray wondered.

'Not necessarily.'

'You were dropping in on the chance of getting a bit of good conversation. Someone interested in Roman history, or politics, or something like that.'

'It's not quite the same class of people as come into the Shot,' Beltane said calmly. 'Although I might have met you. What took you there?'

'I was looking for a woman called Mary O'Bannion.'

An unevenness of the pavement made Beltane miss his step. Recovering, he asked, 'A professional secret? I don't suppose you would tell me why.'

'Not because I'm a man with a weapon,' Murray said. 'That's how the whore back there called it — he hits her, she hits him.'

But although Beltane made a grimace of disgust, he said nothing.

'I had a spell in hospital,' Murray went on. 'It gave me time to think. Putting one or two things together, I decided that Blair Heathers might occasionally use a frightener. A man with a foreign accent who frightened people in the worst possible way. And something else I'd been told made me wonder if he might be running a stable of girls. Then I looked for a name to fit.'

'Kujavia . . . Billy Shanks gave you it.'

'Not necessarily,' Murray said in his turn.

Beltane pointed down the side street they were crossing. 'Deacon Street. Where they found the first body. One of these charming ladies might be Jill — She Who Rips.' He bowed generally, and a woman with her hair in curlers gave a flustered grin.

'When you've visited the Crusader, have you ever come across Mary O'Bannion?'

'A whore.' Beltane filled his mouth with the word, made from it an orotund song. 'An old fat whore. A very fat smelly whore. She lives with Kujavia — so I've heard. You were right about that.'

They crossed Moirhill Road and turned into Baird Drive, climbing the steep hill towards the public park.

'Below, that's the kingdom of the whore master,' Beltane said. 'Deacon Street, Florence Street — all around there. Those letters that have been coming to Billy's newspaper signed Jill are from that kingdom. Jack the Ripper had a passport for it a hundred years ago. He was a client gone wrong — like the Yorkshire Ripper, Sutcliffe. Why shouldn't our Jill be returning the compliment? A whore who hated customers, police, pimps — hated men. It's always seemed to me whores must be full of hate — down there in the dark kingdom.'

An image came to Murray of Frances Fernie, sitting on

168

the edge of the bed watching without protest as he threw her possessions on to the floor. 'Prostitutes aren't like that,' he said.

They were walking now in the shade cast by the line of beech trees on the other side of the railings.

'Who can be sure what they're like?' Beltane asked. 'Even the patron saint of repentant prostitutes wasn't a prostitute at all. Saint Lucia − she was tortured and killed by the Romans for being a Christian. Whether she was or not, her boyfriend denounced her to the authorities because she wouldn't go to bed with him. The earliest recorded martyr of the permissive society.'

'I'll let you be the expert on the subject.'

In response, Beltane made a gesture of scooping at the back of his hand with a fingernail. 'I wouldn't like to give you anything you could use against me,' he said. 'You could make a man very sorry if he ever confided a weakness to you.' He made the dabbing gesture again on the back of his hand. 'You're a scab picker.'

They turned into the park. The attack had taken Murray by surprise. It was not a description of himself he recognized. Underfoot, the grass, barbered close, was waiting for autumn and rain to recover its fresh greenness after the summer crowds.

'If we go up round this way,' Beltane said, 'there's a bandstand at the top. It's sheltered and catches the sun.'

'You know around here well.'

'As a child I played in this park.'

'You − Billy − Eddy Stewart − Blair Heathers − did everyone in this town manage to get themselves born in Moirhill?'

'Oh, not in Moirhill!' Beltane, taken by surprise, sounded prim and conventionally shocked. He pointed ahead. 'We stayed over on the other side.'

'Where the rich people live.'

'Hardly rich. Bungalow land.' A woman on the path ahead of them knelt and took three dogs off the leash. Yapping, the smallest, a chow, pursued a borzoi and an old leisurely labrador across the grass. 'I hate dogs,' Beltane said suddenly. 'Droppings that blind children. Sins of the mothers in this case. Middle-class dog fondlers.' His breath came harder as they climbed and his sentences shorter. 'That bloody fool Columbus importing syphilis. Took the fun out of things for four and a half centuries. What put it back? Not the pill, that's surface stuff. Deep grammar of it − a shot of penicillin in the bum. That's what made the permissive society. Even so − we can't get that fifteenth-century innocence back.'

'Do you have Mary O'Bannion's address?' Murray asked. 'I'm not interested in how you got it.'

As if he hadn't heard the interruption, Beltane went on, 'Think of rabbits and myxomatosis.'

'Rabbits?' Murray asked despite himself.

'Healthier than ever. Bounding about, the size of terriers. So there's always a worry. *Locomotor ataxia* is a terrible affliction. Gogarty's joke about the syphilitic sprat with delusions of grandeur − thought it was a salmon. The ingenuity of the malevolent spirochaete. And now bloody Aids − Venus is a fearful goddess.'

They had arrived at the summit of the park. Below, ahead of them, a neat grid of bungalows stretched to where high flats like exclamation marks punctuated the middle distance. The roof of the bandstand was in process of caving in; but as they walked round it they came on a bench placed where a side wall gathered the sun's warmth. Seated on it, they looked back the way they had come, a vista of chimneys and slate roofs, among which were deceptively open places that might have been gardens but were only the rubbled lots left behind when the old tenements had been torn down.

'At this distance, on a day of clear light, it looks handsome,' Beltane said. His breathing had settled and he leaned his hands on his knees contemplatively. 'Those old masons who cut the blocks of red sandstone or white were craftsmen who knew what they were about.'

'If you did give me her address, that would be it. Nobody would know where I'd got it.' As he said this, it occurred to Murray that it wasn't necessarily true, since the man in the Crusader had seen them going off together perhaps. It wasn't a thought he felt he had to share with Beltane.

'It's nice in the sun here.'

'I can sit in the sun anywhere.'

'It comes back to being brave again, doesn't it?' Everything Beltane said in that resonant tone sounded well. 'Twenty years ago Mary O'Bannion was Kujavia's alibi for murder.'

One of the things that Murray had learned was that when people broke certain silences about the past it was for their own reasons; the wrong question could stop them in their tracks. He waited and said nothing.

'He beat one of his women to death with an iron bar. He'd used it on her before — as well as on the others. But this time he went too far. When he stopped, she was dead.' He gave Murray a strange glance. It was as if he was ashamed. 'Can you conceive a man who beats women with an iron bar? You'd think he would kill everyone he touched. I can't imagine it. But they say it was only that one who died.'

'She was someone you knew.' Murray offered it quietly, as if confirming something obvious.

'Can you imagine even beating a woman with your fists? It'll be easier for you. You're a violent man. I didn't have to be told that about you. I've always avoided violence . . . that's possible even in this city. Yet for all these years in between I haven't been able to help myself from thinking about that iron bar. Beating down, beating down . . .'

'What happened to Kujavia?'

'Nothing. I told you — he had an alibi. He wasn't arrested. He didn't even get his name in the papers. But the girl was dead.'

'I don't see how you can know it was Kujavia who did it.' Beltane stared blankly, not understanding.

'The girl was dead,' Murray said. 'Kujavia was never accused. I don't imagine he confessed to you. How do you know he killed her?'

'I waited for something to happen.' Beltane said. From beyond the trees, Murray could hear the chow yap itself

171

into hysteria like a toy that has been too tightly wound. 'I couldn't believe there wouldn't be justice, God's or man's. I waited for him to go to jail or be run over by a bus. When it was almost too much for me, Billy Shanks sat me in a car one day and said, "That's him". And this ugly little man walked past. It didn't seem real – that he was the man. You read about things, see them on a screen . . . Only what you feel in your own flesh is real.'

When it seemed as if he wouldn't speak again, Murray took the risk and asked, 'She meant something special to you?' It was a question, but the tone was so mild, almost uninterested, that he made it sound as though the answer was a knowledge they already shared.

'I was twenty-four years old and had never been to bed with a woman. There were a lot of us like that back in pre-history. I was walking through the city centre – going home to Mother – and I saw this girl standing under the light of a corner. She was too skinny for anybody to be afraid of her. Even at a distance she looked hungry. I knew what she was. We went down a flight of steps into a basement area. She wanted me to wear a sheath – as if I would have had one. She said something about the other women letting her stand there. I thought, It's her very first night! I got it into my head she'd run away from home or maybe from some kind of institution. The light slanted down through the railings on to her face and there was a bruise round her eye. I asked her what had happened and she said, A man gave me it. Who else but a man? She had such a strange expression – a wince, a sneer, a poor sort of bravado. I took her up against the wall. She was so light and thin but I drove into her with all my strength. I wanted to split her in two. It was the most terrible excitement of my life.' He turned his head and his eyes swam back from the lost distance. 'I know what you must be thinking. How much that must make you despise me.'

'You're not the first man to get it up against a wall,' Murray said.

'Once a policeman, always a policeman . . . I'll tell you
172

something that will make you think worse of me still. I saw her again. As often as I could find her. She was an obsession. That went on for a year almost . . . until . . .'

'Until she got herself killed. She was the one Kujavia beat to death.'

'Oh, no,' Beltane said, as if it should have been obvious. 'She – the girl I was obsessed with – was Mary O'Bannion. The woman who was killed was older. She was quite different – she came from Belgium. She had children. It was even said the trouble might have started over the children – Kujavia interfering with one of them. But they were very young.'

'It was Mary O'Bannion who told you all of this?'

Beltane's face contorted. Later Murray would think the face of the girl in the basement must have looked like that: a wincing bravado. If you glanced away from him, however, the resonant hypnotic note was there just the same as before. 'I have no doubt all whores hate their customers in their hearts. It's perfectly possible, of course, that some of them don't realize. The golden-hearted ones. It would be better for them not to realize.'

'You've known all these years that Kujavia killed the girl. But if Mary O'Bannion gave him an alibi, then Mary O'Bannion could take it away.'

'Did you know that Billy Shanks was a kind man?' Beltane wondered softly. 'He came across me while he was checking up on Mary – Mary O'Bannion. He was starting out as a reporter, only at the beginning of his career. He wasn't any older than I was, but he helped me . . . I didn't understand things then.'

'So you found out?'

'About myself.' Beltane stood up. He moved away so quickly that Murray had to hurry, catching the first words as they drifted back to him. 'Now I sit on my arse shuffling papers for the Region. All nonsense. A nonsense life. As if you bought a ticket for a journey and boarded the wrong ship by mistake. If a young man came to me, I'd tell him to be a doctor – or an engineer – anything that will stick

173

your nose in the world. Don't shuffle papers – better than that, do anything. Bone a carcass. Chine a loin of lamb. Get blood on your elbows. At least you'll learn how a man is made.'

The lady and her dogs had gone home. Afternoon shadows slanted across the grass.

Approaching the gates of the park, after a long silence, Beltane stopped abruptly. 'Maybe it's time,' he said, but so quietly Murray wasn't sure of what he heard. He watched as Beltane pulled out a thin pocket diary, and turning to the back scibbled three or four lines. 'That's what you wanted.' He tore out the page and started towards the gate.

Murray glanced at the page; it was an address. Catching up, he said, 'I won't mention your name.'

Beltane stopped and fumbled a silver flask out of a side pocket. 'It's not often I arrive at the door of a pub and walk away.' He unscrewed the cap, poured, held it out. 'Reinforcements.' Murray made a gesture of refusal.

'Have you always been teetotal?'

Murray shook his head.

'No. Billy said something that made me think you weren't always a teetotaller. It's not a pleasure I could give up. I can't imagine life without it.'

Murray stood a step or two ahead of him on the path. He said impatiently, 'Can't you?'

Beltane laughed and began walking again, the flask open in his hand.

'Isn't it bloody marvellous,' he said, 'how we unburden ourselves to strangers?'

CHAPTER SEVENTEEN
Suspect

SUNDAY, SEPTEMBER 16TH

'You live in the past,' Mother said to Murray, whose head felt as if it had been split and packed in the seam with pieces of burning coal. Passing a long watch one night in an hotel outside Memphis, just before Seidman's wife turned the key in a car ignition and got herself blown away, a black guy from the Witness Programme, a dapper young lawyer offended by the South, had shouted how primitive wasn't the same as stupid; and ruffled, where normally he was as smooth as an FBI man, had given his African examples, all kinds of ways of making things with simple tools and devices – like hollowing out canoes with fire – stuttering as the fleshy red faces split into grins. Thinking of that, he suffered the image of a stripe of slow fire consuming the trunk of a great felled tree. The wood was hard, remarkably hard, but fire ate it out.

When he arrived, he had bent and kissed her and she had smiled and put her hand up to his face.

'Should you not still be in hospital?'

'I signed myself out. You couldn't get a decent cup of tea.'

'First Malcolm and now you. My two wounded sons.'

'Beds are scarce. They were glad to get rid of me.'

'I don't understand what's going on.'

'There's nothing to understand. Accidents go by twos.' No, he thought as he said that, accidents go by threes; drawing her with him through the tiny hall. 'Now that I'm here, I feel fine. I couldn't miss my Sunday visit.'

And it was true that settled across from her with a cup

of tea, he fell into a disbelieving kind of peace, fingering its presence like stolen jewellery. The headache unclamped its bands.

Out of a drifting unguardedness, he told her, 'There was a dream I kept having while I was in hospital. I was in a wood like the one at Coirvreckan, only much bigger. It kept wakening me out of my sleep . . . It was a nuisance.'

'A wood at Coirvreckan,' Mother said dismissively, 'there wasn't any wood at Coirvreckan. It was a bare place.'

At once he knew she was right. It was a long time ago, and he had only been a child; yet it was a strange mistake. The land around that croft worked by his father's three unmarried brothers would have challenged even the imagination of a child to conjure up a wood. There were only a few trees and what there were all pulled to the side by the wind.

'This was a forest – even while I was walking I knew it would take me days to walk out of it. Then I'm lying on the ground and there are people looking down at me. They . . . want me to sing.'

'They would be out of luck there,' Mother said. 'You could never carry a tune.'

'The dream isn't too bad until then. But then a man pushes his way through the crowd. He has rings that flash in the sun and he leans down and puts his hands over my eyes.' The rings, dazzling lights in the sun, and then darkness. 'At first, when he's pushing his way through – I see his hands first – I think I'll know him, but when he bends over I see he's got no face – not a proper one. It's a turnip lantern, like Hallowe'en. The kid's stuff you get in dreams . . .'

The white flesh of the turnip shone in silvery stripes where the tough outer integument had been hacked off. Gouged rectangles for the eyes, a triangular vacancy – a syphilitic gap – for the nose, the mouth an untidy gash. Instead of hair it wore a festal crown of black spikes, and the light from the candle inside shone out through the mouth and nose socket, but not through the eyes. The eyes were dark.

Mother said, looking at him attentively, 'I'm worried about Malcolm. He wasn't looking well last Sunday – when you weren't here.'

Murray waited a moment, took a deep breath, before saying carefully, 'That would be because I was in hospital.'

'He keeps things from me. He thinks I would worry, but I can tell when something is wrong.' She leaned forward, her blind-seeming gaze accusing him. 'I would expect you to tell me.'

'He's old enough to tell you what he wants you to know.'

'You are the elder. A brother should care for a brother.'

'Oh, I'm in good shape for looking after him.' He raised a hand as if to touch the bruised envelope of flesh by his eye, but, realizing what he was doing, did not complete the gesture. Embarrassed, he said, 'It must have been all that fresh air when I was young.'

If then any thought came to mind, it was of his father's changes of duty from one lighthouse to another, continual changes, to edges where the land made a fist of rock and ended or across the sea to islands, every move exchanging one remoteness for another, heads turning as you walked into another class of strangers; but Mother, fixing her gaze on his lips, said, 'Your visits to your uncles did you little good. I know what kind of place you were in when you got that hurt. Calum and Angus are dead now, but not your father or any of his brothers would have stepped inside a place where drink was sold.'

That was so ridiculous, it made him want to laugh and he was surprised to hear it come out as a groan. 'That's not you. That's not you now, not any more.' The headache reasserted itself with a sharp discomfort. 'When Malcolm brings his bottle of wine this afternoon, will you refuse a glass from it?'

That was childish. In her presence he regressed arms whirling shrinking down a tunnel eat me drink me . . .

'If your father could hear you now,' she cried, matching his anger.

'But he can't. He's dead. And whatever you think, it wasn't anything to do with me.'

177

He had been in Glasgow when it happened; the fifteen year old son who had run away from home. What blame could he have for that accident? A man falling from a high place, arms whirling, shrinking down the clear air to the grey rock.

They shared their dismay in silence until she explained it away to herself.

Gazing at him with an air of being offended, she said, 'You live in the past.'

And when Malcolm arrived with Irene, later than usual, he came with empty hands. There was no bottle of wine. 'I had to stop on the motorway for something to eat. You didn't forget I was away on a course? They put in an extra session this morning and it trailed on. Irene ate because she was tired of waiting. We were sure you would have eaten too.'

'No,' Murray said quietly. 'We waited.'

'We were sure you would have eaten, Mother,' Malcolm called.

She came to the door of the kitchen carrying an oven glove. 'I didn't buy in anything special. But there's always plenty. I have a pound of mince and sausage rolls and six slices of Silverside. And York ham – a half pound and a quarter. Bits and pieces that have to be eaten up.'

There seemed no way of preventing her from buying unrealistic amounts of food. Wilfully, she bought and stored and had often to throw away meat, fruit, pastries, sweet biscuits, of which she ate surprising amounts.

When she turned back into the kitchen, the three of them were left to study one another. Malcolm cleared his throat. 'You don't look as bad as I'd expected. Irene said you were looking terrible.'

'It's worse than it looks,' Murray said, exactly reversing the sense of what he had intended to say. He squinted evilly at his brother out of the Chinese slant of his injury.

'I was sorry I couldn't get in to the hospital. Did you have many visitors?'

'Eddy Stewart.'

'I was sorry I couldn't manage in.'

'I had plenty to think about,' Murray said.

178

Irene laughed.

He was conscious of her in a way he did not want to be, every movement of her shoulders, every inclination of her head, a gesture in which she enclosed the palm of her right hand in the fingers of the left. Because he had wanted to look only at her since she came into the room, deliberately he had kept his eyes turned away as if they had quarrelled. Now when she laughed, she lifted her chin and stretched the white smoothness of her throat.

She said, 'Murray's going to find who killed John Merchant.'

'You know that's stupid,' Malcolm said.

'Look for then. Blair Heathers is paying him to do it, isn't that right, Murray?'

'Why would Heathers do that?' Malcolm asked blankly. 'What on earth could you find out?' Another idea struck him: 'Was that what you were doing when you got attacked?'

'No,' Murray said. 'I was asking questions about Frances Fernie.' In the stillness, he could hear the clatter of a pot being put down in the kitchen. 'I couldn't understand why she'd claimed my brother was sleeping with her. That was before I knew she was a friend of Irene's, of course.'

'Mother doesn't know anything about this,' Malcolm said. 'We've kept it from her.'

'I can understand that. When I saw Francis Fernie, she told me it was you who introduced her to John Merchant. Was she telling the truth?'

'You're the one who's supposed to care about Mother,' Malcolm said bitterly. 'All right, all right. Why not? They hit it off.'

'Is that the new name for it – fixing your boss up with a whore?'

'For God's sake!' He let his voice rise, so that Murray, despite himself, glanced uneasily in the direction of the open kitchen door. 'You're unbelievable. People don't think that way about relationships any more. Sex isn't dirty any more.'

Irene laughed again. 'Oh, Murray,' she said. 'Your mouth's open. You're staring at him as if he'd gone mad.'

179

Taking heart from her support, the younger brother cried, 'You've spent too long spying on bedrooms in third-rate hotels. Too many divorce cases – you think the whole world's a dirty little keyhole.'

In a flush of pure rage, Murray gathered his weight under him to spring up. In the same instant, however, he saw the colour drain out of Malcolm's face. Settling back, he said in the tone of a man offering information, 'You're behind the times. People don't need that stuff for a divorce any more.'

Although – that's human nature – for other reasons they still want to know; and will pay someone to pry . . .

Mother came out of the kitchen, taking off her apron. 'Did none of you hear the door?' They had put a light in the kitchen for her that flashed when the front door bell was rung. 'You're all so busy talking,' she scolded, smiling.

They heard her opening the door and then the deep note of a man's voice.

'It sounds as though she's letting someone in,' Malcolm said in surprise, and Murray twisted in his chair to see the tall figure of Ian Peerse precede Mother into the room. Behind him, he heard his brother blunder to his feet.

'I was explaining to Mrs Wilson,' Peerse said, studying them all from his great height, 'how sorry I am to disturb you on a Sunday.'

'What is it?' Malcolm sounded panic-stricken.

With an unhurried movement, Murray too stood up and came between Malcolm and his mother. Smiling at her, he said quietly to Peerse, 'Did you tell her you were a policeman? What makes you think you can get away with a stroke like this?'

Peerse bent courteously over the old woman. 'This is my first chance to see Murray since he came out of hospital. We're old friends, though he left the police and I stayed on.' And, with a glance at Murray. 'It was good of you to invite me in, Mrs Wilson.'

'A friend of Murray's?' She was bewildered. 'I thought you said you were Malcolm's friend. I don't hear as well as I used to.'

It was unprecedented for her to admit her deafness.

'You can see I'm fine,' Murray said. 'Thanks for looking in.' He made a move as if to walk back with Peerse into the hall.

'We were just going to sit down at the table,' Mother said. 'Would Mr Peerse not like to join us?'

'No—' Murray began.

'If it wasn't too much trouble? I think Murray feels it might be too much for you.'

'There's plenty,' Mother said firmly. 'I always make sure there's plenty of food in the house. I'm always being told it's wasteful.' She glanced indignantly at Murray. 'But there you are, you see. It means you never have to worry if someone comes in unexpectedly.'

'It seems as if you're joining us for dinner,' Irene said, smiling up at Peerse. 'Since you're an old friend of Murray's, you can sit here opposite him. I'll set another place, shall I, Mum Wilson?'

Settled at the table, Malcolm said, 'My mother doesn't know – about what happened last week. She doesn't know about – Francis Fernie – or – any of that. We've kept it from her.' He spoke just too softly for her to hear.

'You surprise me,' Peerse said, taking the cue for the pitch of his voice with cruel exactness. 'I don't see how you'll be able to keep that up.'

Mother had refused Irene's help in bringing food. Murray saw her hesitate now at the kitchen door, and that her eyes were fixed on Peerse's mouth with a painful attentiveness.

'My mother's deaf,' he said softly, 'she's not senile. She's trying to find out what's wrong.'

As they ate, however, Peerse began to question Malcolm, choosing his moment and always in that maddeningly exact lowered tone.

'I don't swallow,' he said, chewing with neat pursed lips and, in fact, visibly passing the bolus down the long passage of his throat. 'I don't go at all for the story that you were with the Fernie woman.'

'It's not the kind of thing you tell lies about,' Malcolm said bitterly.

'Don't answer him,' Murray warned. 'This isn't official. He has no right to be here.'

'It's not the kind of thing a man would want his wife to know about,' Irene offered, with the air of a woman making a point on her husband's behalf.

'So why didn't he deny being there?' Peerse asked, very reasonable in his turn.

'Shut up,' Murray said in a harsh whisper. 'Leave it!'

At which Peerse raised his voice to compliment Mother as she sat down again. 'That was very nice, I enjoyed it. We were talking about the case I'm working on just now. I'm afraid it's murder – not the best subject for Sunday dinner.'

'Oh, no,' Mother said, 'I'm not a great reader, but I like watching television. There's a lot of good programmes – and I like the detective ones.'

'This case of mine was about an alibi,' Peerse said, taking a cream cake from the plate she had set down and dividing it neatly in half. Somehow Murray had never thought of him as having a sweet tooth. 'A man was found dead in the street at five o'clock in the morning. From other evidence, we knew he must have been left there at some time after midnight, and the doctor's best guess was that he'd been killed around nine o'clock that same evening.'

Mother was listening with a frown of concentration. 'Wait now,' she said. 'Would that man be the man Malcolm worked for? The one who was killed – by that woman, Irene, the one who killed the other man?'

'I think you're right, Mum Wilson,' Irene said. She laid her hand on Malcolm's arm. 'I can't imagine who else it could be.'

'John Merchant,' Peerse confirmed. He was silent for a moment and certain secretive little pouchings of his upper lip suggested he was licking cream from his front teeth while keeping his mouth decorously shut. 'He had a mistress. I was the one who had found out she existed, and so I went to see her. Talking to her, I knew there was something wrong. I have an instinct; she couldn't hide it from me.'

'You felt it was her that did it?' Mother asked. With this topic, it seemed all her suspicious uneasiness had vanished. Remembering how she enjoyed the crime series on television, Murray could have sworn that her eyes had brightened. With something to make her alert, she seemed younger; and it came to him with a pang how featureless her life must be. 'She was the one that killed him!'

'It seems not,' Peerse said, nodding down at her, 'since she has this wonderful alibi. Merchant wasn't the only man she went to bed with – there's this other one who claims he came to her room at eleven that same night and stayed with her until the next morning,'

'Wait, wait, but,' Mother cried, 'and even supposing that's true, she still could have killed him, couldn't she? For I'm sure you said a minute ago that Mr Merchant was murdered about nine o'clock. Well, that's before this other man was there at all.'

'But it's just the time when somebody must have taken the body and left it in the street.' Peerse stretched out his hand, hesitated, took another of the flaky pastries full of cream. 'I know I shouldn't. It's greed.'

'There's not a pick on you. You're lucky. You can eat as much as you want to,' Mother said impatiently. 'Maybe there was two of them, and the other one took the body away.'

Peerse sighed. 'There's a general opinion that's not likely. This is the second murder, you see, and both of them were . . . messy. It's natural to assume we're dealing with a madman. And the mad don't work in pairs. That's what they tell me . . . and it makes sense . . .'

'But you have a hunch,' Mother said, relishing the word.

Before he could answer, Irene intervened. 'Mad*man*? I thought it was a woman. Murray's friend Billy Shanks calls her Jill the Ripper.'

'Journalists,' Peerse said, offering just the single word as if the disdain he put into it were a sufficient explanation; but then inconsistently added, 'Physically, there's no reason why it shouldn't be a woman. It doesn't take strength, not with the right knife. With a butcher's knife properly sharpened, meat falls apart. The first blow causes shock – and there's a possibility that in Merchant's case it actually paralysed him without killing him, which let them do other things to him before he died. That may mean specialist knowledge, or perhaps it was nothing more than luck.'

'Luck?' Malcolm exclaimed incredulously. 'For God's sake!'

Loudly then, Murray began to talk about television. He had no set and so he had to talk about what he had seen in the States. Once started, he couldn't stop; and heard himself, under Peerse's ironical gaze, describe chat shows, baseball, American football, a documentary about a deaf girl that had stuck in his memory. He carried the conversation like a burden until the old lady pushed into a brief silence to ask Peerse, 'Would you like to have more tea now? Or coffee instead? Malcolm always has coffee.'

After these Sunday meals, it was the custom for Murray to make a second pot of tea for Mother and himself and coffee for Irene and Malcolm. He avoided her eye until reluctantly she rose and went into the kitchen.

'You don't want more coffee,' he said to Peerse. 'You've remembered an appointment.'

Malcolm leaned across the table towards Peerse. 'I don't know why you won't believe me,' he said. 'I was with her all night. I wish I'd never seen her, never been near the place, but I was and that's the truth. She didn't have anything to do with this terrible thing. Can't you accept that, and leave me alone?'

'Does your wife accept it?' Peerse wondered, staring not at him but at Irene. 'It doesn't bother her at all, where you were?'

'It's because they believe in relationships,' Murray said as the tray with the pot of tea and coffee cups were set on the table. 'It's only policemen who have dirty minds.'

'In my house,' Mother said, fixing her pale gaze on her elder son, 'I expect people not to mumble.'

'I was saying it was a pity Mr Peerse – Ian – had to go.'

'But he hasn't had his coffee. He has to go?'

Peerse shrugged. 'Yes, yes. Thank you for the meal. I enjoyed myself, Mrs Wilson.'

As Peerse got up, Murray rose with him. With the relief of it being over, he was suddenly gripped by the anger he had been restraining. Unexpressed, however, it was like a poison exhausting him.

It was in this slack off-guard moment he heard Mother say, 'That man who gave the woman an alibi, I wouldn't be surprised if the two of them were in it together. I was thinking about it while I was making the tea.' Again, adding to Murray's disorientation, the pleasure of this involvement had altered the expression of her face, like an echo of a memory out of his childhood. 'And that solves it, you see, because they'll have done the murder together. I don't know why you didn't think of that.'

He had been only a child and they had been standing on a bridge across a river. Had it really been a river, or was that a child's memory making everything larger than it had been; perhaps it had been nothing wider than a burn, and the bridge made of wood with a low handrail on either side? She had put back her head and laughed at something he had said; and looking up at her he had *felt* not thought: how young she is, how clever she is, how beautiful my mother is. He had been no more than seven or eight, but of the truth of that part of the memory he had no doubt.

The moment held him, wrapped and helpless, so that he had no energy to intervene. He listened as Irene spoke.

'Oh, Mum Wilson, someone who is mad has to do it all alone. First, Polly Nicholls at the end of August, and then Annie Chapman on the eighth of September. That's what Jack the Ripper did – Billy Shanks wrote about it. And then at the end of September he killed another two women, I can't remember their names, but he killed them both in the one night. He just walked from one street to the other and did it again. Billy Shanks says that poor man they found dead in Deacon Street was like Polly Nicholls, and then there was John Merchant. So, you see, we only have to wait . . . If it happened again, and if two men died in the one night, then we would know. It would have to be someone who was mad then, wouldn't it?'

It was a diversion and Murray was grateful for that.

As they walked along the lobby, Peerse smiled above him. 'Odd marriage your brother has.'

Murray opened the door and waited. He could not afford the luxury of anger.

'We know he was there at the woman Fernie's flat,' Peerse said. 'I believe that bit. The taxi drivers confirm the times for the evening and the morning.'

'Taxi?' Murray asked, taken by surprise.

'He had a car in the garage, that's right, and he phoned instead for a taxi. And another in the morning – no buses for your brother.' Peerse sniffed. 'He offers reasons, of course, but I find it odd. It's almost as if someone wanted to make sure he could prove he was there.'

Murder cases were littered with irrational behaviour – but so was daily life; and no one thought twice about it until something happened and policemen and lawyers arrived asking for things to be logical. Murray was too tired to try to explain any of that, and it wouldn't do any good to try. He said, 'He went to visit the wrong woman on the wrong night. He's not the first man to make that mistake.'

Peerse gazed down on him speculatively. 'You were some kind of a policeman once. I wonder if you're as ignorant as you're pretending. He didn't go off to visit her on impulse – not off his own bat. If we can believe him, once Merchant got interested in her, he stopped seeing her. He's a careful fellow your brother. Hadn't seen her for months. According to his story, *she* phoned him that night. Said she was lonely and wanted him. He doesn't seem to be very good at resisting temptation. He went, they had intercourse . . . more than once – he felt he could be quite frank about that.'

Murray stared at the closed door. He wondered if it had been Frances Fernie who had told Malcolm to take a taxi.

186

Everyday life was a muddle; he believed in chance and accident. It was his job to listen, and most times when he heard people blame or congratulate themselves it seemed to him they were talking about their luck, the kind it was.

For Francis Fernie, however, the coincidence had been extraordinarily convenient.

CHAPTER EIGHTEEN
Mary O'Bannion

MONDAY, SEPTEMBER 17TH

It took a lot of people a lot of years going down to wear down stone. These stone steps were worn down in the middle where Murray climbed. He had slept rough in the back entries of tenements like this. He had wakened in them cold and lonely when he made his fifteen year old boy's flight from the lighthouse to the city. Once, wakened with sunrise he had come out of a close where he had dozed on a couple of flattened carboard boxes and found the tenements curving away like a wall of cliffs, golden in the honey-coloured morning light. People had brought up families in them, now the families were in high-rise flats or in harled semis on the vast desolate estates of the outskirts; it had been a city of tenements; what made it unique belonged to them. And the tenements were dying.

This tenement in this street in the wasteland of Moirhill smelt of death.

He gave no outward sign of hesitation as he climbed from one landing to the next. There was no nameplate on the door, but he had been told to expect that. He rapped with the side of his fist and it opened at once.

'Hello, Mary,' he said.

She was gross and from the darkness behind her drifted the sweet stench of unclean flesh. A fat smelly whore, Tommy Beltane had said.

She yawned and turned back into the flat. The hall was narrow and her bulk rubbed the walls on either side. She eased herself out of sight and he glimpsed a lavatory bowl and then she pushed the door across, not bothering to close it. There seemed to be only one other door at the end of the lobby and he pushed gently so that it swung open, and after a moment stepped inside.

Dirt crusted on the single window dimmed the light of the outer world. An electric bulb suspended at an angle from an overhead flex glimmered pallid yellow on the sink and cooker, on a chair draped with underwear, a table heaped with the remnants of meals. On its side an emptied bottle of vodka lay precariously near the edge. At first glance, it appeared a figure was lying on the bed, but it was only an accident of tangled blankets and his heartbeat slowed.

As he listened for the lavatory to flush, she waddled through unannounced and settled into the chair, mumbling, 'You were lucky. I was going a place or I wouldn't have let you in.'

She reached up a bottle from the floor and poured into a tumbler. As she sucked drink, her hand was unexpectedly small against the sliding mounds of her lower face and neck.

'For a pee,' she explained. 'I was going for a pee or you'd still be out there.'

She was not pathetic but monstrous. He remembered the woman in the Crusader: a weapon – Big Mary – she hits you and you hit her – are you a man with a weapon?

'Who sent you?' she asked and lifted the glass to her mouth again, cupping it in her little hands, rims of black showing under her fingernails. 'Should I know you?'

When he did not answer, she laid down the glass and looked up at him. Her eyes were squeezed under heavy pale lids of oddly creamy flesh. She blinked and stretched her face down in a grimace that pulled her mouth into a gaping rectangle. As if the ugly movement had cleared her sight, she frowned at him. He had the impression it was the first time she had looked at him properly.

'Did you say who it was sent you? I would remember you.'

'Tommy sent me.'

Her head lolled back to rest. 'Tommy? I don't know – don't even bloody know – anybody called Tommy.'

189

Her eyes were almost closed. He glanced from the bottle among the debris on the table to the other one almost empty at her feet. It was impossible to tell — her head thrown back on the side rest of the chair — whether she had genuinely drifted off into a sleep. He winced at the thought of touching any part of that loose sprawl of evil-smelling obscenity.

He had seen a woman built like this drink hard men under the table and show no effect. That much flesh could soak up a lot of alcohol.

He wondered about using Tommy Beltane's full name to her; but, coldly, set that aside as being of no advantage. Instead, he said, 'What about Joe then? When is he coming? I'd like to talk to Joe.'

The thin slices of eye under the heavy white lids widened and contracted in an instant. It was a reflex movement, the effect like the glare and narrowing of a cat's pupils.

'You're not frightened,' she said. It was a local idiom: it implied — but you should be. 'I've got protection. I don't get fucked about.'

'Joe wouldn't like it?'

Instead of answering, she lifted the glass and tipped it into her mouth like a tiny bucket over a well.

'Supposing,' he said, 'I told you I had a message for Joe?'

Her breath wheezed in and out, a melancholy little tune as she thought about that. 'What message?'

'You don't want to worry about that. Just tell me when he's going to be here. I'll give him it myself.'

She hitched herself to the edge of the chair and struggled to rise. She used her arms to lift her weight and when she was half up he knocked the inside of one elbow. Lopsided she settled like a Zeppelin that had sprung a leak.

She whistled curses.

'There's no need to swear,' he said reasonably.

For some reason, this seemed to astonish her. Eyes and mouth popped open. Given something puzzling, she went on overload, shorting all the circuits of her cunning.

'I don't think you're all there,' she said.

'That's just because you have a bad conscience.'

Streams and ponds of sweat shone in the bread-coloured plains of her cheeks. 'You're from the police.'

'I'm a detective,' he said carefully.

'No – none of them would come here on their own. It would be two of them or more likely three.' She made it sound like a boast, and then another thought seemed to strike her, so forcefully that she blurted it out. 'That woman sent you. She was too frightened to come back so she's sent you.'

His first reaction was to ignore this as a diversion, for he had been preparing the way to question her if she had ever heard Kujavia mention the name of John Merchant. He stared at her without expression, giving her no clue to his response.

'You were stupid to come here, whatever she paid you,' she said. 'Joe nearly went mad when I told him about her coming here.'

If it mattered that much to Kujavia, it was worth pursuing. Mary O'Bannion believed the mystery woman had sent him. That might be useful, but it created problems in questioning her.

'She wasn't afraid,' he said contemptuously. 'You told her what she wanted to know. After that she didn't like the stink in here. It made her sick.'

'She's a liar,' the fat woman wheezed. 'That blonde bitch ran like a wee scared rabbit. She thought I was going to keep her here. But she was too quick for me.' She brooded on her failure. 'If her hair had been longer, I'd have had a grip of her.'

Small. Hair cut short. Young, it seemed, and blonde. Perhaps it was because he had been thinking of John Merchant . . . sometimes for Murray a spark would jump from fact to fact, person to person. I have the second sight, he had told a client once, and been amused when she took him seriously. Now he had an image of a young blonde woman sitting on the edge of a bed watching him tumble her clothes out on to the floor.

Sometimes though it happened that the spark jumped the

191

wrong way. When it did, he wasn't better than average at his trade, but a lot worse.

'By that time, you'd told her what she wanted to know about Joe,' he said.

'She didn't know anything about Joe,' the pursed lips spat out the words. 'Nothing. She knew nothing. She just knew about me because my name was in the papers. It was me that helped Father Hurtle with the children.'

'Tell me about it.'

'Ask her. If you're that anxious, ask her that sent you.'

'That's not the idea, Mary. The idea is you tell me, and that lets us know if you tell the same story twice.'

He tried to read the expression on her face but the drooping folds of flesh made a mask out of its abundance. After a moment, he saw to his astonishment a plump tear leak over the bottom lid of her left eye and run the downhill slalom of her cheek.

'Poor wee things. Even if I didn't really like Annie,' she wheezed, 'those two wee ones were lovely. She was a cunt though and a right snob. I was dirt. I was ignorant. I'd never been anywhere. I couldn't even cook.' She made the last charge sound particularly venomous; whether because it had hurt most or out of a memory of how the woman Annie had spoken it was impossible to tell. 'I still haven't been anywhere. I never seen Belgium or Germany or anywhere. And I still can't cook. But I couldn't have been that bad at learning. For I'm still here and she's away.'

And with the tear still drying she broke into a cracked cough that he took a moment to recognize as laughter.

'But you looked after her children?' he wondered aloud. He frowned, trying to remember the name of the priest she had mentioned. 'You didn't like her, but you got Father Hurtle to arrange for them to be adopted?' It was an obvious guess.

'God help them,' she cried falsely. 'Poor wee motherless things. Father got a good home for them.'

'And you kept in touch?'

'Eh?'

'You took an interest in the children?'

If he had thought the choice of phrase might flatter her, he was mistaken. Lady Bountiful farted and said, 'Father wouldn't tell anyone where they were going. And why would I care?'

'Children grow up,' he said. 'They want to find out about their real mother. Adopted kids do that sometimes. They come looking.'

With the effort of thought, the fat woman's mouth hung open and her tongue lolled out over the bottom lip. 'That wee blonde? One of the kids? Annie's daughter?' She gave the barking cough that parodied laughter. 'Annie thought she was a lady. Her girls were going to be ladies. That one was no fucking lady!'

A young blonde woman staring at him from the edge of a bed . . . There was a simple way to discover if one of the children had grown up to be the woman calling herself Frances Fernie.

'Up. On your feet.'

Her only response was to let her great thighs sprawl apart. The smell of gin from a pub door snaring him in the bad time and the young policeman buying the bottle and taking it back to the empty room to be drunk in secret – never with anyone else for that would have been weakness. The smell that rose from her was unclean but spiced with the odours of the body's hidden places. A jungle smell, a taint of the swamp, sick flowers of corruption that drugged the air and drew a man face down among them to die. Out of the dead past the smell drifted to him from the bodies of whores.

'If you make me,' he said softly, 'I'll soil my hands on you. You can get up the easy way or the hard way.'

As if there could be any easy way for her to hoist up that gross hill of flesh. She sighed and strained, heaved and was on her feet.

'I'll need a coat.'

There was one thrown across the chair by the bed near where he stood, but when he picked it up to pass to her he saw that it was ludicrously too small. It was a woman's coat, however, and he said to her, 'That's not yours. Does Joe wear it?' which was only a piece of mockery until he caught the look on her face. It was a cloth coat, dark green in colour, not new but of reasonable quality, the kind the better chainstores would sell. Holding it, he remembered what Barney the paperseller had told him: that Kujavia did this, cross-dressed for a disguise or some private satisfaction. It made him more grotesque, not less frightening; it had been hard to believe, thinking of that lumped white face, the smell of dirt. 'If he does,' Murray said almost to himself, 'he must be the ugliest woman in the world.'

'Mine's ben the room,' she said, taking the coat from him and throwing it back across the chair.

He followed her into the lobby. It was not surprising that he had overlooked the second door. Whatever colour it had once been had faded to a drab shadow in the darkest corner.

'I'll get my coat,' she said, and opened the door.

She was so wide that she blocked the sight of what might be in the room. It was only the noise that warned him. Scrabbling, clicking nails on linoleum, a gusting of breath, the woman called out and as she squeezed to the side the dog writhed past her. The impact of its weight and the blow in his hand were felt as a single shock. By instinct he had thrown up an arm to guard his throat. He staggered under the hurled weight of the beast, managed to stay upright and, turning, got it pinned against the wall. Everything seemed to be happening with extraordinary slowness. Its hind legs would have torn him, but he held it upright locking his free hand round its throat and leaning into its belly with his knees. He shook his head at the woman, warning her not to interfere, showing his teeth at her like a dog, and without a weapon she hesitated waiting for him to be pulled down. There was only a little time, and yet everything in that time held still. A wolf's head all eyes, the dog glared its hate. His blood sprang out along its muzzle. Every part of his attention poured into the grip of his left hand, the weaker hand, but he tightened his grip and leaned his weight into the wall. Roughness of hair, cords of muscle writhing against

194

him. The choked voice of its snarling trembled against his palm. It began to die but it was brave and a little mad from being locked up and it would not release its bite. Suddenly blood and clear snot came from its nostrils and its teeth ground on the bones of his hand in its last agony.

He knelt by the dog and freed himself. As he stood up, she was turning back through the door with a bottle in her hand. He reached out and took it from her. There was the least of noises, a soft light tap like metal on metal, as he laid it down gently on the coal bunker in the corner. She retreated before him. As she did, she wheezed in a breathy small-girl whisper, 'That dog was fucking crazy.'

'It's not the dog's fault.'

'Joe trained it.'

Since a cheque from Heathers had arrived, he had hired a car. Mary O'Bannion spread across the seats like a tide of sludge.

'You'll have to get that hand attended to,' she whispered solicitously. 'Get a jab at the hospital or it'll go bad on you.'

He grunted. The pain in his hand was something his will could control; later he would get treatment for it.

'The blood's coming through that cloth,' she said, looking at his hand where it rested on the wheel. 'You should take me back again, and then go to the hospital.'

'Later,' he said. 'We're going to have a look at somebody first – and you'll tell me if you've seen her before.'

After a time of silence, working that out, she seemed to lose her fear and become talkative, almost cheerful.

'I like big cars. There's no rubbish about them. I like the smell of them.' She patted the radio with her grimy hand. 'There used to be this Dutch guy. He would take me in a Rolls-Royce. He'd come from the airport and fetch me. He was a businessman, see? Money was no problem. He could buy anything except a ride. The first time I saw his dong I nearly lost my eyesight.'

Murray was worrying about what would happen when they got to their destination. He wondered if he could get her to climb the stairs to Frances Fernie's flat; and only then, belatedly, did it occur to him that meant showing her where her mysterious visitor lived; and if she knew then Kujavia would be told. He remembered what Tommy Beltane had said: an iron bar beating down; beating down on a blonde head. But if she wasn't the visitor, it wouldn't matter . . . And how else could he find out but by going to the flat . . . The pain in his hand made it hard to think.

'I got a fright,' Mary O'Bannion was saying in her high childish voice. 'You're not putting that into me, I told him. No, he said, I can't find anybody to take it. If I could find somebody to take it, I'd make her rich. Jesus, maybe,' she said, 'if I met him now. I was awful young then. But it was terrible big. Like a bloody great length of hose and as thick as your arm. He drove up to Loch Lomond and back while I wanked him. I mean it never stopped. It just kept coming all the way.' She gave him a sideways glance. 'After him, I was ready for anything.'

'Close your dirty mouth,' he said, but casually as if she could not disturb him.

When he came to Moirhill Road, instead of turning north towards Frances Fernie's flat he swung the other way. It might not make any difference, but, despite the burning in his hand, he did his best to take a roundabout route. Still hoping to confuse her, he stopped a street away from the flat.

'This is it.'

'I've only my slippers on. You didn't give me any time to get my shoes on. I've no coat.'

'It's not far.'

She groaned and struggled to turn off the seat, her bulk sagging and catching at every obstacle. With his undamaged hand, he made a fist and struck her a blow like a stick on a cow's rump.

Out of the car, he herded her by a grey stone wall. Muted, the noise of traffic from the main road played background to her sighing and muttering and the slap of her carpet slippers on the pavement. As they rounded the corner, they came in view of a group of people standing on the pavement at the entrance to Frances Fernie's close. There were half a dozen young women, and two men, one grey haired and the other not much older than the girls. There was a workshop of some kind up there, he remembered; it was late afternoon and, finished for the day, they lingered for a moment in the sunshine talking before going home. He saw the younger man turn the round thickness of his glasses towards them and say something. The others looked and floated their surprise and amusement like a set of matched pink and white balloons. Through their eyes he saw a man in a shabby blue suit escorting an enormously fat woman, shoeless, floundering, coatless in a flowered dress too short to hide her white fish-belly thighs mottled red with sitting too close to the fire.

'Where is this fucking place?' she gasped.

'It's not far.'

She stopped and dribbled obscenities while the group stared towards them.

'I'm not making a fool of you,' Murray said, too softly.

'What? I can't fucking hear you.'

The pain in his hand was at a distance; but the pain in his skull was himself, threatened to replace himself. Street and watchers queasily spread and separated. 'Move,' he snarled.

But as they approached the entrance, he saw that the grille had been pulled shut and locked. He would have to ask for it to be opened. As they hesitated, no one in the group smiled; it hung silent around them. At close quarters, it did not find them funny. The wounded animal was dangerous. The woman something corrupt accidentally exposed to the light.

He could not bring himself to speak.

As he went on, the stillness was so absolute that all he could hear was the sigh of the woman's breath by his side. After a dozen steps, she came to a halt.

'I've had enough of this,' Mary O'Bannion said.

'Yes.'

She billowed around to stare back the way they had come.

'Was it one of them? You never fucking said. I didn't look at them right.'

Under her gaze, the group drew together as if for protection.

'I've changed my mind. Forget it,' he said. 'You can find your own way back.'

She made no pretence of not taking the point or of being shocked. On questions of humiliation and punishment, experience had sharpened her understanding. Like rancid butter melting, tears of sweat leaked out from every grey enormous fold of her cheeks. 'I knew you were a right bastard.' The words squeezed out between the little gasping suck of her lips. 'At least give me the fare for the bus.'

His will that had brought them there unclenched. Between one moment and the next, he lost any faith in the possibility that she might identify Frances Fernie. What had persuaded him was gone and seemed absurd. More importantly, in his distress, suddenly it seemed better to do nothing. Blair Heathers was paying him to do just that, to keep out of the way and quiet. Anything he did might harm Malcolm instead of helping him.

'I can't walk,' Mary O'Bannion said.

'Find a customer.'

With the rest, he spectated as she struggled away, wallowing and limping under the burden of that great weight as if already her feet had begun to bleed.

CHAPTER NINETEEN
Double Murder

SATURDAY, SEPTEMBER 29TH

'My name? Call me John.'

He was going to die soon but he did not know that so he was able to joke. He knew that women of a certain kind spoke of their clients as Johns. And despite her refinement, her voice and clothes, he thought of her in that way; if she was an amateur, he expected her to be an expensive one. On the other hand, he was so comfortably able to pay that it complicated pleasantly the question of who was using and who was being used.

He did not expect her to give him her real name — that was part of the impression he had taken of her — and so, when she began to offer one, he stopped her and said, 'I'll call you Belle.' It was another of his private jokes.

She lingered on what he had said as if considering its possibilities. It was so exactly the reaction he might have hoped for that his jaded appetite stirred. 'I didn't expect to be given another name.'

'We're not the same person all the time,' he explained to her. 'We're all the pieces on the board. Why should they all have the same name?'

Double doors at the end of the reception area swung open releasing on a thick apostrophe of cigar smoke the fat chuckling anger of the crowd watching the fights.

'They're well pleased.'

'I didn't know it happened,' she said, 'having a boxing match in an hotel like this.'

'It's big through there. They have the ring and all the

tables set out around it. They lay on a good meal. You can drink and sit in comfort while you watch — not that everyone bothers to watch.'

'It sounds as if you would prefer to be there instead of here with me.'

'I've eaten,' he said, and with the gesture of someone sharing a joke ran the tips of his fingers down her arm with a light pressure. 'I was reaching for my wine when a spot of blood fell on the white cloth between the bottle and the glass. It put me off.'

'You must have been very close,' she said. 'I'm sure that's not supposed to happen.'

'Oh, they're quite keen,' he said, deliberately misunderstanding her, 'on them bleeding. So I came out here and saw you. And remembered you.'

'But not my name.'

'Parties are like that.'

'And, of course, I was there with my husband.'

He wondered if that was true. Seeing her alone here, he had remembered her and decided that he had missed a chance. Expensive whores were an occasional feature of old Blair Heathers' parties.

'And now you're here,' he said. 'Belle de Jour.'

They set out for her place and he took it for granted that even if there was a husband he would be somewhere else. A double life after all needed more than one roof over its head. He had indulged himself in the delights of explanation as she drove: 'I named you after a film. It's about a rich young lady who loves her husband but is fascinated by the idea of prostitution. She's afraid of it — horror-stricken really — but she can't resist it, not once the idea is there in her mind. And she does find her way to a brothel. She can only go there in the afternoon, of course. It's the only time she has free. So the madame — she's the one who christens her — gives her that name, Belle de Jour. The girl who's only available in the afternoon.'

After all that, she said, 'I'm not rich,' which made him laugh until, easing himself on the seat, he was disturbed

200

by the musty unexpected tang of his body's secretions.

'What happened to her?' the woman asked.

Everybody enjoyed a story. Made up, it gave you a beginning, a middle and an end; quite often in the right order. In real life, on the other hand, you employed someone for years; one morning you came on him crying at his desk and were too tactful to ask why; not long afterwards he handed in his notice and disappeared. Or Jackie, when you were boys at school together, who took every dare however rash or crazy – the schoolmaster thrashed him and, panting, grinned, 'The VC or the gallows'; but twenty, God, thirty, years later you opened a paper and read about some traveller in cosmetics dead in a car crash and recognized the name.

'Well? What happened to her?'

'She was disappointed,' he said. 'That's what usually happens, isn't it? The madame admires her because she's "a lady" – and even hints at the prospect of a partnership – a profitable business. The girls when they're not working play cards, drink tea and gossip. A lot of the men are grateful – which isn't the idea at all.'

He tried to read her expression but rounds and lozenges of light tumbled across her profile like a series of carnival masks.

'And then?'

Or back there at the table while they were eating, Leo offering nudge and wink stories about poor John Merchant to his new masonic buddy; some kind of policeman, what was the name? Standers, sweating and flushed with steak and wine, full of claims about leads and hints about the state of the body. In a murder, policemen must always start its story at the end; getting back to the middle would count as one of their successes; beginnings, presumably, they would leave to do-gooders or defence lawyers.

'Everybody loves a story.' He laughed. The sound of his own voice weaving the complexities of his thought around her was pleasant to him. 'A young tough – a crook – what the Parisians called an *apache* – takes her one afternoon. He's a real animal – and he comes back for more. Buys her over and over again. Reality suddenly gets to be a little bit like what she had imagined.'

'And then?'

The simple insistence disappointed him. It happened that way: a woman caught his interest, appeared different, and it was all a pretence and paper thin.

'And *then*,' he went on, with an ironical stress, 'and then one fine day he follows her home. Attacks the husband. Cripples the husband – but gets himself killed. I think the moral for tough guys must be, don't fall in love. For wives . . . you shouldn't try to live out what you imagine.'

'She seems to have got off lightly though.'

While he was wondering if it was worth testing her with the point that the poor husband, paralysed and speechless, knew about his wife's infidelity, they arrived at their destination. She introduced the blonde woman who came through from what he assumed would be the bedroom as her sister, but about that he reserved his opinion. The idea of sleeping with sisters might be taken as an added inducement, something that would put up their price.

'My sister will go to bed with you. I don't do that,' the woman, Belle, said.

Standing close, smiling at one another, it seemed possible the women might after all be sisters. It was not simply that there was a certain resemblance – make up and a shared hairdresser could do that for women – it was something that stirred between them, as palpable and indeterminate as the smell of two people who have just come from the same bed. They could be sisters. Or lovers.

Naked, the second woman's body was unexpectedly fine. He was in the habit of disappointment; unclad breasts that dwindled, bums that drooped, warts, blemishes, a rash of pimples across the shoulders. The sister's skin was clean and unmarked. Her breasts were firm and pointed and, because she was not tall, they seemed large. He turned her round and ran his hands down from neck to haunches, and then knelt impulsively and stroked with his tongue the skin that covered the round clean bone at the cleft of her buttocks. Close, her skin was glossy with good feeding and youth, and even there her body smelt sweet. With his hands on her waist, he urged her forward into the bedroom attending to the swaying play of her muscles as she walked. Yet it was not this nakedness but the other woman being there and fully clothed which excited him so painfully. By the bed, one on either side, they undressed him. At last, crouching, each slipped a hand under the waist of his shorts and eased them out and down. The erection unconstrained leapt out, slick, mushroom capped; 'Ready for count down,' he whispered, grinning, but his voice trembled foolishly; and the woman Belle unsmiling stroked both hands along its length. The sister lay back across the bed and, as if this was unfamiliar to him, Belle drew him forward until he lowered himself between the open legs. His erect flesh was cherished in her warmth as if by a boneless hand, but because he had felt no resistance as he entered her there was no danger of him loosing his seed. Instead, he could be attentive absolutely to the sensations produced by those muscles she knew so well how to use in clasping and squeezing him. Lying on her, in such unexpected control of himself, he had a sense of power so great that it felt like happiness. Even when he felt Belle nudge his legs open, when he felt her legs and the cloth of her skirt against the insides of his thighs, when her hands rocked him, even when he felt her finger pressing into him, the ragged little pain, the indignity, even when he had surrendered and shuddered, the happiness grew. He buried his face in the woman's hair and whispered. As he did, he felt the pressure at his neck and then a sting, but before he could react the woman's body under him began to shake and he thought she was in orgasm until she gasped, 'Don't!' and 'He wants to be tied up!' and lifting himself up so that he could see her face he saw she was laughing.

He slid out of her slowly. He had not gone down at all. So enormous was he that it seemed he would slide out of her forever.

'Before anything else, I have to pee,' he said.

'We shouldn't let you,' Belle said as if considering the

203

possibility of stopping him, but, of course, he could not allow that since it would have caused real discomfort. Anyway delayed urination could damage the bladder or the kidneys. He supposed it was even possible that urea retained in the bloodstream might adversely affect the brain. You had to be careful about such things.

In the bathroom he could not relieve himself in the ordinary fashion. Taking his weight on one hand, he had to lean at an angle over the pan. It intrigued him that he was so large and had kept his erection. He stood spread legged over the washbasin and ran cold water out of his hand, impressing himself with the fancy the water was turning to steam. You haven't changed since you were a boy, he whispered to the face in the mirror; but it was a lost innocence that told him, Those women are your creatures. Even if they tie you up, it's because you will them to; you invent them; what ideas would they have left, left to themselves, but the tired clichés of a commercial script? They are the creatures of your fantasy. Despite all this, the face in the glass looked afraid, but he understood that an edge of fear was part of this complex of feelings, and anyway most of that clown's look of fright was because the flourescent light around the mirror shone as a white circle in the pupil of each eye.

As he turned away, he noticed a smear of blood at the side of his neck and paused to pat it dry. Turning a corner of the towel red, he remembered the little sting as the sister cried, Don't! and wondered if Belle had nipped him with her teeth.

First, he stood at attention like a little soldier and they bound his legs together working up from the ankles. They tied his wrists and then bound his elbows which for some reason alarmed him.

Yet it was all in the script and at any moment all that pain which was no great pain, and that absurdity and the humiliation which was at the same time real and unreal, he could have gone back to the little philosophical puzzle which had pleased him so much to consider: who was using whom?

As it happened, he was too busy for that kind of thinking, and then Belle produced the knife and the script was torn up and the worst that he had ever been afraid of happened and the humiliation and the pain was nothing he had ever wished, being real and with nothing in it of make believe.

When in Conference Room One, Chief Superintendent Frank O'Hara, head drooped forward as if brooding over the knotted arthritic knuckles of his big hands, argued that the second killing of the night was unlikely to have been done by a woman – what woman would risk going into that fucking place by herself? – naturally, he knew nothing of what had happened between Constable Weyman and his partner.

The news about the dead man was passed from beat to beat from just after one a.m. until it reached Constable Weyman about fifty minutes later. By radio, of course, he had heard about it earlier and he and his partner had been reporting on vehicular traffic since, but the kind of detail which is unofficial comes on foot. From the spot in Carnation Street where it had been found, it was no more than a twenty-minute walk along Barnes Street and round by Merse Street to the pavement outside Matt's Bar; but news about the condition of the body had travelled cater-corner like a game of linked hands where people met until it arrived at Constable Weyman.

After he had heard, he went back across the street to where his partner was waiting.

'He'd been tied up. There weren't any ropes on the body when it was found, but they could tell by the marks. That's three now.'

They walked on slowly, more or less in step.

'Marks?'

'On his legs and arms. Where he'd been tied up.'

'Oh.'

'What marks were you thinking about? Were you wondering if Jill had cut off his prick. The second one had his prick cut off.'

205

'No,' his partner said. 'Merchant had been mutilated, but he wasn't castrated. He'd been sexually abused — but not castrated.'

Something in the tone of that irritated Weyman.

'I thought she'd cut it off him,' he said.

'No. You should read the sheets.'

'I read them.'

They went through a close and checked along the back of the row of shops. There should have been an open court in the middle of this rectangle of tenements; instead, a hundred years ago for profit, another tenement had been built in the open space, and people still lived there although its windows everywhere faced walls and even at noon the light was shut out. Buildings like that were known as backlands. There weren't many of them left and they were all due for demolition. The squatters who lived in them paid no rent, but then they had no lighting or heating or water; they didn't pay rates either. Looking up in the dark, he saw the glimmer of a candle in a broken window. Some of the squatters were dangerous. All of them attracted predators. By stretching out, Weyman could touch with one hand the back of the shops and with the other the derelict backland. The place between was a narrow passage down which they followed the pale circles of torchlight. It was no place for two young people even if they were in uniform, not at two o'clock in the morning; not after a body had been found a quarter of an hour's walk away — a man naked with rope burns on his ankles and wrists and his throat cut at last. Still with his ornaments though; she hadn't cut them off; he had been lucky that way. At the thought, Weyman smiled to himself. It was not much of a joke, but then it wasn't much of a smile either.

Constable Weyman hated this beat and this section of this beat and having to cover it on this shift when it was as dark as hell. Most of all, he hated having to cover it with this partner. Not that it was her fault — any other woman would have been as bad. It was the Region's policy now the force was at full strength to put a presence back on the streets, constables on foot patrol; and with equal rights, women, who got the same pay, did the same job. He understood that; he was an intelligent man; intelligent enough, if he could hold on through this time, to go to university, fees paid by the force, get a degree, work his way up. He could make a success of a career in the police force. It was even possible he might discover a talent for detection. Certainly, he would make a first class administrator. All these hopes lay on the other side of what he had to do now.

When the noise came, some things about it were certain; it was a yell that sounded once and stopped, it was human not animal, it was the deeper note of a man.

'What's that, what's that?' he cried as their torches jiggled patterns on the enclosing walls.

'I can't see anything,' his partner said. She was trying to squint between the boards that were nailed across the nearest window opening. Behind it, when families lived in the backlands, there would have been the front room of a room and kitchen.

'I can't see anything. The light doesn't reach.'

The torch held by her cheek threw shadows up across her face. It was like the trick children used at Hallowe'en to frighten.

'We'd better go in and check.'

'Don't be fucking stupid,' he whispered.

Some things about the noise were uncertain: among these: whether it was a cry of fear or pain or anger, or whether whoever had made it was still in there.

'Somebody might be hurt.'

She moved along to the dark entrance and went inside assuming that he would follow. She must have realized that he was not at her back for he saw the indistinct shape behind the torch and was dazzled by its light on his face. As they stood, they heard feet on the stairs inside stumbling upwards.

'There you are,' he whispered. 'He's gone.' He raised his voice. 'And get that bloody light out of my eyes.'

For some reason, he kept the light of his own torch out of her face.

'I'm going to have a look,' his partner said. 'Somebody might be hurt in there.'

'Why are you so fucking stubborn?' His voice whispered anger. 'You heard – some old cunt fell over and got a fright. Now he's taken off.'

'Maybe, and maybe somebody's hurt in there. Whoever ran away might have left somebody.' Left somebody hurt? Christ, left somebody *waiting*?

'Are you coming?' she asked. She was stubborn.

'You waste your fucking time, not me.'

She went into the close and he was left alone. He listened to the knock of her feet on the stone floor of the passage. Faintly then, heard its note change on to wood as she entered the flat behind the boarded window. All of that seemed to take a long time through which he waited in a curious blankness of attention, though all the while straining eyes and ears; and then his partner was coming back and he heard her talking in the dark, not to him and he knew how bad it was. A voice crackled answers and 'We've to wait here,' she told him. 'Till they come.' Her voice was stressed and thin, but there was something else there also as if her shock was waiting its time to turn to exhilaration. 'It's four killed now.'

'I'd better look.'

'If you like. I don't suppose it'll make any difference.'

But he stepped round her. There was only one flat on the ground floor. Its entrance had been locked and boarded and broken in more than once. There was nothing to stop him going in. Since there was no hall, the room was immediately beyond the smashed door and he saw the body at once where it lay parallel to the far wall. One arm was stretched towards him with the palm up. The lid on the nearer eye had been cut away; on the other eye, the little flap hung back like a tiny scar pressed against the temple. A wide red stare watched him edge closer. The belly had been cut open and the sickening spillage gathered up and thrown across the left shoulder.

There was the smell.

The light trembled on an ugly mess between the legs. This time some part of it had been cut off him.

There was the stir of rats disturbed at feeding. It had not been the murderer's steps they had heard, but someone who had stumbled on this and fled.

He recognized the dead man – a derelict called Old Danny who appeared in the district and vanished again according to some calendar of his own. In the spring, he had seen him one of a group of three on a bench near the social security office in Riverside Avenue. A woman and two men, lost drunks with the faces of idiot children. Later the bench had a scattering of beer cans under it, and the old man had it to himself, eyes shut, flat on his back, with his knees up so that it was only as you got closer you could see he had the fingers of one hand inside his fly rubbing himself. In that public place, the look on his face was naked in its privacy. Not on duty, you walked past, the sun was shining, it was the first day of good weather that had lasted all summer long and you walked by a French restaurant and a dress shop and three girls were joking as they came down the steps of the library and one of them, in pale brown cotton skirt and jacket, was the most beautiful girl you had ever seen. You would never forget her, and she passed you without a glance, the golden girl, walking with her friends towards the bench on the corner . . .

By the wall behind the door as he retreated, there was a scatter of clothes – Old Danny wore layers of coats – tangled in a worm cast like another corpse.

All of it was terrible, but it was the wet little smear of flesh on the dead face that made it Constable Weyman's last night on the beat. His partner had been wrong.

Going in to look made a difference.

BOOK FOUR

CHAPTER TWENTY
Mourning

TUESDAY, OCTOBER 2ND

'Cold enough for you then?' Barney asked.

'It's cold,' Murray agreed, and took the paper the old man gave him.

'Bloody cold.' And grinned an old man's empty grin, cried, 'Terrible murders – la-atest!' and dropping back into normal pitch went on hoarsely, 'Like winter, i'n'tit? And it was summer yesterday. Nothing in this bloody country makes sense.'

It didn't seem as bad as that to Murray, but it was true the wind had changed direction and overnight covered the city under a lid of low grey cloud. It might be that the long Indian summer was over at last.

'You're getting rid of the papers fast enough.'

'Two in a oner, but it takes two. Just a murder doesn't sell papers any more. We could do with two every night.'

'You wouldn't have anybody left to buy one.'

'There's a million buggers in this town. Plenty to spare. Kill two of them every night make no difference. Kill ten for me – kill as many as you like,' he offered malevolently. He coughed and spat; with a change of mood, added, 'But the old guy was a liberty. I mean he wasn't looking for trouble or wanting his hole. Just an old dosser.'

'Could've been you, Barney.'

'Away to hell!'

Driving, Murray made a bargain with himself not to rub at the ache at the base of his skull until he had passed the canal bridge. The gesture had become automatic. He lost.

After that, he came among neat little bungalows clinging to a slope so that the best of the front gardens had been turned into rockeries set with heather. Farther up, the houses took more space to themselves and at the top where the fat man lived there were walled gardens and glimpses of fruit trees.

The fat man himself opened the door.

'What the hell do you want, you bastard?'

He had been drinking, still held the glass trembling in his paw. His eyes were red with weeping and his cheeks had the high flush of a man getting ready to have a stroke.

'Just a few questions. Nothing that'll take long. I know you're upset.'

'This is a house of grief,' the fat man said. As if impressed by his own words, he released a plump tear from the corner of each eye. 'And you can fuck off.'

Murray put a hand on the edge of the door and held it seemingly without any effort against the fat man's pressure. 'I can't do that, Leo. I'm working for Blair Heathers and he'd like you to answer a few questions.'

Not at once, but slowly as he thought about it, the fat man stopped trying to close the door. Inside, the hall was square with a passage to one corner running through to the back of the house. There was a door on the right lying open.

'Yes?' Murray asked and went in first.

It was a big room but even so there was too much furniture in it. With sunlight through the bow windows, it might have seemed more inviting; on an afternoon when the weather had changed, it was bleak.

The woman by the window was dressed in mourning.

'Oh, Leo,' she said, 'put on the lights. I can't sit in the dark any longer.' She came forward. 'We've been sitting in the dark,' she explained.

'It's not a friend,' the fat man Leo said.

'Would you like coffee? A drink instead, perhaps?'

She was the perfect hostess.

'For Christ's sake,' Leo snarled. 'Don't you listen? He's not anybody. He shouldn't be here.'

He took her by the shoulder and propelled her out of the room.

'Nice lady,' Murray said. 'She reminds me of your wife.'

'That bitch,' Leo said, but not as if his heart was in it. He sat on the sofa, spilling from one cushion to the next, and held up his face wet with shameless tears. 'Why do you have to be like that? Ask your questions and leave me in peace.'

'Your brother and you depended on Blair Heathers, and that—'

'No. No way.' The fat man's cheeks quivered with the force of his denial. 'My brother didn't depend on anybody. He didn't need anybody. My brother was hard.'

Murray stared down at him reflectively. 'Seventy per cent – call it just seventy per cent – of the work your firm does is for Heathers. Take that away and you don't have a business.'

The fat man threw off glittering drops of tears and sweat as he shook his head.

'You forget,' Murray reminded him, 'I went over the books for your wife.'

'Stole them! So that shyster lawyer could get his hands on them. You cost me a fortune, you bastard.' But his heart wasn't in it.

'You shouldn't have put things in her name.'

'My brother was hard. I'm soft. What am I going to do now? He knew what to do. He knew what to do about everything . . .'

Murray regarded him with distaste. 'I'm sorry about your brother. It was a bad way to go. You want whoever killed him to be caught—'

'*Her*! Do you not read the papers? Jill the Ripper. Ripper . . . Christ!' He covered his eyes with his hand.

Murray waited, but he seemed ready to shelter behind that hand indefinitely. 'Had anything happened in the business? Something he was worrying about?'

'You say Blair sent you here?' The folds of his cheeks creased in bewilderment.

'That's right.'

'Blair's never had any complaints.'

'Maybe things have changed now your brother isn't going to be around.' Murray watched the fat man quiver. 'How about John Merchant? Your brother was tied up with him, wasn't he?'

'That was Blair's end,' the fat man said. He wiped his cheeks dry with the palms of his hands as he tried to think. 'I don't get any of this. What does Blair want?'

'He's a good citizen. He's trying to find out who killed John Merchant – and your brother.'

'All right. But where do you get off asking questions about the business?'

'It's a funny coincidence,' Murray said. 'There's a million people in this city – and Jill chooses John Merchant and your brother. And they both did business with Heathers.'

'I don't want to talk to you any more.'

'Crazy people – the ones who hear voices – kill strangers,' Murray explained. 'There isn't a reason why any of their victims should know one another.'

'They might,' the fat man said argumentatively. 'What about those guys who kill prostitutes? Don't some of those women who get killed know one another?'

'Being on the game together, that's possible. But it's not the pros who are getting killed this time – it's the clients,' Murray pointed out. 'Why should the clients know one another? Do you think there's a lodge for poor creeps who have to pay for it in Moirhill?'

'My brother . . .' Goaded, the fat man struggled to find the right words while Murray waited interestedly. 'My brother wasn't like that.'

'He didn't go with whores?'

'He didn't have to pay for it.'

'What about amateurs? Did he pick women up?'

Disdaining to reply, the fat man sneered instead.

'Maybe he had special tastes?' Murray wondered. 'He wasn't married, was he?'

'There was *nothing* wrong – not with my brother.'

216

The pain sounded real enough. As Murray studied him, the fat man tried to hold his glance until he began to weep, heavy shuddering gasps that got worse as he fought to control them.

'My brother was hard,' he sobbed, 'he crawled to nobody. What does it matter if he knew John Merchant? That old tramp didn't know John Merchant. Neither did the first guy who was killed.' He wiped at his cheeks with an oddly child-like gesture. 'I don't believe Blair sent you here.'

Murray frowned. 'The first guy? The one that was found in the lane off Deacon Street? What do you mean he didn't know Merchant? He's never been identified – they don't know who he is.'

'Oh, yes, they do. You can ask them yourself.'

'Ask who?'

'The police,' and saw something in Murray's face that made him smirk through his tears, 'they're coming here this morning. I've made a list for them – people my brother knew, friends, business, anybody I can think of. That's why they're sending someone.'

It was time to go.

Outside a car engine roared briefly and was cut off. Doors banged on either side of the silence. It did not have to be the police. At a time like this, people called, old friends, relatives, wanting to commiserate.

As the fat man had pointed out, this was a house of grief.

CHAPTER TWENTY-ONE
The Risks They Run

TUESDAY, OCTOBER 2ND

'That was cheeky.'

Detective Chief Superintendent Jackie McKellar had taken over the Jill case from Standers after the death of John Merchant. Standing in front of his desk since he had not been invited to sit down, Murray was in the process of deciding that he disliked the man intensely. He stared at the place where the scalp of the Chief Superintendent shone pink through the wispy grey hair. In the situation he found himself in, concentration on that kind of detail sometimes helped.

'The people out there have had all their leave cancelled, right? And the days off. We've got the full team here from half nine in the morning till half nine at night – and after that there's still people here. We're tired. And then we've got you.' The smart thing to do would have been to grovel, but the best Murray could manage was to keep his face expressionless. 'They tell me you were a real copper once.'

This time McKellar waited until there was an answer.

'A long time ago . . . I was in Eastern.'

'I started in that shop. Nobody ever taught me to behave like a cunt there. I hear you went to America – is that where you learned to be a cunt?'

'I went to America,' Murray agreed stolidly. Twenty years ago, because he couldn't stand yes-siring authority, he had left the police. Now he was standing in front of a desk again; it was as if he had never been away.

'I send officers to interview a witness and they find him crying.'

'When I got there, he was crying. He was fond of his brother.'

'I've got your number. You see yourself as a hard character,' McKellar said. 'You're one of the bully boys.' He made a mouth of sour disbelief. 'Who paid you to go and see Leo Arnold? And don't give me any crap about confidentiality.'

'Blair Heathers.'

McKellar blinked; he controlled everything but that twitch of the pale sandy lashes.

'He hired me after Merchant was killed. Not for anything fancy – just to check on a couple of things.'

'Things,' McKellar said by way of acknowledgement, not recording any kind of opinion. Instead of leaning forward, he settled back, studying the biro as it turned end for end between his fingers. Murray had heard enough about him to know that he was straight; but Blair Heathers' name made him cautious. Murray was impressed.

'Arnold says he's had bother with you before.'

'I'd worked for his wife.'

McKellar pulled a sheet from the pile and glanced at it. 'He's divorced.'

'This was before, at the end of last year. They'd been separated, and she'd decided to protect herself. She wanted everything in the business checked out before the settlement. It was interesting . . . that firm wouldn't have survived without the contracts Blair Heathers put their way.'

'I thought Heathers was your client,' McKellar said.

'You told me not to give you any crap about confidentiality.'

'I wonder if you're so stupid you're trying to get clever with me,' McKellar said, but he didn't sound in a hurry any more. When the interruption came, he waved to a chair by the wall. 'Sit there – till I've time for you.' And to the pot-bellied sergeant, who decided it was politic to allow himself a grin, 'This is a detective. He's going to tell us if he sees a clue.'

Murray sat while they came in and out. McKellar went away for a time in the middle. At intervals to different people, he explained that Murray was a detective. Everybody seemed to enjoy the joke. With time to think, Murray thought of other and better ways he might have handled the interview. He thought of getting up and walking out. There might be something a man of his age not trained for any trade, without professional qualifications, could find to do. After a time, instead of concentrating on what was going on, which anyway was all routine, he became obsessed by the smell of food. Because of the size of the operation, they had reopened the old school kitchen as a canteen. A smell that was warm and savoury made Murray's nostrils widen. He knew it was an illusion: the nose's equivalent of a mirage; in the canteen, if he could have gone through, there would be pies of slippery muck, dry occluded pastry, plastic puddings, sandwiches. Still his nose told him differently. Over the long wait hung the tang of stew and fresh baked loaves making his mind wander. Some detective.

'Some detective.'

'It's a living.'

'We were talking about Leo Arnold. Your story is that Blair Heathers told you to go and ask him some questions.'

'No. He didn't tell me.' There was no point in trying to make that lie stick. 'But his instructions covered it. If there was anything he should know – money worries – that kind of thing.'

McKellar looked sceptical. 'Money worries. In the middle of a murder enquiry. You picked a funny time.'

'I didn't learn anything,' and as McKellar sneered and nodded his lack of surprise at that, Murray added foolishly, 'except that he was fond of his brother.'

'How about your own brother? How do you feel about your brother?'

Murray stared back blankly. Caught off guard, he could not stir his wits to find an answer.

'Your brother knew John Merchant,' McKellar said, 'and Merchant's girlfriend.'

In search of a diversion, Murray said, 'Merchant was afraid of a man called Joe Kujavia. Have you heard of him?'

220

'Pimp. Strong-arm man. Are you telling me he had a connection with Merchant? A business connection?'

'Not business.' For Malcolm's sake, the last thing Murray wanted was any probing into Merchant's business connections. 'Back when he was a student in Poland at the beginning of the war, Merchant was put into a concentration camp . . . I can't remember its name, but I can get it for you. I took a note after Merchant told me. Kujavia was a guard there – and Merchant recognized him, even though it was so long ago. He saw him kill a young boy and he never forgot him. He could have identified Kujavia as a war criminal.'

McKellar was smiling.

'A war criminal,' he repeated, and the corners of his lips twitched and he had begun to laugh. It sounded horribly genuine, even if rusty; but then he couldn't have found much to laugh at in the last three weeks. There was even as he continued the hint of a tear in his eye. 'You're a joke, Wilson. I didn't expect you to make me laugh—'

This time, however, the interruption was a final distraction. The heavy-bellied sergeant was nodded in and laid a brown envelope on the desk in front of McKellar. He was wearing the familiar plastic gloves used to handle evidence or, even oftener, to search a drunk and disorderly or verminous down-and-out in the station. Behind him, other men came in and congregated in a half ring in front of the desk. None of them paid any attention to Murray and from where he sat he could see McKellar, his own hands gloved now, open the envelope. He slit it at the wrong end; if a tongue had been used to seal the flap, forensic might establish a blood group from the mucus. Gently squeezed and tilted, the envelope gave up a length of folded paper. As McKellar spread it open, his expression did not change, only he kept it in front of him too long, like a man committing something to memory. When he held it up, they recognized the spiky variable script that carried the signature 'Jill'. It had been addressed to him and he would take personally whatever it had contained of mockery or of

221

warning. He laid the letter in one compartment of the white plastic evidence tray and held the envelope again over another. He had to shake it more than once, turning and easing it until the little packet inside came free. The first impression was that it was red and then they saw that this colour was streaked upon a ground of white. As McKellar turned it, Murray recognized the Royal Bank logo and '£5 silver' written underneath in blue. In smaller letters at the bottom, it would carry the injunction: Re-usable bag. Do not discard.

The tray had a dozen compartments of various sizes. McKellar held the bank envelope over one of the two longer rectangular ones in the middle. The envelope had a tuck-and-gather flap and it took him a moment to unpick it. Watching, Murray could see he was not very deft with his hands. A wad of cottonwool and what it held slid out into the compartment.

It was then, remembering, or reminded by chance as he glanced up, that the Chief Superintendent told Murray, 'Get out.' And added on the next breath, 'And watch it. You're on a short rope.'

Despite which, Murray went to the canteen. There were no prime rib steaks, so he took a hot meat pie which was neither and a plastic beaker of tea. The big men overflowed the furniture, shadowing tables with their shoulders and hanging their bums over chairs like pastry waiting to be trimmed. Pale lines on the walls marked where there had been transfers of birds and animals when this had been the school dining hall. It was visiting day in wonderland.

'What the hell are you doing here?'

Murray had chosen a corner table with his back to the room. Looking up, he saw the plate and cup slide perilously on the tray between Eddy Stewart's startled hands.

'Sit down before I get that stuff in my ear.'

'No way. I don't want to be even seen anywhere near you, pal.'

'You'll get your pension, Eddy – and you're too old for a promotion!'

'They shouldn't have fed you. That shit's subsidized by the taxpayer.'

'I put on a disguise.'

'You even smell like a cop – McKellar make you sweat?'

'You knew I was with him?'

'There aren't any secrets in this place.'

'McKellar got distracted.'

'Eh?'

Murray gestured with a thumb at his crotch. 'Somebody sent him a present. All wrapped up in cottonwool.'

'Bloody hell!' Stewart said appreciatively. He glanced round and sat down. 'I heard the buzz there'd been a letter, but – So the Gaffer got a wee present from Jill? A prick for a prick.' He laughed and hefted the tray as if ready to get up again. 'He'll be as wild as hell.'

'Hold it, Eddy.'

'Make it quick. I'm nervous sitting here.'

Murray hesitated. 'John Merchant told me he'd recognized a guy as someone he'd seen before. A guard in a concentration camp. You know, like an SS man? I think the guy he was talking about was Joe Kujavia.'

'Do you tell me that?' Stewart said in a tone of respectful astonishment.

Murray studied him suspiciously. 'I decided to tell McKellar. But when I told him, he laughed.'

'Aye, well, he would, wouldn't he?' Stewart's deadpan cracked into a grin. With amusement, his face, beefy and pale from too many hours on his feet, reddened so that he looked healthy and cheerful. 'Let me tell you, Ian Peerse's father and Jackie McKellar hated one another's guts. This is a while ago – they were both inspectors – and Andrew Peerse got the same idea you've got there.'

'Where did he get it from?'

'No problem.' Stewart's grin widened. 'From the man himself. Kujavia used to boast about it. So Andrew Peerse took him seriously. He did a lot of work on it apparently. In his own time as well – bloody idiot – like father like son, eh?'

'So what happened? I haven't heard the joke yet.'

'Jackie McKellar did a bit of enquiring of his own. He traced Kujavia's first conviction. For pimping. In London. In 1939. I mean, before the bloody war at all, right? He got a lot of satisfaction out of making a cunt of Peerse. No wonder you had him laughing.'

'You'd better eat that pie,' Murray said. 'It'll be getting cold. It's all right, I'm just going.'

Stewart cut a wedge of the pie and shovelled it into his mouth. A wedge of white grease had begun to congeal round the edge of the crust. He made a face and swilled the mouthful down with tea.

'One other thing, Eddy. It'll only take a minute. Is it true they've identified the guy who was found dead off Deacon Street? The one that had the wheel over his face.'

Eddy burped, and put another wedge of pie into his mouth. Indistinctly, through it as he chewed, he said in disgust, 'For all the good it did. An old guy called Lester Rose. Worked as a book-keeper or something with MacKinlays – the engineering firm, know it? Once they could check with the dentist, there wasn't any doubt. He'd had a lot of fancy work done on his teeth.'

'No connection with John Merchant?' Murray wondered.

Stewart stared. 'Why should there be? Just a wee clerk. He wasn't anybody. They wouldn't have known who he was yet if the daughter hadn't reported him missing. She'd come all the way over from America because she'd written to him and hadn't got an answer.' He burped again. 'She was in a hell of a state apparently. She seems to have been fond of him.'

He came out of a side door into what must have been a children's playground once, and walked along by the line of trash silted against the wall. Until he got a view from the corner, he was puzzled by a thin, plaintive persistence of women's voices.

There were six of them, gathered in a line on the edge of the pavement. One was fat and four were thin; and five were young, in their early twenties perhaps, though Murray found school kids fooled him now. The last one had hair almost entirely grey with only traces of its original red. She had a lot of hair and when it was all red men must have turned to look after her in the street.

As he crossed the playground, the women started to clap their hands keeping time to his steps. It was a kids' trick, but an effective one. On the far side of the road, the usual idle group of the curious were watching. Making a fool of him seemed to be the game in favour that day.

When he came through the gate and stopped, the clapping tailed away. Close up, the younger ones didn't look all that young. The one facing him had a T-shirt with the legend: My Name's Rita not Jill. She had dyed blonde, very soft hair that fluffed up like a halo round her head. There were placards too; home-lettered; the older women held the biggest: Women's Collective Protest – and a lot of words underneath too crowded to read easily.

They stared at him uncertainly. None of the men going in and out would have stopped. It was natural, though, as Eddy Stewart had pointed out, for him to be mistaken for a policeman. He looked the part.

'Does it matter more because it's men who are being killed?' the older woman cried at him. Her face was very passionate and earnest with sincerity. 'Would you care if it was one of these girls instead of some man?'

The smart thing would have been to move away then.

'If anyone's degraded, it's not the women, it's the men,' she cried.

'You're talking rubbish,' he argued. With McKellar, he had been smart and kept quiet. 'It doesn't matter whether it's men or women. It makes no difference.'

In their excitement – and it must have been boring standing there for so long without a response – they crowded him, although the older woman shrilled, 'Don't block the pavement. We're not blocking the pavement. Don't cause an obstruction, girls.'

The blonde Rita shouted, 'A woman's got a right to self defence.'

From the babble, another one screeched, 'You're a fucking liar. All of you fucking liars. Who says a woman did it? You're protecting some fucking man!' She looked the youngest of them, a raw-boned girl with a big nose the cold wind reddened.

Self defence. Liar.

'You want to make up your minds,' Murray said helplessly.

They all wanted to make a point, and made them together. Three times in the uproar he heard the word 'degraded'.

Degraded . . . degraded . . .

And then he too was shouting and the bull roar of him knocked their mouths shut. '*Cut*. Don't you understand he was *cut*? And—'

But to his horror he might have wept.

Cut – a farmer's word. The old derelict found in the backland had been cut, libbed like a horse; worse, not gelded, but amputated. The bloody remnant poured into McKellar's tray, a toy for Forensic.

In the silence a voice said, 'You don't understand the courage of prostitutes. The risks they run every day.'

He looked and the speaker was the older woman. The mane of grey hair with its streaks of red had shaken loose around her shoulders and she seemed like a crazy Joan of Arc.

To her, as if there was no one else, he said, 'This city has the ugliest whores in the world.'

For her, too, they might have been alone for she held him with a look of hurt and shock. It was as if she were terribly disappointed. Just then a group of detectives came out of the school and stared across to the gate, and seeing them the women fell back to their previous line at the edge of the pavement.

226

CHAPTER TWENTY-TWO
A Taste of Alone

THURSDAY, OCTOBER 4TH

Even though he had left the city, it had not been difficult to trace Father Joseph Hurtle, who twenty years earlier had been a young priest in the parish of Moirhill.

The wind faltering across the square smelt of the sea and clean. There was a bank on one corner, a fountain in the middle, an hotel and two pubs, in one of which he had been given directions. 'Father Hurtle seems a decent sort of man,' the landlord had offered unasked. 'But there's not many RCs in Beaton. I don't suppose you would have found half a dozen before they built the chipboard factory. So most of them are incomers. Not that some of them haven't settled in very well. It must be a real change – out here in the country from what they're used to. We got the chipboard factory and then we got the new houses. I suppose that's what they call progress.'

He went out of the square by the bank corner and the directions were good for soon he found himself among a cross-hatch of new council housing, all the doors painted the same shade of brown and the hedges low and meagre. His destination was set on its own, across the road from the last of the houses. On the one side, it faced the sea, and on the other a low undulating landscape was blurred under a grey mist, except where on the nearest hill farm machinery, like a box of red and yellow toys, was laid out in lines as if waiting to be sold. The chapel was determinedly modern with a pleated roof like a paper aeroplane and, as he went round the side, he wondered which pleat hid the untowered bell.

From some childhood urging, the thought came into his head: I won't call him Father. Tucked on the other side of a neat stretch of lawn, there was a house which bore a cheerless resemblance to the scheme through which he had come. Before he could ring, the door was opened by a thin-faced man with a head of curly black hair and an air of being flustered. Murray saw the clerical collar and next that the man was holding up his right hand in his left, and that it was wrapped in a white cloth.

'Father Hurtle?'

'Yes, but – Did you want to see me? Yes? Would you like to come with me?'

'The thing is,' he explained, hooking the door shut with his little finger, 'I've cut myself.'

He set a nervous pace and Murray at his side made sympathetic noises.

'It's the kind of accident that's easily done. I was going to use garlic salt and I banged the container to loosen the salt. Things get damp. And the glass broke in my hand. It's quite a bad cut, as a matter of fact.'

As Murray looked, the cloth streaked with sudden red.

'If you wouldn't mind, I don't much feel like talking at the moment. Perhaps if you could—'

'That's all right. I'll walk you down to the doctor. When you're losing blood, it doesn't do any harm to have someone with you – just in case.'

'Oh, I really don't think there's any need, though it's kind of you. I'm just going in here. Not so far as the doctor. One of my parishioners who's a nurse.'

The house was identical to its neighbours. Murray accompanied him along the path as if it was the most natural thing in the world, and the priest accepted him without further protest. Perhaps he was glad of a distracting presence as he explained to the plump little woman how he had come by his injury.

'Garlic salt?' The woman shook her head. The priest rested his behind on the edge of the kitchen table as she unwound the cloth from his hand. She repeated the words as if memorializing something outlandish. Her attitude towards him was protective, touched with the incredulity one offers a child.

'Mrs Sweeney and her husband – Mary and Willie – are very good to me. I think I eat in their house more often than my own.'

'You should really get stitches in this . . . At least when you eat with us you get plain wholesome food.'

'Oh, no,' Father Hurtle said, 'not stitches surely? I don't want any fuss.'

'This will sting. I don't see . . . there's no glass . . . I don't think, no. That's okay. I have butterfly plasters somewhere . . . There we go . . . and there, and one more.' She was wearing an apron and took a roll of bandage from the pocket. As she began to bind the hand, she asked him, 'Do you know where this bandage came from?' She was very pleased with herself and mischievous. 'From the hospital. It's just a small hospital,' she explained, taking account of Murray. 'Well, eighteen geriatric beds and twelve general – heart attacks and things like that to give you a bit of variety. When one of the old people die, you tie up their ankles before the undertaker comes. And when you cut off the bandage, you pop the rest of the roll into your pocket. Then you forget and bring it home with you.' She laughed with delight. 'That's you all wrapped up in stolen bandages, Father.'

But, with a change of mood as they were leaving, she asked him, 'Did you go on Saturday, Father?' She shook her head more in sorrow than anger. 'And wasn't Willie right? Didn't you find yourself being made a fool of by a lot of Communists?'

'They're building a nuclear power station along the coast,' Father Hurtle said, glancing at Murray as they retraced their steps.

'What was happening on Saturday? Some kind of protest demonstration?'

'I hadn't realized the place was so large. They'd hidden it behind a great rampart of earth so that you couldn't see

229

it from the road. I simply hadn't realized.' He sighed, and turned his head as they passed the last of the houses to look at the sea. A white haar was rolling in towards the shore. 'Isn't it strange that we can't vote on what really matters? All those young people on Saturday marching and singing – it won't make any difference. In the evening, I saw them straggling away over the fields like an army in retreat. No country has ever held a vote before it declared war.'

'Did you get anyone to go with you?'

'Two ladies,' Father Hurtle said.

In the presbytery, he offered tea and, as he sipped the delicate fragrant liquid, some of the colour began to come back into his cheeks.

Murray tapped his tongue softly against his palate. 'Lapsang souchow,' he decided appreciatively.

'You know your tea!' The priest was excessively pleased, as if he had been prepared to apologize: and indeed hurried on, 'I don't usually offer it to – I felt the need of it just now. Most people prefer something more familiar, so I don't offer it. I keep it to myself – not selfishness, just that I know it wouldn't be enjoyed. It's my tipple.'

'Mine too.'

'Ah, you live alone.'

Some unexpected acknowledgement not to be admitted passed between the two men. They drank in silence, by accident raising the cup to their lips and putting it down again in unison.

'How can I help you?'

'I'm not a Catholic.'

'No.'

'I'm a private enquiry agent. I've been hired to trace the whereabouts of two children you helped to an adoption – this would be about twenty years ago. It was when you were in Moirhill . . . The mother was murdered.'

'Annette Verhaeren.' The name came without hesitation. That puzzled Murray. It was twenty years ago, and yet the reaction had been immediate. 'I can't help you.'

'It would be to the children's benefit.' Murray offered

the cover story he had devised. 'I've been hired by a relative of the mother. There would be money in it for them, if they could be found.'

'I hope you don't understand what you're trying to do,' Father Hurtle said. 'Surely if I explain it to you, you will give up this thing. Let her children alone. What would you tell them? It's my prayer they have no idea now who their mother was.'

'Have you any right to decide for them?' Murray asked quietly. 'Don't tell me you've never heard of adopted children wanting to find that out.'

'I can tell you about their mother,' the priest said. 'Oh I haven't forgotten. She was born in Belgium, and during the war – she must have been very young – sixteen perhaps – a German soldier fell in love with her and somehow got her to his parents in Bavaria. He was sent to the Eastern Front for his pains and died somewhere in that confusion. Working all the daylight hours, she was trapped on a farm with his parents who hated her. I was her priest, you see, and she told me these things.' Closing his eyes, he rubbed his forehead as if he was suddenly tired. The fingers were long and thin; like the man himself, to Murray they seemed fragile, as if they might be too easily broken. 'A British soldier rescued her from that – and married her. The marriage lasted on and off for years and it's possible he was the father of the older girl. When I wrote to him . . . afterwards, after her death, he sent me a letter saying he knew nothing about the kind of life she had been living. He was remarried and had begun a second family. He wanted to have nothing to do with the children. You couldn't blame him.'

'Everybody deserves to be remembered,' Murray said. 'Why shouldn't her children learn about Annette Verhaeren?'

'Do you know where they found her body?' Father Hurtle asked. 'Have you ever lived in a tenement in a place like Moirhill?'

Murray nodded.

'Do you remember the open stone sheds in the common

yard at the back of those tenements, the ones they use for storing bins of rubbish? The body was clothed, but the buttons were crammed into the wrong holes – the garments were put on clumsily. The police said she had been beaten when she was naked. They could tell it had been done with a bar of metal – wood would have splintered in her flesh, you see. If it had been started methodically, it ended in a kind of frenzy. Her body was a bag of broken bones. It was summer and the refuse men were on strike. She was found among the stinking rubbish that had spilled over from the open bins.'

After a moment's silence, Murray sipped at his tea, but it had gone cold.

'You know I can find them without your help,' he said. 'Coming to you is just one way of doing it.'

Further Hurtle got to his feet slowly, as if his body were a burden. 'I'm going for a walk along the beach.'

'Would you mind if I kept you company?'

'No.' Unexpectedly, he smiled. 'But I won't change my mind.'

They picked their way down the slope to the shore. The mist was now hiding most of the sea. Their feet sank into the white sand where the wind had gathered it at the beginning of the beach.

'I am sorry you have made your journey for nothing,' the priest said.

By common consent, they started across the sand to the water's edge. A glance at the priest labouring by his side forced on Murray the unwanted resemblance to Billy Shanks: not just that they were both above average height, both too thin, but something in them flayed and vulnerable; and it was this quality in Father Hurtle which made Murray recognize it as being in Billy too, for it was more evident in the priest, as if he had gone further along a road the two men were to share. When he stopped by the water, Father Hurtle drifted two or three paces apart. The little waves shushing into the sand at their feet made an enclosing and private sound.

'I don't like to remember that time.' The priest's voice came faintly, a white thread almost lost in the sea's noise. The mist was all round them now, and from the far hidden end of the beach there was a sound of children calling. Father Hurtle turned his head towards the sound. 'They're playing truant.' Still looking away, he said, 'I wasn't a success in Moirhill. There was so much unhappiness. If you are ill, you want the surgeon to cut with a steady hand. You want help, not pity. I was full of pity.' Turning his back on the sea, he pointed, seeming in no doubt of the direction although the haar had swallowed the last of the landmarks. 'Over that way is where Duns Scotus was born. I think of that when I'm walking among the new houses here.'

He moved off so abruptly that Murray was taken by surprise. Hurrying in the mist, he strayed on to low rocks covered in tar-coloured seaweed that slithered underfoot. The first slip taking him by surprise shook him, so that he picked his way uncertain of his balance and by the time he caught up Father Hurtle was already seated on one of a litter of concrete slabs, the collapsed remnants of defences against an invasion. The half circle of children listening to him had something odd in their expressions, something careful, wary, a little blank and cautious.

'. . . When I was a boy at school that was the word we used when someone told tales to the masters. I was just the same as the other boys, I hated a fellow like that.' To Murray, it was strange that the priest's voice had altered into exactly the timbre of the minister's sermons he had been forced to listen to as a child. 'For if you gave in, you know, the masters hated you for it, whatever they said, and just as much as the boys. Don't ever by a clype.'

The children's eyes shifted beyond the priest to question Murray, and with a noiseless gesture like a man shooing geese he urged them away. Released, they scattered and one boy at a safe distance muddled all he had felt into a single cry of animal defiance. At the sound, the priest startled in fright and then at Murray, as if he had forgotten who this man was taking the place beside him on the concrete bench.

'I can't remember the name of the older girl,' he said. 'Poor Annette named her after her own mother. The younger child was called Urszula.'

'Was she named after anyone?'

'It's a Polish name.'

They sat in silence. The children were gone, leaving not even a lingering echo in the mist. It was very quiet; Murray waited for the other man to speak; he was good at waiting. From somewhere on the point behind them a foghorn began a melancholy lowing.

'Not that the names will do you any good,' Father Hurtle said.

'The people who adopted them gave them other names – to make them seem their own.'

'More paper work. When you're tracing someone, that helps.'

'I was poor Annette's priest,' Father Hurtle said. 'Do you think I didn't know who had killed her? I knew his name and his face – filth and cruelty. He was her pimp.' Whispering, he leaned closer. 'He beat her with a bar of iron. But afterwards I saw him walking the streets of Moirhill. They said he had been out of the city when it happened. They said he had some kind of protection. No God, no justice. I thought he was under the protection of Satan. But I was ill . . . when I believed that. I had to leave the city, you see, because I was ill.' Murray felt the warmth of his breath, and perhaps he leaned away for the priest drew back and then got to his feet. 'I can't help resenting that you came here,' he said.

—I'm sorry: that should have been easy to say: but Murray sat silent watching him go, a black stripe like a branchless tree, until he lost form in the mist.

CHAPTER TWENTY-THREE
Jill

SATURDAY, OCTOBER 6TH

It was parked on a double yellow line, but Murray had remarked before that the bigger the car the less chance of a parking ticket in this city. He recognized the chauffeur, sitting in a familiar pose with his head tilted forward as if reading a book, and ran up the stairs expecting to find Heathers at the door of the flat or on his way back down. The door of the flat was unlocked as he had left it, not wanting to give Irene an excuse for going away again if she did come; and so, even inside, he still thought he would find him waiting. He walked from the back room and through the lobby to the room he used as an office. Puzzled, he went to the window and inclined his head trying to see if the car was still there. Behind him there came a deferential double knock and a discreet clearing of the throat.

'I hope I didn't give you a fright, sir. The door was open, sir.'

Out of the car, the chauffeur was smaller than he had looked at the wheel. The uniform was cut to emphasize the breadth of his shoulders, but it could do nothing about the shortness of his legs. Cap in hand, he fitted anybody's idea of a servant.

'I didn't think, sir, you'd mind me coming in, sir?' The tough nasal Moirhill drawl sounded to Murray uncannily like Blair Heathers' tone.

'Where's your boss?'

'Oh, he wouldn't be here himself, sir. He's a busy man. He wanted you to get this, though, right away, sir.' The little respectful word, gargled far back in his throat as 'sur', was being repeated too often. He held the envelope but did not come forward, making Murray cross the room to take it from him.

There was a single sheet of paper inside:

Following our discussion of 14 September, an arrangement was made. That arrangement is terminated.

'It isn't signed,' Murray said.

'The thing is you've been making a nuisance of yourself. Going to see the wrong people, sir. At the wrong time, like. A time of grief, sir.'

All round, visiting Leo was turning out to have been a mistake.

He spread the envelope with two fingers and looked inside. 'Where's the cheque?'

'There's a complaint from the bereaved. And then the police lifted you, and you shot off your mouth to them. It really wasn't what was wanted, sir.'

'You're quite a talker yourself,' Murray said quietly. 'Tell your boss I expect to get paid up till this date. I'll send him a note of my expenses.'

The chauffeur looked at him wisely. 'You do that,' he said. 'Only I've a feeling Mr Heathers has told the police you weren't working for him at all. I can't see him bunging you any more money . . . sir.' And the grin that had been struggling to escape from the start, came out as he retreated.

It wasn't a conscious decision to go after him. Lightly, as if carried, his body went forward on a reflex of anger so fast that the chauffeur reaching to open the outer door had no chance to defend himself. He caught the man by the back of the neck and lifting him like a doll ground his mouth and nose against the boards nailed across the broken panels.

At his desk, he took a bundle of bills out of their clip and spread them out. Staring at them with unseeing eyes, he kept hearing the sound of feet stumbling away down the stone flights. Nobody owned him. Without anybody's help,

236

he had stopped himself drinking. Among men who cursed as casually as breathing, he made a fetish of being clean-mouthed. Above all, he had learned to control his temper. Lose that . . .

When he looked up, there was no way of telling how long Irene had been watching him.

'You should have a fire on in here,' she said. 'It's cold outside and it's getting dark.'

He put on the lamp on the desk, but because its light was focussed downward and fell between them it made it harder to see her.

'It's an office,' he said. 'We can go into the other room.'

'It's not any better. Unwashed dishes. A child's game on the table. You don't make yourself comfortable.'

'Chess.'

'What?'

'It doesn't matter.'

She came forward and took the seat on the other side of the desk. It was the place where clients sat, people who came to him because they were in trouble, and it seemed strange to see her there.

'Here I am,' she said. 'But I don't know why. Couldn't whatever it is have waited until tomorrow at Mum Wilson's?'

'I expected you yesterday.'

'I told you when you phoned I'd come if I could manage. There wasn't time yesterday. And we'll be at Mum Wilson's tomorrow.'

'I waited here for you all day,' he said.

She crossed her legs in the circle of light that fell from the lamp. 'Shouldn't you have been working? I thought you'd be out working on the murders. I thought you might be going to tell me what you'd found out.'

'I don't work for Heathers any more. He sent someone to tell me I was fired.'

'Nothing to tell then. No solutions. I'm sorry.'

'I've been fired before. Heathers today. Somebody else yesterday.'

Bittern, in the morning, phoning to tell him he was off

the Foley case – 'lack of any visible progress'. Even when he had tried to tell the lawyer about the letter from Mrs Beddowes the stubborn old man had paid no attention.

'Being fired twice in one week,' Irene said, 'you must feel terrible.'

'I've no complaints. I was hired to find a guy who'd run off with his partner's wife – and the profits. I got too involved with other things even to try.'

Reaching up, he re-angled the lamp, turning it towards her face. With an intimate unselfconscious movement, she tidied her hair, raising her elbows and using both hands to smooth it into place. He had never noticed how black her hair was; coarse black hair, thick and glossy like a peasant's; if you ran your hand over it, you would feel it crackle with life under your palm. Almost you would be frightened to stroke hair like that. Undiscomposed, she looked with wide and candid eyes into the light.

'Other things?'

'I got interested in a woman called Annette Verhaeren.'

Had he startled her? With that light on her face she could hide nothing. He was sure he had, and then she looked at him so candidly he was not sure at all.

'Annette . . .?'

'Verhaeren. Just a whore. She got herself beaten to death by her pimp. He used an iron bar on her and then dumped the body in a back-court midden among the rubbish.'

'The rest of the rubbish.'

He did not understand.

'That's what you make it sound like – as if you were saying, "among the rest of the rubbish".'

He nodded slowly. 'Does that bother you?'

'Oh, Murray,' she might have been irritated, but then she was laughing, a glittering sound. 'You never say "fuck". Malcolm says it all the time – well, except at Mum Wilson's, of course. I sometimes can't believe you two are brothers.'

'That happens,' Murray said. 'You could have two sisters who were very different from one another.' He could not stop watching her mouth, which was full with just the

238

smallest hint of the pressure of her teeth behind the upper lip. He looked at her lips which had shaped the word 'fuck' and spoken it to him. 'That was something else I found out about Annette Verhaeren. She had two children.'

'Sisters.'

'Half sisters. I think they each had a different father.'

'Well, then,' Irene said, 'you wouldn't expect them to be very like one another.'

'That's what I'm hoping.'

He expected her to ask why, but instead she said, 'What happened to them – after their mother was killed?'

'I'm still finding that out.'

'Maybe they're dead.'

'No I don't think so.' He leaned forward, resting his forearms on the desk. 'The younger one was called Urszula – but the people who adopted her changed her name. She'll be a woman now.'

'How did you find out about her?'

'That's my job,' he said. 'I traced the priest who worked in Moirhill then.'

'And he told you where they went when they were adopted.'

Murray shook his head. 'He wouldn't do that.'

'Why not?'

'He feels they should be left alone. If they've forgotten, he wouldn't want them to be reminded.'

'Well, that's why they were adopted in the first place, wasn't it?' she exclaimed. She sounded again simply impatient. 'Their mother dying in that horrible way – you wouldn't want them reminded of it – why would you want to?'

It was darker now, but since she in her turn had leaned forward he had the sense of them as bound closer in the circle of light. If he had wanted to, he could have stretched out and touched the soft pads of her lips. 'I don't think she's forgotten,' he said, quietly as if working it out for himself, in the husky intimate whisper a man uses to the woman by his side before sleeping. 'I think she came back with her

239

sister, and they've been looking for the man who killed their mother.' The outside bell rang and rang again. With a startled movement, furtively small as if between conspirators, he motioned her to ignore it. 'Unless you know how, though, it's not easy to trace someone in a city. That's the job I do – even without Father Hurtle's help, I could find the place they were sent to be adopted. But for them, that kind of thing would be hard. I'm sure they haven't found the man – but, by this time, he'll know that they're looking.'

The bell rang again and her eyes widened staring at him, and then she had stood up, out of the light, and was walking to the door.

When she came back, she put on the overhead light and all the shadows retreated to the corners. Blinking, it took him a moment to recognize the woman she had brought into the room.

'There doesn't seem to be anybody else to care,' Mrs Beddowes said.

She was in her middle forties and her figure was good, but there was something that made it seem as if she would have been happy under other circumstances to let it go a little. Inside her there was a comfortable woman, a mothering woman, constrained. When he had interviewed her, he had been surprised by her lack of bitterness. It was true she and her husband were separated, but she still had an interest in the business which she had helped him to build up; and now, just as much as the partner Foley, was left looking at an emptied bank account and a list of creditors.

She said, staring in front of the desk, 'I know where he is. She's left him.'

'Mrs Foley you mean?'

'She didn't stay with him. I never expected her to. And now he's on his own.'

Belatedly, he got to his feet. 'I'm not involved any more. Your lawyer's taken me off the case.'

'There doesn't seem to be anybody else to care,' she said again. She looked at Irene as if in search of support. 'He's there on his own.'

240

'How did you find him?' Murray asked.

'He phoned me.' And looked again at the other woman as if for understanding of the obvious: what else would he do? 'From an hotel – in Oliver Street. I know where it is, I can take you there. They took a room and stayed there under a different name.' She put a hand to her cheek in distress. 'I can't remember. He told me, but— The room number is 12a. Room 12a. They were pretending to be husband and wife, only now she's left. He wanted me to come.'

Automatically, Murray had noted on the scratch pad the name of the street and the number of the room. Round the two he added a box of broken lines. 'Are you afraid of him?'

'No.'

'What is it then? Do you want me to make him tell what he's done with the money?'

'It isn't anything like that.'

As she struggled to find words to explain, she turned again to share what she felt with the other woman. Murray was struck by a curious blank intentness with which Irene was watching; it didn't seem as if she was conscious of the appeal which was being made to her, but he could not tell what she was thinking. Like a stone in a stream rubbed and fretted smooth, the human face had learned from the enmity of its kind to hide what it felt.

'He may kill himself,' Mrs Beddowes said. 'I don't want to go by myself into an hotel room and find him dead.'

'You don't give me any choice,' Murray said, looking not at her but Irene.

'I'll pay you.' She sounded timid, as if the relief was so great she could not believe he was not about to change his mind.

'We have that other piece of business still to finish,' he said to Irene.

To his astonishment, she came forward and put her arm through Mrs Beddowes'.

'That's all right. I'll come too. Perhaps I can help.'

There was a grass strip alongside the pavement and he crossed that to get to the access road for the terrace. The first house showed a brass plate incised with the name of four different businesses, next door was a doctor's, and then came two hotels side by side. The second was the one she had pointed out to him.

At first, he thought the front door was locked. The upper panel of tinted glass gave no view of what lay inside. As he looked for some kind of bell, he tried the handle again, twisting it the wrong way this time. The door opened on to an unexpectedly spacious hall. At the entry there was a letter board, empty except for a bill filed under M – N. No one was in the hall or behind the reception desk. There was a lot of dark varnished wood and he caught a lingering smell of cat. In the registration ledger open on the desk, he found that the last entry was for room 12a; it had been taken the day before by a James Belford. That was close enough; giving a false name, for most people it was going to be Smith or one that resembled the sound of their own.

He climbed the stairs quietly and fast. The place was so deserted there was the uneasy sense of violating a private house. There was nothing public about the feel of the dark hall or the stairway. He went up as alertly as a burglar.

On the upper floor, he was faced by a door labelled Residents Lounge and glimpsed drawn curtains and chairs like islands in the dim light. To his right there was a short flight of steps and what looked like a dining room. He turned the other way along the corridor and almost at the end of it found 12a.

At his knock, a voice called, 'Myra?'

Murray knocked again, waited, called back: 'Mr Beddowes? I'm here from your wife.'

His voice echoed in the corridor; he looked both ways, but no one appeared. All the doors stayed shut. He rapped with his knuckles and listened. Room 12a gave nothing away. He had a sudden idea the man he had been paid to find was standing just the other side of the closed door, holding his breath he was so afraid of being heard.

'Mr Beddowes?' He put his mouth close against the panel. It was as if he was whispering into the man's ear. 'Your wife is outside. She came, just like you asked her. But she wants you to see me first.'

'Why?'

'I don't know why she doesn't want to talk to you first, Mr Beddowes. You're the one who must know that.'

There was a long pause, so long he was getting ready to try again, when the man inside asked, 'Who are you? I don't know your voice.'

'My name is Murray Wilson. I'm an enquiry agent. Your wife came to me.'

'I don't believe you. Jimmy sent you. Is he out there with you?'

Murray tried to remember what the partner of Foley's first name was.

'Are you there? What are you doing?'

The voice rose in fright.

'I don't have anything to do with Jimmy whoever-he-is. Your wife came to see me. You phoned her because you needed help.' He kept it flowing with the insistent reasonableness you would use on a child. 'That's how I knew you were here. How else would I know? You do need help, don't you?'

The silence from behind the door ached. Barely loud enough, so that he had to strain to hear, the voice said, 'Jimmy's threatened to hurt me.'

Quickly, Murray worked out that the room must face out to the front. 'Forget Jimmy. Believe your own eyes. Go and look out of the window. You know your wife's car? It's parked across the street.'

It was back then to waiting. Even if he saw his wife standing by the car, Beddowes might still decide it was all a trap. Her concern for him, the adulterer and thief, was a woman's miracle.

With a tinny rattle, the lock released and, under nothing more than the impetus of its own weight, the door eased back. Murray stepped inside and pushed it shut again with a hand behind him.

A pale man in pyjamas slumped on the near side of the

bed. His head was bowed and he peered up without raising it, giving him the look of a turtle trying to retract into its shell. Thick black hair covered his forearms and showed between the unbuttoned jacket.

'Go and tell her to come up.'

'I can ask her. But you'll have to answer some questions first.'

'I want to see Myra.'

'What about Mrs Foley? Where is she?'

'In hell.'

The hair on Murray's neck bristled.

'In hell, for all I care.'

'She didn't come here with you yesterday?'

'She was never with me. I have to speak to Myra. I don't want to be on my own.'

The tone of self-pity set Murray's teeth on edge. 'Before you came here – where were you staying? In another hotel? Is Mrs Foley still there?'

'I don't know where she is.' He pulled the halves of the pyjama jacket together and held them shut. 'When I woke up, she'd gone.'

'With the money?'

'Money?'

He looked bemused.

'The money that belongs to Jimmy Foley. Jimmy has the funny idea he needs it to pay the creditors – otherwise he goes bankrupt.'

'Myra didn't talk to you about money,' Beddowes said with an absolute conviction. 'You're working for Jimmy.' He didn't move, but the cords on his neck came out again and this time it looked as if he might get his head to disappear.

'All right,' Murray said. 'Let's talk about your wife's share of the money. Did it go with Mrs Foley when she went?'

Beddowes slid along the edge of the bed and fished up his jacket from a tangle of trousers, shirt and soiled underpants. He held out his wallet. At the invitation, Murray moved away from his position by the door and took it from him with no more than the caution he kept as a habit

244

from so many confrontations. There was a ten-pound note and a five folded in half and in another compartment four singles.

'She left me my credit cards,' Beddowes said. 'So I won't starve.'

Murray flicked the wallet so that it fell on the bed. At the movement, Beddowes ducked as if expecting a blow.

'There are a few people I'd feel sorry for before I got round to you.'

Behind him, there came a light insistent tapping. A woman's voice called from the corridor.

'It's Myra,' Beddowes said. His face sweetened with relief; the cavalry had come over the hill. Looking at him, Murray shook his head in disbelief.

'I saw him at the window,' Mrs Beddowes said. 'Let me talk to him.'

He closed the door on the happy couple and walked slowly back along the corridor. As he went, he thought about what he would say to Irene, but when he crossed the street her car, which was parked behind Mrs Beddowes', was empty. He could not understand it; almost at a run he went to the corner and then walked back, looking into the shops as he passed.

The hall of the hotel was still deserted. He circled impatiently until he found a public phone tucked in the darkest corner under the stair.

'Mr Bittern's still at dinner. We have guests.' It was a querulous female version of the lawyer's voice; there was even the familiar bleat on the vowels – 'gu-ests'. 'He doesn't take business calls in the evening.'

Persuaded to come to the phone, Bittern sounded unwelcoming.

'I have something Foley might be interested in hearing.'

'You're off that enquiry. I made that perfectly clear.'

'I think he might want me back on it again.'

'I would regard that as irregular, highly irregular.' The successive 'eh's' lengthened like a sheep giving warning.

'I know where to find Beddowes.'

'. . . Oh, yes.'

'My information is that Mrs Foley has left him and taken the money with her.'

'That would be unfortunate.'

'I can find out from Beddowes where they were a couple of days ago. That should give me a chance of finding her.'

'Why should Mr Beddowes co-operate?'

'What else can he do? I'll tell him if we get the money back the business can still be saved for all of them. He's afraid of Foley – but then he doesn't know how often the husband takes it out on his wife instead of the other man. I can persuade him.'

Bittern was non-committal, but climbing the stair he felt as if he might be back in business. He decided to give Mrs Beddowes more time with her husband and pushed open the door of the Residents Lounge from which he could keep an eye on the landing. It was dark inside and he felt on the wall for a light switch. He touched only the rippled surface of a heavy paper, but instantly a standard lamp beside one of the chairs came on.

'Didn't you hear me call?' Irene asked. 'I watched you going down the stairs.'

'Why are you sitting in the dark?'

The question came out too emphatically. There was something about the suddenness of her appearance which he felt as uncanny. More startled than he wanted her to see, he took a deep breath and tried to slow the beating of his heart.

'I was thinking,' she said. She was curled with her legs under her into a corner of the big chair, and he noticed how its leather had dried and begun to split. 'Malcolm's told me you'd killed a man once.'

He shook his head.

'Oh, yes,' she said. 'In America.'

He sat opposite her. An ashtray was balanced on the arm and he put it on the floor beside the chair. The mash of stubs in it surprised him; it was hard to imagine a Resident venturing in here where the chairs kept their distance in the underwater light. Perhaps it had been Beddowes, tired

246

of lying on his bed staring at the ceiling, who had sat here smoking last night. Whatever happens, I did him a favour, Murray thought; but it was like a verdict on someone he did not expect to see again.

'You know I think Frances Fernie is your sister,' he said.

'And do you agree with your friend Peerse? Do you think she was the one who killed John Merchant?' She spoke quietly, sounding almost indifferent as if the problem was his and he had asked for help. 'Does that make her Jill? What does it make me?'

'You're not like her.' She was his sister-in-law, who sat with them on Sundays at Mother's table. 'Your lives are different.'

'She was a prostitute in London, did you know that? After the woman died—'

'The woman?'

'The one she stayed with.'

'The woman who adopted you both?'

'Yes. After that, she met this man and lived with him in London. It was all right at first, but then he asked her to oblige his friends. She told me that's how he described it. And she did – if she'd obliged them any more they'd have had to invent another opening . . . That's what she said to me.'

He got up and came close to her, standing over her. She stared up, waiting, but he could find nothing to say. What he felt was irrational – that she felt she could say anything to him, as if he was without sexuality. I'm a man!; but his rage was too confused and humiliating.

'That was the life *she* was leading,' Irene said. He watched the movement of her lips. 'But I was a secretary. I don't mean in the typing pool. I was a private secretary to one of the directors. I had started with nothing but I got qualifications. I taught myself how to talk and to dress. Nobody did anything for me.'

'But you knew about Frances.'

'Oh. Oh, no.' She sounded eager to make him understand. 'One day in my lunch hour, I saw this girl and recognized her. It was just by accident.'

On a station platform, in a restaurant, people could meet by chance. It was possible to believe her; and that, given the smallest change of circumstance, she and her sister might not have met again.

'I married Malcolm and he brought me here. She came after us. I wasn't to know she was looking for this man who killed her mother.'

'Your mother too.'

'The detective,' she said. 'Oh, you're the one who knows.'

Elsewhere, like a signal from the hotel's hidden life, a door banged shut. Startled, he glanced towards the landing, but no one appeared. Beddowes presumably was still being comforted by the wife who had been given some reason to separate from him even before he stole from her. The look on his face when he had heard her voice: It's Myra. Myra.

A snatch of music from a radio ended with the closing of another door.

'There are a lot of things I don't know about,' Murray said.

'Like whether it's really Frances who has done all these murders?'

'It's possible.'

'You think she would have killed John Merchant? And those other men? You think she could have done all those terrible things to them? But if it was her, wouldn't she do it again? Kill someone?'

And, of course, he wasn't sure. How could he be, remembering the submissiveness of a woman watching as he threw her possessions scattered on to the floor?

'It's possible,' he said stubbornly.

'Malcolm's with her.' Irene reached out and touched his hand. 'She phoned this afternoon and he told her he would come. He's been with her all this time.'

CHAPTER TWENTY-FOUR
Blood on a Mirror

SATURDAY, OCTOBER 6TH –
SUNDAY, OCTOBER 7TH

After they had waited for a time without an answer, Irene produced a key. She saw him look at it, but said nothing; if it was a challenge, this was not its time.

From the first, the flat felt wrong to him, even before they put on the lights and went from that room along the passage to find the bedroom empty. The bed was disturbed, but there was no way of telling if it had been used or left unmade from the previous night.

'They may have gone out somewhere,' she said.

'Where?'

As a couple, Malcolm and Frances Fernie had no right to exist outside this flat. They were only bodies that came together. One of the pillows was dragged half-way down the frozen wound of the bed; a woman might have done that, gathering it under her to raise her buttocks. He looked up and met Irene's eyes.

'It seems,' she said, 'as if we have the place to ourselves.'

The bathroom was empty, which was only what he had expected; but as he turned to go out, he caught sight of his face in the round mirror. Across his nose and cheeks, there was a stain like a tribal scarring. He put on the flourescent strip around it to see better, but there was only the single mark like a smeared handprint. It was in the front room beside one of the chairs that he found a dark circle of spots.

'He'd been hurt and fell here or bent forward.'

He sought out with his finger for her each separate indication.

'He?'

'There's blood in there too. On the mirror in the bathroom.'

'But she wouldn't hurt him,' Irene said. 'And neither of them are here.'

'He's been hurt.' He saw Malcolm's face in the mirror tattooed with blood. He kept his voice steady, but at the last word he felt a pulse shake his right eyelid as if a shock had been carried into his whole system.

'What about Frances then? What are we going to do?' she asked.

He was paralysed by the impossibility of telling Mother that Malcolm was dead.

'We can't stay here,' he heard her saying.

He could not decide. In a crisis, when other people panicked, he had always been able to act. Now in the nightmare he could not decide.

'Your friend Eddy Stewart would be able to find out if anything's happened to them,' she said.

'Eddy?' He stared at her stupidly.

'You know where he lives, don't you?'

He nodded.

'We'll go there then.'

Sitting beside her in the car as she drove, he said, 'When I was a boy my father would say to me I had hands like shovels. You'll never be a gentleman with hands like that, he said to me. I went back to the house for his funeral when I was sixteen. Malcolm was just a baby and I had never seen him, so I went into the bedroom and picked him up. He was all wrapped up in white and he jumped in my arms like a fish. I dropped him.'

Gaping at the doorway in terror then, he had seen the figure of judgement.

—Oh, Mother, I've killed the baby.

When Lynda Stewart had been a kid who laughed easily,

250

with long blonde hair that wasn't washed often enough, skirts had been worn long and over the months her growing belly had gradually raised them at the front. After seven months of pregnancy, Eddy Stewart had married her and as things went in Moirhill that was luck.

'I didn't come from Florence Street,' Lynda said.

They were waiting for Eddy to come home.

'Carnation Street,' Murray remembered. 'It was Eddy – and Billy Shanks, of course, who came from Florence Street. Just round the corner.'

Back then, rather than watch her marrying someone else, Murray had chosen to go away and leave the city, so there had been luck in it for him too, though no way of being sure which kind.

'Different. It was different!' Even in her sudden animation, she was careful to keep the left side of her face angled from them. She had taken a chair with its back to the light, which made no difference since when she opened the door they had seen the black eye and the ugly bruise on her cheek. Pride was a strange thing. 'Don't compare it to Florence Street. My mother would shout at us – if we did something dirty when we were wee – "They wouldn't do that even in Florence Street." They were right rough in Florence Street.'

She seemed to have finished, and Murray was about to say something, when she burst out, 'They were *rubbish* in Florence Street.'

From somewhere upstairs, plaintive and discordant, noise skirled female like a wounded cat. With an inarticulate cry, Murray leaped to his feet.

'It's Sally,' Lynda Stewart stared in fright. 'It's just Sally.'

Sally . . . He turned in a kind of bewilderment from her to Irene. He remembered Eddy Stewart with his face sagging in pouches of self-pity, complaining about his marriage: 'Sally – a magic wee kid . . .'

'Sally,' he said and sat down again, ashamed. 'According to Eddy, she's a daddy's girl.'

251

'She's bothered with nightmares,' Lynda said.

As if suddenly too tired to pretend, she lay back in the chair; like that she looked younger. He stared at her breasts and at the way the nightgown fell between her thighs and at the dull flare of the bruise on her cheek.

'I went to the Marriage Guidance and said I couldn't stick it any more,' she said dully. 'The stupid bitch asked me if I wouldn't be lonely. I told her I'd had practice . . . It's bad enough when they're in uniform, but once they're in plainclothes you've no life at all. He was never here for the kids – not even when they were ill. And when he was here – you watch a policeman's children – they all expect the third degree, they're used to it, that's the way they get treated at home. He made Jenny feel as if she was a prostitute until she walked out. Peter wouldn't have joined the army if it hadn't been for him.' She got up and went behind him so that he had to twist around to see that she was opening a drawer of the sideboard. Beyond her, he saw Stewart in the doorway. 'Peter wrote to me,' she said, searching.

'Postcard,' Stewart said, pointing his finger at her, 'because your big son is too fucking idle to write a letter.'

He had been drinking and wasn't carrying it as well as usual; or maybe he had come to the point Murray had seen in other hard drinkers when all the bottles over the years started to catch up.

'Has that bitch been crying on your shoulder?' he asked.

But it was Irene who explained and persuaded him to come with them out of there, and, following the two of them through the hall, it was Murray who glanced up and saw the white triangle of a sick child's face watching them from the landing. Little Sally had got out of bed to see what was happening.

'The world's gone fucking mad.' Eddy Stewart pushed up his cheeks with both hands as if he could squeeze out tiredness like water from a sponge. 'Why the hell should anything happen to your brother?'

Murray, who had taken over the driving, was conscious

of Irene in the seat behind him. It was as if she was a prisoner; as if he had never left the police force and his old partner Eddy and he were taking in a prisoner; as if everything in his life had been different and he would not have to tell the old lady her son was dead.

'Your brother should have stayed in his own bed,' Eddy grumbled.

In the last hour before midnight, Moirhill Road was busy with cars; groups of young men spilled off the pavements; there were girls still walking home alone. He swung in where the side streets curved into ambushes of darkness. Outside the school, they stopped and Eddy Stewart got out. Busy with their own thoughts, they waited for him to return with whatever he had discovered. Murray wiped steam from the window in an arc using the edge of his palm. Just here, he had been shirricked by the group of women demonstrators: *Women don't kill!* And the tall one with the wild grey hair, like a crazy family doctor, eyes wide and shining: *Jill uses violence to make you face the truth!*

Make up your minds, he should have said.

The track he had wiped in the steam was filling with a haze of tiny pearls of moisture. Dimly he made out a figure crossing the yard.

'Let me speak to him.'

But when he got out, it was not Stewart but Peerse erect and reproachful who strode through the gate.

'The man was off duty, but you brought him back.' Peerse gave what passed with him for a smile. 'That's what happens on this kind of enquiry. Conscientious officers do more than anyone could ask of them.'

'Is there any news of my brother?'

Peerse bent to peer into the car. 'That's your brother's wife in there? Take her home.'

As he straightened, Murray grabbed him by the upper arm. It was so thin his hand closed around it. 'Tell me. Has something happened, you bastard?'

Above his head, Peerse said, 'I'll deal with this.' Grouped in the gate behind him, three plainclothes men, beefy, crumple-faced and scruffy, hovered uneasily. A yellow carpet of light spilled from the side door of the school they had neglected to close as they left. Murray let his hand fall to his side. The nearest of them farted, muttered 'pardon' into the silence, and then under Peerse's stare they broke and moved off, bulkily unconcerned.

'Take her home,' Peerse said, speaking even more quietly than before. 'Her husband could be sitting at home wondering where she is. I'll send a car after you to check it isn't a false alarm. Meanwhile, I'll go and have a look at the Fernie flat for myself.'

'There's blood on the floor in the front room – and in the bathroom – on the mirror.'

'Your brother should have paid heed,' Peerse said. 'I warned him about the woman Fernie the day I came to your mother's house.' Perhaps despite himself, his voice was full of anticipation. 'If she has harmed him, she's made a big mistake.'

As Irene got out of the car, she must have heard only the last words for she said, 'Is it all right?'

'You've to go home,' Peerse said. 'I'll be along later to ask you some questions.'

'He doesn't know anything,' Murray said quickly. He was afraid that she would blurt out that Frances was her sister. It was as though he was in conspiracy with her against Peerse. 'They haven't had anything reported.'

'There isn't anything you can do,' Peerse said. 'As soon as we know about your husband, we'll be in touch.'

'They might both be hurt,' she said.

'Both?'

'Come on,' Murray said. 'I'll take you home.'

'What about Mary O'Bannion?' Irene asked.

Fat drops of rain splashed on the bonnet of the car beside Murray. As Peerse stared down on them, about to stoop like a predatory bird, Murray felt his mind go blank, then blurted, 'I've been telling her about Kujavia.'

'That's a story he's been telling everyone,' Peerse said. He sounded bitter. 'Did he tell you about the concentration camp?' He turned from her and put his face down close to Murray's. 'McKellar told me all about it – he thought it was very funny. He said it reminded him of my father.' He straightened. 'Do what I've asked, Mrs Wilson, and go home. Believe me, you haven't anywhere else to go.'

But in the car she said, 'It's not far away, is it?'

The rain was falling heavily now, pouring from the edges of the wipers on each upswing. All those years ago on the beat, the night the mob had cornered them, Peerse on the ground, twitching like a daddy-long-legs when you opened your fist and it was too injured to take off. Peerse had seemed too fragile to last . . .

'He's right,' he said. 'There wouldn't be any point.'

'I want to go.'

'Why?'

'Because I don't know anywhere else,' she said.

Above his head from the bracket on the landing wall, the gas mantle glowed white except where from one broken corner a blue discharge flared and swayed. It hissed in the stillness as he waited and the smell from the flat, worse than memory had prepared him for, licked out from the crack of the open door as if the dead dog had been left where he dropped it to rot heaving with blind white maggots. He hit the door with his full weight and heard the chain rip out. The edge of it hit something solid and it gave until, staggering, he stood inside.

The bulk of Mary O'Bannion foundered in the ghastly light of the flaring lamp, the waterfall of flesh that was her face decomposed with shock. Covered only by a dressing gown, wine-red with decorative detail in gold thread picked out on the cuffs and neck, she cradled in both hands a great exposed flop of breast where the door had struck her.

'Where's Kujavia?'

He pushed her aside moving fast to keep the advantage of surprise, and felt her roll at his touch like a sack of milk. As he forced his way past, she groaned recognition, 'It's you – ya bastard!'

255

He had a choice of the room where the dog had been or the kitchen. He was prepared for two possibilities: that the place would be empty or that he would have to deal with Kujavia. On the hand that knocked wide the kitchen door, the marks of the dog's teeth had left a ragged half circle puffed and pink like a burn that would not heal.

A third possibility that he had not considered was that Mary O'Bannion would have a customer this late into the night.

Beyond the table with its litter of uncleared dishes, a naked man, tall, fleshy, bent a little forward facing the sink and the window black above it. His back was ridged with fresh stripes and the white strokes of old beatings. The long muscles stood out on his sides and flanks like a man in the stress of a task. At the opening of the door, he had wrenched to look over his shoulder, turning only his head so that each eye showed a streak of spooked white. The full mane of hair spread out like a soiled halo.

'Ah, no,' Tommy Beltane groaned in disbelief and vexation.

For Murray turning away was an act of involuntary decency. The recess bed was a tangle of blankets and outdoor coats. It was noisome but unoccupied, and there was nowhere else to hide in the room.

'Look at him. I tell you look at him.'

For a crazy second, he thought she was calling on Kujavia, and saw him, a column of shadow, in a corner where he could not be. Sweating malevolence, she waved at Beltane the bulging slab of her arm with its incongruously tiny hand flapping like an excretion of sick flesh. Unheld, the dressing gown slipped to reveal breasts, shaking belly, a cascading enormity of thighs with at their juncture a patch of hair, folded and crushed amidst her fat, the light colour of which suggested some trace of the lost girl Tommy Beltane had bought.

'Turn round so he can see you.'

Very slowly then and laboriously, a puppet worked by her drunken scream, he began to edge round, one foot and then

256

the other, inch by inch it seemed until he faced them. Crouched forward, knees bent, hands braced on his thighs, he supported from a thong tied around his testicles, drawn out from a thick bush of white hair, a bag looking very like a housewife's shopper made of string. The shopper was half full.

'More weight. He keeps crying on more weight.' Mary O'Bannion cursed him. 'He'll go on till one time it'll pull the balls off him. Not that he'll know any fucking difference.'

'Jesus wept,' Tommy Beltane said, and grinned with a horrible wincing bravado.

Murray could not bear the sight he made. 'Tell Joe Kujavia—' he began, but the fat woman made a noise like a spitting cat.

If she comes, I'll punch her out, Murray thought, and closed his fists with a serious exultation.

She glared, ropes of saliva twining from her lower lip as if like a monstrous tabby with a mouse she would sink her teeth in him. Physically she appeared to swell with malice, but an instinct of self-preservation at the last moment deflected her rage. With a rush that defied her bulk, she threw herself at Tommy Beltane. Though she held out her hands against him, most of the damage was done with a great swing of her belly like the comedian in an old-time movie. Beltane staggered under the impact, his hands lost their support, and with a squeal of anguish he came down on his knees.

That finished Murray.

'Get up,' she screamed. And slowly, groaning, he began the effort of rising to his feet. 'Oh, I'll make you pay. You'll pay, you bastard. I'll have them off you.'

Even going down the stairs, her voice pursued him. Taking them two at a time, he stumbled on the second flight and saved himself by clutching the banister. Shaken, he stood still and then, instead of going on, turned his head to listen.

The crazy tirade had stopped as abruptly as the turning of a tap.

Poised, straining to catch any sound, the second room where the dog had been caged came into his mind. If someone had been hidden there, Mary O'Bannion's obscene rage would have been a way of distracting him. If Kujavia . . . The broken gas mantle sputtered in the stillness overhead.

He had taken the first step up when he was arrested by the clatter of feet mounting towards him. Irene appeared on the landing below, stopping with a catch of the breath as she saw him above her.

'Stay in the car.' His whisper echoed harshly between stone walls. 'I told you — stay in the car and lock the doors.'

'Eddy Stewart's down there.'

'What?' the sweat burst out on his forehead.

'They've found them.'

'What about Irene's car?' Murray said dully. 'It'll get vandalized if it's left there.'

Vaguely, he was conscious of Stewart's quick appraising glance. 'No problem. I'll get it picked up.'

The police car gathered speed, barely paused at the intersection, began to go faster. Stewart muttered something in answer to Irene, and Murray leaned forward to listen.

'Where they've been found. Not anything else, I don't know anything else.'

Not if they were dead. Not anything.

Murray sank back. They had already been told that. There was no point in her asking. He thought they were heading south, but he couldn't recognize any of the buildings.

'Almost there,' Stewart said, sounding relieved.

They bumped over a ramp and the car began to sway and jolt. Around them there was a sudden impression of space, of darkness, as if you might look up and see the stars, yet he knew they had not travelled far enough to shake free of the city. Getting out of the car, he looked up and glimpsed the moon and scarves of cloud drawn ragged by the wind.

'What's wrong?' Stewart caught his arm as if to support him.

258

'I'm all right.' He felt Stewart's grip let him go slowly as if reluctant.

The dizziness came and went as they crossed the broken ground. Cars were drawn up in a haphazard curve around the arch of a tunnel. All the headlights were on and as they passed in front of each car they swept long shadows into the entrance.

'It's all right inside,' Stewart said. 'We told those bastards who are on strike to get the lights back on in there.'

The last words echoed as they entered under the arch. They went on not asking questions, since the answers would come soon enough. When Murray glanced back, there was nothing behind them but the tunnel and the lamps on the walls drawing together in the distance. It had been cold when they got out of the car and then warmer out of the wind, but now the air around them was chilling. It felt like walking down into a grave. The breath rose white from their mouths. Unmistakable, the erect figure of Peerse towered in the middle of the way about thirty yards distant from them. Seeing their approach, the woman between the two men, he raised his right hand and moved it in a gesture so ambiguous it was impossible to tell whether he was calling them forward or imploring them to go back.

BOOK FIVE

CHAPTER TWENTY-FIVE
Cold Malcolm

SATURDAY, OCTOBER 6TH –
SUNDAY, OCTOBER 7TH

Once he had come back to the car from visiting Frances and found the side window broken and bright splinters of glass scattered inside. He had swept the seat clean and driven away in guilty haste. When he got home, Irene had turned his hand and he had seen blood beaded from a fine slice along its edge.

Walking that street tonight had been like falling, he had so many good reasons for not coming back to see Frances.

'I shouldn't have come,' he told her.

'You'll come, you'll come, you'll come.'

Her face under him was stupid with lust. It had never been like this with her before. Instead of being excited, he was chilled by her need. 'Just get it into me,' she gasped, driving her pelvis against him. 'No tricks, just put it in. Put it in!' In impotent revenge, he laid his full weight on her, that she raised with her loins using the strength of a coal heaver, until realizing what was happening she began to curse 'bastard bastard bastard' and lift him in her spasms higher with every curse. Until with a final grunting scream she was finished and dwindled under him; to complain in a moment, 'Ease up. Christ, you're smothering me.'

He rolled off her on to his back. What in prospect had drawn him, attracted and repelled like a dog to vomit, was going to make a bad meal in memory. At the thought of food his mouth filled with water; not steak or fish with fine wine but a hot pie, the kind they ate on terracings at football matches, holding it in both hands, the grease running between their teeth.

'I locked the door behind you, didn't I?' she whispered.

'It's locked.' He lay with his arm covering his eyes and his head turned from her. 'Both locks and all the bolts. Not forgetting the chain. You put the chain back on as well.'

She turned and pressed herself against his leg. He edged away.

'That's all right.' Her voice was quick and placatory, with no resentment. 'You don't have to bother. Just hold me.' She tugged at his fingers to draw his hand over her. 'Put your arm round me.'

'What's wrong?' He had never seen her like this and it made him uneasy.

'Last night someone tried to break in. I heard noises. I got up and stood behind the door.' She touched his shoulder and her hand was cold. 'I didn't put any light on. *Scratching noises*.' She shuddered against him. 'And then I heard the lock turning back.'

'Did Irene know this when she asked me to come here?'

'And then,' her whisper hardly reached him, 'then I heard the second one go too. I knelt down and put my hands over the bolt that goes into the floor. The door was shaking and I pressed my hands down, then it stopped and I thought he had gone away. Only after a while it started again . . . but just for a little while.'

He hitched up on an elbow to look at her. Her face was pale and seemed shrunken until it was no larger than his fist. There was nothing left of her prettiness; it was gone like a conjuring trick.

'I'm going home.'

'Please,' she said.

He lowered himself back on to the bed. He stared at the faint outline of an old stain surfacing in some enigmatic shape through the white plaster of the cornice.

'We can do anything,' she said, 'you can do anything, if you won't leave me.'

His decision, though, had been made. He dozed and

264

imagined that he had risen and dressed. It occurred to him that he had not been able to enter her because she belonged to John Merchant and so he did not have the power; but Merchant was dead, and to meet that objection Merchant changed at once to Bradley. The big Yorkshireman Bradley was dead too, of course, but for some reason that did not matter. She belonged with Bradley and with Merchant and so he did not have the power. This explanation comforted him and lapped in warmth he slept.

At some time later, he wakened out of a dream full of turning locks and the sounds of bolts being drawn back. The bed beside him was empty.

A debtor to mercy alone he'd learned that for Miss Geddie *of covenant mercy I sing* all of them had learned *nor fear with thy righteousness on* he sang and the words turned to ice and erected themselves in silver spears glittering from his lips *my person and offering to bring* learned it out of fear, they were all terrified of her, as a child learned it well to remember always *the terrors of law and of God* who turned in his arms with Frances, two women side by side, Miss Geddie so strong, he saw her hand on Frances, cold it was colder than anyone could bear, colder than anyone could live and bear, anguish, spears of ice thrust in him, a cold agony *with me can have nothing to do* and he held a naked body in his arms and went forward through the passage that pulsed like a living thing only the pulses were round eyes of glass picking up light from the torch behind him and he carried her in the body of the giant, the ice giant, so cold, forced down like a mouthful of chewed meat in the pulsing tunnel and got here at last, to the belly of the giant, mummy, a belly of ice *my Saviour's obedience and blood* Jesus, was she smiling at him with those teeth striped with blood, so strong Miss Geddie, her hands on Frances, two women side by side, and then the blood came out of Frances's mouth, bright blood striping her skin, covering her teeth, she came close to him, he would warm himself upon her naked flesh, he knew her body, felt the little gristle under the left nipple

265

roll between his fingers, put fingers in her mouth in her arse in the crack of her sex, erected the cold spear of his prick to stab into her into her warmth melt in her, sorry, Miss Geddie, sorry, Miss Geddie, Frances came on top of him, her fault her fault, and was colder than any ice, colder than regret colder than righteousness, colder than Miss Geddie when you were naughty *hide all my transgressions from view* spears of denial lifted into the glittering air from his lips, not naughty, a man, not to be frightened by their bogeys by their lies, the I thing, melting in Frances, listen for the truth in the dark, holding darkness in his hands, her lips open over him

—What is love?

she moved on him, lay on him, rubbed her breasts and crotch on him; when she laughed, he choked on the foulness of her breath.

FRIDAY, OCTOBER 12TH

For Murray, it seemed that each waking of his brother was like a journey. All of them were impossibly far, and often he would open his eyes and be gone again, turning back. Watching Malcolm's head roll and the querulous thinning of his lips, it was easy to wish for him more peace than waking could bring.

Seated by the bed, Murray found the quietness disturbing. Even in the white hours of the early morning, the wards he had been washed into as a victim had sighed, bustled, clanged, groaned. In this room it was quiet. The loudest noise was the altered sound of Malcolm's breathing.

With a start, he realized his brother was watching him.

'Where's Mother?'

He had to bend close to catch the words.

'She's not gone long. She'll be back soon.'

'Why are you always here?'

The whisper was puzzled and fretful.

Murray got up and went across to the door. Through the glass, he could see into the short length of corridor. It was deserted.

'I'm supposed to let them know when you wake up.'

Malcolm looked in the direction of the bell. His head and then his eyes moved very slowly, with an underwater slowness. It's not going to be any good, Murray thought. Even if I get time alone with him, he'll remember walking through the streets to her flat, perhaps a little more than last time, but we'll hit the barrier again. On the other side of the black line struck through that night, there was only a kaleidoscope of lunatic fragments.

'Why isn't Mother here?'

'She'll be back.'

Murray waited, he was good at waiting. After a time, a dry spasm of coughing jerked Malcolm's eyes open.

'Frances isn't here?'

'How could she be?' Murray explained as he had before, 'Frances is dead. You were found with her in the Underpass, tied together. Until you opened your eyes, I thought you were dead too.'

'Tell me . . .'

A white glitter of lamps and the cold at the end of the tunnel. Men crouching over an ugly shape like a badly tied carpet, that fell apart into the two bodies, one looking as dead as the other. The sparkle you could not help seeing of frost in the bush of black hair over the woman's groin. A man's voice: 'Christ, look at his arm!' A man's voice: 'There are tracks from out there near the middle.' 'She's been a looker.' 'Fancy getting up against her now?' 'Christ, no, she looks frigid.'

Laughter. He had glanced at Irene, but she seemed not to have heard, standing apart with Peerse who was frowning over her head at the smothered incongruous sound; looking back then and seeing Eddy Stewart among the group, the grin slackening his lips.

'I don't remember anything that would help you,' Murray said.

The head turned from side to side on the pillow. It had been a full-fleshed face, a little soft round the mouth, good looking in one of the conventional ways; the kind of man who reminded women as the night wore on at parties of some singer or actor. Now the most noticeable feature of his appearance was his teeth. Square and white they were too large for his mouth. His lips could not cover them.

'I carried her . . .'

'That's right.' Murray leaned forward to hear. 'You could have done − it could have been that way − through the tunnel down into the Underpass.'

'I'd been there before . . . that day with Heathers . . .'

The thread of voice slipped away and Murray came so close his cheek almost brushed his brother's lips and still he could not be sure that what he heard was, 'Poor girl. Poor girl.'

'Frances?'

'The poor black girl . . . poor girl . . . I carried her . . .'

'Black girl? There wasn't any black girl.'

Malcolm's eyes opened, suddenly clear and rational. 'I told her to look out through the peephole . . . Because it was a woman she let her in . . . She wasn't afraid of a woman . . .'

'That was in the flat,' Murray said, confirming it. 'Frances went to the door and saw this woman through the peephole − and because it was a woman and you were there, she let her in, is that right?'

'Yes.'

'Did she have a gun, this woman? Was that how she forced you? How could she force you to drive the car − and then to carry Frances? Can you remember?'

But his eyes had closed again, showing only a thin slice of white under each lid. After a pause, during which Murray thought he had slipped away again to sleep, he whispered, 'I had to drag her . . . It took a long time.'

A long time. Whatever else was lost, they knew the kind

of time it must have taken him. Out of the tunnel, somewhere in the open area; he had been struck from behind,
a desperate blow. He must have come round lashed ankle
to ankle, bound face against the naked corpse, his wrists
fastened behind its back. He would not have been able to
stand up; there was no way of getting free without help.
Probably he had tried to shout. There was no one there to
hear him. After a supervisor had used his fists in a dispute
the previous day, every worker on the site had walked out.
There wasn't any way of predicting a thing like that. Was
there some way the killer could have learned of it? Or come
there by chance; was that kind of coincidence possible? It
had been cold, colder than anything he could account for,
cold beyond reason. One eye stuck shut with blood from
the head wound, Malcolm must have known how close he
was to dying for even in that terrible bewilderment he had
begun to drag his burden inch by slow fought inch. When
he was found by a partner in the specialist firm, he had made
it almost back to the mouth of the tunnel, but it had taken
a long time. By then, given the way he had lain while
unconscious and the tightness of the cords, the damage had
been done.

'It wasn't anything to do with Irene,' Murray said. 'She
was with me.'

Suddenly, he realized that he had spoken aloud and
glanced down at his brother with a reflex like an acknowledgement of guilt.

'Mother?' Malcolm whispered.

As if it were moved by a separate intelligence, and one
not willing to deceive itself any longer with weakness or
Murray's questions, Malcolm's left hand crept out from
under the covers, passed across his body and felt down his
right side.

'Mother?'

—I want this hurt to go away.

Given three wishes, in the child's world of mysterious
powers what was wrong could be set right.

In slices, catching the corruption as it ate its way upwards,

269

the surgeons had exchanged Malcolm's right arm for his life. He would live, but there was no kiss-and-make-better to return what was gone. The last operation had taken the arm off at the shoulder.

With a convulsive spasm, he half raised himself and fell back.

'You didn't tell me.'

'You knew,' Murray said. 'It's just that when you wake up you don't want to remember.'

The doctors had been impressed by him; not enormously though, since hospitals, all things considered, witnessed astonishing amounts of courage. Malcolm's had been of the male stoical kind. Now he stared up, hopeless and afraid and full of hate; but it was all right to be yourself with family.

'You should have looked after me, Murray,' he said. 'Mother thinks you should have looked after me.'

Malcolm's glance showed how much he discounted that possibility, and yet its bitterness was unreasonable as if his weakness had drawn him into the child's world of belief.

'No more operations,' Murray said. 'I've spoken to the surgeon. They'll give you an arm – a prosthesis, it's called.'

'A *prosthesis*,' Malcolm mocked. But went on with a change of tone, 'You're telling me they'll hang a lump of tin and plastic on me.'

'They'll fix it so you can work it with the muscles of your back.'

'Oh, God,' Malcolm groaned and shut his eyes.

Be grateful for it, Murray thought, and that you're not a manual worker. And for six months full pay, and six months half. The benefits of a steady job. He listened to the sound of his own breath. It went in and out so quietly that it was only when he forced it gently on the out breath that he heard it sigh in his nose. It was a little noise but in the stillness he heard it as his own, not lost in the rasping snore of the crippled man.

'Is it true she was dead?'

Murray thought for a moment, then said, 'When you were tied to her, she was dead.'

'I thought she spoke to me.'

'With the wounds she had, she was dead. The ones in front were enough to have killed her – and you were covering those.'

A spasm of coughing shook the man on the bed. It went on until he began to choke. Murray held him up and gradually the fit eased. He slumped in the support of the cradling arm.

'I feel my elbow itching.'

'I'll scratch it for you.'

'If you can find it.'

It took a moment to recognize the thin squeezed note as laughter.

'It's in the other arm. My God, I can feel an itch in the arm that isn't there.'

Murray laid him down. 'That happens.'

'Will it happen once I get my prosthesis? Will the elbow of my prosthesis itch?' Malcolm asked contemptuously.

'Maybe.' Murray stood up and stretched. He rubbed his neck where it had gone stiff. 'I'll get somebody.'

'You want to know what I regret – really regret?'

With his hand on the door, Murray hesitated. Through the glass, he saw his mother accompanied by a nurse coming towards the room. She was moving very slowly. In all her long life, until this time when Malcolm had been hurt, she had not needed the aid of a stick.

'Mother's here.'

'Murray? You know what I regret? The women I haven't had. And the ones I could have had but passed up. Murray? Who's going to look at me now?'

Letting the door swing shut behind him, Murray stepped out into the corridor.

Mother came waveringly, feeling forward with her stick at each step. Yet those milky eyes, he knew, missed nothing of him. Groping forward, she held him in her blind gaze and with her stick beat, beat, on the roof of his skull.

CHAPTER TWENTY-SIX
The Children of Annette Verhaeren

SATURDAY, OCTOBER 13TH

The gull screamed a savage brainless cry and flew up almost into his face as he entered the gate. Startled, he watched it rise beyond the spire, a blunt tower of grey stone that matched the overcast sky, as if the church was a fortress set on this hill above the sea. When he looked down, he saw that he was being watched. Erect among the stones marking the lairs of the dead, a man stood motionless, resting his weight on the handle of a spade.

'Could you tell me where I would find Mr Sinclair?' Murray asked. He had seen the name on a board at the gate.

The only response was a tightening of the lips. At a distance, Murray had imagined this might be the minister himself, but the cuffs of the trousers were frayed, the boots cracked, a curve of torn lining showed below the old jacket. Close up, white hair and deep lines scored on the cheeks marked him as old.

'What about that then?' the old man asked.

'Mr Sinclair,' Murray repeated. 'I was wondering where I'd find him.'

'That's a berberis bush. Would you describe that as bonny? Sometimes we just have to take a minute to look at things.'

Spiders' webs by the hundred were strung between the narrow spiky branches. Each line was beaded with drops of moisture that caught a fraction of the light so that the webs made a shawl thrown across the bush.

'I haven't seen that before,' Murray admitted, recognizing the need for diplomacy.

'It's the kind of thing you miss if you're aye in a hurry.' Honour satisfied, he took account of the question. 'You want the minister?'

Murray nodded.

'I doubt you'll not catch him. Did you try the manse?'

'I will if you tell me where it is.'

'Down the road a bit – behind the wall on your left. Before you come to the village. Here, you know why it's out there and not in the village?'

Professionally patient, Murray said, 'No idea.'

'So he'd never have to pass a fisherman's door to get to the kirk. A minister passing the door when the boat was out being bad luck, you ken. In the old days, the only time a minister would be in a fisherman's house was for a funeral – and then it was all right for all the boats would be in the harbour. The young men don't bother about that stuff. They've been too lucky for too long.' He eased the spade to and fro in the earth. 'It's a gey while since a man's been drowned out of this village.'

'You've been here a long time. You must have heard of a couple called Fletcher.'

The old man coughed sardonically and hawked a loop of green phlegm among the silver webs. 'Only a hundred first to last. It's all Fletchers, did you not know that? Or Thomsons. Two families of Hillises, but they're incomers . . . Or Grahams. There's aye Grahams,' he offered grudgingly with the manner of a man making an admission.

'The couple I'm thinking of adopted two girls. This would be more than twenty years ago.'

'Sandy Fletcher: And Grace – that was Grace Hillis before she married.'

'I had an address, but the house is empty.'

'That whole row's empty now. And will be till the winter's by. They're all holiday cottages.'

'Where have the Fletchers gone? Have they left the village?'

273

'I'll show you Sandy's place.'

With the slow rolling gait of a ploughman, he led the way, offering obliquely phrased enquiries that Murray parried with the ease of practice. At the church porch, they came on a younger, more rumpled version of Murray's guide, standing with his head back staring upwards. The chain for the bell hung from the tower down the wall, but the hook that should have held it up out of reach was twisted and sagging loose.

As they came up, the man lowered his gaze to them. 'Aye, Bob,' he said. 'I've been thinking – all this talk about the Lower Paid Worker,' he gave each word an emphatic capital, 'it's awful degrading, ken.'

Murray walked on a few steps. The white marker stone in front of him was incised:

To a
Merchant Seaman
Of the Second
World War
August 1940
Known Unto God

Behind him he heard the man's complaint: 'Even if they do get a productivity agreement, it's not right. You're digging a grave and he's there with the stop-watch. And you stop to dicht your brow and the watch stops. And it starts when you start – but it's just impossible to dig out a hole without catching your breath. And then he says to me, Now the box is such-and-such so I'll allow you a time that takes that into account.'

At last the old man plodded to join him. Taking it for granted that Murray had been listening, he said, 'Oh, it's sacrilege' – the word took Murray by surprise – 'just sacrilege. Folk should be allowed to go in peace, not pestered with watches over their coffins and burial places.'

'You were going to show me where the Fletchers stay.'

'Ah . . . where Sandy bides now.'

His tone gave it away for Murray even before he pointed to the stone. It stood beside the one to the dead seaman.

Sacred to the Memory of . . .

'That's Sandy. Grace lives with a sister now – somewhere down South Shields way I've heard, but I couldn't swear to that. He turned Catholic when he married her, but he turned back later – and that's why he's there.'

'Did Mr Sinclair know them?' Since there was no Catholic church in the village or even near, the minister – assuming he had been here and possessed even of normal curiosity – remained the likeliest source of information about the Fletchers' adopted children.

'Certainly. And he knew his father as well – he's buried over there.'

'I'll try the manse then.'

'Ah, but he's not there. He's away down to Miss Sturrock's. You can see the gable end of her house from here. You'll have missed them though. He was in an awful hurry.'

But as he came to the house, a stout white-haired woman in a tweed skirt and anorak was drawing the door shut behind her. She had a stick tucked under her arm and a binocular case of scuffed leather slung over her shoulder. Only her ankles, disappearing into sturdy boots, seemed vulnerable. She directed at him the look of a woman who would not welcome an interruption.

'Miss Sturrock?'

For an uncharacteristic moment under that steady gaze, he wasn't sure if he had caught her name correctly.

'Should I remember you?' she asked.

The oddness of the question made him hesitate. 'My name is Wilson. It's the minister I'm looking for – Mr Sinclair.'

'You've missed him by about half an hour.' At his look of frustration, she relented. 'But we'll catch him, if you don't mind a walk.'

Despite the thin ankles and the boots, she set a brisk pace.

'If I hadn't been in the middle of a baking, you wouldn't have caught me either. He's had a sighting of a yellow-browed warbler up by the loch.' She gave him a sharp glance, looking for a reaction. 'You're not a birdwatcher yourself.'

'I'm a city man,' Murray said with a sour private smile.

They turned off the road on to a grudging space left between the barbed wire edging a field and the grey stone of an eight-foot high estate wall. He fell into single file on the path behind her.

'I used to take the children up here on summer days,' she remarked over her shoulder.

He grunted.

They squeezed through a gate swung in a half circle of iron guards to keep out sheep. It was like stepping from a room into the open air. Below them, the sea was patterned light and dark from the scoured valleys that lay under its calm surface.

'We're high up,' he exclaimed in surprise.

They were standing at the top of a cliff.

'We'll be higher still before we're done. All the way up by there, and then down again to the loch.'

The path took a long upward curve, close all the way to the edge of the drop, towards the summit of a sheer face of rock whitened by generations of guano. He recognized common gulls, herring gulls, guillemots, razorbills, kittiwakes, stirring and squabbling and swooping from it. Farther out, a gannet folded its wings and plunged towards the water. His breath began to come faster. Striding on, the woman pecked at him with her glance. 'You don't get a climb like this among city streets. I've walked this Head in all weathers for thirty years. And, since I've retired, my time's my own.'

At the summit, they turned their backs on the sea and jolted down a slope towards a rocky shore. They skirted a steep hill rubbed with slides of stone among the coarse grass.

'Over there – to your left. It's the only decent shelter on the Head. Everywhere else the winter winds are too cruel for trees. Alex Sinclair should be somewhere about there – that's where the sighting was.'

On the side they approached, the ground sloped down sharply into the loch. The trees were thinly ranked on the other side; and they made their way round, jumping a meagre stream. The loch was about a mile in length and beyond it to the north there was a glimpse of the sea. Among the trees, they could hear the noise of water lapping into the loch over a little weir. They went slowly through the thin cover without a sight of either quarry, man or bird.

'Never mind,' Miss Sturrock whispered, crouching to peer up through angled branches of willow.

As Murray contemplated the forbidden possibility of planting a kick on her tweed-bound rump, the connection that had been niggling at him fell into place.

Up here with the children . . . Miss Sturrock . . . retired . . .

'Were you the teacher? In the village school?'

'Sh-ssh,' she hissed. 'I wonder — could that be — if it would move — I think it might be . . .'

But it wasn't, and she admitted, moving cautiously between the bare trunks, and not distracted but freed by the other activity of searching for the bird, that, yes, she had been the teacher, later the head teacher and at last the sole teacher in the village school.

'Do you have any memory of two girls who were adopted by Sandy and Grace Fletcher?'

She stopped so abruptly that he almost touched her.

'Aah.' Her breath sighed out. 'What has Alice done?'

'Alice?'

'Francesca and Alice,' she said impatiently. 'The Fletchers adopted them.'

'Frances, yes. But the other child's name was Urszula.'

'Oh, Grace Fletcher wouldn't have that. It was foreign. Grace couldn't have felt she belonged to her — not with a name like that. It seemed such an odd name anyway — I mean, I knew the mother was Belgian. Alice is such a pretty name, I told the child. It's the name of a little girl like you who passed through the mirror into Wonderland.'

'Did everyone know who their mother had been?' If that

277

was so, Father Hurtle's vision of setting them free of the past had gone wrong from the start.

'How do you keep a secret like that? How do you keep any secret at all in a village where everyone's related on one side of the blanket or the other?' With the binoculars, she swept the opposite bank as she continued, 'After his brother's wedding last weekend, Jack Graham gave his wife a beating – hands *and* feet – because she'd danced with Peter Hillis. Of course, poor Margaret didn't even know they'd fallen out. They quarrel over fouled nets or over berths in the harbour – one thing or another incessantly. And it was the wrong time of the month for Jack. All that family go funny at the full moon. It's the in-breeding. I'm not local here, you understand.'

After thirty years?

'The village knew that the mother had been murdered?'

'I don't know how much difference it made. Perhaps the damage was there already. But, of course, people did know. And then Sandy Fletcher had his accident – not on the boat, but in his car coming back from the Harbour Inn. Drunk naturally – but before that he wasn't a heavy drinker. Just normal for a fisherman, there are no drinkers like fishermen. But after his accident . . . he couldn't work, they left the house in the village – for a while they lived over there,' she pointed between the bare hills across the loch, 'in a miserable place. Afterwards they went to Braefoot – that's about twelve miles up the coast. By that time, Sandy was a different man altogether, pathetic really. It's one thing to want to be good and another to be good. And I always suspected it was Sandy who dropped the first hint of where the girls had come from. One night in the Harbour Inn just before he fetched them. So maybe, as well as the accident, it was guilt. He wanted to be a good man, but he could never be a wise one.'

'When I mentioned them, why did you ask if . . . Alice had done something? What were you expecting me to say?'

'You didn't say anything though, did you?' They had come almost to the end of the trees. 'I didn't miss that.'

'I'm a private enquiry agent. I've been hired by a relative to try to trace them.'

'After all this time?' She looked at him sceptically.

'An uncle – in Belgium. There were reasons for the delay. He had troubles of his own. He was too friendly with the Germans during the Occupation.'

'Why would he want to find them now?'

Murray shrugged. 'He doesn't seem to be short of money. He may want to help them.' It was a reasonable cover story; on the way down, he had worked out a different one on the assumption no one would know their background.

'It might be better for him if you don't find them,' Miss Sturrock said abruptly. As Murray glanced at her, she turned her face away from him. 'I never met another child like her. She would say to the others, "When I go outside, you will all hit me and I shall cry – but you will get into trouble." A child of six. It was like an invitation to them to hit her. She was so strange. Sometimes I think of her and wonder if one day I'll open a paper and read that she's been murdered. Unless, of course, by this time she's learned some protective coloration. Learned to pretend to be like other people.'

'You said she was only a child.' Murray's voice was tight with suppressed anger. It took him by surprise; but he did not want to think about why he felt it.

'I don't understand why Alex Sinclair isn't here,' Miss Sturrock said. In every direction they were alone. 'I think I'll go back. There isn't any point in looking.' After a step or two, however, she swung about and faced him. 'There isn't anything I could tell you that would help you to find them. They were glad to get away and that was the last we heard of them. Alice went first although she was the younger, only sixteen. The man left a wife and child behind. Frances went too, but that was later. I always thought Frances was fond of Grace Fletcher.'

'It was – Alice you found strange.' He remarked on it casually, spoke quietly, trying to undo the harm he had done; yet he saw her hesitate. The wind came up, rattling

279

the branches, so that he had to raise his voice, 'You must be curious about what happened to her. And that's what I'm trying to find out.'

'She was . . . clumsy,' Miss Sturrock said. 'Such a little girl and she kept bumping into people. The boys would kick her with their heavy boots. Spat . . . she spat when she was talking. She sprayed them and they got angry. Yet she was pretty, like a doll − and intelligent. More intelligent than they were which didn't help. She would say, "You are only the son of a common fisherman." *Stupid* was a favourite word of hers. I've never met another child like her before or since. She seemed to know what the weak spot would be.' The old woman gave a laugh that after so many years had not lost its edge of irritation. 'Don't imagine I was exempt. "You don't speak like the lady on the radio − you speak like the village children" . . . She had no sense of self preservation.' Again she fell into the precise, oddly assured child's voice she reproduced for each of the girl's utterances. ' "You know Princess Andrea in the story? She is me." Not "I am she" − it's the ordinary boastful childish statement gone wrong. "*She* is *me*". She lived in a fantasy world and none of us mattered.'

'None of that sounds so bad to me,' Murray said. 'She was only a kid, and she was having a bad time.'

She shook her head, a brief sharp movement. It occurred to him it was the gesture she had used when a child was being slow; as if she might cry to him, 'Don't you *see*?'

Instead she said, 'You've missed the minister. He's not retired like me, perhaps someone caught him before he could escape on to the Head.'

'That's all right. I don't suppose he could have told me more than you've done.'

'You're a good listener,' she said grimly. 'I'm going back. You go on over the hill − that way − and you'll get a look at the house they lived in after Sandy Fletcher's accident.'

'I don't think,' Murray began, 'it would be worth—'

'I don't want you walking back with me. You make too

280

much noise. Go on over the hill, if you want to understand the life they had.'

After a moment he shrugged and began to walk in the direction she had indicated.

'I say!'

He turned.

'What have you seen while we've been talking?'

He stared back uncomprehending.

'A wheatear — there with rust on its throat. Didn't you see?' Triumph reddened her leathery cheeks and she watched him maliciously. 'Or the moorhen? Or the coot there?' A dark bird tugged a caravan of ripples under the bank. 'And so much to hear! You don't know where to look unless you listen. Don't preen yourself,' Miss Sturrock cried. 'Don't preen yourself on being clever about getting a silly old woman to talk so much. Of course, I think about her. But I can't see how anyone would have made a difference.'

CHAPTER TWENTY-SEVEN
The Knife

SATURDAY, OCTOBER 13TH

They hadn't drawn the curtains in the house across the road. He could see, as if held in a frame, a table uncleared from the evening meal and a woman with a boy who might have been her son, their heads close together as if sharing a joke. In a moment, the father, shirt-sleeved, came through the open door from the kitchen and with his hand raised to his mouth bit a piece from something and stood watching them as he chewed. Dull suburban home movie; but in Murray's fatigue it had an hypnotic effect that was hard to break.

'Travelling,' he said without turning his head. 'I spent some of the day travelling. And I went for a walk along a cliff.'

At his back Irene said, 'You're so tired you can hardly talk straight.'

'I've had a long day. I went looking for a minister and found a schoolteacher.'

'And then you came to see me.'

Armoured by routine or indifference, the actors in the playlet across the street seemed to have no need of privacy. Reaching up with his arms on either side, he drew the curtains shut. 'I came anyway,' he said, 'but I wasn't sure you'd be here.' When he turned, he moved abruptly as if to take her by surprise. He had thought she was standing, but she had seated herself on the couch and he had not expected that. 'You might have been at the hospital. Or at Mother's.'

'He hasn't made up his mind whether he wants me to

visit,' Irene said. 'He thinks I should have stopped him from going to Frances when she phoned.'

'Does Malcolm know she was your sister?'

'He didn't go there for my sake,' she said.

'I know what he went there for.' Saying that, he heard himself, harsh, dry, a voice full of dry rage. He saw the heaviness of a man pressed down like a burden on the outspread body of a woman. It came between him and Irene so that he looked away from her as if she might read the unwanted vision in his eyes.

'Did I ever tell you,' she asked, 'that Frances expected to be fucked by you that day you went to her flat? While you were asking your questions, she kept waiting for you to start hitting her. After that, she expected to get fucked. She couldn't have stopped you. Instead you poured her stuff on the floor.'

She got up and walked through into the kitchen. He followed and stood just inside the door watching her. She set down a bowl half full of a grey greasy mix beside the carcass of a chicken on a tray and began to lay beside it knives from a drawer, each coming down with its sharp separate knock on the wooden surface.

'It's not for me,' she said. 'I don't like chicken. It makes me squeamish.'

Tiredness gathered to a single ache at the base of his skull. The surface of the mix in the bowl was covered in flecks of green. Staring at it, he felt a drop of sour vomit rise into the back of his mouth.

'Finding out things is my business,' he said. 'I know who killed Annette Verhaeren. It's not a great secret — only his name doesn't appear in the papers.' But that wasn't what he wanted to say first. He had come to tell her about being in the village. 'Finding things out . . . I had a contact who helped me to trace where Annette's children had been taken for adoption.'

'Billy Shanks?'

She was working with a knife on the chicken carcass. She reached in with the blade first at one side and then the other,

283

sawing to cut. With the knife she held back the skin at the top of the aperture and used her fingers to wrench the bone inside to and fro. The grey skin wrinkled back in folds under the pressure of the knife and the forked bone tore free at last crusted with brown meat stained with blood.

'Do you have to do that just now?'

'I read up,' she said, 'so I do things properly. I'm taking the bone out before I cook it and that makes it easier to carve.'

'Miss Sturrock said you were clever.'

'. . . Miss Sturrock.'

'She was the teacher in the village school. Maybe you don't remember her. But she remembers.'

'What would she remember from all that time ago?'

'An awkward girl who bumped into other children and spat when she talked.'

'Frances is dead. It's not kind to talk about her that way.'

'Not Frances – she was talking about you.'

'No,' Irene said. 'Not me. That was Frances.'

'Do you remember the cliffs above the village? Miss Sturrock took me up there. Do you remember how high above the sea it is? And then we went down to the loch. That's the only place where there are trees.' But the face she turned to him told him nothing; a pretty woman looking round from a kitchen task; he wanted to take her flesh between his fingers and mould some expression he could understand. 'What about the house then? Don't tell me you forgot the place you lived in. Miss Sturrock told me where to find it. I've never seen a lonelier place. You couldn't have been any lonelier on an island in the middle of the sea.'

A barbed-wire fence jumped, he crawled across a child's landscape patted out of plasticine, a heathland that sagged and rose in soft swellings as if the earth had bruised. He recognized everything, it was all the places he had lived as a child, scoured places, where even the flowers crouched under the wind. In a place like this his father had died, swum down the gull-crying air.

'It's not something I ever think about,' she said.

It was incomprehensible to him; even while they were talking she had her back to him, working at what was in front of her on the kitchen surface as if it was all that concerned her. She was taking the last soft portion of forecemeat and pressing it into the bird. Finished, she folded across the flap of the neck skin.

'When they were adopted, they weren't allowed to keep their own names,' he said harshly. 'The village liked familiar names. Like Frances. Or Alice.'

'The girl who went through the looking glass.'

The silence lay between them.

Swum down, fallen or jumped from a high place. He had left home and that had happened to his father. What would her reaction be if he said to her, none of the things she might expect, but, I have never known if my father killed himself or if it was an accident. What he remembered were their quarrels. That he might have been loved so much was not a possibility he had ever been able to bear.

She had turned and he saw that she was staring at his hands. He had clenched his fists.

'When you're there during those long waits in the hospital with your brother, does he tell you what Frances was like in bed? Do you like to listen to that, Murray?'

'Someone like you doesn't have to talk like this.'

Unexpectedly, she laughed. The noise grated on him like the squeal of a cat. 'I don't understand you,' she said. 'I haven't understood anything about you from the day I met you. What kind of detective are you? What do you do if a witness says "fuck"? What about "fuck"? How do you feel about "fuck", Murray?'

'I do my job.'

'Do you put your hands over your ears?' She closed her eyes with the tip of each forefinger, very gently in mockery.

Baited, he swung his head from side to side. 'I can do my job.'

'But you're no good at it. If you were any good at it, Frances would still be alive—'

'I can do my job,' he said again, clinging to that. 'Half the cops in the city are—'

'I'm talking about you.' She reached out and struck him softly on the chest. 'If you were any good, you would have known by this time who killed Merchant and the others.'

'Maybe I didn't want to know.'

He shouted into her face, all the pain and weariness forcing it out of him. And then in silence, he listened to what he had said.

She sighed. 'It was *that*,' she rested her hand lightly on the big muscle of his arm, 'and the broken nose that fooled me. I've solved you, Murray. Inside you're a mummy's boy—'

She ended on a gasp as he lunged forward and pulled her against him. He crushed his mouth down on hers.

When he raised his head, she said with what might have been triumph or contempt, 'You needed that.'

He felt her body against his, not as a woman's — compounded of hardness, softness, swellings and incurvings — nor even as a body at all, but as a pressure that conveyed the beat of his own heart and resonated that beating until he shook to its drum of lust and rage.

'No,' he said, 'I needed this,' and moved too quickly for her to stop him.

'Poor Malcolm,' she said.

They were back in the living room. Everything was the way it had been before. Except that he wanted to say to her, That wasn't me. I'm not like that. He wanted to go over to the couch and sit beside her and draw her head down on to his shoulder. The trite sentimental image of togetherness presented itself to him, vividly, painfully, lingeringly. When, ashamed, he bundled it away, its trace was left behind the rings of fading light from a lamp when the eyes close.

'He was so anxious to be a success,' she said. Listening to her voice, he edged the curtain aside. The window was splashed with fat drops of rain; he watched it fall slanting under the street light. 'Did you know how ambitious he

286

was? He called that man Bradley ''the boss'' – and he was desperate to get his job. But they were going to put Bradley in prison, except that he cheated them by getting cancer and dying first. They were ready to arrest him. Poor Malcolm didn't know that.'

'How do you know what was going to happen to Bradley?'

'Peerse – that policeman who came to Mum Wilson's – the one who told us to go home and he would find them – he's been here twice. He's angry because he was sure Frances was Jill – and she spoiled everything by getting herself killed. Now he doesn't know what to think. He explained all that to me – he likes to explain things.'

With a shrill gust, the wind burst rain like shrapnel across the glass. In the house opposite they had drawn the curtains at last. Everyone had something to hide.

'He told me how Jack the Ripper killed a woman called Mary Kelly on the 9th of November. Peerse is waiting for the 9th of November because he thinks Jill will kill someone else then. Mary Kelly was a prostitute, just like the others, and he killed her in her room and cut her to pieces. Because it was in a room and not in the street, he had more time. The room was like a butcher's shop with her blood. He even hung bits of her flesh from the nails in a picture frame.'

He heard her get up and turned to follow her out of the room, but stopped after a few steps as if he had come up against an invisible wall. He had to force himself to enter the kitchen for the second time.

'Watch your feet,' she said. 'There's broken glass on the floor. That could be dangerous.'

Not stepping among it, she stretched out to reach the tray with the chicken. 'Open the oven door.'

'Peerse didn't have the right to come here,' he said. 'Not unless it's official – and I don't think it was. You don't have to listen to him.'

She slid the tray into the oven and closed the door. 'I didn't know I had any choice. He says that after Jack the Ripper killed Mary Kelly the murders stopped. They waited for another one to happen, but it didn't. And Jack the

Ripper wasn't ever caught. They still don't know who he was. Peerse said there were all kinds of theories – that it was a surgeon or a lawyer called Montague John or a duke – one of the royal family. All kinds of theories. Even one that it might be a woman. But there weren't any more murders. Maybe the person who'd done them went abroad. Or died. Committed suicide. But not ever caught. Peerse is waiting for the 9th of November—'

'Only he won't rest unless he catches somebody.' On impulse, he added, 'He won't have to wait till November. Don't ask me why, but I feel that. It'll end before then.'

'That means someone will have to be killed sooner.' She said it as simply as a child. 'Your friend Peerse says there has to be another one. And no one will be caught, but afterwards whoever did it will stop. That'll be the end of it.'

'No . . . that kind of murderer is like an animal that's tasted blood. Maybe not here any more, maybe another city, maybe even another country – it wouldn't stop. The temptation would be too strong.'

'That's not true,' she cried. 'She could go away and start a new life. She would just disappear. She wouldn't do it again . . . and that would be the end of it.'

'That doesn't sound to me like Peerse.'

She stared at him and said, 'Oh, yes, he told me that – something like that. I'm sure he did. You said yourself there are murderers who aren't ever arrested – like the man who killed that woman you talked about.'

'. . . Annette Verhaeren.'

'Yes.' She knelt and began to brush the fragments of glass into a dustpan. As she picked up one of the larger pieces to drop it into the pan, he saw that it had opened a thin cut along one of her fingers. Without looking up she said, 'I know about him – he works for Blair Heathers. One night in bed, Malcolm was crying. Kujavia had taken him to that flat – the one the fat woman was in. Malcolm wanted to see the black girl who'd been at Heathers' party. Only when he told me what Kujavia had done to her, he started

288

to cry. But not even that could make him stop wanting to have Bradley's job for himself.'

'He's not ambitious now,' Murray said. If it was a defence of his brother, it was a brutal one. 'He told you – and you told Frances. That was a bit of luck she had; it's not easy to find someone. Not when you come back to a city as a stranger after such a long time. But when she went to Mary O'Bannion's, Kujavia wasn't there. Sometimes he sleeps there, but he uses other places as well. He had to be careful. Billy Shanks told me once – if that bastard got himself killed, half of Moirhill would come out into the streets and dance.'

She swung open the mouth of the bin. Glass glittered, turning as it fell. She licked the blood from her finger.

'What makes you think Frances wanted to find him?'

'Because she knew he had killed her mother. Because,' he hesitated, 'it's possible she had nightmares about him.' Tufts of black hair in a carnival crown of spikes. 'Maybe she saw her mother being killed – the way she was killed. She had to do something about him.'

'Poor Frances.'

He nodded, watching her.

'She's dead,' Irene said. 'There isn't anything she can do now.'

'He is a dangerous man. There wouldn't have been anything she could do. She was lucky she didn't find him.'

'Even although he knew she was looking?'

'Did he?'

'That's what you told me.'

Murray remembered. 'Going to Mary O'Bannion's,' he said slowly, 'that was probably a mistake. She shouldn't have gone there.'

Somewhere he heard a sound of music, a radio being played too loudly, as if a door had just been opened. He was so concentrated upon her, however, that for the moment it did not register.

Inconsequentially, she said, 'Tomorrow I'm going to Blair Heathers. He phoned and asked me.'

'Why would you go to Heathers?' He stared at her in bewilderment. Always she surprised him, left him shut out, excluded. 'There isn't anything for you there.'

'I can't go to Mary O'Bannion's,' she said. 'I'm not as brave as Frances.'

But as he tried to understand, she turned away.

—I'm here bitch I'm here bitch I'm here I'm here I'm here.

Before he could speak, she said, 'Mum Wilson must be coming down.'

'What?'

'I'll take her to the hospital tomorrow – on my way to Heathers.'

'Mother? She's been upstairs all this time?'

The music stopped as if a switch had been turned. Straining, he heard a door bang shut. She was coming down.

'Didn't you realize? I couldn't leave her on her own. That wouldn't have been right. Tomorrow I'll feed her chicken before we go.' Irene smiled. 'She had to rest. I thought you knew . . .'

When he let her go, she said, in what he heard as contempt, 'You needed that.'

He felt her body against his and shook with lust and rage.

'No,' he said. 'I needed this.'

He was too quick for her. With a boxer's reflex, he swept away her hand as it hooked for his face and with his weight crowded her back the length of the kitchen until the wall stopped her. She had nowhere to go. She was in jeans without a belt so that, when he popped the button and pulled, the zip peeled down to the crotch. She didn't speak but grunted with the effort of striking at him. Her hand swung round his back; some corner of his mind recorded that she was using only one hand; her left hand hit him again and again just over the kidneys. 'Get them off.' And he used both hands to drag pants and jeans down her thighs. 'Ah, yes.' 'You,' she heaved against him, 'prove – nothing – prove nothing you bastard – bastard – ' And with that

he turned her and laid her belly down across the work
surface. Her body made its own space, smashing neatness
into debris, sending aside a glass that rolled until it fell and
exploded on the floor by their feet. With his hands he held
her legs open and by some accident of dexterity put himself
into her without any fumble or searching; a terrible shameful
relief unblocked his loins, for his rage had been shot through
with fear that he would fail to enter her, go soft. Instead,
with that hard muscle filling her, he began to beat up,
bending his knees and driving up so that he lifted her from
the floor with every stroke, and it was not her, not her body,
it was his heart he drove against, beat against, that drum
stick – beaten by lust and rage, whose pace raced against him
until one or the other had to surrender and he, for survival,
released all his need and suffering in a shuddering discharge
that seemed as if it would never let him end. When it slowed
he was still full of tension and kept her split on that thick
rod from which he dangled her. He had her left hand in
his and drew it up high between her shoulders bunching
up the bright shirt so that he looked down the stretch of
her naked back from their intertwined fists to where the
hair of his groin foamed black against the white globes of
her buttocks. With the other hand, he gripped her by the
nape of the neck and now turned her head so that her cheek
lay against the board and she sought him with her eye. 'Do
you know what's happened to you? What I've done to you?'
he asked and tightened his grasp. She said something but
he was too excited to listen. 'You've been fucked. Your
word, not mine. Fucked.' 'You may as well stop,' she
gasped; this time he heard. 'There's no one there.'

Unstrung then, he bent forward and laid himself gently
down until he rested on her. A great sweat burst out of him,
issuing from his long need and loneliness, oiling the junction
of their bodies and thighs. Her hair surrounded his face and
he drew a strand between his lips and blew it away softly;
and saw her hand clenched by him on the board. Because
it was so close, the hand was out of proportion, grotesquely
large, little hills of knuckles, and the knife it held glinted

like a rapier. In reality only a kitchen knife with a blade five or six inches long, but honed on either side and drawn to a point. A blade for sticking or slicing . . . He remembered her hand punching into his back; her left hand; the knife was in her right.

He straightened and eased out of her. With a little grunt of complaint, she pushed herself upright. She faced him, not trying to cover herself or put on the jeans and pants tangled round one ankle.

'I'm sorry.'

'I don't ever have an orgasm. If that's important.' Her hands hung empty by her sides.

'I'm sorry.'

'You want me to cover myself?'

She bent and took up her pants, settling herself into them comfortably and smoothing the shirt down over her flanks. She pulled up her jeans and fastened the button, then fished out the toggle to draw up the zip moving her hips up and forward with an intimate movement as if she was alone.

'If you had hit me with the knife,' he said hoarsely, 'I would be dead by now.'

It lay where she had discarded it beside the bowl and the broken scatter of stuff on the surface, and she reached out and swung its shining blade away from them.

'I forgot I was holding it,' she said.

CHAPTER TWENTY-EIGHT
At Heathers'

SUNDAY, OCTOBER 14TH

'Deal?'

'What else? When he has something to celebrate, Blair likes to have the world and his wife joining in.'

'Wife? Did you bring your wife?'

As the two men laughed, framed between them Murray glimpsed Irene on the other side of the room. As he moved, the group round the piano surged back surrounding him. Trying to push through, he found himself encircled in a cleared space, alone with a woman who was wobbling her buttocks as some kind of entertainment. Holding out her hands to him, she mewed an invitation. The spectators yelped applause. He tried to pass her and she hooked plump fingers into his sleeve. He was held. She parodied excitement. Time stretched. He saw their mouths yawn like muzzles and heard them yap.

With a convulsive blow from the side of his hand, he broke her grip. Her powdered jowls shook as she panted into his face. A loop of saliva linked her parted jaws and, showing her teeth as if she might worry him like a rabid bitch, she smile-snarled, 'Shy? Are you shy?'

The party was afloat.

Against the sober man, latecomer, gate-crasher, the noise swelled. In the room next door there were more people, but Irene wasn't among them. Hurrying, he brushed by a table and set the ornamental spray of fine wires trembling in a shimmer of changing colours. From decanters and glasses light swung at his eyes. Pushing his way across the room, a pulse of pain began to tick inside his skull. The sharp prod on his shoulder came as a relief; but when he turned, disconcertingly fast, ready, it was only an overweight stranger, who stumbled back a step as if in fright.

'That was my friend.' Like a full sponge, the man leaked moisture. His cheeks glittered. 'The one you refused to dance with.'

Murray stared at him in bewilderment then remembered the fat woman.

'Are you listening?' the man asked, poised between aggression and flight. 'She doesn't need that stuff.'

On impulse Murray said, 'I wouldn't piss on your friend,' and heard a snort of amusement. Glancing round, he discovered Eddy Stewart, red moon face split in a grin.

'Take my advice. Don't argue,' Eddy said, grinning. 'This is an old mate of mine, and he's a bad bastard.'

Glaring, the man looked from one to the other and began to retreat. Over his shoulder, tremulously malevolent, he piped, 'Why did you fucking come, if you don't want to have fun?'

'That's the story of your life, Murray,' Eddy said.

'What are you doing here?'

'Mr Heathers wants to see you.'

'You have your hand on my arm.'

The big man smiled and took his hand away.

'Nobody asked you here,' he said. 'You came without being asked. But Mr Heathers is willing to have a word. So what's the problem?'

As Murray went with him, he had the illusion that time had flowed backwards and they would go outside and Peerse would be waiting in the police car to ask him why he had been to see John Merchant and the call would come and they would go to where a body was lying with its head smashed in on the dirty cobbles of a lane off Deacon Street. But John Merchant was dead and that seemed a lifetime ago. It got quieter as they went towards the back of the house. By an uncurtained window, two boys and a girl passed a cigarette and gazed out like

294

philosophers at the blank darkness over the garden.

Outside a door half-way along a passage on the first floor, a man watched their approach with the attentive lack of curiosity of a sentry on duty. He was big, over six feet, with the used features of those who live by trading in punishment. For a moment, Murray thought he recognized him as one of the men who had beaten him in the club the day Merchant died; but he couldn't be sure, and anyway it made no difference.

By contrast, Murray had forgotten how small Heathers was. Red in the cheeks as if he had been treating himself as part of his celebration, the little man swayed heel-and-toe in front of a big log fire.

'You're a silly bloody man,' he said. 'I've been talking money the last four days like telephone numbers. I'm a one man fucking solution to the unemployment problem. I've got a crowd of hangers on waiting to suck my arse. And then I've got you. What the hell do you think you're playing at coming here?'

The flush on his cheeks heightened dangerously, giving him the look of a man preparing to have his first stroke.

'Can I talk to you alone?' Murray asked.

The heavy squad had stayed outside, but Eddy Stewart had come in with him and stood to one side watching. There was a television set behind Heathers and he turned to the tray set on top of it and half filled a whisky tumbler.

'You must think I'm stupid,' he said.

From the depths of one of the three leather armchairs grouped round the fire, there came a snicker and Murray realized a man was slumped there. Although the sound had been turned off, the cassette film was still showing so that it was uncertain whether the man had been amused by Heathers or by some complication in the tangle of naked bodies on the screen.

'Go back to sleep, Peter,' Heathers said. 'You're drunk.'

'Never, sir.' The man reared up and showed them a fine head with a large nose. 'Not the sex to get drunk. Testosterone has target organs other than the testes. One

295

of them being the kidney where it induces the production of alcohol dehydrogenase. Now since that breaks down alcohol in the body and since women don't, not yet at least, not quite yet, thank God, have any balls to speak of – *I* can handle my drink like a gentleman and they *can't*.'

He said all this quickly and fluently in a voice that was deep, unslurred and authoritative. Finished, he blinked once or twice and gave an enormous yawn. Clearly he was very drunk.

'Aye, and I can say "the Leith bloody police dismisseth us",' Heathers said indulgently. 'Go back to sleep.' Drinking, he studied Murray over the tumbler's rim. 'You wouldn't be planning to do anything silly, would you? I had to pay for a new set of bridgework for Denny after you smashed his face.'

'Denny?' Murray asked, genuinely puzzled.

'My chauffeur. I reckoned that left us square.'

The pain at the base of Murray's skull flared and settled.

'I just want to talk,' he said, 'but not with him here.' He nodded towards Eddy Stewart.

'You can say anything in front of Eddy.' Heathers' tone was matter of fact.

'Policemen are funny people,' Murray said. 'You can't trust them – not even to stay bent.'

He heard Stewart curse softly, but kept his eyes on Heathers, who chewed his lip and asked, 'Just talk?'

'About a visitor you're expecting. A lady you invited.'

'Uh huh . . . Look, Eddy,' Heathers said abruptly after a pause, 'no use you staying here to be insulted, eh? Go and have some fun. Find yourself a woman.'

Without turning his head, Murray heard the door open and close. He crossed the room and sat in one of the three chairs by the fire. It was very comfortable and the leather felt slightly warm under his hand. In the other chair, the man had slumped down with his eyes shut.

'Can we get rid of that clown as well?'

'He's no clown!' In something oddly like alarm, Heathers glanced down at the man in the chair, who licked his lips and sighed, settling down deeper still. 'Started from nothing like me – I've known him since we were kids. In the medical world, he's a big man. He saved my sister's life. He's somebody. You're the fucking clown.

That was possible; it wasn't a description Murray felt like arguing over.

'What did you want to see Irene for?' he asked.

Heathers drank and wiped his bottom lip with his finger. 'To tell her I was sorry about her husband.'

'That was all?'

'I might have mentioned Alex Shepherd to her.'

The name meant nothing to Murray. 'Why would you do that?'

'You've no idea who he is, have you? He let slip to me the other day that your brother had done a favour or two for him in the way of business last year. Apparently your brother and his wife got away for a wee continental holiday last summer. Alex Shepherd was the one that paid for it.' Perhaps as a result of the warm fire and the whisky, Heathers had become flushed. 'I told him to watch his mouth, I mean keep it shut. It looks as if your brother's going to need his pension . . . and we wouldn't want him to lose it.'

'She won't be interested. She's not the grateful type,' Murray said. 'She's coming to see you because she wants to find Kujavia. Get a message to him maybe.'

'Why would she want to do that?'

Ignoring the question, Murray said, 'When she asks you, I don't think you should tell her. Not how to find Kujavia. It's not something you would want to have on your conscience.'

'People are always asking me for something.' He turned away to refill his glass. Murray heard the bottle knock on the rim of the tumbler. 'You do something for me, I do something for you. I can talk to anybody, rich or poor, crack a joke. Me, I like everybody to be happy. Christ, that's the way I am. I can't help my nature.'

As Heathers gulped at his drink, Murray saw with an

unpleasant premonition that the hand which held the tumbler was trembling.

'Just don't help her to find him. He's a madman. You know how he treats those women of his.' Murray ignored the head shake of denial. 'He killed one of them, right?'

'I never heard he killed anybody,' Heathers protested. 'He's like everybody else, he just wants to make money. Why would he do something stupid like that?'

For a moment, Murray was sure he could not be serious; but Heathers stared back at him with the innocence of an enormous greed:

'You don't control him.' he said at last. 'He's an animal.' In desperation, he cast around for some way of persuading Heathers. 'One of his tricks is to dress up as a woman. John Merchant's mistress, Frances Fernie, she was afraid of Kujavia – never mind why. She wouldn't have opened the door of her flat at night to let a man in . . .' He hesitated. 'But she might have opened the door to a man dressed as a woman.'

'How many murders is he supposed to have done according to you?' Heathers' attempt at laughter sounded bad and quickly he gave it up. 'Did he murder Merchant as well? Is he Jack the bloody Ripper or Jill or what?'

The man in the chair opened his eyes. Glancing at him, Murray found their gaze fixed on him, and his heart jumped as if he had been caught doing something wrong. The man was slumped deep in the chair; even the flesh of his face sagged, under the cheeks, in folds down to pouches drooping on either side of the mouth. In the middle of that general surrender, the eyes were clear and hard; blue-grey, the marksman's colour.

'Jill rips Jack, Jack rips Jill,' the voice said unslurred. 'In Yorkshire, Sutcliffe was a cowardly boy – and even when he got a man's muscles, he couldn't deal with a woman without a hammer – he had to be *sure*. You can pay too high a price for love poetry. There's a little worm that lives in the sea and at dawn a week before the full moon in November it breaks in two. The front bit where the brains

298

are stays where it is, but the bit at the back floats up. All of them do that – millions of them. The sea's like soup, and then whoosh! out come the sperm and the eggs – like milk all over the surface. Sex soup. But the *brains* aren't in the soup – they stay down among the coral where it's quiet and a worm can think. Not like us. We want to be kind to one another – but how can we be? Don't blame Jack – or Jill. Compared to the worms, we're not well arranged,

The deep voice unwound without hurrying, hypnotic in its certainty that it would not be interrupted; and then the eyes blinked, the mouth gaped in a yawn – and all the authority vanished.

'Be quiet, Peter, you're drunk,' Heathers said mechanically.

He had unnoticed taken a seat, and Murray was surprised by the change in him. He looked old and shrunken in upon himself.

The deep voice muttered a reply as if to itself, '. . . not the *only* arrangement, didn't say it was . . . could do what the fire-worms do off Bermuda and *burst* – the two sexes come together and burst . . . shredded . . .'

'You're too late,' Heathers said. 'You should have come earlier. She was here, I gave her a number to phone. Whatever happens, it's nothing to do with me. Get that straight. As far as I'm concerned, she wasn't here. I don't want to know.' He sucked at the last of the whisky and his upper lip creased in anticipation of the deep cut lines of extreme age. 'I didn't mean to tell her. I didn't want – I wish I'd never met the bitch!'

'Columbus saw them on the night he approached the New World,' the man in the chair said aloud. 'Sending out signals of light before they burst,' He began to giggle like a child, a noise so unexpected that Murray's skin crawled. 'Oh, the lights, Columbus said. Oh, the pretty lights. Look at the lights!'

CHAPTER TWENTY-NINE
Various Wounds

MONDAY, OCTOBER 15TH

When he slipped and fell, he saw between his outflung
hands cigarette stubs, soft paper gobs into swirls like marine
life and by them fat splashes of snot, white, with thicker
centres – tiny eggs broken on the pavement. Irene hadn't
gone home last night, or returned when he checked this
morning. He had no idea where she was. Now he sprawled
at the entrance to the close that led to Mary O'Bannion's
flat; he had knocked and waited and knocked, no answer;
coming out, he had been in too much of a hurry and fallen.
Irene or Kujavia, he had to find one or other of them before
they came together. If they hadn't already; but he couldn't
afford to consider that. All he could do was keep looking.

There wasn't much time.

'Hairdressers,' the woman said, rolling down her tights
as she sat on the edge of the bed. 'Or that's what they
claimed they were. I hate fucking amateurs. . . Do you want
the blouse off next or the skirt?'

'Whichever you like.'

'You don't care which?' She gave him an unexpectedly
shrewd look. 'Take the top off, will I?' Without standing
up, she began to unbutton the blouse. It was less like a
strip-tease than the unthinking movements with which a
mechanic unpacks a tool kit. 'So the two of them had a right
big tip for themselves. Specially the younger one. Gave me
this patter about when they went back with this bloke and
how he tried to get funny. We smashed up his place, the
younger one said. Bloody mad amateurs!' She took off her

bra and glanced down without pleasure at the released flop of her breasts. 'I think she was a bit touched – the younger one.' She wriggled her bum and the skirt came from under her and slid to the floor. 'I know a head case when I see one . . . well, in this game,' she smiled placatingly, 'you have to, don't you? But I haven't seen them since. Not around here. Just that time and once before – back in the summer before it got cold.'

Murray was not interested, although he understood why she was talkative. Even a whore could get nervous. He hardly listened, trying to judge when it would be right to ask his question.

Unclothed, she stood up to let him look at her. She began to turn then changed her mind and sat down again on the bed. She leaned back resting her weight on her hands in an obsolete starlet pose, and asked, opening her legs, 'You sure you don't want anything else?'

He shook his head.

'You just want me to get dressed again . . .'

She took up the bra and bent forward to let her breasts fall into the cups. As she reached behind to fasten it, he said, 'There is one thing you could do for me.'

Caught like that, she hesitated with her hands reaching up her back.

'Tell me what you want, and I'll tell you what it costs.'

'The answer to a question.' He took out all the money he had left and fanned it towards her. 'I need to find Joe Kujavia. I'll pay for a whisper.'

'Oh, no.' She began to dress, cramming her clothes on in her hurry. 'You've come to the wrong place. I don't know what you're on about.'

'I'm not police,' he said, without moving nearer or raising his voice. 'You know what I am, just a John, another mug. Didn't I pay you already? I'm harmless. Only I need to find Joe – I can pay, here, as much as you—'

'I want you out of here.'

She padded on her bare feet across the dirty linoleum and opened the door that gave on to the corridor.

'Come on,' she said. 'I can get somebody here if I shout.'

'You've already taken my money. Suppose I say you took it for telling me where Joe Kujavia is? You wouldn't be any worse off if you did tell me. Nobody would know.'

'Please.' She had closed the door. 'Just go away. You can have your money back.'

And she actually went over to the dresser and came with it held out.

'You earned it, keep it. I haven't asked for anything back. You've got it the wrong way round – I'm trying to chuck it away. That's how nice I am. You're frightened – but I was joking. I won't say anything – not if you can tell me where he is. Who's to know?'

'Please,' she said again, and added with a desperate reasonableness, 'I want to get out to the shops before they shut.'

All he could do was keep looking. He tried to find Irene.

At Mother's, he let himself in with his key, but knew at once it was going to be no good. Even the air of the flat felt deserted. In the living room, he stared around trying to decide what was wrong; and then realized it was because the table was not set. Mother always had the table set for their Sunday lunches. He wandered through into the tiny kitchen. Searching for a glass, he knocked a jug off the shelf. The crash of its breaking startled him like guilt. – I think you do it deliberately to torment me! Mother would cry, rushing in out of his childhood, tall and young.

When he was in the hall, he intended to go back out of the front door. He stood with the handle in his hand, head bent as if in thought. The handle warmed in his palm, and at last he crossed and pushed the bedroom door gently open.

'There's nothing to steal.'

The voice was Mother's.

With a convulsive movement, he thrust the door wide. She was sitting up in bed. Under a disordered flying scantness of hair, her scalp shone white; the mouth without its teeth had sunk into a shrivelled hole; a claw hand

athered the gown across the wrinkled corded skin of her
chest. He looked on her in horror.

'I thought it was burglars,' she whispered.

'I was sure no one was here. I—' Why had he come in
here then? '. . . I'm sorry.'

'I woke up straight out of my sleep, something had fallen
in the kitchen. And then I heard steps. People moving
about—'

'No,' Murray said, 'it was just me.'

She patted her hair trying to flatten it. At another thought,
she covered her mouth with her hand. From behind it, she
said, 'Upstairs was broken into. All round here. Because
of the drugs, they need money. The couple in the paper
shop, they were tied up. I woke up and heard the noise.'

'I've been looking for Irene. I didn't really think she'd
be here, but — and so when I walked in I was sure there
was no one. I thought you would be at the hospital.'

She kept her hand over her mouth, but she wasn't afraid
any more. She frowned and said angrily, 'I'm going to bring
Malcolm home.'

'Home?' Murray tried to make sense of the word. He stared
round the cramped overcrowded bedroom. 'He doesn't live
here. What do you mean — home? Even the furniture's
new. You don't even have any of the old furniture.'

'Are you drunk?' Mother asked. 'Like your father, are
you drunk?'

There wasn't much time.

It occurred to him that while he was out searching for
her, Irene might be at his flat, locked out, and waiting for
him to come back.

As he hurried past, the old paperseller Barney caught at
his sleeve. 'Hang on, I've something to tell you.' But he
would not risk being overheard and so kept up a monologue
punctuated by the sharp slap of folding each paper before
passing it across. '. . . bloody brother-in-law. Never worked
a day in his life. You know what a parasite is? A parasite.
Now he's getting it posted. The form, I'm talking about.
The form, the fucking form and the giro. Because he's taken

303

her out into the country, he doesn't even have to sign on. They post – Wait, Murray! That certain person – the one you mentioned to me . . .' The change of tone was abrupt as they got the pavement to themselves. 'He's got a wee trick of dressing up like a lassie. I just remembered that. And I hear he can get away with it – even though he's such an ugly cunt.'

Murray stared at him speechless.

'That's what I hear anyway . . .' Barney trailed off.

'That's what you wanted to tell me?'

The paperseller put a hand to his lips in a gesture that, despite the pouched eyes and the grey unshaven jaws, was oddly childlike. 'Oh, Christ, Murray. Did I tell yous that already? I did, didn't I? For fuck's sake, I think my head's wasted.'

'No. It's all right,' Murray said. 'Thanks, Barney.'

The old man grinned in relief.

'Any time. I hear things yous never would.'

The years caught up with everyone. The years and the red wine.

And, of course, Irene wasn't waiting for him outside his flat. He accepted in his exhaustion that it would be Miss Timmey, knocking and knocking on the broken door as he climbed towards her. What she had to tell him, he heard like a message from his own despair.

'. . . his head just looked too big for his wee body, not a stitch of clothes on him, all his ribs standing out, you could have counted them, it was like one of those pictures you'd see of the poor folk during the war in the camps or some wee black bairn in Africa, and he was just bruises all over and what was . . . between his legs, you know, *there*, was hurt.'

'It was a girl they had, it was a girl,' Murray protested, not pointing but holding up one hand as if for protection against the closed door of the middle flat. A girl, happy, healthy, as fat as she could roll; a child of love held between two of the beautiful people, Moirhill version. Every time you saw the couple they looked as if they had just got out

f bed, glossy and replete; you could see how the sight of
them might drive an old woman, a dry spinster, demented;
o that she imagined a child was being tortured, pestered
with what she had imagined she had heard. That was an
asy problem for him to solve, a man who understood
human nature, a detective.

'It was a girl,' he repeated stupidly. 'The child in there
was a girl.'

'Nobody knew, you see, about the wee boy, he was never
et out, they say she had him by another man before she
got married, *if* she *was* – married that is, and they kept
him tied to a cot but something must have happened and he
got out and they found him crawling down the stair . . .
and he was that light, that light, you felt you could pick
him up and hold him in one hand.'

To Murray's horror, the old woman wept.

'I said to the police I told you what I'd heard. They were
ight angry. They'll be coming to see you, I expect. I had
o tell them I'd told you.'

Crossing a vacant piece of ground at the corner of Florence
Street, Murray began to shudder. From somewhere out
beyond the suburbs, the wind carried a sprinkling of snow.
A long time ago in the Northern shop, autumn then too,
and one of the other policemen arguing with him about how
exactly they executed traitors under the old savage laws of
England: thick lipped, emphatic, a white complexion under
ed hair; arguing until he went to the phone to settle it. The
voice of the librarian had replied at once, 'The traitor was
hung and the bowels drawn out and burned in front of his
eyes while he was still alive. Oh, and he was castrated. And
hen—' What had been strange to Murray was that he had
answered at once, without having to check any book, as if
he had been waiting for just that question.

Behind him, the light of the shop window threw a lozenge
of yellow on the wet pavement. It was dark and getting late;
he was running out of time and this felt like his last chance.
Although he hadn't eaten that day, the smell of food made
him feel sick.

305

'Kujavia?' the Indian behind the counter repeated thoughtfully. 'No . . . I do not know that man. That is quite unfamiliar to me.' Despite the beleaguered shutters over the windows, he had the air of a man in transit, passing with cardigan wrinkling over a full paunch from Moirhill to better things.

'Now that surprises me,' Murray said with a tired sour grimace. He made as if to go, then turning back asked almost casually, 'Is the black girl still here?'

Involuntarily, the shopkeeper's eyes widened. He bent his head over the bundle of papers on the counter, and tapped at a face in a picture with a hard brown finger. 'It's absolutely wrong,' he complained. 'Why should educated people still want to read of such a person?' Even upside down, yesterday's monster, Idi Amin, was unmistakable. 'I could not tell you how much I hate that man. We lived in the same street as him. He was our friend. And no sooner were we at the airport then he took all our furniture. Lovely furniture – made in Denmark to our order. We had seven cars.'

'Is that where you got a taste for the black ones?'

The shopkeeper frowned in offence. 'We do not care for them. Not in that way.'

'I've just come from one of Kujavia's whores,' Murray said. 'She didn't know where he was – of course. But she told me she'd seen the black girl coming in here. All I want to do is talk to her – that's all,

Slowly, the large brown eyes turned to look towards the back of the store. A curtain was drawn across the opening. 'She was in distress,' he said. 'It was an act of humanity.'

As he put back the curtain, he heard the shuffle of feet. She was edging away step by step, but the back room was small and it didn't take long for her to reach the end. She watched him with wide fixed eyes, the pupils dilated as if she was drugged or in shock. An enormous bruise distorted one side of her face, and as she sucked in her lower lip with a parody of something appealing and childish a gap showed where a front tooth was gone. She was young, and under

306

the ruin of her face enough was left to suggest she had been fine looking.

'She won't talk to you, you know,' he heard the shop-keeper say. 'I have given her tea. It was an act of humanity. Something dreadful has happened, but she will not talk.'

Murray stepped through and let the curtain drop behind him. The weak single bulb cast a drained light. 'You don't have to be afraid of me,' he said to the black girl. 'Did you come from Mary O'Bannion's?'

She nodded.

'Was Kujavia there?'

She stared at him, blank and fixed as if she had not heard.

'Did something happen?'

In the long moment of waiting, her smell came to him – a female scent rank and pungent; and then something else, a sweet sickliness of unwashed flesh that did not seem to belong to her, but reminded him of the fat woman – and their smells were different yet strangely mingled and confused, partaking one of the other, so that suddenly he had an image of them intertwined obscenely on the fetid bed.

'Did something happen?'

And at last she folded one hand into a long fist as if holding something and swung it in the air.

An iron bar, beating down . . .

'Is she dead?'

Into the gap of the broken tooth, she sucked her lip stroking it with her tongue and then, sweetly, unexpectedly, like a child, she smiled.

'I cannot tell you how much I hate that man,' the grocer said as Murray left. There was no way of knowing if he was thinking of Kujavia or Amin. 'If I had that man here, I would stick pins in him and pour in salt.'

CHAPTER THIRTY
Trap

MONDAY, OCTOBER 15TH

In the corridor where the dog had lain, the mountain of flesh that had been Mary O'Bannion had given up the ghost. One arm was flung out and despite himself he noticed how small it was and fine boned as if it had been spared for a cruel memento. He searched the kitchen and the back room and remembered as he was leaving to check the little lavatory, but no one was in hiding. He pulled the outer door shut and it looked all right although he had broken the locks to get in.

The light on the landing below was out and he felt his way down; the slippery chill of the wooden banister sliding under his palm. Perhaps Kujavia had told Mary O'Bannion that he was going to meet Irene. Perhaps she had tried to persuade him not to go, tried to tell him it was a trap, made of herself a gross barrier to block his way. He had killed her and gone. But where? Where would Irene ask him to come? The risk she was taking; there was no place where she could be safe with him, the man who had killed her sister. Where would she want him to come? The man who had killed her sister . . .

Someone was coming up, a man's steps, climbing fast. It was as if his ears had been closed in a dream and suddenly he heard.

He stepped into a corner of the dark landing. There was a hasty panting, absurdly loud, and he held his breath and felt instead his heart tick in his throat. The shape came from below in a rush. Stepping on to the landing, it was tall, taller

than Kujavia, and Murray let his breath sigh out. At the
sound there was an exclamation of fright and the figure
stretched out a hand towards him and then fled stumbling
upwards. The light from above glowed through a bristling
mane of hair; there was no mistaking that halo.

Tommy Beltane had come to visit again.

Yet he did not believe Kujavia would come.

He prowled from room to room, keeping away from the
windows. In the bedroom, he slid open the drawers in turn.
It seemed he should recognize some of the things he had
spilled out on this floor. The police must have gone through
the flat after she was killed, but her stuff lay in the drawer
laundered and folded, like clothes that had never been worn
waiting for an owner. Soon perhaps the real owners, the
shadowed figures behind John Merchant, would dispose of
the place. There were books on a shelf by a bed, but their
titles meant nothing to him. No more than the clothes they
had anything to do with her: props of the part she had
played for Merchant. From the bottom of the last drawer,
he lifted out the child's doll, old and ragged with only a
tuft or two of yellow hair. As he gripped the scabbed toy,
he had an image of the woman snatching it up, how she
twisted her body so that he was never out of sight. A child
trapped in the desolate cottage by the edge of the sea where
Annette Verhaeren's daughters had been taken would have
needed something to comfort her. Or she might have come
across it in a corner of this flat, discarded by some previous
woman: there was no way of being sure. Gravely, it watched
him out of the one remaining eye in the battered face.

In the bathroom, big fluffy orange towels were folded on
the rail as if she might step out alive from behind the hinged
leaf of marled glass that concealed the shower. There was
a handbasin inset into a black surface; and a circular mirror
above it that showed him a coil of light reflected in his eyes.
He fingered the contents of a shelf: Charles of the Ritz
boxes, Aludrox, a medicine, L'Homme Roger et Gallet,
Crème à Raser, at the end a smokey brown bottle, Eau de

309

Toilette, the cap black and round with a bronze press knob. Like the clothes, like the books, he could not find Frances Fernie. She had seemed wary and not easily to be caught; but she had opened the door that night to a hunter more cunning than herself. Carefully, he pulled the cord to put out even the light around the mirror before he opened the bathroom door, but light flooded in and the shape of a woman straightened from where she was laying her coat on the bed.

'When I came in, I thought you'd changed your mind and gone,' Irene said. 'You've been sitting in the dark.'

'No. I had the light on in here. Not at the front – in case he was watching from the street.'

'He'll be here soon,' she said.

He blinked at his watch. It was exactly eleven o'clock.

'In half an hour, if he's punctual. Where did you go?'

'I just drove around like you wanted me to,' she said. 'When I thought it was time, I came back. If he's down there, he's seen me coming in alone. Wasn't that the idea?'

'He'll be afraid of a trap. He'll be watching somewhere out there.'

'If he was out there when you came in, then he knows you're here,' she said.

Murray shrugged. 'I did some looking myself before I came in. I'm betting he wasn't there.'

Without being sure . . . He had not told her about the murder of Mary O'Bannion. Where would Kujavia have gone after the fat woman's death? He did not think he would come here.

'If he comes at all,' he said to her.

'Oh, yes. There isn't any doubt about that.' She began to laugh. Pointing, she asked, 'What's that you've got?'

He was still holding the doll by an arm, dangling from his left hand. He looked at it in bewilderment. Irene appeared enormously alive to him. The light hurt his eyes and head, he had not eaten since the day before; with an aching floating clarity, he saw that excitement had heightened her into

310

omething that glittered like beauty. She was full of expec-
ation. Beside her he was diminished.

'You're not well,' she said. 'Why don't you go before he
:omes? That would be better. You still have time.'

Instead of answering, he held out the doll. With a move-
nent he would have been ashamed of if it had been conscious,
ae stroked a finger down the yellow hair. 'I found this in
ne of the drawers. It belonged to Frances.'

'I don't think so.'

'I saw her with it that time I came here. It belonged to
her.'

She sat on the bed. 'It doesn't seem worth arguing about.
I mean what difference does it make who it belongs to?'

'I don't know, I was looking for something that would
help me to understand her. It's as though she never lived
here. I was trying to remember her face.' The woman in front
of him, however, his brother's wife, had kept intruding into
his thoughts; now it was as if the two sisters were one;
mysteriously the living and the dead had merged. 'But I
only met her that once. It'll be different for you, you'll
remember how she looked.'

'Suppose I did? Why should you care?'

'She killed men. I was trying to understand what might
make a woman who would do that.' He flicked the doll and
it sprawled on to the bed beside her with legs apart and one
hand flung up above its head. She tensed at the suddenness
of it then relaxed. 'She was your sister. Didn't you see her
playing with that when you were kids? It must have meant
something to her, something special. Did you get it from
your mother, from Annette?'

'I don't remember,' she said, so emphatically that
he accepted it as honest. She stood up. 'It's almost
time.'

As if she could not keep still, she yawned and stretched.
She went back and forward two or three steps one way then
the other. A stranger brilliant with some dazzling expectancy
smiled at him and took up the bag thay lay beside her coat
on the bed.

311

'Here, Murray,' she said. 'You're so anxious to understand everybody. I'll make you a present of that.'

It was a pocket diary with Frances' name in front; but
there were only notes of hair appointments, a visit to the
dentist, an entry: 'Walked in the park'. Even these jottings
became less frequent, stopped at last in May, so that most
of the little book was blank.

'He'll come,' she said. 'We have to be ready.'

He followed her along the passage. A door that he had
not remarked at the end on the right led into a very small
narrow space like a pantry. In the corner, there was a
window that looked into the living room. It was set deep
in the wall like part of an old conversion, and was covered
on either side with a net curtain.

'You could watch from here,' she said.

Without answering her, he went out and through into the
living room. Set high, dirty, the window in the corner wasn't
anything to notice. Glancing that way, the attention was
taken by the painting of brown fields with a tiny cold
moon-sun low over a hill. Through the open door, along
the short passage, he could see the bed with her coat thrown
on it.

'But you can't be in *here*,' she said, coming after him.
For the first time, she seemed uncertain of herself. 'Not
when he comes. I have to see him on my own.'

'We want a confession.'

He would play out the game until she realized it was
hopeless and Kujavia would not come.

'You know if he sees you it won't work. You said yourself
he'd think it was a trap. He'd go away — you'll spoil —
I didn't want you here. Please, please—'

She almost wept in the distress of her frustration. He
thought of the men who had been killed, of fat Leo Arnold
weeping for his brother, of Merchant. 'If Frances wasn't
worth it . . .' He wanted to comfort her. He wanted to
hold her.

'No!' She swayed back and struck away his hand. 'None
of that.' Her lips writhed as if getting rid of filth.

Three spaced knocks beat against the outer door.

'Now,' she cried softly. 'Please, please. He's here.'

Because he had not believed Kujavia would come, the sounds went through him as separate shocks each one like a blow. He rubbed at the side of his head and caught himself in the act of that unconscious gesture which had become a habit with him.

In a sudden alteration, she brought her body close to his. She put his hand on her breast. 'I didn't mean that just now,' she whispered. 'We can make love, afterwards, we can, I won't mind, anything, afterwards.' In her urgency, she pressed herself against him.

The drum beat in Murray's skull. On the outer door, the fist beat steadily.

'If it is him, he's here to kill you,' he said.

She stepped back, needing room for her great moment.

'He's my father.' And she nodded, eager to share it. 'Not Frances – just me. My father. Mine. I've always known that. There's no way he wouldn't come when I told him that. He won't hurt me.'

But Mary O'Bannion was dead. What she said was impossible, a crazy thing. He struggled to find the words, a man in an alien country, that would make her understand.

'And Annette Verhaeren?'

An iron bar beating down into the flesh that had mothered her.

The knocking on the outer door stopped.

'He'll go away,' she cried in the same soft hasty whisper. 'Oh, you bastard, why don't you go in there, before it's too late,' she began to push at his chest, herding him backwards, 'please, before he goes away, you fucking bastard – I didn't mean that – you're right.' He was the mirror in which she might glimpse these alterations. 'You're right, he's here to be punished, we'll punish him, there's a lane at the back, and I've parked my car close – please, please, he's going away – it won't be difficult, with two of us it'll be easy—' She had actually driven him back by

313

the strength of her desperation. With her hands fluttering at his chest, he stepped into the narrow pantry-like space. Giving in, he moved away from her unurged until he was by the window. Through the droop of soiled curtain, he could see into the room they had left. 'He'll be just another of them,' she whispered. 'Just somebody else found in Moirhill.'

Out of the dark, Kujavia came, a small man, hardly taller than the woman, but very broad. He was wearing a suit rumpled enough for him to have slept in it, but the material looked heavy and of good quality. When he unbuttoned the jacket, braces showed curving over a little high paunch. His shirt was open at the neck with a scarf knotted at the throat. And Murray knew him: with his lumpy potato face, dull, malicious, brutal, those erected spikes of black hair, he was the one from the nightmare out of the circle of standing men, a silver club glittering in his hand, the arc of his arm carrying darkness. A small man, not much taller than the woman, but very broad.

Apart from one glance round as he entered, Kujavia seemed unsuspicious. Perhaps he had been watching and had seen her arrive alone. In any case, it did not seem to occur to him there might be anyone else in the flat.

Behind the glass, they moved and gesticulated. The woman came nearer and then, as if surprised, retreated. The man's face was distorted by a heavy jeering contempt. His mouth moved and he showed his teeth like a dog. On his side of the glass, Murray listened in the silence to the uneven thunder of his heart.

—Did you ever set a trap, Kujavia? You go back and it's been sprung. When you're very young and sqeamish, it isn't a nice sight. The bar beaten into the fur of its neck. The paws stretched out like small hands. I was so squeamish, being young, that I picked all of it up by the edges of the wooden base, in a piece of newspaper so I wouldn't really *touch* anything, and threw it in the bin, trap, mouse and all. The mouse dangling like a glove, boneless and empty. Mother was angry at the waste. She made me go out and empty it (the horror in case the dead thing clung) then fetch it inside. A trap for every time – that would be expensive. She said to me, You have to learn to live in the real world.

—And it always caught them across the neck. Crack! and you saw the pink show of its tongue. And a tiny pile of shit at the back, so little you might not notice it as you lift the trap away. It must nibble the cheese and release the trap and then *jump back* – for if it didn't the bar wouldn't land exactly there on the neck – *crack!* Believe me, it's worked out. Whoever makes these traps, works it out. But suppose the mouse, when the trap moved, froze still? That might save it. Nobody's ever imagined a mouse that kept still when the trap went.

—But whatever, whoever, would be able to stay when the great terror whistled in the air?

—Nature was against it.

When he opened the door, it seemed Irene was as startled as Kujavia. They were standing as close as conspirators or lovers interrupted in guilt. Kujavia took three or four trotting steps backward, groping behind him, feeling for the door. 'Oh, fucking bitch,' he spat venomously. 'You do this. You do this to me.'

It was the moment of surprise. It was cripple or kill time and never a better chance. The knowledge was mapped into the memory of his muscles. Yet he let the precious time of advantage pass though he had been trained so it came more easily to act, his body, like the bodies of so many men, made over into an obedient animal prepared to slip the leash. Yet he stood, the animal was forgetful; his will tangled in the strangeness of their resemblance, as if beauty and ugliness could be confused.

And as the moment was lost, Kujavia made his own act of recognition.

'Sure . . .' He struggled with it, the thick pulpy brows drawn down, then showed a row of yellow teeth. 'Sure! I give you a small lesson when Mr Heathers ask me, then he take you on. He hire you. What is it? Does she pay you?

315

Is that what she promise? She doesn't have any money. She talks fancy, but I know her. She's nothing. I pay you. I'm a rich man.'

'I was going to tell you he was there,' Irene said on one breath, like a child pleading.

'What do you care about this, mister?' Kujavia asked contemptuously. 'It's not your business. Is she going to sleep with you? I give you plenty of women.' He turned the black deadness of his gaze briefly on the woman. 'Or her. I can give you her. Blair Heathers is a rich man – like me. But I know how to handle the women.'

'I don't want you to be afraid of him,' Murray heard Irene cry. 'I don't want you to be afraid of anybody. He told me you killed—'

'You be quiet,' Kujavia interrupted her, without raising his voice. 'I don't tell you to speak. Keep your mouth shut.' He began to sidle forward, addressing himself now to Murray, keeping his attention fixed on the other man's eyes. 'You go away now. You and me don't have quarrel. Forget you ever been here. I deal with her, okay? You don't hear of her any more. You take some money. That's what you want. That way you have no problem, no trouble. I'm a rich man.'

Murmuring, he crept forward. It was too obvious a trick. Yet Murray waited inertly, his hands by his sides, his body slack. He was barely conscious of the words or what they meant . . . *at first you could hear men all round you hidden among the trees and then there was only your own breath and the sounds of your feet made on the iron floor of the forest . . . In the morning, a father and his sons came with blood on their boots and hands* . . . Merchant's nightmare and his own fused . . . A murderous peasant who would kill him.

He was saved by the sweet smell of human dirt tickling the nostrils like sickness as Kujavia took the last step. It released the animal in the body. He knocked away Kujavia's fist with its deadly armour of rings striking for his throat. It was a forearm block and done with such force it took them

316

off their feet and crashing to the floor with Murray underneath. As the terrible little man hooked for the eyes with his thumbs, Murray caught him by both wrists.

Like that, locked in an effort so great that they were held in a matched stillness, Murray understood that he was going to beat Kujavia. He was younger. He was stronger. All the frustration and doubt were burned away; the confusion was burned away in violence. The fear of death that the eating pain in his skull had taught was gone. Everything was simple. Steadily, remorselessly, he forced up his right hand to turn the other man. Kujavia panted, began to slobber with the effort, but little by little was being twisted. Each of them knew how it was going to end. They saw in one another's eyes the same knowledge.

Kujavia swooped his neck and open-jawed went for Murray's nose with his teeth. He was quick but Murray's response was faster. The hard crest of his forehead smashed into Kujavia's face as it came down. He felt the cheekbone splinter and sink. In the shock of pain, Kujavia reared up and Murray saw above them Irene holding a knife.

The handle of the knife was brown. In the kitchen a set of them were laid out in the compartments of a drawer. Each had a brown handle and its blade sheathed in a plastic cover. He had passed them over as ordinary kitchen knives, but now, recognizing one, he identified all of them. They were butcher's knives for severing, boning, chining. Honed, such a knife was sharp enough to slice meat without pressure: flesh melted under it. Holding one of them, a woman was a match for any man. Like a silver club, the knife shone on the arc of her arm. Murray heaved up in an effort to escape and in the same instant Kujavia writhed in the air like a blind worm.

The trap shut.

With a mortal scream of anger, Kujavia collapsed along the length of Murray's body, who bore his weight, felt him shudder and sigh until with a final threshing of the legs he groaned and lay still. He had bitten off his tongue and blood flowed from his mouth on to Murray's face.

317

In a convulsion of terror, Murray threw off the body. He jerked it away at Irene forcing her back and off balance. In the same movement, picked up by fear's hand, he was on his feet and had caught her by the forearm with both hands. As he squeezed, she released the grip and the knife fell to the floor. Struggling for breath, they leaned together.

There was no way now of telling if his life had been at stake.

CHAPTER THIRTY-ONE
The Last Victim

TUESDAY, OCTOBER 16TH

'Tommy Beltane?' Murray asked.

It was a bad omen.

'There's Eddy,' Billy Shanks, distracted, was watching a group of men coming out of the building and starting across the yard. 'If I could get him on his own, I might learn some of the details.'

'What did he phone you about?'

'Who?' His attention elsewhere, Shanks was puzzled. 'Oh, Tommy – phoned this morning – I don't know – Hell! There's Peerse come out as well. I wonder if Eddy will be going with him . . .' He gave a little muffled snort of laughter. 'Would you know he was disappointed? Peerse doesn't bend – but he's had the leaves blown off. He had the idea Jill was his big chance – now it's over and—'

'Have they arrested her?'

'You're hurting me.' Murray had to force his fist to unclench off Shanks' arm. 'They're looking over. You'll get us arrested, Murray. It was all a nod and a wink stuff from McKellar in there, but they're looking pleased with themselves. All except Peerse – I think he's coming over.'

The tall figure, followed by Eddy Stewart, detached itself from the group. As he watched their approach, Murray put his hands in his pockets to hide their trembling. He had not seen Irene since he had lifted the awkward weight of Kujavia's body out of the car. When he came back, groping down the unlighted stair, she had driven away, either frightened off or abandoning him according to some plan of her own.

'What's he been doing? Crying on your shoulder?' Eddy Stewart jerked a thumb contemptuously at Murray.

At the harshness of that tone, Billy Shanks' arms flew up from his sides as if he would pull his two friends together. 'On my shoulder for what?' Billy cried in distress.

From his great height, Peerse's gaze drifted over them, chilly and remote.

'Billy's the one who's been doing the talking,' Murray said. 'He tells me I'm innocent.'

'Were you accused of something?' Peerse wondered mildly. 'You were asked questions. If you're found wandering about Moirhill at one in the morning, you must expect to be asked questions.'

'Have you been held all night?' Shanks asked, suddenly understanding. 'We just met,' he explained impulsively, 'when I came out from the briefing. He was here and he asked me for a lift—' He broke off and cleared his throat nervously.

'It's all right, Billy,' Murray said. 'You're innocent too.'

'What did they hold you for? Just for walking down the street?'

'He had blood on his clothes,' Eddy Stewart said.

The words created an odd lengthening silence. The other men had left the yard and they had it to themselves. Although the sun had come out, it was cold in the long morning shadow of the building. A police car slid across the gate entrance and stopped. When Peerse looked towards it and then at him, Murray understood and fell into step at his side, walking towards the gate. Something unspoken was communicated between them.

'If I'd been there,' Peerse said, nodding back in the direction of the building they had left, 'during the night, I'd have asked you different questions.'

'Yes.' Murray made the simple acknowledgement; it was a fact they recognized.

'Would I have got different answers?'

'Maybe, then.' As he spoke, Murray was conscious of Peerse's gaze turning down to him. 'Not now.' They crossed the line of the shadow of sunlight. 'As a matter of fact, there weren't all that many questions. I spent most of the night in a room, waiting. Some time after it got light outside, they started. But pretty soon, this guy came in and whispered something – and they went and left me. That was it. I think they forgot about me, until just now when they let me go.'

As they came nearer the car, the driver started to get out, but, at a gesture from Peerse, scrambled back, closing the door again. Through the glass, Murray saw him staring straight ahead.

'Kujavia was found dead last night,' Peerse said. 'That's why they left you alone. Mary O'Bannion was found lying beside him. Would you like to offer a theory for that?'

'They quarrelled about something. Did he use that bar of his on her? It's surprising he hasn't killed her with it before. I don't know how she got him.'

'Did I say she was dead? You're right though, and about the iron bar. Only while all this was going on, she managed to stab him. They found the knife in her hand. It was quite a special knife apparently – and so they've decided she was Jill.'

'Mary O'Bannion?' Murray was so genuinely astonished that he could not hide his incredulity at the idea.

'The psychologists will explain it all to us,' Peerse said. 'She was taking revenge for a lifetime of being abused. They're not much help while you're looking – but if you can give them a name, they'll fit an explanation to it for you.'

'None of that sounds like proof.'

'Oh, proof,' Peerse echoed ironically. 'You don't understand. It doesn't take a lot of evidence to convict a dead woman. There isn't going to be a trial. Not that they won't be cautious, nobody's going to say anything for the record. Not just now. They'll wait and see, let time pass – if there aren't any more Jill killings, that's all the proof they'll need. Some time during the night, McKellar decided to see it that way; after that they all did. Shanks and his crowd got to read between the lines this morning. Nothing official. But from now on, everything runs down.'

'Unless there's another killing.'

Peerse shook his head. 'I'm an exceptional man in a profession that values mediocrity,' he said, without any particular emphasis, 'but I don't wish that. I should, believing in justice. Maybe I've been pretending not to be different for too long – with just enough showing to make myself distrusted and do the damage anyway. Maybe I'm not exceptional any more.' He contemplated that possibility. 'I think it's possible the killings might have stopped – if so, we'll never know why. But McKellar will close the file. That fat clumsy whore will have killed them all. Did you ever see her walk? She wore slippers all the time, but she got rid of the bodies in back alleys in Moirhill. It's wonderful what a fat cripple can do. So it's probably over.' He stood, impossibly tall, and asked, 'Are you sure there isn't something you want to tell me?'

'Not if it's solved,' Murray said.

Peerse nodded abruptly and got into the car. He had to duck his head because he sat up so straight.

As Billy Shanks drove back into town, Murray stared out at the mean shop fronts of Moirhill Road flowing past and wondered where Irene might have gone. Had she gone home, back to the house she shared with Malcom? He had to see her.

'That was a long talk Ian Peerse had with you,' Billy said, jerking the car to a stop at a red light. 'Yes.' He whistled tunelessly, leaning forward over the wheel to watch for the lights to change. 'It wasn't like Peerse somehow . . . Yes. He seemed to be doing most of the talking. That's not like him. Not like him, eh?' He smacked into gear and wrenched the car forward. 'He's an arrogant bastard, but I could see he wasn't happy this morning. Not with any of it. What did you think?'

'I think,' Murray said, 'that I prefer Peerse arrogant.' But it was more than that.

What would you find to say to Billy, if he was able, if he could make himself be different?

—I thought that Peerse was the hunter who would not get tired. Without knowing it, not until now, he was the one I had put my faith in: so that whatever I decided or did, in the end he would make it be right. I knew, you see, he believed in justice, Billy – like me – only I didn't expect him to get tired. I thought he was an exceptional man.

'It's always just the one way with you, Murray,' Billy said. 'But if you want to get information, you have to give a little. That's something I've learned.' He concentrated on joining the traffic coming off the bridge; grey concrete legs of the flyover flicked past. A lorry laden with gaping pipes hung over them. They ran into a tunnel and out again. 'Eddy wouldn't come. I don't know what's happened between you two, but he sounded as if he hated your guts. I'm sorry.'

—Because I said he was bent. Or maybe it wasn't even because of that: after all, Eddy's been on the take for a long time: that's something all of us know about Eddy. Because I wasn't polite to him in front of Blair Heathers – perhaps that was it; a man has his pride. But, Billy, aren't you supposed to be the one who hates Blair Heathers? You should be on my side, not Eddy's. My friend, not his. My friend.

'Come where? Where was he supposed to come?' Murray asked.

'To the Shot for lunch with us, of course. I told you I have to go there. To see Tommy Beltane. I told you he phoned.'

If he had been told where they were going, he had

not understood. A feeling of weakness went over his arms and legs, as if all the power had been drained from them. Strangely, it was not an unpleasant sensation, any more than floating when he had swum to the end of his strength. He wondered if Beltane had recognized him in the corner of the dark landing, if he had pushed at the unlocked door of the flat above, if he had gone in and found Mary O'Bannion. It would be strange if, instead of Peerse, Tommy Beltane was to be the hunter.

'Look at that,' Billy said. He put on the wipers as rain battered against the window. 'The sun was out a minute ago. It's going to be one of those days that change.'

For the rest of the journey, they talked about the weather and then about finding a place to park.

It was early yet, and the Shot wasn't busy. They saw Tommy Beltane at a table with two other men. Murray had expected him to be alone. He hadn't expected him to be talking just as he always did. If he faltered when he saw Murray, he corrected it so immediately there was no way of being sure. As they sat down, nods were exchanged, but, as if by complicity, without interrupting the flow of that wonderfully impressive voice. It was like a thing apart, not a possession but possessing the man, made to create an audience.

'. . . No after life. No hell or sweet heaven. Our true horror movie? I'll tell you the last ghost story. We'll be gathered round a corpse engaged in some conjuration we've made possible. Something scientific naturally, or how could we hope for a miracle? The channel opens and we listen to discover what lies beyond the gate of death. We're prepared for anything. Anything but silence . . . Our horror will be the silence, a stillness that has no waiting in it nor any place for expectation.'

'Tell me one thing,' Murray said into the silence, 'That body they used, was it a fat whore? One who had gone on because she was too stupid to do anything else.'

324

One of the men Murray didn't know laughed uncertainly, then trailed off.

'That's harsh,' Tommy Beltane said, combing his fingers through the full patriarchal beard.

'I would rather load dead meat in the market,' Murray said, 'than let a whore lay her dirty hands on me.'

The words came thick in his mouth. He felt their stares.

'Murray's a Calvinist,' Billy Shanks said with an uneasy difficult smile.

'That's a word we use too glibly in this city.' Over the hand smoothing, smoothing his beard, Tommy Beltane watched Murray. 'All of us mouthing that particular cliché with an air of rightful ownership as if Calvin had been born up a close in Moirhill and burned his first heretic outside the City Chambers. What do we mean by it? Ask us and, if we have what passes here for an education, we'll stammer out something about predestination. Only by that we mean nothing but guilt – and that every pleasure has a price higher than we ever wanted to pay.'

'I heard you had something you wanted to tell Billy,' Murray said. 'I heard that you phoned because you had something you wanted to tell him.' But the man he had thought of at first sight as the Prophet shook his head. 'No . . . no, you don't have anything to say. You talk a lot, but you don't say anything. A patter merchant. A voice in a bar.'

'Waiting for closing time.' It was a wonderful voice, masculine and commanding, and whatever he might have wished, even against his will, Tommy Beltane was given an audience. 'Isn't that what we're all doing? What makes you think you understand me? I don't claim that about you. If I spend all of a long night trying to understand, that's the only conclusion I could come to – I think some of us are not . . . at home . . . in these bodies. We should be kind to one another. I was at a conference lately and after the welcome, after the first meeting, after dinner, I couldn't bear it. I looked round this room and there were

325

people at a piano singing, but all of them were younger than me and I didn't know the songs. I went up to my room and repacked my case and came down. I wanted to go home, but I couldn't find my way outside. I went along corridors that had locked doors. And at last I was in a corridor where the side wall was all of glass and I looked across a darkened courtyard and I saw them crowded in that room singing. It was so quiet I heard the hum of one of the lights, failing, flickering. I stood there with my case in my hand watching their mouths moving. I couldn't find my way out. And so in the end I went back to my room and unpacked and lay on the bed, waiting for it to be morning.'

He was crying.

Something in their reaction must have made him realize. He put his fingers to his cheek with a glance of dolorous bravado. It was a look most of them had not seen before and it was not pleasant to see. It said that although a man could have secret lives and separate selves yet in the end they would come together necessarily and be one.

'You shouldn't be angry with me,' he wept. 'Somebody I loved is dead.'

They watched him go.

'You didn't have to talk to him like that.'

'Maybe I know some things about him you don't.'

'I know some things . . . but I admire him,' Billy Shanks said. 'And he's a kindly man – I know some of the good things he's done.'

'I've seen some of the things he does.'

'He lives his life with style. That's my definition of courage.'

'Even the sight of him makes me want to vomit.'

'If I had to choose, Murray, I think I'd choose Tommy. He's better company.'

Murray stood up, then hesitated. 'I need to get to my brother's house,' he said. 'But I don't have enough for a taxi.'

With a familiar clumsy looping movement, Billy pulled

out a handful of crumpled notes from a side pocket and held them out uncounted.

'I'll square it with you when I see you.'

'Fuck you,' Billy said bitterly, 'don't bother.'

It was true that the day was changeable. As they crossed the city, crowded pavements clenched against the rain turned leisurely in a truce of sunlight.

'The nights'll be drawing in soon,' the driver said.

On instinct, he stopped him at the corner and walked the rest. It would have been easy to miss the house among its neighbours, small family houses built in the thirties; some had put a dormer window in the attic to get another bedroom; somebody, some time after the war, had set the fashion of adding a porch. The car, sitting on the tarred slope by the front door, was what he recognized; and the shock he felt made him realise he had expected it to be gone. During the night in the cell and the interview room, what Irene had said about the murders had run through his mind like a refrain. While they were questioning him, what he had listened to instead of their voices was her voice saying: 'She could go away and start a new life. She wouldn't do it again . . . that would be the end of it.'

He moved swiftly up the path, carefully keeping the car between himself and the window. When he touched the front door, it gave under his hand. It had been lying a fraction open, and that dismayed him. He stepped into the hall with the soft step of a hunter. In the current of air that came with him, dry stems of withered flowers rattled in a vase. He passed through the living room and in the kitchen found tea and cups laid on the work surface, but when he put the back of his hand against the pot it was cold. The car in the drive proved Irene had come back here; it did not mean she had stayed. There was more than one way of leaving a house. Perhaps like him she had taken a taxi, or walked to the end of the road and caught a bus; the right bus could go to a railway station or an airport; a bus could be the beginning of a

327

long journey. Back in the front room, he heard a car door slam outside and ran to the window; outside the house opposite, a man was locking the driver's side of a red Ford Escort though it was parked in the drive, a careful man. The sky had darkened, preparing for rain. Murray watched the careful man go into his house and the light went on and he could see him sitting down at the table with a boy who must be his son home from school for lunch, and the woman between them leaning forward resting her hands on their shoulders.

There was no reason to go upstairs. He stood with his foot on the first step and his head bent as if in thought. There would be no reason to go into the room where she had slept, where the faint smell of her body would cling to the things she had worn next to her skin. Incoherent images, of clothes spilled on a floor, of the intimate private life of a woman's hips as she eased up a zip as if she were alone, held him in an oblique suspended attentiveness like a man who would not acknowledge a shameful thing but peeped at it from the corner of his eye. The outer door lay open and he reached out and struck it so that it closed with a crash like wakening.

From above, a voice called out: 'Is that you, doctor? My son's up here in the bedroom.'

'Mother?'

When he went in, she was standing by the foot of the bed. His brother lay still with his eyes closed like a dead man. Startled, she put up a finger to the lips painted on the old bright mask of her face.

'For God's sake, what is Malcolm doing here? He should be in hospital.'

'Oh, no. I'm going to look after him. Irene helped me to bring him home this morning.'

'Irene?'

There was a sigh of breath; at the sound of his wife's name, Malcolm was smiling. Against the white pillow, his face was a yellow axe. His eyes opened and closed again as, sedated, he was pressed down into sleep.

328

As if released, the old woman began to thrust Murray from the room. If it had not been for her expression, there would have been something comic in the reiterated rail shoves that sent him stumbling back. 'Don't you come looking here for her. She's gone. Don't come looking here for her. She's gone.' She wanted to drive him back to the head of the stairs and then out of the house, but he stepped aside into the next room, not resisting her otherwise.

'Did you expect her to stay after what you did to her? Did you think she would be ashamed to tell me? You've ruined your brother's life.'

'What is it? What is it?' Murray asked helplessly, stumbling back from her assault.

'You threatened her with a knife and took her – You know what you made her do. Don't deny it – she told me. There wasn't anybody to stop you. Your brother couldn't stop you, you coward.'

'It's not true. It wasn't like that—'

'Don't tell me lies. Who could believe you?' his mother demanded. 'Who would believe anything you said about her? You've driven her away.'

There was no mercy in her justice.

He was at the end of his retreat. The room was not large; Malcolm had used it as a study for there was a table with a file box on it and a battered second-hand office desk against the wall. One of its drawers was pulled half out and the key in its lock still swung back and forward from being brushed against as they came in. As a speculation of his trade, like a memory of an earlier life, it occurred to him that there could have been a shared bank book locked in that drawer and that Irene might not have left empty handed.

'You've ruined your brother's life.'

The old woman beat at him with brittle fists of folded bones.

As the only refuge left him, he turned his back on her. Through the livid air, rain burst on the panes and leapt up in glistening rods from the curve of the road. The voice faded behind him; he refused it; but what it said had no need of words. While he watched, lights came on in more of the houses opposite because of the storm. It was over there he had seen the woman linking her husband and son at a set table. Thinking of that, he leaned forward until his forehead pressed hard against the cold of the glass, but it made no difference.

There was no way of seeing her from where he was.

THE END

BROND
By Frederic Lindsay

'Undoubted power and atmosphere . . . Brond and the nightmare consciousness of the narrator linger uneasily in the mind'
Isobel Murray, The Scotsman

Glasgow: a strange alien light hangs over the city, the grimy tenements and derelict factories.

A student watches a child leaning from the side of a bridge as an indistinct shambling figure limps into sight; suddenly the figure pushes the child off the bridge. The student stands transfixed as the eyes of the murderer fall on him, daring him to denounce him, but he remains paralysed, incapable of action. From that time on he has fallen thrall to the sinister spell of the murderer, the ambiguous Brond whose web of violence stretches out from Glasgow, drawing the innocent and the guilty to their bloody ends.

'A cryptic, fast-cutting thriller'
Gerald Mangam, The Times Literary Supplement

'The outstanding new voice is that of Frederic Lindsay in *Brond*. Its opening is masterly. It combines the sense of nightmare city of Alasdair Gray with the pent-up violence of William McIlvaney and the results are frightening'
Douglas Gifford, Books in Scotland

0 552 12795 7

THE SMOKE
By Tom Barling

When a Maltese assassin buries Archie Ogle, London's 'Godfather,' under a collapsed building, thirty years of peace are swept away as the old gangland loyalties end in a bitter struggle for supremacy.

Now everybody wants a piece of the action. Eyetie Antoni dreams of a Mafia empire in the West End. The Troys from Bethnal Green want Archie's Mayfair casinos while the Harolds want to destroy the Troys' control of the East End. The Tonnas from Toronto want Archie's international money laundry, the Triads see London as the drugs capital of Europe, and a shadowy City financier plans to forge his own organisation from the shambles.

Only one man - Charlie Dance, professional villain and Archie's top gun - stands in the way of all of them. Divided by greed and the brutal lust for power, they are united in one common aim - KILL CHARLIE DANCE!

The Smoke sweeps from climax to climax: across the battle-scarred map of London, through the drug networks of Asia to a final explosive confrontation in the diamond fields of South Africa where Charlie Dance makes a last desperate stand.

0 552 12504 0

LIE DOWN WITH LIONS
By Ken Follett

A haunted pair flee across ice-shrouded mountains in Ken Follett's thrilling new novel about deadly intrigue and deadlier love in a small, embattled country.

A young Englishwoman, a French doctor, and a roving American each has private reasons for arriving in Afghanistan where mountain-bred natives fight a fierce guerilla war against the Russian invaders. At the centre of the battle is an elusive leader named Masud - the guerillas must protect him, the Russians must kill him.

As Masud sweeps from his hidden eyrie, bringing down death for the enemy below in the Valley of the Five Lions, treachery seeks its prey. A brave and beautiful woman finds herself trapped between two spies - one is the man she loves, the other is her husband. Follett builds the menacing tension to the breaking point, leading to a confrontation that echoes all our nightmares.

'A true master of espionage fiction'
New York Times

'A master of the romantic thriller'
Daily Telegraph

'A fast-moving adventure thriller'
Irish Times

'Never a dull phrase'
Police

'Highly readable . . . rich in detail and full of surprises'
Washington Post

'Genuine excitement'
Sunday Times

'Action and throbs galore'
The Observer

0 552 12550 4

THE SALAMANDRA GLASS
By A. W. Mykel

The heart-stopping novel of international suspense and intrigue by the author of *The Windchime Legacy*.

Michael Gladieux thought he'd finished with The Group, a highly specialised unit he'd served with in Vietnam . . . until his father is murdered, his body found with a note accusing him of Nazi collaboration during the war and a glass pendant anchored to his heart with a shiny steel spike.

Who was Michael's father? Why are Washington and The Group so interested? Michael's search for answers leads him on a terrifying quest - to find his father's killer. What he uncovers is far more deadly, as he becomes the one man capable of stopping the twisted legacy of THE SALAMANDRA GLASS.

Rivals Ludlum at his best!

0 552 12417 6

DAI SHO
By Marc Olden

A man looking to unravel the mystery of the death of an Asian woman he once loved . . . a Japanese secret society linked to a multinational corporation . . . a brilliant artist determined to restore his country's ancient glory . . . a boy with an eerie sixth sense . . . an exotic American woman with even more exotic tastes . . . a Chinese triad that rules the Hong Kong underworld - mix with *bushido*, the samurai code of the Japanese, and the explosive results is *dai-sho*: 'big sword, little sword,' a confrontation of East vs. West, a struggle whose only resolution is in the ultimates of life and death.

The new novel of roller coaster action and stupefying suspense by the author of Giri.

0 552 12541 5

A SELECTED LIST OF FICTION NOVELS FROM CORGI

THE PRICES SHOWN BELOW WERE CORRECT AT THE TIME OF GOING TO PRESS.
HOWEVER TRANSWORLD PUBLISHERS RESERVE THE RIGHT TO SHOW NEW
RETAIL PRICES ON COVERS WHICH MAY DIFFER FROM THOSE PREVIOUSLY
ADVERTISED IN THE TEXT OR ELSEWHERE.

☐	12504 0	**THE SMOKE**	*Tom Barling*	£2.95
☐	12550 4	**LIE DOWN WITH LIONS**	*Ken Follett*	£2.95
☐	12610 1	**ON WINGS OF EAGLES**	*Ken Follett*	£3.50
☐	12180 0	**THE MAN FROM ST PETERSBURG**	*Ken Follett*	£2.95
☐	11810 9	**KEY TO REBECCA**	*Ken Follett*	£2.95
☐	12795 7	**BROND**	*Frederic Lindsay*	£2.50
☐	12417 6	**THE SALAMANDRA GLASS**	*A.W. Mykel*	£2.50
☐	11850 8	**THE WINDCHIME LEGACY**	*A.W. Mykel*	£1.75
☐	12855 4	**FAIR AT SOKOLNIKI**	*Fridrikh Neznansky*	£2.95
☐	12307 2	**RED SQUARE**	*Fridrikh Neznansky & Edward Topol*	£2.50
☐	12541 5	**DAI-SHO**	*Marc Olden*	£2.95
☐	12662 4	**GAIJIN**	*Marc Olden*	£2.95
☐	12357 9	**GIRI**	*Marc Olden*	£2.95
☐	12800 7	**ONI**	*Marc Olden*	£2.95

All these books are available at your book shop or newsagent, or can be ordered direct from the publisher.
Just tick the titles you want and fill in the form below.

Transworld Publishers, Cash Sales Department, 61-63 Uxbridge Road, Ealing, London, W5 5SA.

Please send a cheque or postal order, not cash. All cheques and postal orders must be in £ sterling
and made payable to Transworld Publishers Ltd.
Please allow cost of book(s) plus the following for postage and packing:

UK/Republic of Ireland Customers:
Orders in excess of £5; no charge. Orders under £5; add 50p.

Overseas Customers:
All orders; add £1.50.

NAME (Block Letters): ....

ADDRESS ....

....